James Humphreys grew up in Cambridgeshire, in a village on the edge of the Fens with its own fair share of local passions and simmering feuds. He has travelled as a sales rep in Latin America and negotiated environment legislation in Brussels. Now he works at 10 Downing Street and lives in north London with his wife and baby daughter.

SLEEPING PARTNER

Clarissa Morland is twenty-seven, attractive, shy — and standing trial for the murder of her ex-lover John Grant. John was shot at dawn as he answered the door of his isolated farmhouse, but all Clarissa can remember is being cut free from the wreckage of her car that same morning, after what looks like a frantic getaway. As intimate details of her life and relationship are laid bare for the court, even Clarissa finds it hard to believe she is innocent. But murdering the man she loved in cold blood? She's just not that evil — is she?

A courtroom thriller.

JAMES HUMPHREYS

SLEEPING PARTNER

Complete and Unabridged

ULVERSCROFT
Leicester

First published in Great Britain in 2000 by
Macmillan Publishers Limited
London

First Large Print Edition
published 2002
by arrangement with
Macmillan Publishers limited
London

British Library CIP Data

Humphreys, James
    Sleeping partner.—Large print ed.—
Ulverscroft large print series: thriller
    1. Trials (Murder)—Great Britain—Fiction
    2. Detective and mystery stories 3. Large type books
    I. Title
    823.9'2 [F]

    ISBN 0–7089–4651–8

Published by
F. A. Thorpe (Publishing)
Anstey, Leicestershire

Set by Words & Graphics Ltd.
Anstey, Leicestershire
Printed and bound in Great Britain by
T. J. International Ltd., Padstow, Cornwall

This book is printed on acid-free paper

Monday Morning

The mirror cuts my face into a dozen pieces. As I move my head, fragments of nose, cheek, and dark brown hair slide over each other. At the centre, the glass has turned to diamond, a disk of tiny glittering fragments. I wonder if it was a fist that smashed it, or perhaps someone's head. Even in pieces, I look pale and ill, which is just how I feel. Tired out, too; really wrung out with tiredness because I haven't slept well for months, since the accident, and the last few days have been worse, waiting for today. I splash water on to my face, only to find that the roller towel by the door is sodden, smeared with filth. I stand dripping, unable to think what to do, close to tears although I know it is only water and hardly matters at all.

A nurse looks round the door and tells me to hurry up, and then asks someone further down the corridor *what the fuck they think they are doing.*

* * *

1

Breakfast is a mug of tea and because we are leaving early I'm treated to a bacon sandwich rather than the usual tea and toast. I don't know how people can be vegetarians in here, though some are. They would only get the same roll with the bacon taken out. I have to gulp both down in a rush before we go towards the reception area. I follow the nurse along a succession of corridors, each unusually empty, our steps echoing off the linoleum and the brick walls. I find my shoes unfamiliar after weeks in a hospital bed, then in slippers or trainers. Dressing up in a suit reminds me of going back to school after the long summer holidays. The jacket doesn't seem to fit very well any more, so perhaps I've lost more weight than I thought.

I wait in the reception area while some paperwork is shuffled. The night shift is about to change and the staff behind the glass screens are too tired to chat. We stand by the door, looking out into the half-light, waiting for the transport to turn up. I wish I had saved a letter from yesterday, or brought a book, or anything new to read. I say a few words to Miss Elliott who is on duty, but she isn't very chatty at the best of times. We lapse into silence, waiting patiently. I'm used to this now, after weeks of it. Except that you have too much time to think.

The first thing I can remember is being in the car, in a ditch, hanging upside down from the seatbelt with the whole dashboard and steering wheel in my lap and my head an inch or two above water. The water was almost black and was flowing through the smashed windows in swirls which showed up the rainbow colours of petrol on the surface. Everything was very still, except for the ticking of the engine as it cooled.

Even though I couldn't move and I was so close to the water I was very calm at first, I suppose because I wasn't in any pain. But the water kept coming in, and soon I was scared that the car would fill up, that I would drown in a few inches of water. The smell of petrol became worse and worse, making me gag, filling the car with fumes. I knew that a spark from the battery, the heat of the engine, anything might be enough to set it off. My skin crawled, waiting for the fire. I imagined the moment when the air would start to burn, the heat and the pain. I watched for the lick of flames spreading across the water beneath my head, or the first trails of smoke from the engine. I tried to struggle free, but I could hardly move, and I tried to shout out for help, but I couldn't even whisper.

Then there were voices and people I couldn't see trying to get me out, splashing down into the ditch. One of them tried to pull me free and the pain came then, absolutely unbearable, as if I was being torn to pieces. I must have screamed because they left me there until the ambulance came, and I thought I was dying because the pain was still there and because blood was now running down my face and into my hair and dripping into the water below, even darker than the water. Then the police came, and a doctor, then an ambulance, the men splashing and cursing in the ditchwater, and by that time I hardly knew what was happening, but one of the policemen kept talking to me and telling me I was fine while the doctor gave me an injection and the firemen cut the car to pieces around me with giant shears. I felt really sorry for the car and I whispered to one of them to ask if it could still be repaired, and they laughed and that made me think I would probably live. And the policeman kept wiping the blood off my face so it didn't go in my eyes.

In the end, they cut away the steering wheel. I slipped free, held in their arms, covered in blood, and was lifted out screaming into the air.

* * *

Finally, a minibus turns up and we set off, the road still almost empty. No one says anything, so I watch the wide expanse of floodlands, the high banks of the dykes, and the sun hanging just above the far horizon. The light slants down on to a fresh and empty world. It is going to be a lovely early summer day.

We are going quite slowly, and every now and again a car speeds past, taking advantage of the long straight stretches of road. We pass a village of dull-yellow brick cottages, and I try to work out where we are, but we are out into open country too soon. I stare out of the window for as long as my neck can take it, then look down at my feet. I am wearing smart suede shoes, and I decide I like the change, that I'm even enjoying the journey in a strange kind of way. It's like being a child, taken on some adult business that means nothing to me, but pleased at the break in routine. This thought brings back a sharp memory of a journey in childhood, sitting for once alone in the back of my father's car — I don't know where my brother was — and I was wearing a dress I particularly hated. I try to remember where we were going, but it's gone.

We've come three junctions round the ring road, and now turn off towards the city centre. I've made this journey several times before, but never so early, and instead of the usual delays we speed up London Road. I catch a glimpse of the towers of the football stadium, where I've never been, and of the Star of Bengal Balti Restaurant, once almost my second home. Soon we're past the passport office, and as I glimpse the roof and grey spires of the cathedral to our right we turn off the road, through a high, grey, steel-mesh gate and then into the loading bay. The window goes black.

Inside, I get a mug of coffee, and it is still only eight o'clock so we sit and wait, the others reading the papers and chatting, while I just dream. The coffee is much better than at Whitemoor, where everyone lives on tea, so after a while I summon up the courage to ask for another. Bill, who's been here for years they tell me and is now a bit of a character, says I should pop upstairs to the public gallery, where there's a vending machine. This seems to amuse everyone, and with true comic timing he tops it by recommending a café in the city centre, right by the cathedral. But there's no malice and I smile along with it and I get my coffee. I've learnt that these are ways of reducing the tension, and the staff use them whenever they can. And if you play along, and joke, and ask what's in the paper, or what's the latest in *EastEnders*, then everyone's happy.

At nine, I'm led through to a small room with four semi-comfortable chairs, and a scratched table, but again no window, where Andrew Macleod is waiting. Usually he smiles a lot, but not today, though he does try to look encouraging. He is a lawyer but also a friend of my brother Nick. I have known him a little for a few years. As usual, he asks how I am and he tells me my family are fine.

'Oh, and I saw Chris and Caroline yesterday.' Caroline is my glamorous cousin. 'We had lunch at Ian's.'

'How are they all?'

'Fine. The kids were smashing the place up as usual.'

'Are they missing their Auntie Clarrie?' I hate to hear the bitterness in my voice.

'They're only kids.'

He looks like he is going to say something else, but thinks better of it. We are saved from more of this when Charles is shown in, though I don't recognize him at first. I hadn't seen him in his gown and white bands, and it makes him look older and less overweight. Behind him trots Sarah, who is about my age, maybe older, maybe taller, certainly fairer.

She too is in a wig and gown over a dark and formal suit and is carrying a wad of brown files bound in pink tape.

'Ah, Miss Morland. And how are you?' Charles asks, as if surprised to see me.

'Fine, thank you.'

I don't know if I like him; but because he is confident, and arrogant, and has the kind of Oxbridge bray that sets my teeth on edge, I believe he is good at his job. He bustles around, makes some bland observation, then remembers his junior.

'Yes, you've met Miss Martin, I think.'

She's one of those people who don't say much and look secretly amused a lot, as she does now, because he's said this at least twice before. The three of them take their seats, looking cheerful and confident, and they tell me again what's going to happen today, the procedures, what I have to say. They ask me if I've read through the bundles of papers and I lie and say I have, and they ask me if I have any questions, but I haven't. Instead, I want them to go away and leave me alone, let me go to sleep, stare into space, anything but more questions.

In the end they go off, and my ever-present guard leads me gently by the elbow back to the waiting room. There's a copy of Saturday's *Evening Telegraph* lying around

8

and by the time I've leafed through that, and gone to the toilet and cried a bit and tried to smarten myself up again, all this with my guardian angel looking on, it's five to ten. We stand around by the door that leads to the steps, like a pantomime demon ready to climb up and scare everyone, and Bill is saying how his son went to see United play on Saturday and they were crap, and why he went he couldn't say, but he'd be back there next week, except that they were playing away at Exeter. They were a rough lot down there, Exeter, and he hoped Tony wouldn't go, but he was only young and he wouldn't be told. Then they get a signal of some kind, I still don't know how it comes, and we go through the door, up the stairs and into the daylight.

The courtroom is, in its own way, quite beautiful: all light oak and ash, lit from clerestory windows high above us, and with the benches and chairs upholstered in rich deep green. It glows with a clean, Scandinavian sense of fairness and order. In front of me is a kind of pit, filled with a large square table piled with bundles of documents and thick, expensive legal textbooks, and a couple of computer terminals looking out of place. Beyond this are the chairs for the court reporters and the clerks to the court. To my right are the benches for counsel — mine and theirs — and beyond those the public benches, the press benches, and the gallery behind. The benches are full of people, above and below, but I quickly look away in case I recognize anyone. Everything will be all right, I know, if I can treat all this as theatre where I play a part but walk off afterwards back to my real life. I don't want to see my family or friends. Or his. So I keep looking straight in front of me, at a wooden box, empty except for two rows of seats where the jury will sit. The audience chat, stare around, stow away their coats, position bags of sweets easily to hand, settle down for the show. And to my left, against the wall and beneath a huge and rather naff royal seal, the lion and unicorn so brightly painted that they shine like plastic, is the bench for the judges. That too is empty.

Almost at once the clerks and counsel exchange glances and a small door opens to let in the judge, dressed in red and ermine and a stupid wig, under which his face is surprisingly small and sharp. We all stand, I and the guard at my side, the audience clutching coats and papers and drinks and sweets, the lawyers in their wigs and flapping gowns. He looks around the court, a swift glance, which rests briefly on Charles, and then on me, and then on the gallery. He sits.

Everyone else sits. The clerk to the court stands.

'Clarissa Abigail Morland, you are charged on this indictment with murder and the particulars of the offence are that, on the twentieth of October last, you killed John Darcy Grant, of Manor Farm, Upton, in the County of Cambridgeshire contrary to the common law. Clarissa Abigail Morland, are you guilty or not guilty?'

I have always been Clarrie, a diminutive, a child's name, not the name of a murderer or even of someone you'd allow to take their driving test. For a moment I want to laugh, to explain that they have the wrong person, that they want some Clarissa who is glamorous and smokes and has a fast car and kills people. I am conscious of all these people watching me, listening, breath drawn in and held. But I know my lines and, outwardly, I am calm and so I speak in a soft clear voice I can hear coming from a thousand miles away.

Not Guilty.

There's a sigh around the court as the audience realize they won't be denied their sport, that there is to be no tame guilty plea, and a remanding in custody for psychological reports and sentencing at some later date, but the real thing, a murder trial, the best show going. I shiver, feeling a little sick that a

11

thousand eyes are watching me. I look up a little, tensing myself to resist the stares and the speculation — *Did she do it? How could she? And like that!*

Now there's some business about my medical condition and fitness to stand trial, which I ignore. This is what most of my previous court hearings have been about: endless submissions on my head injuries, my medical state, the extent of permanent and temporary memory loss, with doctors and psychologists and other experts disagreeing over it all with real professionalism. Three days in all, though I don't remember much about them because I was feeling even worse than today, really out of it and I was on serious painkillers because of my leg. Anyway, most of what they said was incomprehensible, all about medial lobes and interrupter cells and post-traumatic suppression. All that was to see if I could stand trial. Charles argued that I shouldn't, because I wasn't yet well enough; and that if I was well enough, I shouldn't because I wouldn't have a fair trial because of my amnesia; and even if I was tried, the jury shouldn't take my silence or the fact I couldn't answer any questions as an admission of guilt. We lost on the first two points, and the judge said he would rule on the third at the end of the full trial. Charles seemed pleased with the outcome. I was just glad it was over.

Now Charles is saying something which makes the judge look over at me. His face and his hands are very grey against the scarlet robes, and there's no real expression on his face except perhaps curiosity. I remember what Andrew told me about how I should act in the dock to make the best possible impression on the judge and the jury, things like how I should look alert, not shift about in my seat too much, and react as you'd expect an innocent person to react when people told lies about them, but not say anything or shout out. It reminded me of drama classes at school, when we were taught how to stand on stage when you had nothing to do, how to find a posture you could keep up for minutes on end, and how to follow who was speaking, and how to have a bland but interested expression on your face, and let your mind wander on to something calming, relaxing, while still listening with half an ear to the dialogue.

So while the legal stuff goes on I think of holidays, when I was a child, going each year to the same village on the North Norfolk coast, two weeks in a cottage, or for a couple of years in a big caravan, which my father always called a static home because he

13

thought a caravan was a bit beneath us. We'd be right on the sea, with only the dunes and a few pine trees for shelter from the wind. I can remember so clearly the first day of each holiday, always the same, walking along the footpath to the beach, sand already in my shoes, and then the sharp blades of the marram grass stinging my legs as I ran up through the dunes, and the moment when I reached the top and could see the sea, spread out, always seeming a long way away because the beach sloped so gently and I knew the holiday had begun.

Each middle Saturday of the two weeks Granny — my father's mother — would come over and look after us while my parents went off somewhere (now I think about it, we never wondered where). She'd take us into Sheringham, which had a seafront and fish and chip shops and ice-cream machines on every corner, and a funfair, and we'd waste our money on games and rides, especially the helter-skelter, and she'd make up what we'd spent at the end of the day, so we still had some money for the rest of the holiday. Then we'd go back to the cottage to be spoilt, sitting up playing Scrabble and eating the secret box of chocolates she brought with her, which my parents weren't supposed to know about.

In my mother's house there was a framed photo of me and Nick playing about on the beach, both impossibly thin, big grins and mops of hair so you can hardly tell us apart. I wonder if it is still there, if she can bear to look at it. What if I had a child who had ended up here? The innocent little girl dragging her toy spade through the rippled sand, smiling up from under her fringe, all in sunshine, now the woman who killed her lover with a shotgun on a cold dark morning. What would I do? Could I sit there in court and watch it all being made public, wondering over and over again what had gone wrong? I think of her sitting at home, in the familiar living room which seems so cold and empty, too tidy and unused since my father died and since Nick and I left home, and her seeing the picture and crying. It makes me want to cry too, but instead I sit with the right expression on my face, breathing carefully, trying to remember how to look the picture of innocence.

One by one the jurors are called forward to swear that they will bring a fair judgment and true in the case. David Morgan and Peter Harrison and Nafiseh Rajah and George Dennison and April Killen and Sharon Picton and Terry Lewis. The lawyers huddle, but they don't give any sign they want to challenge any of them. Peter Furness, Phil Watney, Frank Crosby, Jean Rye and Kader Ali. I glance at each as they shuffle into place, and they look ordinary, people off the street. As each sits, they stare about them in curiosity, taking in their new role, a special audience which is there to watch but is part of the show too, raised up in the jury box. They glance furtively at the judge, and the usher, and a couple even look across at me: a rat-like man whose gaze darts around and looks more like a criminal than I ever could, and a man in a sports jacket, who seems interested and amused by it all. The rest of the jury settle down: a couple of pensioners, a beefy bloke with balding hair clipped short who could be a builder, a fat, sandy man, two middle-aged women, a couple of people nearer my age, one obviously a student, the other perhaps a professional in her suit. A group of twelve people who look so lost and random that they would hardly make do as a bus queue. I wonder what they will do to me. I don't suppose there's much doubt.

I look away again, and catch sight of the sky, a thin sliver of blue through the window high above me, the same sky spread over the fields and villages beyond, the Ashbrook and the woods behind, and my own cottage. It's almost five months since I was last there, since I last slept in my own bed or picked one of my books off the shelf or listened to the *Archers* or looked at the vine I was trying to get to grow up the back wall or spent an evening alone, reading, sitting in my favourite wicker chair, enjoying the evening light. By now, none of my old life seems real, though sometimes I can remember it so clearly.

I have to struggle to bring my attention back to the present. The lawyers and the judge have been going through some exchanges, and I tell myself I must try to concentrate, that this is like an exam, and I can pass it if I pay attention. So I listen as the prosecution counsel stands and nods to the judge and begins to speak.

'May it please your lordship, members of the jury, it is the submission of the Crown that the accused was responsible for the murder of John Grant on the twentieth of October last year. As the case for the prosecution unfolds, you will hear evidence which establishes that Mr Grant was shot quite deliberately as he opened his front door at around 6.30 in the morning. The shot wasn't immediately fatal, and the accused fired a second shot at Mr Grant as he lay in agony on the ground. Chillingly, she waited probably a minute or more before firing the second shot. Why she waited we can only speculate, but whatever the reason it is hardly possible to think of a more callous and horrifying crime.

'The village of Upton where the murder took place lies in a quiet, prosperous rural district, where crime is generally a matter of an occasional theft or drunk driving, or some rowdiness on a Saturday night. This crime was on quite another plane, of quite startling viciousness, and utterly unexpected. If some of you might think that the accused is an unlikely person to be on trial for murder, then they should bear clearly in mind that the crime itself was a most unusual one.

'Members of the jury,' she goes on in her smooth, rich voice, 'the Crown's task is to demonstrate that the accused killed Mr Grant knowing full well what she was about and is therefore guilty of murder and should take the consequence for this crime. To this end, the Crown will seek to establish means, opportunity and motive. You will hear that the accused owned a shotgun and ammunition of the same kind as were used to kill Mr Grant. No less than three reliable witnesses were able to identify the accused at different stages of her journey to and from the farmhouse on that morning. You will also hear forensic evidence which will likewise indicate that the accused was in the vicinity of the farmhouse.

And finally, you will hear a considerable body of evidence from a series of witnesses and from documentary evidence to establish a clear motive for the crime.

'I should say at the outset that there is no direct witness to the crime. No one will appear in this court and swear that they saw the accused actually shoot Mr Grant. The murder took place at an isolated farmhouse, in a sparsely populated rural area, and early in the morning, when the accused could have counted on there being little risk of being directly overlooked. The farmhouse is almost a quarter of a mile from the nearest road, and the front door is sheltered from a nearby footpath by a line of trees and in part by some outbuildings. But a series of witnesses are able to place the accused at the scene of the murder at the time when it took place.'

None of this would be happening, the judge and the jury would be listening to another case, an affray or burglary or common assault, if only I had pleaded guilty. As the prosecution barrister sets it out, it is all so clear and convincing. John was cheating on me, ripped me off as well, and so I killed him and in trying to escape I crashed my car and was caught. I don't remember any of it, but there's the match of the gun and the mud on my shoes and the rest of it. I'm sure Charles thinks it's all a waste of time, and perhaps Andrew too, though as a family friend he has to stay loyal. But because I cannot remember a thing, they've convinced me to go to trial, and hope for something to turn up, and trust that it doesn't make things worse if and when it comes to being sentenced.

Meanwhile, the barrister is still setting it all out.

'John Grant was a man of determination and drive, in his early thirties, and already successful in his career as a property developer, specializing in smallscale but up-market housing developments in Northamptonshire and Cambridgeshire. He was educated at Uppingham School and then took a course in estate management at Cirencester College. He then worked in London and in Wiltshire for several years before returning to live in Cambridgeshire about five years ago.

'At that time, he quite naturally met up again with several old friends, many of whom he knew from school. A group of these met regularly in one of several pubs in the area, usually on a Friday night, and others would drop by every now and again. One of these was Nicholas Morland, the elder brother of the accused, and a contemporary of Mr Grant at school.'

I have a file of papers in front of me, with coloured index flags and a neat label on the spine which reads 'R vs. Morland'. Inside, the front page lists the barristers and solicitors, myself and the judge, Mr Justice Kerr. Charles and his junior are sitting at a desk below me and to my right, and behind them are Andrew and a young woman I don't know but who is probably some kind of trainee on a day out. I don't suppose Andrew's firm get many murder cases, so I hope she is grateful to me for the experience. At the next table to them is the Crown team. Again, two solicitors seated quietly behind the two barristers: Mr Gerard Williams sitting down, dark, running to fat though still young, a flash of gold watch beneath his cuffs and gown, watching his leader without expression. And Miss Ruth Acheson, on her feet, occasionally turning a page with one hand as she addresses the jury, her voice rich and cultured and surprisingly deep as she sets out the case against me.

'The character of the accused is equally germane to the case. Clarissa Morland grew up in the village of Normanton, only a couple of miles from Manor Farm where John Grant was killed. She was educated at a private day school in Peterborough, where she did well academically and took part in several school plays, being considered an accomplished

21

actress. She went on to university and then took a postgraduate diploma in housing management. She worked in housing for six years, first in London, then for the last three years at the Forest Housing Association in Oundle, a few miles from her home village. Her colleagues describe her as pleasant, very able, an extremely good planner, level-headed, but also shy, withdrawn, stand-offish. She had had several relationships before John Grant, but none that lasted. She may have felt that, with Mr Grant, she had found the stable, long-term relationship that she was looking for, and this may have made the final split, and the way in which it ended, more difficult to take.'

I feel my face burning with shame and with anger that she should talk about me in this way, slyly make me out to be screwed-up emotionally, while being a ruthless planner and a good actress. I realize now what Charles had meant when he warned me that the whole of my life was fair game as far as the court was concerned.

'It may be worth mentioning that the accused had lived in Normanton until she was six, and again from the age of eleven until she went to university, and that after returning to work in the area she rented a cottage in the village of Woodwalton, a few miles from Upton. She knows the area around the scene of the murder intimately, perhaps in the way that only someone who has explored it as a child can do. The accused is a keen cross-country runner, and regularly runs in the area. She is also a member of a local shoot, owns her own shotgun, and is experienced in shooting both clay pigeons and also live targets, such as pheasants and rabbits.'

The barrister pauses, letting the jury linger over the picture of me blowing the heads off fluffy little bunnies.

'The accused and Mr Grant had known each other for years, meeting occasionally at parties and in the pub, perhaps once or twice a year. At one such meeting, at an art gallery in the summer of last year, this casual acquaintanceship began to develop into something more serious. Within a few days they then met again at a barbecue party given by a mutual friend, and spent the evening together. It was that night that Mr Grant and the accused became lovers.

'At about the same time, Mr Grant and the accused entered into an agreement about the development of an area of land owned by the accused known locally as 'the Doles', in the village of Normanton, a couple of miles further away from Upton.'

The barrister has this trick of smiling to emphasize her points. I find it difficult to guess her age, in her wig, but perhaps she is forty-five. She has very clear skin, and when she looks around the court her gaze is quite startlingly direct, though mostly she talks to the jury.

'The ins and outs of property development may be something of a mystery to many of us, but the Crown will call expert witnesses to explain the various agreements, and to give a valuation of the land. You will hear testimony as to the nature of the property deal which Mr Grant planned, including from the director of planning at Rockingham Forest District Council.'

The barrister goes on describing the deal, and I think of the Doles, a field on the edge of the village, running down to the river, not good for much except keeping horses, or the odd apple on the trees at the bottom, if the wasps didn't get them first. Sometimes, if it wasn't rented out, my grandparents used to let me and Nick and friends from the village play there during the summer. And in the winter, if it snowed, the long slope was brilliant for sledging, if you kept clear of the trees. We had a sort of camp at the far end, where there were still the foundations of an old hut, or shed, and so nothing grew there except brambles and nettles.

'So, in brief, you will hear evidence that, had the Doles been sold on the open market, in full possession of the facts as to the potential for development at Normanton, the accused could have expected to have gained not the £16,000 she actually received from Lioncrest Developments, the company set up and controlled by Mr Grant, but at least £310,000.'

The audience shift in their seats and rustle. I'm more and more conscious of them, ranked around me, waiting to be entertained. I steal a glance at the gallery, but I don't recognize anyone.

'The accused, then, lost some hundreds of thousands of pounds. But this motive was compounded by the fact that, at the same time, the affair between Mr Grant and the accused had turned sour. You will be presented with evidence concerning the two weeks before Mr Grant's murder which shows that their relationship was over, at least as far as he was concerned. You will hear testimony from Mr Grant's sister, two of his friends and from two members of his staff to the effect that the accused persisted in phoning him and even visiting his offices between the twelfth of October and the eighteenth of October. The Crown invites you to conclude that Mr Grant lost interest in the relationship and that the accused came to believe she had been misled and that she had been used.'

I flick through the files in front of me at random to take my mind away from this. There are witness statements, copies of letters to and from John's company and Mountgrove Homes, copies of the legal agreements between John and I. One page catches my eye: at the bottom are our signatures, mine scrawled in biro, his florid, signed with the fountain pen I had bought him.

I turn on, past police reports, pages of transcripts of interviews, forensic reports, until I come to a group of maps, one showing the Doles, another of the area around Upton and Normanton and Woodwalton, with all the roads and rivers and woods and tracks marked in, and finally one of the whole of Eastern England, showing Peterborough and the roads to the coast ports, from King's Lynn round to Felixstowe, and also the airports at Norwich and Cambridge and Stanstead. These names are so familiar from road signs on our trips to the Norfolk coast, years ago, when my father was still alive.

The last time we went, I was fourteen and we were staying not in our usual cottage but in Sheringham itself, where some friends of my parents had a flat right on the seafront, from where you could watch ships on the horizon creeping up the coast, or the breakers sweeping in over the shingle beach. It was poor weather most of the time, and my father was moody and irritable and used to snap at us and then go off by himself on long walks along the cliffs, and my mother would look sick with worry. He had left his job and we thought he was stressed about finding another one and about money. Now — too late — I know it was because of his illness.

The holiday was also different because Nick had brought along his new girlfriend — I can't remember her name — and they would go off on their own, not wanting me hanging around. These friends of my parents had two boys who were also staying there, Dominic was older than Nick, Aidan just a bit younger and I thought he was really cool. He was tall, and had black hair and could look a bit moody, which suited the holiday weather of squalls of rain. Sometimes we would all hang around together, pretending we had to stave off boredom like real teenage rebels, sitting over a coffee in a steamed-up café, or mooching about in one of the games arcades, where we'd watch Dominic working on his score on the rally-car simulator.

One time, towards the end of the holiday, it

had turned cold and the sea was up high, waves smashing into the sea wall, and throwing spray into the air. It had been raining too, so there was no one around, and we were watching the tide come in, and running in and out of the spouts of water thrown up by each wave. I suppose I was trying to catch Aidan's attention, had probably been doing so for days, but anyway I pulled off the blue Lenin cap he wore, and had it dangling over the edge, and then we horsed around, him trying to grab it, pressing against me and smiling into my face, and maybe if his brother hadn't been around we'd have got somewhere.

As it was, he got his cap back soaked, and he said they'd have to teach me a lesson, and they grabbed me and started to swing me backwards and forwards, Dom holding my arms and Aidan my legs, as if they were going to throw me in. One, two, three. In a way I was scared because the waves were fearsome and there was no rail. But more than that, I was really excited, by the danger, and the way Aidan held me and was smiling at me, and though I was screaming I was laughing too.

Then there was a huge shout from the promenade above, where my father had walked past and seen what he thought was going on. At once, Aidan let go, so I fell on to the concrete. It was so painful, lying there in a puddle of sea water with a bruised arse, and the three of us ashamed, embarrassed strangers again. I can remember the pain, and the taste of salt from the spray and from my tears.

Meanwhile, the prosecution barrister is continuing, her low voice holding the jury entranced.

'Second, you will hear a neighbour of the accused testify that the accused asked her about a murder supposed to have happened some years ago in a nearby wood. As the accused described it, the murder bore striking similarities to the circumstances of the real murder, which took place only a matter of days later.

'Third, you will hear testimony that on the afternoon of the day before the murder, the accused spoke to one of Mr Grant's employees and the accused swore that she would kill Mr Grant.

'These three insights are, the Crown will seek to demonstrate, evidence that the murder of Mr Grant was not the result of a sudden outburst or loss of control but was planned.'

It's my own fault I missed the first 'insight' by daydreaming, and I try to concentrate, but the room is stuffy and I feel utterly helpless, as if all I can do is watch a hopeless drift towards my conviction.

'The accused had a double-barrelled motive for murder. She had been duped into handing over the Doles for a tiny fraction of its true worth. And she had been betrayed and cast aside by her lover.'

Hearing it all set out like this makes it sound like my fault. Like at school, when something got broken, it wasn't the one who'd done it who got the blame, but whoever was stupid enough to still be standing around when the teacher came. So John has gone, and this whole mess, this cheap con trick of a relationship is my fault because I'm the one left to blame. I'm ashamed that I've made this happen, or let it happen, and of what it's done to my family.

I wonder if any of them are here, and I risk a quick look around. I spot my brother sitting near the front, and at first I don't realize that the old woman sitting beside him is my mother. She looks ill, with deep bruises under her eyes and sunken cheeks, and much more uncertain, lost even, than my grandmother beside her. I try and smile at them, at her, and I see her mouthing something, and smiling, and she looks for a moment her old self. But I have to look away, feeling sick. I know that I have done this to her. I can't bear to have to sit here another minute, putting her through this, while the barrister presses on and the whole world looks on whispering and nudging each other.

'You will hear expert testimony that the wounds were made by two shots from a 20-bore shotgun, an uncommon design compared to the much more common 12-bore type, and one used particularly by women. You will also be shown a shotgun of exactly this type, recovered from the possession of the accused.'

I look at the jury, wondering what they are making of all this. I try to think of them not as a block of people, not the way the papers would as a jury of eight men and four women, but as individuals. There's the one who looks like a builder, uncomfortable in his suit, and another who looks like a pig, with bristly, sandy hair. There's the rat-faced one and the bloke in the sports jacket, and an old bloke who ought to have a cloth cap on, next to him a youngish balding man in a suit, a bank-manager type, and an old woman with fluffy white hair. At least they all seem to be paying attention.

'You will hear evidence from the police to the effect that, due to excessive speed, or inattention, or both, the accused crashed her car at a notorious bend on the B1166, near

Deeping St James, some ten miles away, within an hour of the murder being committed.'

She carries on about the crash, and I lose the thread again. What is going on around me seems more and more meaningless. It can't be me she is talking about, and all these people are hearing about, and making notes about, and watching, and judging. I guess that there are lots of little signals that the prosecution are sending out to the court, to the judge most of all, but I don't understand them. I recognize the words, the talk of opportunity and intent and reasonable doubt, I could tell you what a dictionary would say, but I don't know what they really mean.

I feel tired, and really hungry too. It is now about twenty to one, and back at Whitemoor lunch would have been served at midday, like every day. I wonder what the food here will be like. Perhaps there's a canteen, where I'll be surrounded by guards, carrying my tray around in handcuffs. Perhaps I should be surprised that lunch matters more than the trial, after the weeks of boredom, waiting for my day in court. But I want nothing more than to be back at Whitemoor, instead of sitting under the gaze of hundreds of eyes while this woman picks and turns over my life like old clothes at a jumble sale.

'The accused was due at work at 9 a.m. on the morning when Mr Grant was killed, but the route from Woodwalton that she took that day does not lead to her work, and we can only speculate as to where she was going. One possible explanation which the Crown will advance is that this route would take the accused past various rivers and drainage ditches which could have been used to dispose of evidence connecting her to the crime. Another possible explanation is that she panicked after killing Mr Grant and was intending to leave the country and that she was therefore heading towards the airport at Norwich or the ferry ports at Felixstowe or Harwich.'

This is a new thought. I try to imagine what I would have done if I was trying to escape. Would I have had any money? Any clothes? Did I have a passport with me? I think about scribbling a note to Andrew, and I take a sheet from the pile of paper thoughtfully provided for me on the shelf in the dock, but I give up after a few words. I'm too tired to concentrate. So instead I lean back and close my eyes and think of lying in my hospital bed, cared for, and everything quiet. As it was before the police first came.

'You will also hear tapes of the police interviews with the accused, and a mass of corroborative evidence which the police have assembled to support their case.'

I had been in hospital for the best part of a week, pretty much out of it for most of the time with the drugs. I had settled into the routine, being fed, washed, brought drinks. The doctors and nurses said very little except that I needed to rest, though from time to time they asked me what I could remember. I knew, without them saying anything, that they were worried in case I had a really serious head injury. Internal bleeding, or a clot. I can dimly remember being wheeled along to another part of the hospital for a scan. Maybe more than once. But I felt OK, I felt really calm and relaxed. I had one arm bandaged up to my chest, and I couldn't move because of my leg and because of some broken ribs down my left side, but I could just about change the tape in the Walkman my brother brought in. Trying to read made me feel sick, and people talking made me tired and irritable. So I lay there sleeping, or dozing, or listening to tapes.

'Members of the jury, before I conclude these introductory remarks I would like to address directly two points which may give you some concern during the course of this trial.

'The first concerns the circumstantial

nature of the evidence which will be put to you. In a very large number of cases of violent crime, there are no direct witnesses to the crime itself. This is perhaps true of murder above all others. These are crimes that are committed in secrecy, under cover of darkness, in remote and lonely places, or out of sight in an ill-lit alley. The traces are covered over or washed away, the evidence destroyed.

'So we rely on recreating the circumstances of the murder from fragments and traces, from pieces of a jigsaw that was deliberately scattered by the murderer. Not every piece will be found and put in place, but the overall picture of the crime and the guilt of the accused must become clear enough to ensure that no reasonable doubt remains. The prosecution asks the jury to consider and weigh each piece of evidence individually, but also as part of a wider picture. Each individual piece is likely to be capable of more than one interpretation. It may point towards the guilt of the accused, but may also have a perfectly innocent explanation. This can be worrying for jurors, who would not wish to base their verdict on such evidence. But when each piece of evidence is also seen as part of this wider picture, the problem recedes. As each piece is put in place, each individual alternative explanation becomes more unconvincing, or even contradictory, and the one true picture of events should become clear.

'The second point which you are bound to consider during the trial is the character of the accused: 'Could they really have done the crime?'

She starts going on about the psychological profile of the killer. My back is hurting, and I want to stretch out, shift in my seat, but I feel every eye is on me, and I have to look calm, relaxed. Not guilty.

'So the previous good character of the defendant, the testimony of friends and family, and even their appearance in the dock or in the witness box cannot be a reliable guide to their guilt or innocence. You the jury may find it difficult to believe that a young woman, properly brought up, with a university education and a responsible job, could have committed such a crime. But is it not hard to imagine how anyone at all could have committed such a crime? Yet the crime clearly took place. So we have to work from the facts as we have them.'

The old woman on the far right of the jury is watching me with new interest. She reminds me of those grannies who used to clog up the library, taking out piles of detective books, becoming experts in the symptoms of poisonings, fingerprinting and post-mortem techniques. Perhaps she's already comparing me to a Raymond Chandler femme fatale or worse to an Agatha Christie murderess, demure on the outside and with a ruthless desire for gain eating her up inside. With her white hair and her questing nose, she looks a little like Miss Marple. Perhaps she'll take her knitting out in the jury room and explain to the amazement of the other jurors how and why I did it, and how I hoped to get away with it.

'In summary, then, the Crown will seek to establish beyond any doubt that the accused had a strong motive: their business deal they had both joined in had gone sour, and she had every reason to think she had been duped into forgoing a very large sum of money. The sexual relationship between the accused and Mr Grant had been broken off only a few days before. And on the day before the murder, the accused learnt that her ex-lover was having an affair with another woman, and that in all likelihood this affair had been going on for some time behind her back.

'Evidence as to the accused's motive is supported by forensic evidence, which places the accused at the scene of the crime on the day, and which establishes that Mr Grant was killed with the same type of weapon as one found in the accused's possession. It is also, most tellingly, supported by three eyewitnesses, who all saw the accused running away from the scene of the crime at the time of the murder, including the key evidence of one witness, who knows the accused well, who saw her carrying a gun.

'This, then, is the case for the Crown.'

She pauses, and lets the judge catch her eye. He asks if this would be a convenient moment to break for lunch. She nods, he stands, the lawyers and court officials stand briskly, and the guards nudge me to my feet. Around the court, people are standing up uncertainly, looking around to check that they are meant to, like people unused to being in church. With the judge gone everyone begins to relax, the jury are beckoned out by one of the ushers, and I am taken backstage, down to the holding area.

★ ★ ★

I am put into a cell, locked in with a tray of food and a plastic cup of watery orange squash. The guard tells me the food is 'Mexican Shepherd's Pie', followed by apple turnover, and from his look I guess he has to eat it too. The pie is mashed potato on top of chilli beef and red kidney beans, and although it's gone cold around the edges I manage to eat some of it in four or five quick forkfuls. There is a plastic spoon to match the plastic fork, and it takes me another minute to eat the turnover, a greasy pastry around apple jam, and drink the squash. Another hour, at least, before the court starts again.

I push the tray to one side and open up my diary. I haven't written anything since the accident, in part because I was ill, and then hearing about what had happened to John and that I was the only suspect. After I was arrested Andrew said I shouldn't write anything down unless I was sure it couldn't be used against me. He'd told me they could search my belongings, use any notes I made in court against me. I shouldn't talk to any prison officers, or police, or other prisoners without assuming I was being listened to.

'There's all sorts of ways of getting at prisoners,' he'd said. 'Say you wanted to see your child, or your boyfriend, and the prison authorities said, yeah, sure, but you share a cell with Morland and we'd like a bit of help in knowing more about that murder she did.'

So I spoke to no one about it, wrote nothing down, and hoped I wasn't talking in my sleep. The only time I could relax was in the weekly meetings with Andrew, or when I had a visitor, which was almost never once I'd moved from the hospital to the prison.

So instead of writing in my diary, I've filled it with letters and cards and notes and photographs, to add to the things already stuffed into it, programmes from the theatre and ticket stubs and the plan of the gardens at Wimpole Hall where I went with John and the receipt from our first meal out, with his strong, illegible signature at the bottom. It holds everything I've been sent by my family and my friends. A card from my brother Nick of a winter scene by Brueghel, a heavy dark sky and bulky figures in bright clothes walking about in the snow. It reminds me of when we both used to go skating on Deeping Fen with my father, when the fields between the drainage ditches were flooded, and froze over, and you could skate outdoors, for mile after mile, in the open air, until your legs ached and your throat burned, and we were called back to the car.

Next to it I put a card from Claire, my oldest friend, which arrived on Friday. A card with a drawing of a penguin on the front, again with ice all around, a penguin with big mournful eyes but with a bright warm beak of red and yellow. Inside she had written, 'Dearest Clarrie, I'll be thinking of you next week and always, I know everything will be

40

fine and this will be the end of it all and you'll soon be back with us. Do write if you have any time. All our love, Claire.' And next to that one from my friend Kate, who's seven months pregnant and says she's the size of a whale, and the card has a whale on the front, splashing about in the Pacific, to prove the point.

Near the back is a card with a spidery cartoon my friend Seb has drawn of my house, cut down the middle to show all the different rooms, with plates piled in the sink and hats spilling out of the wardrobe and smoke billowing from the stove and a line of empty wine bottles snaking around the kitchen and me lying asleep on my sofa with my head underneath a magazine.

My cottage is on Main Street, which I know sounds American but nothing could be more English, with a Norman church at one end and a pub halfway along. All the houses are in the local stone, with slate roofs, and all have been there for hundreds of years, so that they mostly still have long gardens where you could keep a goat and some chickens. My cottage has a front room you come into straight off the street, a kitchen you go to through a door with little window panes set into it, and stairs up to the two bedrooms and the bathroom.

Sometimes I worry about it more than anything else. Nick visits every week or two, has the heating on for a couple of hours, checks for leaks or anyone trying to break in. Kate stayed there for a few weeks when she was moving house, and Seb has been working there some days to make the place look used. Ever since I woke in hospital and thought the police had come because it was broken into, I've wanted to go back to see it and know it is all right, that my books and records and pictures are all still there, and the brass candlesticks Sarah gave me for my birthday and the pot from Jay, and all the rest of it. I want to hear the cistern fill in the special way it has, waste half an hour trying to light the wood stove when the wind's from the North, maybe eat the tin of cassoulet that has sat at the back of the larder for years. I want my life back.

Monday Afternoon

Andrew brings his sandwiches down to one of the interview rooms. He has also brought me three green apples which he says are to keep me going, though he doesn't say that it's because I look so unhealthy from the prison food, the endless chips and tinned vegetables, and being inside all the time. He seems cheerful as he leans back and tells me that everything is going fine and that I look very calm and am making a good impression. I have difficulty finding anything to say in reply. I don't want to talk about the case.

'Are you OK?' Andrew asks.

'I'm fine. I just feel a bit out of it.'

'It's always very difficult at the start, having the prosecution making the running. Ruth is excellent, although I don't think the CPS and the police have prepared the case that well.'

'Who's Ruth?' I ask.

'Their QC. For the prosecution.' He looks at me more closely, perhaps concerned that I'm not paying more attention. 'She's the one who's been setting out the case all morning.'

'Oh yes.' I want to tell him that I feel worse than I have for a long time, that I can't

43

concentrate for more than a few minutes. But I can't find the energy, and there's nothing he can do anyway. He asks if I feel up to going through some post, and I shrug.

'You've got a council tax assessment, a begging letter from your university, a letter from your ex-employers, and another delaying letter from your car insurers.'

'What do they want?' I ask.

'More medical evidence. And asking if you can recall any more about the crash itself.'

'I've told them. I can't remember anything.'

'Shall I write back?'

'Yes, could you? Whatever.'

I can't even reply to a letter about the crash. I wonder how I will ever be able to give evidence. Best not to think about it. I look at the letter from Forest, and it's painful to see the familiar headed notepaper, and read the first few lines about the grounds for my dismissal. I can't concentrate on this either, and drop it back on the table.

'Do I need to do anything?'

'They are contesting the evidence in your application to the tribunal. I'd recommend you wait until after the trial before making any decision about what to do next. There's no rush.'

After the accident Jeremy Taverner, who

44

runs Forest, gave me sick leave and then unpaid leave, but when he heard that I'd asked one of my colleagues to do me a favour with finding a flat for one of the other prisoners he took the chance to sack me. All of the prisoners I've met were sacked, those who had jobs at all, even if they were only on remand. And I'm lucky that I've got some savings and have been able to pay the rent on my house, so I haven't lost that as well.

'What about Baz's tenancy?' I ask.

'That's all sorted out.'

He digs out a fax from the council's housing department, and it's strange to see the name Fiona Gallagher typed out. Everyone calls her Baz, even the prison officers. We met when I was first in the hospital wing and she was on cleaning duty, and we got on really well. She'd tell me all sorts of stories from her past, really funny ones, although they were mostly about her taking drugs and nicking stuff to pay for it, and this cast of weird characters she used to hang around with, and I'd never know how much to believe. And I'd tell her about my own life — she was always fascinated that I lived in a country village, with a duck pond and a vicar, like on TV.

She's the only real friend I've made in prison. I'm glad to have been able to do something for her in return, even if it's only so she has somewhere to stay on release. But it makes me sad as well, because it reminds me of my old job, my old life.

★ ★ ★

David is very tall in the witness box, neat in his suit and tie, and showing the right amount of cuff. His voice is strong and confident, and he looks straight at Ruth to answer her questions, except when he addresses a sentence to the jury or to the judge. He works in the City, he explains, and comes back to Oundle most weekends. He likes to get away, meet up with the gang, sink a few pints down the Ship or the Seven Stars.

'You knew John Grant well?'

'We were at school together, same year. Not in all the same classes, but we played in the same rugger team as well. We were pretty close.'

'You must have been very upset when you heard about his death?'

'It was a real shock, I can tell you. John was a lovely fellow, really funny, a really good friend.'

'And you had no reason to think such a thing would happen?'

'Oh God, no. No, not at all. It was — well,

still is — absolutely unbelievable. I mean, I'd known him for twenty years. I saw him the weekend before. We'd spoken on the phone only that Monday, about playing in a scratch team. Some charity event he was organizing.'

'And am I right in thinking you know Nicholas Morland too? That you were at school together as well?' Ruth has a lovely, chocolatey voice, like a jazz singer. David is eager to please.

'Yes. We were all there at the same time. Of course, Nick left in the sixth form, but we were still friends. We would all meet up at parties and things.'

'And did you all meet up at a party last summer, on the sixteenth of July?'

'Yes, it was over at Sibberton, the other side of the A1. A friend of ours called Peter Barnett borrowed his parents' house for a party. They've got a swimming pool with big glass doors that open up on to a patio, and you can set up a barbie outside, get a fire going, bit of music, that sort of thing.'

'And you, John Grant and Nicholas Morland were all present.'

'Yes.'

'As was the accused.'

'Yes.' He doesn't look at me.

'Was that unusual?'

'A bit, yes. Clarrie Morland was quite a bit

younger than the rest of us.' I notice I *was* younger, like I'm dead. Perhaps, as far as he's concerned, I am. 'And she wasn't really one for parties. She'd come to the pub sometimes, but she was a bit stand-offish.'

Some of Nick's friends, or rather friends of friends, mainly from school, were real wankers, so I remembered evenings in the pub rather differently. The blokes would end up all standing around by the bar being large and blokish and talking in loud voices, with the girls and girlfriends sitting in a corner, surrounded by coats like refugees. Not wanting to be snogged by some pissed tosser is apparently being 'stand-offish'.

'They were down by the pool,' David is saying. 'I didn't go back down there because it was pretty clear he was chatting her up.'

'Could you elaborate on this?'

'Well, I suppose I mean he was making a real effort. You see, Clarrie wasn't really one for joining in things, games and the like. I don't remember her having any serious boyfriends, and she was a bit prickly. She could be quite sharp-tongued as well. And I wouldn't have said she and John had much in common. But they were talking quite a bit during the evening, sitting down by the pool, and they were getting on really well.'

I hate the thought of John's friends all

watching us and talking about us as we sat there.

'Were you the only one who noticed this?'

'Oh no, a couple of us were joking about it. And we — well, Andy Calder it was, I think — he asked John about it.'

'And what did Mr Grant say?'

'He said, 'Clarrie's a lovely girl,' or something like that, but really deadpan, as if it was some sort of private joke.'

'So did you form any sort of view about their relationship?'

'Well, I suppose we thought it was a bit odd. It wasn't that she wasn't good-looking. She was . . . well, simply not his type. Or the other way round.'

'Did Mr Grant ever discuss his relationship with the accused on any other occasion?'

'One time he said something which stuck in my mind. We were in the pub, and someone was ribbing him a bit about going out with Clarrie, I can't remember exactly what they were saying but the upshot was that she must be fantastic in bed because otherwise they couldn't understand what he saw in her. And John said something like 'You'd be surprised,' but the way he said it made me think he sort of agreed at the same time. Like you'd bought the wrong car, or something, but you had to stick with it and in the end you sort of came to like it.'

'They were not well matched, then?'

'No.' As if charmed by Ruth's interest, David makes a real effort to explain. 'You see, John always went for the same kind of girl. Pretty and fun, someone who'd fit in, get on with his friends and his family. Flowers and meals out and all that. Attentive. I didn't think Clarrie'd be one for being charmed like that.'

It's odd that I have to be here in court before I hear David say something perceptive. I wonder why I didn't work it out for myself at the time. I suppose I wanted to believe in John. I was charmed — by him, by the evening, sitting around by the pool. Usually I'd have been with my friends, or on my own, so to have someone to talk to who was different and a bit exciting was great. The others all went off and we just sat by ourselves by the fire, talking or watching the flames.

Next in the witness box is Andy Calder. I've never made any secret of the fact I dislike him. I have a nasty idea he is about to take great pleasure in getting his own back.

'Yes, I knew John very well. For years. I knew Clarrie Morland a bit too.'

'You were present at a party at Sibberton in July last year?'

'Yes I was. They were both there too.'

'Did they come as a couple?'

'No, but they got together during the evening.' He smirks.

His story is much the same, except it's much worse coming from his lips. Andy is slim and works out a lot and looks after himself, and he screws around. His favourite trick is picking up foreign-language students, the ones who aim for Cambridge and end up in Peterborough, thirty miles out, hanging around in a couple of the bars near the market and the cathedral. So I used to tell people he was gay, because I knew it'd annoy him so much, and I guess he found out it was me. I look at the jury and wonder if they can see how he's enjoying himself.

'I asked John about it a day or two later, down the pub. He asked me what I thought of her. Of Clarrie. I said I wouldn't go out with her myself.'

I guess that what he really said was, 'I'd give her one but I wouldn't go out with her.' He once said much the same to my face.

'John then said, 'What if she were an heiress?' meaning, would I go out with her then. I said that she wasn't an heiress, was she? She worked for a charity and she can't earn much doing that. I thought at the time he was being a bit funny about it. He

51

definitely seemed to be up to something. Like there was a big secret, a big joke he wasn't telling me.'

Charles doesn't put any questions to Andy either. I am torn between wanting the whole thing to be over as quickly as possible, and wishing to put him on the spot, make him suffer for what he's said, or more for his coming along and giving evidence against me. I wonder who else will be testifying, and flick through the list of witnesses at the front of the bundle. John's mother and sister. Victoria from his office. Names I've never heard of. A couple of doctors, who I take to be expert witnesses of some kind. Sam Tyson from the Royal Oak, and some neighbours from the village.

I want to look around the court, to see if they are there, but I can't bear to look at my mother again. Charles says that if it goes against me I might have to serve anything from six to fifteen years. But how could I ask my mother to come into prison, through the searches and all the rest of it, to see me sitting there for twenty minutes when we can't even touch or say what we feel because of the guards standing a few feet away? It makes me cold to think that she could be nearly seventy before I see her again outside prison, or more. Or she could be dead.

I take deep breaths, and think of writing her a note, telling her how sorry I am, and I scribble a few words and ask one of the warders to pass it to Charles. He looks at it briefly, and leaves it in front of him. I cannot believe it, that he would read it or that he wouldn't then pass it on. And I want to call out to him, but he gives me such a cold look. There must be some rule against passing notes, but no one told me and it's so unfair of him to be angry.

'John wouldn't have taken advantage of anyone.' John's father is speaking. 'But he was very good at business and he'd expect anyone else to be just as careful.'

I sit back, close my eyes, and try to still the pain in my head. The whole room feels airless and for a moment I think I might be about to black out. But it passes, and I let my mind drift, silently humming snatches of songs to myself. I think of how I will go travelling when the trial is over, planning a route around the world. Or maybe driving across the States, taking in all those places that I've only ever heard of in songs, like Kelsey or Cripple Creek, Evangeline or Anchorage. Or down into South America, down to the far south. I once watched a programme about the albatross, and it stuck in my mind so clearly that I can see the giant seas and the huge black cliffs of Tierra del Fuego, all drenched in wind and sun, with these birds floating by without any effort, not like the flapping, fluttering birds of England. I want to see them, to sit right on the cliff edge and watch them, arms wrapped round my knees. Once there, I know everything will be all right.

In my picture, I know the cliffs are a little like the Norfolk coast of my childhood. There is a lighthouse, the same springy turf. And although there are cliffs, there are dunes too, and a wooden shelter in peeling green paint, and an ice-cream van.

I doze like this for most of the afternoon. Once or twice I look at the judge, who is always looking at the witness, even when Ruth or Charles are actually speaking. He watches them lick their lips, and dart little looks around the court, and shuffle their feet. If any were lying, I am sure he would see, which is reassuring, except that none of them are. They may be against me, and loyal to John, and they may only be saying what helps the prosecution and builds up the case against me, but they clearly believe it. And in the end, what they are saying is true. He screwed me, and I found out. But did I then kill him?

★   ★   ★

Roger Turner is the last witness of the day, one of John's friends, in fact more a business associate, which makes him sound like someone from the mafia. He put up some cash to fund the land and options John had bought, and had bought a couple of pieces himself, as a front for the consortium they had put together. Property developers, it seems, are always short of cash and want as little money as possible tied up. John had told him about land at the Doles, and about the plan to rip me off, though Roger doesn't put it that way, of course.

'He said that he knew the owner, and that he was sure we could buy the land.'

'Did he suggest how he would do this?' Ruth asks.

'Not exactly.' He thinks for a moment, then adds carefully but with a hint of a smirk, 'I got the impression that they were having an affair, and that she might therefore be more . . . amenable to his suggestions.'

He really is an oily shit.

'Did he say anything about what the accused might do when she found out what was going on?'

'Yes he did. I asked him if she would cut up rough. He laughed, and said she might, but he was betting she'd go off and hide and lick her wounds. Something like that, anyway,' he adds, as if it doesn't matter much.

* * *

There's another unexplained delay, and we wait while the lawyers and the judge discuss a point of process I don't follow at all. I guess the jury are even more bored than I am. The twelve of them sit in silence, obediently watching this discussion or staring about them. The Builder and the rat-like man whisper to each other, though they don't dare snigger. The old man in the row behind looks half-asleep, with his arms folded and his chin down on his chest. He has thick, snow-white hair and a ruddy face and reminds me of someone who used to go to the local pub when we were in the last year at university. He had a lovely voice and at any excuse would start to sing, especially if it was a lock-in and he was 'among friends', and because his favourite song to warm up with was 'Danny Boy', that's what we called him. We thought he was great, Emily and Hannah and me, because he always asked how we were or cracked a joke as he passed by on the way to the bar or the Gents.

Without the evidence to distract me, I feel so naked sitting here, feeling all these people staring at me. I can't pretend they're not there, because there's a constant noise of shuffling, rustling, even breathing. And I've nothing to do, either. If it were like on stage, with the audience blacked out by the stage lights, it might be OK. My mother and brother are on the side nearest me, with Sophie, Nick's girlfriend, next to him. Nick grins, winks and my mother smiles at me as much as she can. I don't know what I feel about my mother being there. It's like with visits in prison. They upset us all, me most of all in a way. It isn't so bad when it's Nick, but I was really freaked out when my mother came in. She tried to cover up how much it shocked her to see me there but she isn't a good enough actress. She looked quite ill by the end and I asked Nick to say to her not to come again. He made up something about being on a different wing and having fewer visits.

★   ★   ★

Inside the bundle of court papers is a series of photographs of my car, or what was left of it after the crash and after I had been cut free by the fire brigade. One shows the inside, the driver's seat and steering wheel and the dashboard jutting out at all angles and various struts and bands of hanging rubber, and I wonder that I could ever have been inside and lived. The photographs seem to prove the case against me. Maybe that's why they are always in the papers. The idea of the devil looking after his own — or her own. Or of fate striking down the fleeing murderess.

★ ★ ★

At the end of the session I was taken back to the cells to wait while the van picked up the prisoners from the magistrates' court. Charles came down briefly to see how I was and if I had any questions. I was so tired that I couldn't make any effort, and he soon went off. He has a strange, bluff manner, perhaps because he's used to dealing with such difficult people — depressed, violent, stupid. He reminds me of one of the surgeons in the hospital, who seemed to understand his patients, was always cheerful, always had a pleasant word, but somehow you could tell he'd learnt how to do it. It wasn't meant. I can imagine Charles coming into hospital in his sports car, a wink to one of the nurses, putting on his white coat so that his cuffs still show, and then doing his ward rounds, half-listening to his moaning patients, flashing a warm smile, saying *Yes, yes, splendid, soon have you up on your feet.*

By now, the male prisoners have all gone, the voices and occasional shouts have gone too, but the van I'm booked on has still not arrived so I am moved to the holding room with a warder I've not seen before. He is tall and young and unfriendly, with his peaked cap pulled down just over his eyes, and all he says to me is *You, sit there, and don't say anything* and then sits by the door and reads the newspaper. I do exactly as he says.

For a few weeks I was moved out of the hospital wing and into the main prison, while they argued over whether I'd recovered or not. And because I didn't know my way around, and hadn't had the training in secure units and young-offender institutes, the other prisoners — the ones Baz knew, mostly — kept an eye out for me. They made a point of telling me the same thing: keep out of trouble, keep your nose clean, don't try to fight back.

And I haven't, I've endured it all: hospital, then prison, then back to the hospital wing, and now I'm set on enduring the trial, the stuff in the papers, what they say in court. I know that shouting back does no good. They leave you locked up. Like a cinema advert I remember of a girl — in some kind of cell — who kept trying to speak but whose words

59

were muffled and distorted, and who was more and more upset. The ad stuck in my mind because it was so horrible and because everyone at college said she looked like me. At the time, I thought they were maybe getting at me, as if I was the type to be phoning the Samaritans.

Rather than think of that, I lean on the table and try to relax. I imagine the jurors leaving court, walking down the underpass to the bus station or picking up their cars from the car park, perhaps doing a bit of shopping on their way home, picking up a ready meal and a bottle of wine from Marks and Spencers. I think of the man who looks like a pig. He'll have had his mousy wife waiting outside in the car for at least twenty minutes. Or the rat-faced one, off to the pub to see his mates, thinking of some way of fiddling the expenses for jury service. Or the one who looks like a student, cycling off to his bedsit, except he can't be a proper student because the city has no university, and the site they were going to build it on has been sold off. They are building a new prison there instead.

Monday Evening

Back at Whitemoor, instead of driving round to the hospital wing we pull up at the main entrance. Miss Barker — they are all 'Miss', even if they are married — leads me into the reception area and tells one of the younger POs to take me up to D2.

'But I'm in the hospital.'

'Not any more.' She says this with real satisfaction, making a show of reading a clipboard, waiting for me to ask why. I don't, so she has to go on. 'You're better now, aren't you? You can stand trial, so you can be on the main wing with the others.'

'What about my stuff?'

'It's gone already.'

In the van I'd decided to ask for some medication, some tranquillizers. They're usually only too happy to hand them out. Before now I'd kept off them, but I want anything that'll help me through the trial. But she tells me I can't see the doctor. He's busy, they're all busy, packing up and getting ready to move. And she's not interested in any backchat, neither. I can't go back on the hospital wing, even for five minutes, and anyway there's no one free to take me, they're short-staffed, so that's that.

I don't bother saying any more. It was like this the first time they moved me from the hospital. They said they reckoned I was better enough, which means that they wanted the hospital bed or felt I was pushing my luck. I was told to move one day, with ten minutes to gather my stuff together, and then marched down on to the wing. It was during the free association hour, so I was under the gaze of a dozen or more prisoners, a few pretending to be disinterested — uninterested, whatever — and the others staring at me quite openly. Some of them asked me who I was, or asked the warden, and I was amazed at it all. It wasn't the atmosphere I'd expected, not exactly friendly, but much more open, more natural, less controlled, very different from the hospital wing.

But I still couldn't answer their questions, or talk to anyone, that first night. Even in the hospital, I could kind of imagine that I wasn't really in prison, though it was horrible and frightening in its own way, with shouts and screaming every night, and being on your own all the time, and the nurses worse than the POs, always snapping and pushing you about. But on the open wing, I was in with all the other prisoners, the prostitutes and fine defaulters and crack-heads and dealers, the drunk and disorderlies, the petty thieves and fraudsters, and that was that.

She turns and goes into some back office and I'm led up into the main wing, a four-storey block in yellow brick, with a pantiled pitched roof, trying to look local but having the same charm as a rural Tesco superstore. This is Block D, the newest block at Whitemoor, the only one occupied by female prisoners, and soon to be closed and refurbished for young offenders. Already the prisoners are being moved across to the new jail in Peterborough. The corridors and staircases are empty, none of the usual activity, few people wandering around, none of the activity and confusion I remembered.

Each corridor of the block is long, with lino floors and brick walls and windows filling the walls at each end, so that during the day everyone coming towards you is in silhouette. Perhaps that's why they stare. Or maybe because the corridor is like a village and any new arrival is a source of interest, something to stave off the long hours of boredom.

We pass through the doors and the gates that bar each corridor, the PO unlocking and locking each one, until we come to the second floor from the top: D2. Another officer, Miss Allen, is standing by the last gate, chatting to another prisoner, who is holding a mop and who I don't recognize.

'Hello, Karen,' my guard says to Miss Allen. 'This is Clarissa, Clarissa Morland. Transfer from the medical centre.'

'I know this one of old. How are you, then, Clarrie?'

'Fine, Miss Allen.'

She was on this floor when I was here before. I like her, she is very cool and fair and seems to take more of an interest than some of the others who are friendly enough but who treat it as another job. The other prisoner, a black woman about my own age, looks at me with curiosity but says nothing.

'I'm sorry we can't give you your old room,' she says as she unlocks the furthest door, and ushers me into the cell. 'But I've put you in with an old friend. She asked after you specially.'

I know at once that it must be Baz, though I've no idea how she could have known about my transfer. The cell is empty, with my stuff neatly piled at the end of the bottom bunk. There are sheets and blankets piled there too.

'Was this the first day of the trial?' she asks. I nod. 'OK, let's get this made up.'

She helps me make up the bed, flicking out the sheets and tucking them in neatly. I find I am shy, but still manage to ask her about getting some tranquillizers.

'Have you had them before?' I shake my head. 'Ach, then I wouldn't bother with that muck. Are you worried about sleeping?'

'Maybe, but it's more I just feel sick and can't concentrate. I feel too wound up.'

'Have you eaten?'

'Yes,' I lie. I'm not hungry, and I can't even think about food.

'What about exercise? You used to go running, you told me.'

I'm surprised she can remember. 'Not since I . . . I came in here.'

'Right, how about a run in the morning, before you leave for court? That'll set you up. OK? I'll fix it up with Mr Newton. He's on the morning shift.' The bed is done, and she nods and is gone, as if she feels she has shown too much kindness.

The room is pale cream, the paint scuffed and the wooden bed and table and chair chipped. The one bright spot is a cluster of creased posters and pages from magazines on one of the walls, of moody singer-songwriters and indie girl-bands. There is a single window, made up of several long, narrow slit-windows with brick piers between. They aren't obviously bars, but they do the same job. You can open two of the slits for a bit of air, but could only get an arm at most through them. Still, during the day there is a view out towards the fences and the fields beyond.

After a few minutes sitting on the window ledge, watching the night fall and the reflection of the room in all its strip-lit glory, the door opens and Baz comes in. I get down but am surprised as she gives me a crushing hug.

'God, it's good to see you. How are you? What's been going on? Why are you back in here?'

She talks on. I'd forgotten how the prisoners talk, the words tumbling over each other, questions put without any time to hear the reply, to make up for the long hours alone each night, from seven through to the following morning.

'I'm fine, I'm great.'

'How's yer leg?'

'Fine.' She still holds me by the shoulders, smiling but also looking at me searchingly. She looks no different than the day she left the hospital, still stocky under her T-shirt, her dark hair, even shorter than mine, still slicked back. Still full of restless energy.

'I've been going mad in here. The whole place is closing down, did you know?' I nod. 'No new arrivals for three months, the whole of D4 and D5 empty, and I'm the last one

66

from before, since Vikki and Haggis left last week.'

'They've gone?' In fact I don't remember them at all.

'Yeah, the only ones left are those off out this month. Or on trial like you. I'm going on Thursday, you know. Shit, can you believe it, after two years I'm off out. Fuck it. Two fucking years.' For the first time she slows down, then looks at me again. 'Your trial started today?' I nod. 'How's it going?'

I don't really know what to say, so I mutter something about how difficult it is to follow what's going on. Baz agrees, and starts telling me about her own trial, and how she only met her counsel a few minutes before the start, and how her shite solicitor wouldn't tell her what to do or what was going on, and when she gave her evidence she screwed it up by trying to argue with the prosecuting barrister.

'He kept asking us all these questions, and they all pointed one way, like I was going to be trapped by them, and then repeating what I'd said so it sounded like I was lying, even when I wasn't.'

It makes me feel a bit more grateful to Andrew for the trouble he's taking.

'How did you pick the solicitor?' I ask.

'Fuck, no choice there. She were there

when I came down the nick, and that were that. I had her from then on, see, though I asked for a change. I knew she was no good straight off, like. She kept saying as how the evidence were dead against me and how I'd have to say I was guilty. I kept telling her, I'll do that for the possession, sure, maybe, but never for the dealing, no way. But she never told us what to do, so I got well screwed over that, eh?'

She smiles, but I can see how angry she still is. She'd never talked about it before, and it isn't one of her funny, half-made-up stories.

'Did you have your family there? Your friends?'

'Aye, one or two. But not me real friends, like. They'd legged it when I was nicked an' weren't going to be seen in any court, you know?' She smiles. 'But I'd me uncle Billy there, to look after me mam.'

This reminds me how hard it is with my family sitting there, having to listen to all the evidence, and how I wish more of my friends could have been there, to help them and to make me feel I wasn't alone. When I was in hospital, even after I was charged, they were around a lot at my mother's, and called Nick a lot too, and sent cards and stuff. Then more of them sort of faded away. I think it was being moved to the prison. Perhaps it made them realize it was for real.

'You look awful, girl,' Baz says. 'Real tense. And here's me gannin' on.'

She sits me on the bed and takes something from her locker.

'Come on and lie down here.'

She pushes me down on the blanket, and though the rough hairs tickle my nose I let her pull up my shirt and massage my shoulders. She pours on some scented stuff and rubs it in, telling me all the time about how much the wing has changed, what's been going on, who's been split up from who by the moves. I close my eyes and feel her fingers seeking out little knots of muscle in my shoulders and rubbing them apart. The oil and the rubbing are warming, comforting.

Baz asks me again how the trial is going, and I tell her it's going fine, and then I admit that it isn't, that the prosecution have got so much evidence and I'm sure I'm going to be convicted. I can't see any way out.

'Why not give evidence, then? Tell 'em what really happened?' she asks.

'That's the whole problem. I can't remember anything about the day, why I was there, or anything that really matters.'

Baz doesn't say anything for a long time, but I guess she is still thinking about this because she is still kneading the same part of my back.

'So maybe you think you did it?' she says at last.

'I don't know,' I say, but this isn't enough. Not after a day of sitting in the dock, reading the evidence, hearing the prosecution setting out its case. I've felt the mood of the audience, the press, and the jury change. They know I did it, now.

'I suppose I do,' I add, glad I have my face in the pillow when I say this. I hadn't admitted it out loud to anyone, and hardly to myself. 'I can't believe it, but it seems pretty clear I must have.'

She has stopped touching me altogether now.

'What about pleading guilty, then?' she asks.

'I thought about it. But it would be so awful for my mother, my whole family, my friends. You see, they can think — even if I'm found guilty — at least they can think that it's all been a terrible mistake, a miscarriage of justice. However much the evidence is against me, they can at least believe that I'm innocent and that they don't have a sister or daughter or friend who is a murderer. And particularly like that. Did you know I'm supposed to have shot him twice?'

'Yeah, I heard that.'

'Well, they say I shot him, and then I stood over him, watching him die, talking to him or taunting him or whatever, and then I made him look at me, and then I shot him again. Shot him in the face.'

'Shit.'

'Yeah, right. It wasn't provocation, it wasn't the heat of the moment, but I planned it all out. And I enjoyed it. That's why I couldn't plead guilty.'

Baz sits back on her heels, then gets off the bed and wipes her hand on her towel. I don't move, don't look up. I'd talked a bit about John and about the murder before, sort of in passing. Several of the prisoners, even some of the staff, have asked me what he was like. Normally they don't ask about crimes, about what you have done, rarely about anything outside prison. But there must be something about killing your lover that fascinates them. What they want to know is *what's it like to kill someone you've screwed?*

But I've a feeling growing in me that I've made a horrible mistake, talking like this, being so open about what I'm thinking. I should never have said anything, and now from having found a friend and ally, I've made things even worse than before. I'm too drained to speak or cry or even move. Then the lights go off, and I hear and feel Baz climb into the upper bunk and get under the blankets, and I do the same. She says goodnight, though her voice sounds odd, and I whisper something back.

In the dark, I lie on my bed, half-dreaming, remembering feeling this miserable when I knew John was breaking it off with me. That night I'd talked to Claire, saying the stuff about him I'd said a hundred times before, about whether he was really committed, whether he took me seriously, but not wanting to admit to her that it was really over. I'd made a huge bowl of pasta as comfort food and had a couple of glasses of red wine, though I wouldn't normally drink on my own like that, and when that hadn't dulled me enough I even had a whisky, and lay under a duvet in front of the TV. I can't remember going to bed, or anything more until I woke up in hospital. Except the crash itself.

Tuesday Morning

I'm woken at 6 a.m., and I feel terrible, with a headache, a foul taste in my mouth, and aching shoulders, but Mr Newton has no pity and gives me two minutes to get ready for my run.

Outside in the exercise yard it is raining, a fine drizzle that makes haloes around the security lights, but I soon settle into a rhythm, feeling the air catch at my lungs. I can imagine the security lights are street lamps, that the asphalt is a road, that I am running along a street in the early morning, as if I am not here at all. My left leg, the one I injured, is more than up to the twenty minutes I have. For that time, none of the last seven months is real.

I used to go running two or three times a week, usually seven or eight miles. I had different routes, sometimes going up across the fields and past the old quarry, or along the old railway line to Normanton and back through Tomlin's Wood. If it hadn't been raining too much I'd take the paths along the Ashbrook, or even as far as the River Nene. I preferred to run in the morning, for half an hour at least, even if it meant getting up before it was really light. I'd put on the coffee and head out, within two or three minutes of the alarm going off, when I had the world pretty much to myself. I might have seen the post van, the milk float, the earlier commuters heading to Peterborough station on the roads, but there was never anyone about walking or running, no one on the paths and tracks.

However cold it got, I'd stay warm until I was back and straight under the shower. I'd have coffee, cereal, and I'd go to work and be there by eight. I could then leave early. I'd have the evenings to myself.

One of my routes took me up past the mill, through Short Wood and on to the road from Southwark to Woodwalton. A few hundred yards along the road is a turning which follows the old drove, eventually passing Manor Farm and joining the road from Upton to Normanton just by Miss Meadows' cottage. They say I turned off there, went up to the farmhouse, and shot John as he answered the door. They say I must have thought I wouldn't be seen, even carrying the gun. Except that I was. It's put beyond doubt because Miss Meadows — who has known me for years, since I grew up in the nearest village to her house and we both sang in the church choir — saw me running away from the farm with a gun in my hand. She couldn't sleep, got up early, and saw me from her kitchen window as she made herself a cup of tea.

I have a shower, and feel much better, and head back to my cell with a real appetite. One of the prisoners serves tea from an urn in the kitchen at the end of the corridor, where there is also a carton of milk, two or three loaves of bread, and a pack of butter marked 'EC Intervention Board Not For Resale'. I make a pile of toast, pour a mug of tea for myself and one for Baz, just as the 6.45 bell goes off, and go back to our cell.

I keep eating, and eventually she climbs out of bed, smiles briefly at me and goes straight off to the shower. I guess she is upset after last night and I want to kill myself for what I said. I was right to tell her the truth about what I feel, or fear, but I can't afford to lose the only friend I have in here, even if she is about to be released. I wonder about leaving her a note, but then Mr Newton reappears, signals me into the corridor, and I stuff down a last piece of toast with a mouthful of tea.

★   ★   ★

This morning there are four of us going to court. I remember Josie from a trip to the magistrates' court. She is weird and supposed to be violent. The others I haven't seen before — an old woman up for being drunk and disorderly and a woman about my own age who can't or won't speak much English and is charged with drug smuggling. She keeps looking at me suspiciously, perhaps because I'm in a suit. We stand around for a few minutes, not speaking, under the eyes of Miss Thornton. She is in her forties, ex-military, and although she is offhand and brusque the others seem to like her. She checks over our appearance, and clearly wants to snap at us to stand up straight and keep our hands out of our pockets. She goes out to see if the van has turned up, and Mr Evans, the custody officer, comes over.

'Morland, you'll want to see this.' He passes me a newspaper, folded open.

LOVER GUNNED DOWN IN PYJAMAS BY JILTED EX

A jilted lover killed her boyfriend in a carefully planned dawn ambush as a double revenge, a court in Peterborough heard yesterday.

Clarissa Morland, 27, used her own

shotgun to kill businessman John Grant as he stood in the doorway of his isolated farmhouse, claimed Ruth Acheson QC, prosecuting.

She fired a second shot to finish him off in what the prosecution described as a terrifying cold-blooded execution.

The two were said to have had a steamy romance in the months leading up to the killing in the picturesque village of Upton, near Peterborough, last October. This ended after an argument over a property deal.

'Morland had a double-barrelled motive for murder. She was duped by her lover into selling some land for a tiny fraction of its true worth. And then she was betrayed and cast aside by him,' said Ms Acheson.

Morland, described as 'quiet and reserved', was smitten by Grant. During their 3-month affair they shared expensive dinners and secret meetings at the £750,000 farmhouse where the murder took place.

When it ended, she planned a cold-blooded dawn killing, hoping to evade detection, the prosecution alleged. But her car crashed while escaping and she was arrested at her hospital bed.

The trial continues.

'Done with that, love?' The old woman nods at the paper, still clenched in my hand. I let her have it, and she reads the page, then turns on without saying anything. I don't mind her or any of them seeing it. But what about my mother? My friends? People at work? Seeing it in print like that makes it all seem so real. True.

I suppose the jury will see it too. Perhaps they're sitting at home at this very moment, leafing through the paper over the cornflakes, spotting the headline or the grainy photograph of Manor Farm, the scene of the crime. *Look, it's my case, in the paper.* I heard somewhere that juries aren't supposed to read the newspapers or watch the TV, but I can't believe they won't. They must be talking it over with husbands and wives and even with the children. *You wouldn't think she could have done such a thing, but there's so much evidence. And the police seem so sure. What about the judge? You can't really tell. But I reckon her lawyers think she's guilty. Isn't it awful the way they'll stand up and lie like that when they know someone's done it?*

★ ★ ★

We go to court in the usual way: first searched, then handcuffed. Today there is a proper van, more like a lorry, with steel steps up into the side and a central corridor with a half-dozen or so individual cells. Each is tall and narrow, and there is no window, only an air vent high above. These vans are built to take male prisoners, but even so there is only just room for me to sit down, so they must be hell for people who are tall or fat. They usually take pregnant women to court in a car or Transit van. My cell has been bleached recently. The ammonia tickles my nose, makes me want to sneeze, but it's better than the usual sweat, or stale urine, or fresh vomit. They're supposed to clean the vans each day, but who's going to waste their breath complaining?

The light is very dim, set behind grimy toughened glass, and it has a subduing effect. They probably designed it that way. So we all sit in individual boxes, saying nothing, while the custody guards and the prison staff sort out the paperwork or maybe have a chat and a smoke. I lean back and try to snatch some sleep. I have had bad dreams most nights since the accident. Sometimes I don't remember them, and only know because I am tired, and other times I wake up and then the dreams stay with me vividly. Last night it was a dream I've had before. I was in a garden, all lush grass and dark bushes, and there was a seat by an old yew tree. I could see myself, dressed all in white for no reason. I sat on the seat, which was also a tomb or a gravestone, and I started to eat the berries off the tree. At once, I had a deep, deep pain in my stomach, like a terrible weight, and I rolled forwards because that made the pain a little less, and I had dark red mess from the berries over my stomach and on my hands. I was looking down on myself as I lay curled up on the grass looking at the berries on the tree. I knew I was dead.

I think I woke up shouting, but I can't really remember and it's so common in prison that no one ever does anything or says anything if you do.

At the court Josie is led off somewhere and the three of us are put in a reception cell. The old woman sits on a bench, staring into space, seemingly at home, but the other woman doesn't know what's going on and perhaps because she's scared she can't sit still, paces around the cell, and then starts calling out, shouting, banging on the door. After a few minutes, two guards come and shout at her to shut up, but she doesn't, instead trying to push past them, so the younger guard grabs her, swings her to the floor and puts handcuffs on her again. She's shouting all the time, and the guard is shouting back, and then the woman stops shouting and starts to cry. I doubt the guards know she doesn't understand what they are saying, and I know I should tell them, but I don't want to get involved and though I feel embarrassed and ashamed, it isn't enough to make me do anything other than watch. In the end they drag her off, and I tell myself that she will probably be fine.

The guards come back for me, and lead me through into an interview room. I can't be sure if it's the same one we were in yesterday. Andrew and Charles are waiting, and it's really odd to see them so calm and civilized and neatly dressed when a few yards away people are sitting staring into space and drooling and being dragged about or being handcuffed to the toilet door so they don't smear shit over themselves. Again, I find it hard to follow what they are saying: something about the evidence during the day, and what I can recall about when I first heard that John had cheated me over the development.

I try, but can remember much more clearly seeing Andrew in his office, with a view over the street leading to the cathedral, one of the few bits of the old city left, and some elegant modern art on the walls, as he looked over the agreement John had drafted, and then advised me against it. He'd never mentioned this since, never said that he'd told me so. In a way, I wish he'd been firmer, had told me straight out I was going to be ripped off. But I know I would have closed my mind, would have signed anyway.

★   ★   ★

There is some delay at the start of the session and I open the bundle of documents again. The leading prosecution barrister is listed as Miss Ruth Acheson and I wonder why she isn't married, or isn't a Ms. I try to see if she's wearing a ring, but she has her back to me, talking to one of the other lawyers, and I can't see her hands. She seems like a real *Cosmo* woman, really at home in the court, and I'd imagined her with two beautiful and talented children and a loving husband, but apparently not. Maybe I would have preferred to have a woman barrister defending me. Sometimes Charles and even Andrew can be a bit too much of the white knight, both in their own way getting off on saving a rather awkward damsel in distress.

The next witness is Victoria and I make sure I don't catch her eye. As well as being at my school, she was John's junior partner, and maybe more. She looks composed, with a hint of bravery, as she takes the oath.

'Would you please state your full name and address,' Ruth asks.

'Victoria Asprey, of Hornbeam Cottage, Higham.'

'And your occupation?'

'Estate agent.'

'You were, I believe, employed by Mr Grant at the time of his murder?'

'That's right. I'd worked for him for three years or so.'

Victoria is dressed in a sombre suit, which goes very well with her fair hair and gives a hint of mourning — which might even be genuine.

'So you must have formed a fairly good idea of the kind of person he was?'

'Oh yes. He was a wonderful man, a really good employer.'

I find myself bristling as she draws her hair back behind one ear once again, her head tilted down.

'Was he generally liked?'

'Yes, he was very popular.'

'Lots of friends?

'Oh yes. He was so considerate and generous. He'd do anything for people, was always putting himself out. A lot of charity stuff, that kind of thing.'

'He didn't, for example, have a sharp temper? Have arguments with people?'

'Nothing like that.' I wonder if Ruth is trying to get her to say something particular.

'Would you say you had a good understanding of the business? His business, that is.'

'Well, yes. We talked things over quite a lot. He liked to ask my opinion on possible deals or developments, or whatever.'

'And would you tend to see his papers, letters and so forth?'

'Very much so. He was out and about a great deal. Off to see clients and sites. So I'd look after the office and deal with the mail and generally handle things for him.'

She flicks her fringe from her eyes.

'You said that Mr Grant was a good employer.'

'Oh yes. He was great to work with.'

And so it goes on and on, as she builds up her role as advisor, partner and confidante, shows how close they were. I wonder about this. I remember the one time I went to John's office. He'd suggested we sign some papers and have lunch afterwards, and we were there only a few minutes. His offices were small but richly decorated, highlighting the original Georgian features, and blending with the solid wood and leather furniture. So different to my own office, with its metal desks and papers and unread reports piled to the ceiling. I can see the three of us there now. John, sitting on one end of his desk while he looked through his messages. Victoria, looking me over and making a point of talking only to John, with little jokes and comments to show how close they were. And me, feeling dowdy and out of place as I watched the two of them. There was something in Victoria's way of looking at me that made me wonder if they'd ever slept together. And I could sense John watching us as we paced around each other, loving it. I had to look away, willing myself not to blush. I'd been grateful to be able to bend over the documents, signing them without a second glance.

'They entered into this agreement,' Victoria goes on.

'When was this?'

'September of last year.'

'And what was the arrangement proposed?'

'Well, John — Mr Grant — was looking to put together a site for development on the edge of Normanton. Marsh Lane. He had bought a piece of land himself, and was negotiating with some of the neighbouring properties. You see, down Marsh Lane all the properties have long gardens, with old bits of paddock and orchard. John's plan was to bring these together into a single block and develop it properly.'

'What was the accused's part in this?'

'She owned a piece of land which John needed for the planned development.'

'Was it a significant piece?'

'Oh yes, very much so. You see, to develop the site, the Council would insist on proper access for vehicles. Marsh Lane was too narrow to put that many extra cars down, let alone the construction traffic. But by using the Doles — '

'By the Doles, you mean the land owned by the accused?'

'That's right. By using that land, you could put in an access road which bypassed the village altogether. And you could put more houses in as well.'

'How many were in the plans Mr Grant drew up?'

'Thirty-six houses. All executive-style, three or four bedrooms, with twin garages.'

They sound horrible, though they would have sold.

'Were you aware of the value of each piece of land on their own?' the prosecution asks.

'Well, I can't remember exactly. I'd need to look at the files. But the five lots at the back

86

of Marsh Lane, plus the meadow which John already owned, plus Clarrie's land, would all come to about nine acres.'

All Victoria's answers are clear and helpful. I have a bad feeling that she is making a good impression on the jury.

'Which would be worth how much?'

'At the time? Well, for agricultural land you'd look to pay £3,000 an acre, and because it was good pasture, most of it, and people always want that for ponies for their kids, perhaps £4,000. No more than that. So say, £15,000 to £20,000.'

'And how much would the site have been worth with planning permission?'

'Maybe a quarter of a million pounds.'

The whole court decides to pay a little bit more attention.

'Is that your estimate?'

'It's how much John thought he'd get. He'd been in discussions with one or two of the big developers. He might have got more by staying in as part of the development consortium, but he wouldn't have got paid out until the properties were built and sold. With the rest of the land, the whole project was worth over a million.'

The jury look impressed too. The Builder is still blowing his cheeks out at the thought of the money, and the Rat, who usually sits staring at his feet, has looked up as if the whole million had been offered to him.

'Had Mr Grant already committed money to the project?'

'Oh yes. Perhaps £50,000 to buy the land he had and to take options on the rest. And then there was his time. He'd worked flat out on this for months. We both had.'

'And all he needed was the accused's land?'

'Yes.'

Victoria is looking a little less confident now. She is playing with her watch strap, and I guess she needs a cigarette.

'When did Mr Grant first mention the accused to you?'

'It would have been in July. He'd found out that she owned the land, and he asked me if I knew her. Clarrie, that is. I said yes, we'd been at the same school, though not in the same year. He asked me if I saw much of her. I said no, I never knew her well. We didn't have friends in common or anything like that.'

'Did he mention her on another occasion?'

'Yes, he did. A week or two later. He said he was looking forward to dealing with her because of where she worked. She'd think she knew about housing developments, and a little knowledge was dangerous. It made people too confident.'

88

'Can you remember his exact words?'

'Yes. He said, 'She'll be easy to roll over.''

I feel cold and sick. Perhaps I am going to be sick. I almost start to look round to see if there is a bowl or a bag, but instead I close my eyes and try to imagine I am walking out of the court, into the city, looking in shop windows, sniffing the sick-sweet smell of frying onions at the stand at the corner of the Market Place, drifting around the stalls, feeling the clothes, looking over the stacks of cheap household goods. Joining the crowds, walking away.

'He also said I should never discuss anything about the business with her, particularly anything to do with the deal at Marsh Lane. Not that I would have done anyway — talk about his business like that — but he made a point of saying I shouldn't tell her anything about their business deal either.'

'So he could well have been keeping something from her?'

'Yes, I'm sure he was.' She nods in emphasis.

'I see.' Ruth makes a note. 'Where did they meet? In the office?'

'No, they usually met for lunch, or sometimes in the evening. That was very much John's style. He wasn't one for working from the desk. He liked to get out and about and meet people. He was always on the phone, or off in his car to see clients or playing golf or whatever.'

'Did you ever go with Mr Grant to any of these meetings?'

'No.'

'To your knowledge, was anyone else ever present at these meetings?'

'Not that I know of.'

'So Mr Grant would meet the accused for lunch or dinner or for a drink or whatever, and discuss this project. Was there more to their relationship than simply business?'

'Oh yes. She was really sold on him, you could see that. She'd do anything for him, was always phoning up, so it was embarrassing for him. But she thought there was far more in it than there really was.'

I want to block my ears, to stop listening, and I look over towards Charles, but I know there's nothing he can do. Instead I think of just the right words for her. *Bitch. Fucking bitch. Poisonous bitch?* Maybe that's it.

'I don't think he encouraged her, at first. Not seriously. I mean, John was a really amazing man, tall and good-looking and with this business he'd built up himself. Really successful. It doesn't surprise me that she might have wished it was more than it was.

He'd have been a real catch for her, after all. And he may have played along with that because of the deal. But I think she simply lost any sense of reality.'

I close my eyes, but memories press in. John taking me to some restaurant, pulling up in his Range Rover. I jump in and he guns the engine, sending us speeding down the lane, the lights making a tunnel in the dark. Where were we going? To the Hayloft for dinner? Or the Royal Oak for a drink? I can see him returning from the bar, having bought us both pints, without me having to tell him I hate being served a half-pint because I'm a woman. Was even that little detail a part of the plan? Did he find out things like that about me, dig them out from my friends, from Nick, and then use them to reel me in?

I open my eyes again, and he is gone, and in his place stands Victoria, pushing aside her fringe again, her wide mouth smiling, as if enjoying my humiliation.

'And how long did this go on for?' Ruth asks her.

'Two months, perhaps.'

'And he kept you up to date with how it was going?'

'Oh yes.' That wide smile again. 'He was quite funny about it, sometimes.'

'In what way?'

'Well, that's how I remember about him saying she'd be easy to roll over. He used to see her on Wednesday evenings, mainly, and he used to say about it being like his Wednesday evening rollover. Like on the Lottery.'

She smiles and looks about her, but no one else seems to find this funny. Ruth quickly moves on.

'Now, during this time, I understand that Mr Grant was negotiating with the accused about buying the Doles. Is this correct?'

'That's right.'

'Did these negotiations come to a conclusion?'

'Yes, they did. Sometime in September, John asked me to arrange with our solicitors to draw up contracts for the purchase of the Doles.'

She tells us all the deal John and I signed, where he got most of the land and I was supposed to get a house built for me, a place of my own at last, rather than having to rent. And all the time he was planning to rip me off.

'Did he say anything when the agreement was finalized?'

'No, not really, but I could see he was pleased. More than that. Really excited. And a bit nervous.'

'And did he say anything later on about this deal?'

'He did. A few days later, he had a meeting in Kettering with Tony Peston, the regional director of Mountgrove Homes. He said that he might come back with the big cheque. He often called it that. The big cheque.'

'When was this?'

'The middle of October. The week before he died.'

'And was he still in contact with the accused?'

'Well, she'd ring up a lot. Two or three times a day. Finally, he told Samantha, our receptionist, to say he was out when she phoned. And in the week he was killed she was phoning up dozens of times a day. She was totally abusive to Samantha and to me.'

Ruth glances at her notes, and Victoria carries on, as if trying to justify herself. Or him.

'You see, to him, it was simply business. If she was going to get emotional, get involved, and read something into it that wasn't there, that was her lookout. And because she worked for a housing association, she thought she knew all about developments and so on. But she was out of her depth. In any case, it wasn't her who deserved to make the money, it was John. He had the vision. He was

93

prepared to take the risks.'

Ruth can't shut her up quick enough. There's something of an atmosphere in the court now, and I look down. I don't want to look at the jury, or my own counsel.

'Can I take you now to the day before the murder? That would be the nineteenth of October. You were at work that day?'

'Yes I was.'

'And Mr Grant?'

'Yes. For once he was working in the office all day. It was horrible weather, so he was going through some papers.'

'Did the accused phone up?'

'Yes, she did.'

'How often?'

'I don't know. All the time. A dozen times, perhaps.'

'Do you remember what she said?'

Of course she can. This is her big moment. Apparently I was shouting down the phone asking where he was and accusing her of having an affair with him, which she says with that nauseating flick of her hair as if the idea isn't that surprising, she being the woman she is, and that I'd finished off by saying I was going to kill him.

'You're sure about this?' Ruth insists. 'That the accused said she would kill him?'

'Yes.'

94

'Can you remember her exact words?'

She screws her eyes up in a stage show of recollection. 'Not exactly, but it was something like 'Tell the bastard I'm going to kill him for what he's done.''

'Could it have been a sort of joke?' Ruth is all sweet reasonableness.

'She wasn't joking as far as I could tell. She was really upset, quite hysterical, and almost screaming at me. It was really frightening.'

'Did you speak to Mr Grant about it?'

'Yes. He was very apologetic and said he'd phone her and tell her not to be abusive on the phone to me again.'

'Did he seem worried, when you spoke to him?'

'Preoccupied, yes. But he cheered up later.'

'He left the office at what time?'

'At about six o'clock, at the same time as me.'

'Did he say what his plans were?'

'He said he was going out, I think. I don't remember very clearly.'

'And you didn't see him or speak to him again.'

'No.'

Ruth pauses to let the pathos sink in before saying she has no further questions. The court as a whole breathes out, people shift in their seats, cough, look about. Charles stands and shuffles through his papers.

'Miss Asprey, did you know much about Mr Grant's private life?'

'A little. I didn't pry, but he'd tell me bits and pieces.'

'And you worked for him for three years, so you'd have a fair estimate of his character.'

'I suppose so.' She is already becoming a little wary.

'Would you say he was a trustworthy man?'

'I think he was honest, yes.'

'Honest in the sense of that he wouldn't break the law?'

'That's right.'

'But he was a good salesman, wasn't he?' Charles is brisk and reasonable. 'If he wanted to sell something, he'd be good at it, and he'd extol the good points and he wouldn't dwell on the bad.'

'Perhaps.'

'He had a wide range of business interests, didn't he?'

'Oh yes.'

'He was a director of twenty-three companies in total, I believe.'

'I don't know for sure.'

'According to Companies House, anyway. And he engaged in numerous business deals, didn't he?'

'Yes.'

'Now my learned friend pursued a line of argument in her questions to you to the effect that Mr Grant pulled a fast one on Miss Morland. Do you find that a convincing line of argument?'

'Yes. I wouldn't call it a fast one, but I know what you mean.'

'Do you think that what Mr Grant did was dishonest?'

'No, I don't.'

'You said in your evidence that 'It was her lookout', meaning Miss Morland. So as far as you were concerned, there was nothing exceptional in what took place.'

'No, it was simply a business deal.'

'And there is no reason to think that Mr Grant mightn't have used the same approach elsewhere in his business dealings, is there?'

Victoria now sees where this is going, and bites back her words. More cautiously, she says she supposes so.

'What I am getting at is that the kind of man who could do what he did to Miss Morland could have done something equally shady to someone else, couldn't he?'

'I wouldn't know.'

'Could have perhaps misled a business partner or client in the same way?' Silence. 'Someone who might have decided to take the law into their own hands, perhaps threaten Mr Grant?' She says nothing. 'Is it not at least a possibility?'

'I wouldn't know.'

'Well, perhaps we could turn now to the events of the day before Mr Grant's death. You said that Mr Grant was in the office, that he didn't go out because of the weather. He was looking over paperwork, and so on. Can you describe the scene in a little more detail?'

'Well, he was in his office facing the high street most of the time, looking over the papers for various developments and also about some property in Ireland he was dealing with. He was quite excited, though, about the big cheque coming in. He phoned the bank that morning to see if it had arrived, and he came to talk to me, talked to Samantha, walked down the street and bought a paper, things like that. Not settled down as he'd usually be. He was sort of mooching about.'

Mooching is a word I sometimes use, and I'm surprised to hear it coming from her until I remember that we went to the same school, and we must have both picked it up there. It's odd to think of us being there, Victoria and I and John's sister Rachel. I wonder what the teachers there make of all this. How they might write this up in the old girl's magazine we get every year. Perhaps a short paragraph alongside the news of degrees and marriages and careers and babies, reporting my conviction and my new address at HMP Durham.

'Did he go out for lunch?'

'No, I went and got us sandwiches at about one o'clock. The bank phoned about the money arriving at three, and then he laughed and chatted for a bit. We all had a glass of wine as a sort of celebration, and then he went back to his office and made some calls.'

'How many, would you say?'

'I've no idea, but for most of the rest of the afternoon. I was out between four and five showing a client over a property, but when I was there he was on the phone pretty continuously.'

'But you don't know who to?'

'No.'

Charles pauses again, checks his notes. He seems quite pleased with all this.

'Now, about the phone calls you claimed to have received from Miss Morland between the seventeenth and nineteenth of October. You said that there were at least two dozen calls, and that she was angry and emotional. You also said that she was quite abusive to you on the call made on the afternoon of the nineteenth. She demanded that you put Mr Grant on and swore at you and at Samantha

Atkins, the receptionist.'

'Yes. Something like that.'

'Well, Miss Asprey, I hope it isn't 'something like that'. I hope this is your accurate recollection of the events of those days. This is an important matter.'

'I know that. I am quite sure.'

'Good, because I am quoting from notes I made of the replies you made to questions put by my learned friend earlier this morning.'

His learned friend is looking a little pensively at Victoria. There is suddenly a quickening of interest around the court.

'My lord, I wish to put in evidence certified copies of records held by BT, Orange and Vodaphone of phone calls made to and from Mr Grant's offices on the seventeenth to the nineteenth October of last year. These records show the date, time and length of call, and the location from which the phone call was made.'

Ruth rises to object, saying the evidence should have been disclosed weeks ago. Charles counters that it was only in the last few days that I'd been able to recall the conversation clearly enough to raise the issue, and that the evidence had only arrived the day before. He adds that this is another example of how my medical condition means

100

I cannot easily defend myself against the murder charge, this aimed mainly towards the jury. The judge looks unimpressed.

'Mr Everard, I am prepared to allow this evidence to be admitted. However,' he goes on, with a dry half-smile, 'I should point out that I am not at all keen on counsel who make a habit of producing undiscovered evidence during the trial. Do I make myself clear?'

Charles bows and mumbles something I don't catch, and then there is a pause as papers are handed around, to the judge, to the prosecution, to me and to Victoria. She is looking over at Ruth, clearly wanting to be told what to do, but Ruth remains seated and expressionless.

'Miss Asprey,' Charles goes on, when everyone is settled again, 'you will see that calls to and from certain numbers have been underlined in green. These are phone calls from Miss Morland's home telephone number, from the offices of Forest Housing Association where she works, and from her mobile phone. You will see that there are two incoming calls to John Grant's office on the seventeenth, three on the eighteenth and two on the nineteenth. That is seven in total. You will also see that there are three calls made from public phones which are marked in red.

Of these, two were made from the same call box in Upton, one on the seventeenth at 17.12 and one on the nineteenth at 11.04. The second time is significant because we know from witnesses and from the evidence of the other phone calls made by Miss Morland that she couldn't have made that phone call as she was in her office all that morning. Indeed, she made a phone call from there to Mr Grant's offices at 10.57 that same morning which you will see marked on this sheet, just above it. There is no way in which she could have left her office and travelled the seven miles to that phone box in Upton in seven minutes, is there?'

'I suppose not.'

'In which case, she cannot have made that phone call. And would you agree that it is reasonable to assume that she didn't make the other call from that phone box either?'

Victoria shrugs.

'Anyway, that leaves us with one call from a phone box in Oundle itself, on the Market Place, made on the morning of the nineteenth October at 9.16. Even if Miss Morland did make that call, and there is no reason to think that she did when all the other calls were made from home or office or mobile phone, that only leaves a total of seven phone calls over four days.'

She says nothing.

'Which leaves me bound to ask two questions. First, how much reliance do you think we can put on your evidence when your recollection of 'dozens' of phone calls over those four days turns out upon examination to be so unreliable? Not dozens, but seven. An average of less than two a day. Is this poor memory, or do you actually want to suggest that Miss Morland was more upset than she in fact was?'

'No, it isn't like that at all. I don't know exactly how many calls she made because I didn't take them all, but there were a lot and she was upset. John himself said so.'

'Well, he isn't here to confirm that, but perhaps we will be hearing from the receptionist Miss Atkins later. However, we can at least be clear about one thing. You said that Miss Morland phoned on the afternoon of the nineteenth and was upset and angry and abusive first to Miss Atkins and then to you, and that Mr Grant said he would speak to her about this. Is that correct?'

'Yes. She was really unpleasant and swore at Sam and at me even though John was out and we'd told her so.'

I remember the call really well, even though Andrew had only thought to ask me about it last week. It's one of the last clear memories I have. I'd spoken to Nick that morning, who'd told me he'd heard from a friend of his that this friend's parents were selling some land behind their house in Marsh Lane to John. The day before I'd heard something similar, though I'd assumed or maybe hoped that it was some mistake, or maybe John doing a quick deal when the chance came up and he'd tell me about it when I next saw him. But then I started to think it all through, though I tried to blank it out. I was sitting at my desk, looking at tenancy lists and maintenance schedules and all the time thinking about what John was up to, picking at it like a scab. Why was he avoiding me? Not returning my calls? Why hadn't he told me about buying the land? What papers had I signed in his office that day? Was there someone else he was seeing? Was it Victoria?

I didn't want to phone from my office. I didn't want to phone him at all, but I had to know for sure. Sam picked up the phone and told me that John wasn't there. I told her to stop messing about and put me through because it was really urgent that I spoke to him, but before she could reply Victoria had snatched the phone from her and started shouting at me, telling me to leave him alone and how I had no right to speak to her like that. I put the phone down. I should have called her a poisonous bitch while I still had the chance, or worse if I could have thought of something, but instead I can enjoy watching Victoria being made to admit that the records show that the call was only fifteen seconds long.

'And in those fifteen seconds, Miss Morland is supposed to have asked to speak to Mr Grant, been told he wasn't there, started to swear and abuse Miss Atkins, who then asked you to take the call, so you come over and take the phone, and tell Miss Morland that Mr Grant really has gone out, very politely, and that she shouldn't use bad language to her staff, and then Miss Morland starts abusing you, claiming to believe that you were having an affair with Mr Grant and that she would kill him, and that after trying to calm her down you put the phone down. All in fifteen seconds.'

Silence. Victoria is sweating. She must be feeling it running into the small of her back, her skin clammy. There's no pleasure in it now, only perhaps some satisfaction mixed with the knowledge that my turn is still to come.

'An alternative view, Miss Asprey, is that you made this up, embellished what was a far more mundane phone call, perhaps in talking it over again and again with Miss Atkins or with your friends and family, or perhaps with the police, and you've added in lots of things which you or she might have said. But you didn't say them, did you?'

'I did! I don't know how long the call took. I wasn't watching the time. But she said all that.'

'When?' We all watch the two of them: the jury and the audience are at least being treated to some drama. 'When did she say it? There simply wasn't time.'

'There was!' The huskiness in her throat has the edge of tears. Charles lets the tension drop as he consults his notes. Beyond Victoria, I can see Ruth muttering to Gerard, though there's nothing either of them can do.

'Now, I mentioned two questions arose from the records of the phone conversations. There is the question of these two calls from the phone box in Upton. Do you remember picking up the calls?'

'No.'

'Do you remember *not* picking up the calls?'

'No.' She is mulish now.

'You have no recollection of these calls whatsoever?'

'None at all. We get lots of calls.'

'Well, let's not overstrain your powers of

recollection. They've not helped much so far. We'll have to leave it for the moment with a single fact. Someone who wasn't Miss Morland and who has not been identified by the police phoned Mr Grant twice in the days before his death.'

'My lord, my learned friend is engaging in comment,' Ruth says, half-standing.

'Yes, quite right, Miss Acheson. I'm sure Mr Everard will not do so again,' the judge says, with a wave at Charles to show he can start again.

'No further questions, m'lud,' Charles replies, and sits, looking pretty pleased with himself. Victoria waits, surprised, not realizing he has finished and that Ruth doesn't want to question her again.

'You are free to leave, Miss Asprey.' The judge is neutral. She nods and steps down and leaves the court, all eyes on her at first, then more and more people turn back, whisper to each other, look around for the next event, and I'm probably the only one to watch her leave the room, the double doors closing behind her, and in my mind I follow her out to the car park and to her little red sports car, the one she drives around far too fast in, with her sunglasses pushed up into her hair. I've no idea if she still has a job, what has happened to John's firm, what she is doing now. I hate her for being able to walk out, but for the first time I wonder if I might still do the same. Another couple of days like this.

* * *

While they call the next witness, I flick through the bundle of documents again, and I notice a thicker, folded page, which opens out into a beautifully drawn and coloured plan of the accident. It shows the road, the ditches and hedges, even the individual trees. The skid marks are there, the path of my car as it left the road, struck a tree, then rolled into a ditch. Beneath it are statements from passing motorists, the firemen and police. Names I have never heard: Terry Williams and Dr Nicholas Campbell and Maria Heggerty and Darren John Miller and PC Derek Fowler. They describe finding me and helping me get free, how I was still conscious and in great pain and a load of technical and medical stuff about the speed I was travelling and the damage to me and the car.

There is another map, showing the route I usually took to work and the way I went that day. Looking at it, I realize that I have driven along that road before. It goes to Weyland, out in the Fens, where my father is buried.

108

Jeremy Hatton is an estate agent who also works part-time for the local council as a district valuer. He is also smooth and inordinately self-satisfied, but this only seems to make him more convincing as an expert in property deals. He starts with a brief historical lecture.

'The land in question is called the Doles because it used to be owned by a charitable foundation, certainly before 1756 which is the date of the first records. The rents from it were used for relief of the poor and the needy of the parish. It was bought from the church in 1896 by a Mr Potto, sold on in 1917 to a Miss Thomas, and then sold to George Grey in 1946.'

That was my grandfather — my mother's father — who bought it to keep his horses on, though they'd gone years before I was born. The Hunt used to meet in Normanton, by the pub, but I don't remember that either. Then my grandparents rented the land out to a sheep farmer for years. When Grandma Grey died, the house went to Nick, and the money and the furniture to Caroline because she had a house and a family, and the Doles came to me.

'I would say that the land would be worth

between £10,000 and £12,000 as pasture and nearer £140,000 if sold with outline planning permission for, say, three detached executive homes. When the potential development behind the Doles and the question of access is taken into account, this could rise to £300,000. But it's not easy to calculate what we call the marriage values of land precisely. It all depends on how much an individual developer would be prepared to pay, what he thinks he would be allowed to build on the land, the state of the market, that kind of thing.'

'So it could be lower or higher than your estimate?'

'Oh yes.' Ruth gets a smooth smile. 'But I would say it was very unlikely to be less, and quite likely to be more. But as I said, this is only my estimate, and with these large developments there is much more scope for individual assessments of the market and so on to have an effect.'

'Thank you.' Ruth sits, quite satisfied, and nothing in Charles's brief questions, pushing Jeremy to admit that such developments often take years to come about and frequently come to nothing, seems to concern her much. She doesn't re-examine her witness, and now the court has had one thing made clear: John stood to make a fortune by getting control of the Doles, and if I had known, I could have shared in it.

* * *

I'm curious to see the next witness. Richard Porter is the head of planning at the District Council, and though he's far too grand for me to have ever met him, I've seen his name at work on dozens of documents and planning letters, always with his initials: R. N. Porter.

While we wait, I steal a glance towards the public seats, the gallery above, the double doors at the end that lead to the outside world and which I may or may not one day walk through. There's a single aisle, like in a church, which the witnesses all walk up, and rows of seats to each side, perhaps eight seats to a row, six rows each side, nearly a hundred people. The seats are nearly full, mainly with people I don't know, unemployed and retired people, or ghouls who want to take a day off work for a bit of fun. A few rows back on the side nearer to me are my family, and today Philip is there too. He's in his fifties, a painter, large, bearded, usually jolly, although he's sitting here quiet and intent, and we always call him my mother's friend, because boyfriend would sound so absurd. Near the front on the other side, the side nearest the jury, is John's father, but thank God not his mother or sister. I don't know how I could face them. There are also some friends of his and some other grim-faced people who might be family or friends. It's like a wedding. I wonder if the ushers on the door ask everyone coming in if they are bride or groom.

Porter comes in and takes the stand, and he is as precise and prissy as I had imagined, though taller and younger-looking. He stands eagerly in the box, leaning forward, stooping a little, as he gives his evidence.

'You discussed the deal with Mr Grant?' Ruth asks.

'Oh yes. It is quite normal for a prospective developer to discuss a project with the planning authority. In fact, we are encouraged by central government to meet developers and explain to them what would or wouldn't be likely to be in accordance with the planning controls and with the relevant county development plans.'

'Did you meet Mr Grant?'

'Yes, on a couple of occasions, I think. And we spoke on the phone.'

'And what did you discuss?'

'Most recently, his plans for a housing development at Normanton.'

'Including the Doles?'

'Yes, indeed. He wanted to know our likely view of a medium-density development in the fields to the rear of the houses in Marsh Lane. We discussed what he had in mind. I said to him that it would be contrary to the PPG to route so much extra traffic through Church Lane.'

'PPG?'

'Sorry,' he says, not sorry at all. 'Planning Policy Guidance issued by the DETR.' Ruth shows no interest in what DETR might be. 'These are central government guidance notes on planning policy. Housing densities, traffic flows and the like. The specific problem for Mr Grant was that there was only a very narrow access road from his site to Church Lane, quite inadequate for the extra traffic created by nearly forty extra houses. The vision splays at the entrance alone would have ruled it out.' The jury let vision splays pass them by.

'Could the road have been widened?'

'Oh no. You see, the access road joins Marsh Lane between a cottage and a barn, both listed buildings. You can see them marked on the plan. That, plus the fact that even if the traffic could have been funnelled into Church Lane easily it would still have caused a considerable loss of amenity to the village, really made it a non-starter.'

He has a bony head, a long face adorned with thick glasses above a small black moustache. He doesn't look like he laughs much. It is all too easy to imagine him politely turning down anyone's application to do anything.

'Did Mr Grant seem upset by this news?' Ruth asks.

'No . . . I wouldn't say so. We discussed whether a lower density of housing might be more acceptable, but my quick estimate was — ' he checks his notes ' — oh, five houses. Yes, he wouldn't have liked that at all. And I was perhaps being a little optimistic.' He smiles at the memory of his own recklessness.

'So what did Mr Grant say next?' Ruth asks.

'Naturally he asked about other forms of access, whether some other route to the site might be feasible. Well, I had a look at the plans of the village as a whole, and I was able to make a suggestion of my own.'

He looks pleased with himself, waiting for Ruth to prompt him, to ask what it was he could see that John, the professional, could not. He obviously doesn't know that the story going round the lawyers in Peterborough, according to Andrew, is that John boasted later that he'd let Richard work out about the access for himself, so he'd be more likely to recommend that it could go ahead.

'I could see at once,' Richard says, 'that only using the land to the west of the school grounds, between there and the river, would provide the necessary access.'

'And when did this discussion take place?'

'Errr . . . ' Wincing, he checks his notes again. 'July the twenty-fifth.'

'And from then on he would have had no doubt that securing access through the land known as the Doles would be the only way to ensure that he could proceed with the planned development.'

'Not ensure it, of course, because all I could do was explain how the planning controls might operate in the circumstances he put forward. The decision would of course have been taken by the planning committee of Rockingham Forest District Council.'

'That decision would have been taken on the basis of advice from you?'

'From the planning department, yes.'

★   ★   ★

Tim Cartwright was an old friend of John's. He seems bewildered, even half a year on, that something like this could have happened to him. His slow, drawn-out voice is still surprised.

'Well, I last spoke to John on the Wednesday,' he says.

'The day before his death?' Ruth asks.

'Must have been. Yes, that's right.'

'How did he seem?'

'He seemed fine. Same as always. You know.'

'Did he mention any concerns? Any worries?' Ruth asks.

'No, nothing like that.'

'He didn't mention any threats or warnings?'

'No, nothing at all.'

'Or that he was depressed, or worried?'

'No. He was fine. He certainly wasn't down about anything. Quite the opposite, really. He seemed to be particularly cheerful, I'd say. Like he'd had some good news.'

'Did he say what it was?'

'No, but we didn't speak for long. He phoned to suggest we meet up later in the week for a drink. Down at the Hayloft. He asked if I'd get the lads together for a bit of a sesh. I got the impression that he had something to celebrate. He said something like, 'Tell them I'm buying, that'll soon round them up.''

'That doesn't sound like a man in fear of

his life or contemplating suicide, does it?'

'Absolutely not. No way would John have done that.' Tim seems quite certain of this at least, and I have to agree.

'Did Mr Grant ever discuss his relationship with the accused with you?'

'Er . . . well, yes he did, once or twice.' He seems genuinely embarrassed.

'Did he ever say why he started going out with the accused?' Ruth suggests, to get him started.

'Well, he did tell me how it happened. He went to some gallery, and she was there. They got chatting, had a meal afterwards at the Great Northern, and it went on from there. They'd known each other for ages, of course.'

'Were you surprised when you heard that they were going out?'

'Oh yes. She wasn't at all the kind of girl that John fancied. I actually asked him about this once, and he asked me back if I thought she was a good-looking girl. I said . . . ' Tim stops, clears his throat. 'Well, I said yes, I suppose so, but not my type, if you know what I mean. Then he said something like, 'Yes, I'd say the same.'' He glances towards me, but not at me. 'Well, this was obviously a really odd thing for him to have said, so I said, 'How do you mean?' He then said, and it didn't really answer the question but he said it anyway, 'The thing is, she's hooked on me, which is nice, and she doesn't moan or complain the whole time.''

I remember how I felt when John phoned me a few days after the barbecue and invited me for dinner. I knew exactly what he had in mind. He wanted to replay that first evening, but instead of dropping me off and going away like the last time, he would come in with me to my house and we would go to bed together. He must have known that's what I would think when he suggested we went back to the Great Northern for dinner. He must have known I would be so excited, would be waiting all week for that evening, so that I'd be rid of any doubts or second thoughts.

I had bothered Claire and Joanne and even Kate, asking them what they thought I should do, and wear, and like good friends should they'd told me what I wanted to hear. Claire had also said that if he was taking me to the Great Northern twice in two weeks, he was serious and he was worth knowing. Not such good advice.

*   *   *

The last witness before lunch hardly looks old enough to drink, let alone have a job serving behind a bar. He grins with nervousness,

118

looks around, does a sort of nod and wink, presumably to his mates in the gallery. Gerald, Ruth's junior, stands to examine him, man-to-man stuff.

'In the autumn of last year, you were working as a waiter at the Hayloft?'

'Yes sir. That's right.'

'Did you know Mr Grant?'

'Oh yes. I'd seen him there several times. He'd come in for lunch quite a lot.'

'And you remembered him?'

'He was a good tipper.' Even the judge smiles at this.

'Do you remember him visiting the Hayloft in the evenings?'

'Yes, he came in one time. In September. He was in the bar, not the restaurant, having a bar snack. I saw him when I went through to get some drinks.'

'Who was he having the meal with?'

'With her.' He nods at me.

'Did you speak to him?'

'No. I wasn't waiting on his table. But I saw him afterwards, in the car park.'

'Could you tell the court what you saw?'

'Well.' He gathers himself, licks his lips, as if he has told the tale many times before but this time he knows he has to get it right. 'Well, I was having a break, and I'd gone out through the kitchens into the car park for a smoke. As I came out I saw him — Mr Grant that is — standing by a car with this woman. The one he was in the restaurant with.'

'You could be sure it was Mr Grant?'

'Oh yeah. There's light from the kitchens and one of them security lights in the car park too. They were mainly in the shadows but I saw their faces.'

'What were they doing?'

'They were kissing. Really giving it some.'

'Not a goodnight kiss, then?' Gerald looks around a little to emphasize his little joke.

'No.' He laughs, suddenly wolfish. 'Nothing like that. He had her pressed up against his car.'

'And to the best of your recollection, this would have been in September of last year?'

'That's right.'

'I've no more questions, my lord.'

*   *   *

Charles comes down to see me when the court breaks for lunch. He tries to be nice and reassuring, but he isn't very good at it, not like Andrew. After a few embarrassing minutes of stilted small talk, he starts to warn me that the prosecution may drag up more of this kind of thing.

'They may try to suggest that you and

120

Grant were in the grip of a strong passion,' Charles says, as if a strong passion were some kind of morbid obsession, rather vulgar, and certainly beyond his own experience. 'Throwing caution to the wind, that kind of thing. Which would explain a violent reaction if you were thrown over. So you see, we have to rebut this quite sharply.'

He then just looks at me. What does he expect me to say next? That we had sex once a week with the light off? That we screwed like stoats at every chance we could?

'We might want to bring forward character witnesses, if the Crown pursues this line. We spoke about this before, if you remember.' I don't, but I hardly remember anything of the preparation of the case. I was still pretty ill, worse than yesterday afternoon.

'It would also help to balance the effect on the jury of hearing from John's friends yesterday,' he adds, and I see what he means. All these people coming forward not to say what a lovely person Clarrie Morland is and how she wouldn't hurt anyone, but instead speaking of John like he was a saint and I was a weirdo he was stupid enough to get involved with. It's the same with the witnesses to come. Miss Meadows. Mrs Tomkins, from the village shop. Sam Tyson who runs the Royal Oak. Even Uncle Brian. All ready to help put me away, but no doubt they think they're only doing their duty. I wonder if anyone could be trusted to speak out for me, or whether they all think I did it, everyone in the village, at work, all my friends. Maybe even my family.

I wonder what they see in me that makes them so sure that I killed him? Maybe they've always thought that there was a twist of evil in me. Maybe my teachers and classmates, the other students at university, all my colleagues from work, would all say the same. *Yeah, we always thought she was a bit odd. It was no surprise when we heard what she'd done.*

'I'll think about it,' is all I can say.

Tuesday Afternoon

We have pork chops for lunch, with roasted parsnips. I wonder whether these come from round here. David Lawrence, a local farmer who used to come on the shoot, grows fifty acres of parsnips, so these might be his. The pork is too dry to taste of much, and cold as well, after coming down from the canteen under a cold metal lid. But I eat it all, followed by the apple pie and custard which had managed to keep its heat. Longer in the microwave, perhaps.

After eating, I feel a little better. I close my eyes and imagine I'm not here, but am sitting at my desk at the office, sorting out tenancies and applications for change of use and reviewing the revenue projections and the arrears. And every now and again I'd sit back with a cup of tea, stretch my back after too long on the keyboard, and chat to Phil or Sue or look out on to the Market Place outside, or at the array of postcards on my noticeboard, landscapes and beaches and sunlit buildings from my friends, and a few paintings too, Burne-Jones and Klimt and Degas. I can even picture the china mug from a local builders', filled with coloured pencils. I wonder if it is all still there, whether I could go back there, in a week or two, as if nothing had happened. Or in ten years or more.

Andrew comes down with his sandwiches, which looks like becoming another routine, but no apples today. He asks how I am, speaking in a different way than when we're with Charles, more like we are friends, or at least contemporaries. I say I'm feeling a bit better, and that Charles being able to stuff Victoria with the phone records was excellent. But Andrew says I shouldn't get my hopes up, that it won't make that much difference.

'In the end, it all comes down to Miss Meadows saying she saw you with the gun.' He has a lovely voice, which sounds Scottish even though I know he is from somewhere in Northern Ireland. It makes what he says sound so normal and sensible.

'Can you think of any reason, anything at all, why she should have it in for you?'

But I can't, and it makes me miserable to think of how little Andrew and Charles have to work with, how they must think I've had it, even if they're able to pretend otherwise most of the time. I worry about this while he finishes his sandwiches. He offers me one, but I'm not hungry now.

'I haven't been much help in putting the case together, have I?' I say after a while.

'Not a lot,' he says, smiling again. 'Good thing you've got such a crack team working for you.' He realizes this isn't what I wanted to hear, so he tries again, more seriously. 'Look, I believe you've a good chance. It all depends on Charles knocking some holes in their evidence and us putting up some alternative theories. Anything else you can remember could be a help, but we should still be OK with what we have. Especially if you feel up to giving evidence,' he adds with a bit of calculation. He and Charles are always on at me about testifying, and though I've explained that I can't do it, they won't let it drop.

'I know you think I must know more than I do, but I really can't remember anything about the day he died. It isn't an act. So I can't give evidence, can I?'

'We'll see,' he says soothingly, and changes the subject, saying how he'd gone with Nick to the Royal Oak over the weekend, and how he'd had to be careful because Sam Tyson, the landlord, was giving evidence for the Crown later today.

'You're not supposed to talk to the other side's witnesses,' he says. 'So I had to let Nick buy all the drinks.'

'What's Sam going to say?'

'Have you read his witness statement? It's in the bundle.'

'Oh yes,' I say, though I've read nothing.

'I was going to ask you if you think that any of the other people there that night might have had something against John.'

Andrew passes me a list of names, neatly typed out, which I'm fairly sure he's shown me before. I can't think of anyone. It all seems so stupid and melodramatic, questions like *had he any enemies?* So I shake my head.

'Can you tell me anything about them at all? What about Alec Frindle?'

'I've never heard of him. I might recognize him, if I saw him. But that goes for any of them.'

'Julian Ashbrooke? You must know him,' Andrew asks.

Julian restores church organs for a living, though as he can't make much from that he must have his own money, and some people say he's the younger son of a lord, or something like that. He has the most upper-class accent and long dark hair like Byron and even wears velvet jackets, but everyone thinks he's all right because he shoots so well.

'Yeah, I know him, but I don't remember John ever mentioning him.'

Andrew makes a note.

'Brian Lindsay?'

'He farms near Upton.'

Uncle Brian's a character too, taking advantage of his early morning milk round to pick off any pheasants straying on to the road. I've known him all my life — he's a family friend — and though he's not a relation I still think of him as 'Uncle Brian'. Again, I'd be surprised if John ever had anything to do with him. Although John lived in the countryside and knew loads of people round about, he wasn't part of the real country. If it had been a prestige shoot, lots of businessmen with Range Rovers and a gamekeeper, all at £200 a day, and with deals being done on the side, he'd have been in his element. But a few farmers, the odd doctor or vet, hacking about in a patch of rotten old woodland, or going down on the common after rabbits, usually when it was raining or blowing a gale or freezing cold, that wasn't his scene.

In a way, it wouldn't have been mine, except that Nick and I loved going with our father, and after he died we wanted to go even more, as if it helped to keep him with us — even years later, when we were both living in London, we'd still come up for a halfday's shooting each season. Most of the others were friends of my father's from years back, and they wanted us to come too. So we'd have an afternoon getting cold and hitting almost nothing because we were so out of practice, and then going on to the pub, warming up with strong sweet tea and sandwiches and slices of pie.

I hand the list back to Andrew and tell him there's nothing there.

* * *

Tony Peston is a large man, standing up straight in a well-tailored suit and dark blue tie with some kind of crest on it, hands on the rail of the witness box, the only slight trace of nervousness the way his left hand slides up and down the rail a little. He works for Mountgrove, the developers John was doing a deal with.

'When did you first meet John Grant?' Ruth asks.

'A few years ago. He was involved in a land deal near to Northampton which we were interested in buying into, but nothing came of it.'

'But you stayed in contact?'

'Oh yes, we put a bit of business his way from time to time. Estate-agency work on one or two of our smaller developments, where it wasn't worth having our own sales team handling things.'

'And you never had any problems or difficulties in any of these transactions?'

'No, none at all. John was very good at his job, very ambitious, very successful too at pushing upmarket property. So no complaints.'

'And you would meet from time to time?'

'Yes, we'd stay in touch. The odd phone call, maybe a meal or a round of golf. Perhaps every few months. We were both in the Round Table, too. Different branches, but my wife and I came over to one or two functions in Oundle which John was organizing.'

'And when did he first mention the development at Normanton?'

'It would be over the summer of last year. End of June or the first few days of July. He phoned me up and said he had a tasty little project in mind, and was I interested in hearing about it over lunch. We met on the tenth of July at the Pheasant in Keyston. I've checked my diary.'

'And he told you about the project?'

'He was a bit cagey about exactly where it was, but he said he'd found land for development in one of the more desirable villages west of Peterborough. We chatted it over, John clearly knew what he was on about, so I said Mountgrove might be interested, if the figures stacked up.

'It turned out from what he was saying that he had already bought some land there, or at least taken an option or something like that. He wasn't exactly desperate, but you see a lot of people in the business who are under pressure and are looking for a good deal to set them up.'

He has a large, square head, neat hair, wide shoulders. The jury watch him with an air of trust as he explains how John negotiated to develop the site.

'When I saw the plans I could see at once that it was a winner. You had the river running alongside, the trees, great views. So then I was fairly sure the figures he'd sent me were realistic. But of course it all depended on access. And that meant buying the Doles.'

'Was Mr Grant quite open about this?'

'Oh yes. Though when we went to look at the site we arrived separately and if anyone asked I was to say I was from the water company. Not that anyone did, of course, but I think he enjoyed all the cloak and dagger stuff. We looked over the site, over the plans, and I told him then and there that if he could sort out the access then we had a deal. We'd take an option. I think we shook hands on it.'

'And when was this?'

'The eighteenth of October.'

'And did you hear from Mr Grant after that?'

'He phoned the next day to clear up a couple of points about the plans. He said he hoped to have the land sorted out in a week or two. We talked about getting the lawyers and accountants in on it and assuming everything was OK about putting the deal to the main Mountgrove board at their November meeting.'

Peston goes on to describe various meetings, and the final negotiations, and Ruth presses him on how John seemed at their last meeting. It's all a bit boring. Even the judge stops writing and finally asks Ruth where this is leading. She starts another line of questions.

'Did he ever mention the accused?'

'Yes, once,' Peston replies. 'In fact, I asked him. I didn't want to get the company caught up in something fishy, though on paper it was all legal and above board. So before we signed I took him to one side and asked him who this Clarissa Morland was, what the whole set-up was, something like that. The name was on the paperwork. He said it was all kosher, and I thought he was going to say something else, but he stopped himself. All he said was that there was something personal as well which he'd tell me about sometime. He said it with a bit of a smirk and I asked if anything bad was going to come out of this, and all he said was there was no chance of anybody saying anything, and it was legally watertight. So I had to leave it at that.'

'Did you draw any conclusions at the time?'

'It was quite easy to work out what he'd done — or so I thought at the time. He'd agreed to buy the land without telling the vendor about the wider development, and if she'd known she could have tried to screw him for more money. Lots more.'

'So you believed that what he was doing was legal?'

'Yes, of course. I wouldn't have had anything to do with it otherwise. That's not how I or Mountgrove do business, I can assure you. If John'd misled her, that was her lookout, but John Grant always struck me as pretty fly, so I guessed it was all fine. People who are made to look like fools aren't usually the first to start screaming about it.'

Ruth talks him through some of the details, and I wonder whether I would have said something or done something if John hadn't died and the development had gone ahead. I think he read me right. To tell my family, or to have had to go to Andrew for advice would

132

have been bad enough. The thought of telling anyone else, of starting an action in court or telling neighbours or going before the planning committee, having my private life spread around and picked over, was unthinkable. I would have swallowed it. Or found some other way of getting my own back.

'I've a couple of questions, my lord.' I look up to see that Ruth has finished and it is Charles's turn. They both seem to square up to each other. 'Mr Peston, would you say that the construction industry was still pretty much a male preserve?'

'No, not really. We have a lot of women working for us.'

'On site?'

'Well, sometimes. I've had girls who are surveyors on site, and I've heard of the odd female chippie or plasterer.'

'But still the overall atmosphere is pretty macho, isn't it? Banter, ripe jokes, riper language.'

'I suppose so.'

'Not the kind of world where people wear their emotions on their sleeve. Unless someone's put a door in the wrong way up or something.'

Charles gets a laugh, even from Peston.

'So when my learned friend asked how Mr Grant behaved at your meeting on the eighteenth of October, and you replied that he did not seem worried about anything, this doesn't tell us much about his real state of mind, does it?'

'No, not really.'

'I don't want to labour the point, Mr Peston, but if you had gone to that meeting with money worries or family problems or even someone from a gang of villains leaning on you for protection money, you'd have tried not to show it, wouldn't you?'

'I suppose I would.'

'That would be the professional thing to do?'

'Certainly.'

Charles turns a page, pausing to mark down the little victory. I see that one or two of the jury are looking interested, wondering where this is going. One is chewing his pen and making a note, and the old biddy is looking over her glasses at Charles. They must be grateful this isn't a six-month fraud case.

'Mr Peston, you've been in the building and development game over twenty years, so you must have seen or heard pretty much everything?'

'Most things.' He is cautious again.

'It's a pretty rough world at times, isn't it?'

'How do you mean?'

'Well, bully-boys, intimidation, protection rackets, that sort of thing.'

'I wouldn't agree at all.'

'You haven't come across this kind of thing? Threats against property, threats of violence, unless business is put towards a particular firm, anything like that?'

'No.'

I look over at Charles, really worried, because our defence is that John could have been killed by some mafia-type people, something to do with a business deal. Charles doesn't look bothered, though.

'I understand that you were working for Mountgrove in their southern region in 1994 when that company was the subject of a series of arson attacks.'

'I was, yes. What of it?' His chin juts out a little more.

'Were there suggestions at the time that Mountgrove had refused to pay protection money on one of its developments east of London, and that it was being 'leaned on'?'

'Something like that was said, yes. The police looked into it, but nothing came of it.'

'So such things are known to happen in the industry? Not every day, perhaps, but from time to time?'

'I suppose so. There's a bit of it about at the rougher end. But Mountgrove doesn't get any more than anyone else.'

'I agree entirely, Mr Peston. Occasional acts of extortion or intimidation aren't unknown in the construction industry, and even a large PLC like Mountgrove isn't immune. So a smaller outfit, a one-man band like Mr Grant — '

'My lord, I would submit that is comment by my learned friend,' Ruth says, with a cold smile.

'Yes, Miss Acheson.' The judge twists around to face Charles. 'Mr Everard, could you refrain from comment. And could you also not ask more than one question at the same time.'

Charles doesn't seem too put out by this, although Mr Justice Kerr is quite scary in his own way. He bows slightly and starts off again.

'Mr Peston, would you agree that it is possible that Mr Grant might have found himself leant on by villains of one kind or another?'

'I suppose so.'

'And if he was perhaps a bit naïve, or stupid, or got in too deep, a murderous attack wouldn't be out of the question? Unusual, perhaps, but not unknown?'

'It's possible.' He turns the thought over in his mind. 'It's not at all common, though.'

'No, but thankfully murders aren't common events either.' Charles moves in to hammer his point home. 'So could we agree that when you saw Mr Grant on the eighteenth of October, the jury shouldn't read too much into your view that he did not look upset?'

'No.'

'And we could also agree that the construction industry has perhaps a little more than its fair share of threats and intimidation?'

'Perhaps.'

'Thank you, Mr Peston. I've no further questions.'

Ruth bobs up to re-examine her witness.

'Mr Peston, could I clarify a couple of points before we finish with you?'

'Certainly.' He adjusts himself again, his hand slowly rubbing the rail.

'Did Mr Grant ever talk to you about threats against him or his businesses?'

'No.'

'Did you ever hear of such threats?'

'No.'

'Have you any reason to believe that Mr Grant was the subject of any such intimidation or threats?'

'No.'

'Thank you, Mr Peston.'

He steps down, strides out of the court. Most of the jury watch without much interest, a little like cattle in the field gazing at the farmer at work, except for the one in the sports jacket, who is whispering to the woman next to him, the one in a suit who could be a journalist or maybe a pharmacist. She is pointing at one of his feet, and when he crosses his leg so she can see his sock better she laughs. I can't see them and I'm consumed by interest. What is so special? A flash colour? Dennis the Menace printed on them?

The usher is speaking again, calling John's mother. She walks purposefully up to the stand, looks about her, makes an odd sort of half-nod to the judge, makes her oath in a firm voice, then turns to face Gerard, pulling her shoulders back to prepare for the ordeal. He starts her off with some easy questions to settle her in, about her and her husband moving from Surrey to Oundle about twenty years ago, how her husband was an accountant there before he retired.

'And your son lived with you until he went to college?'

'Yes.' She looks afraid, although I think it is probably anger. I am sure that if she could she would kill me.

'You were close to your son?'

138

'Yes. Yes, we were.' She opens up a little. 'We're that kind of family. I would see John most weeks, and we'd speak every few days on the phone. We were very close, very open.'

'And when did you last speak to him?'

'Two days before . . . before he died.'

'Mrs Grant, I know this will be painful, but could you tell the court what he said in that last conversation.'

'Yes, of course.' She makes a show of preparing herself. 'He asked how we all were, various things like that, and about some building works we were having done. A new bathroom. And we chatted about other things like that. Family things. Then I asked him how the business was going, and he said it wasn't bad, but I knew he was very pleased about something. I could always tell. Then he said he would know in a day or two if a big project was going to come off. He'd spoken about it several times before, and although I didn't know anything about it I knew it really mattered to him, so obviously I said I hoped it would all go well and told him to tell me all about it as soon as he heard anything.'

'Did you say anything else?'

'Well, I asked after Clarrie.' Her voice has changed, is more guarded. 'I always did, as I knew they were seeing each other.'

'And what did he say?'

139

'He said it was rather awkward. He said that they were no longer going out together, but I shouldn't mention it to anyone at all, and least of all to talk to Clarrie. Not that I would have dreamed of interfering. He said he would explain what had happened at the weekend. He was coming over for lunch on Sunday.'

I watch the jury as she tells them about this last conversation, how he sounded, fighting to remember the exact words. The Builder scratches his arm slowly without looking away from her. Danny Boy's eyes are moist. Miss Marple is very still, a handkerchief crushed in her hands. I wonder if she has a son. Or had.

'Did he say any more than that?'

'No.'

Gerard waits, milking the pathos, and I remember the time we went round to their house for a family lunch. I think John felt more trapped into it than I did, but we had bumped into his parents in the George at Stamford, of all places, and he'd had to introduce me, had had to explain later that we were seeing each other, and then accept on both our behalf an invitation to a family Sunday roast. I'd been really pleased at first, because this was a sign John was taking the whole thing seriously, proof that I was more than just a passing fancy, a fill-in.

So we turned up on a sunny Sunday morning, greeted by his mother on the gravel drive, brought round to the back of the house in a flurry of exclamations to where John's father was sitting in their conservatory reading the *Sunday Telegraph*, and that's where I was left, with a dry sherry, while John helped his mother prepare the vegetables. His father asked me a couple of questions about my job, but was soon bored with this and changed tack, instead rustling the paper to emphasize his points as he railed about the latest idiocy of the government about City regulation, something I didn't know about or care about. So I was manoeuvred into my appointed role as an ignorant leftie, and by lunch the whole family had decided to run on as if I wasn't there. Rachel had arrived and been a bit offhand — we were at school together, and never really liked each other without exactly falling out. She and John chatted on with their mother, holding forth about people I didn't know, and what was happening in the village, and did they remember this and that, and family holidays, and about some weird couple in the same hotel. I smiled along with this, even as she rubbed it in by saying how this must be very boring for me.

'What kind of relationship did they

141

have?' Gerard asks.

'To be honest, I could never make out what he saw in her. She was quite ordinary, really. She had what I imagine to be a rather dull job, and the few times we met she was not what I would call good company. She wasn't at all like the other girls that John went out with. She was awkward. She wasn't . . . Well, she didn't join in. She wasn't any fun.' This in a plaintive voice I remembered all too well.

'So you were surprised when they started going out?'

'I don't think that she and John had much in common.' She says it with bitterness, a real edge.

'Did you know that your son and the accused had entered into a business deal together?'

'John had said something along those lines. No details.'

'Were you worried by this?'

'I was a little, yes. John had done extremely well over the years. He had taken a modest inheritance from his grandmother and used it to build up a thriving business. He was clearly going to do even better in the future. This isn't simply because I'm his mother that I'm saying this. It was quite clear. And I was not at all sure that she was the right kind of person for him, or what her motives might have been. He was quite a catch, everyone said so, and she might have thought there was more to their relationship than there really was. And I don't think she was at all stable, even then. She was nervy, emotional. I could see that.'

The jury aren't so rapt now. The Builder shifts uncomfortably in his seat, and the bloke with the socks has his arms folded and his chin on his neck.

'Did your son ever do or say anything to make you worried?'

'Yes. On one occasion he phoned me up —'

Charles has heaved himself into action to stop her, but although the jury never hear what John's fears were, and are cautioned to ignore what the witness has been saying, and although Ruth apologizes with a smile and almost a girlish giggle for inadvertently encouraging the witness to come up with hearsay evidence, the idea is deftly planted. I might have threatened John, or been caught plotting to marry him for his money, or worse. It doesn't matter if the exact opposite is true, that he was after me for my money, or rather the Doles.

I suppose it must have been that way from the start. I wonder if our 'chance meeting' in the gallery was set up. Maybe not, as he loved going to galleries, and he bought quite a few paintings, had them up on the walls in his house and in his office, some lovely stuff, though always local landscapes, or watercolours of the coast. Never portraits. And then again, going to a gallery is different from a meal or going to the cinema. It's less of a 'date'. Perhaps he was happier being seen with me at a gallery, where it could be that we just shared an interest in art rather than being a couple. Perhaps he knew he wouldn't meet any of his friends at an art show — those friends who seem to have spent their time laughing at me behind my back, pulling his leg, asking him if I was a good lay.

I don't know what to think. I can't get it straight in my head, least of all with his mother standing there, talking about him and me. I look down at my feet, blanking out everything else, feeling how cold my feet are after sitting here without moving for most of the day. They have gone clammy, as if I'd been walking around in the rain, and I suppose I'm cold all over, almost shivering, and I hunch myself into my jacket a little.

When I look up again she has gone and Rachel, John's sister, is there instead. She is younger than him, closer to my age, though you wouldn't know it because she looks older than I remember. Her face is set with the same fixed expression of discontent as her mother.

But she still looks like John. The same colouring, the same shape of head, the same dark eyes. She acts like him too, always self-assured, so that she stands up straight in the box, facing Ruth, as John would have done. And when she speaks it hurts me because their voices are so similar. Hers is lighter, of course, but she uses the same phrases and words and has the same tone, the same confidence. Hearing her makes me realize how much I miss him.

'You had known the accused for several years?' Ruth asks her.

'Yes. We were at school together.' Rachel's voice is a bit hoarse, so that though she looks calm I know she is close to tears as well.

'But you weren't friends?'

'No.' She almost smiles. 'We didn't have much in common.'

'Were you surprised when you heard that she and your brother were going out together?'

'Yes, of course.'

'Why?'

'Well, they were very different. John . . . ' She sighs. 'John was a really lovely person. Lots of fun. Lots of energy. Throwing himself into things, always having a great time, and everyone, all his friends, were like that too. He liked normal things like going to the pub, playing games, eating out, a good film. And he got on with people really well. Never put people's backs up. Always looking out for people, helping them out. Nothing too much trouble.'

For a moment she smiles, and for that moment the hurt and the sullen hate are gone from her face. She looks so sad, remembering something about him, something he said or did, and for this moment he is alive again for her. My eyes prick with tears, but whether they are for him, or her, or me, I don't know.

'But Clarrie was quite an odd person in many ways.' She flicks a look at me, no more. 'At school she was very shy, she never had a boyfriend as far as anyone knew. It wasn't that she was ugly or anything like that, but she was too awkward. She'd say the wrong thing.' Then, more woodenly, she adds, 'Though she was an odd mixture because although she was shy most of the time, she was a really good actress.'

'Really?' Ruth sounds surprised, but I know at once that this is all pre-arranged, so they can suggest I am playing a part now.

'Yes, very good. Almost professional, I'd say. It was like she was all closed up, and that was the one time she could be herself.'

'Was she always like that?'

'No, I don't think so. I think her father's death was a real shock to her. I don't know if she really got over it.'

'When did he die?' Ruth asks.

'Maybe twelve years ago. It was when we were in the third form, so she would have been about thirteen or fourteen.'

'How did he die?'

I look over to my mother, sitting with her eyes fixed forward, blindly. She scrabbles for Nick's hand, and he holds hers as Rachel goes on. I stop myself from listening, and only wish I could stop the whole court, shout out, block their ears, the jury and the press and the rest of them. For a moment I have the clearest memory of sitting on my bed, at home, the night of the day my father died, staring at the shelves crammed with the coloured spines of paperback books and piles of magazines and odd little china pieces and envelopes of photographs and a bashed-up cup for cross-country running and a model clock I'd once tried to build and odd souvenirs of places we'd visited, all jumbled together.

I couldn't sleep that night, and I sat and read loads of cartoon books, *Asterix* and stuff like that, one after another, maybe even the same ones over again, until it was light.

147

'Did you meet her with your brother?' Ruth asks.

'A couple of times. Once at my parents' house, and a couple of times for a drink.'

'Did your view of her change?'

'Not really. I mean, she was very different. Much more assured, with a degree and a job and everything. But she was still very shy. When she was at my parents', she was quite rude, rushing off before the meal was over and pretending she wasn't feeling well. I think she couldn't cope with being somewhere where she felt she didn't immediately fit in.'

Now she sounds just like her mother.

'Miss Grant,' she says, 'were you present on any other occasion when your brother spoke to the accused?'

'Yes, one time I was.'

'Could you tell us what happened?'

'Certainly. I was round at John's, about nine o'clock in the evening. We'd been out to the cinema in Peterborough and come back to his house for some supper. We'd only that moment got back when the phone went. It was Clarrie. I couldn't hear what she was saying, of course, but I knew at once that it was her because John used her name so I'd know who it was. He made a face too.'

'Can you remember what he said?'

'She must've been asking if she could come over because he said no, that I was there, and then he said that later wasn't possible because he was tired and had to be out early in the morning. Then she was obviously trying to pin him down to another time, and he was saying stuff about meeting at the weekend, asking her over for supper, and that must've worked because he was able to get off the phone.'

'Did he say anything afterwards?'

'Yes.' She has it all ready, although she doesn't seem to be motivated by some petty revenge like Victoria. I don't remember making the call, but I am convinced it happened just as she is saying. 'John apologized, and I think I must have asked him how it was going. He said something like 'I don't think there's much mileage left in it, but it'll be hell to have to tell her it's over.' I said something about her being difficult and he agreed and said that she was very intense, she took things seriously. He thought she probably hadn't had as much experience of affairs as she might like to suggest, and she might get hurt. Then he said something that stuck in my mind. He said, 'In fact, between us, I'm really worried about how she'll react. She might try and do me some harm, though I don't know how.''

149

'And are you sure it was the accused that he was referring to?'

'Oh yes. No doubt about it.' She looks back at Ruth, absolutely sure.

'Could you tell the court the date of this conversation?'

'Yes. It was on the sixteenth of October last year.'

'The Sunday before he was killed, in fact?'

She nods, close to tears again.

'Thank you, Miss Grant. I don't need to ask you any more questions.'

★　★　★

There's something so humiliating about being told you've taken something too seriously, that you've loved someone too much — a mixture of stupidity and embarrassment. You still know it was the right thing to do. Better that, surely, than to have held back, calculated how far to go for your own interest. But that's precious little compensation for the hurt.

When I was at university I had an affair with one of the lecturers. If it sounds pat saying it like that it's because it's one of the few emotional mix-ups in my life I've told many people about. I made a point of being open, once I was over the worst of it, because

I thought it would help me to forget. And in a way, perhaps I wanted to punish myself. He was in his late forties, he had a wife he'd been married to almost since I was born, and he had two children still at school.

I didn't feel bad about him cheating on her, or me breaking up their marriage, because he told me from the start that she was having an affair with one of his colleagues and I believed him. So we started seeing each other, going to odd pubs well away from anywhere where students would go, to films at the multiplex on the edge of town rather than in the centre, or meeting in his room, when the chemistry don he shared it with wasn't around, or some other quiet corner of the faculty and drinking red wine from dusty, unmatched glasses and fumbling together with one ear cocked for someone trying to come in. At first I thought it was exciting, stylish, like a French film. The furtiveness was all part of the deal. The fact he was old enough to be my father, give or take, made it seem sophisticated. But after a while I wanted more, I suppose I wanted to see how much I meant to him.

From time to time he'd ask me round to their house with a group of his other students, and I'd go because I was curious about her, and now I think he asked me because he wanted the thrill of me being there, under her nose. I thought she was really nice, and wondered about her affair, and I saw the way that he treated her, that he put her down because she didn't have a degree, how he would lecture to her in the same way as he would do to his students. So I said we should live together, that I should meet the children, that if she had started seeing someone else he'd get custody. I don't think I wanted any of this for a moment. I wanted to know that he really did love me. I wanted to test him.

What happened was so dreary, so obvious, that it's embarrassing even to think of it. He came up with reasons to put off telling her. When we went out, I noticed how he would start to lecture me about things, about politics or art or the film we'd seen or even feminism. He would always think of a reason why it wasn't right to meet his children. Then he thought it was best if we didn't meet so often. At all, for a bit. So we had the scene, playing out our roles, saying our cheap-shit lines. He was a bastard. I was naïve. He'd used me. I'd taken it too seriously. And so on.

Fortunately, I shared a house with some good friends who let me cry and get pissed and feel sorry for myself for a while, then pushed me to revise for the end of year exams and show The Bastard by doing really well. The next year I made sure I wasn't doing any of his courses, and me and my friends would go off to the same pubs and cheap restaurants, or to the out-of-town cinema, and see him with another young student, and go over and say hello, fancy seeing you here, and go back home to laugh about it. And of course I told myself it would never happen again.

* * *

Rachel seems to have been standing there for an age, while Charles asks her pointless questions about John's habits — what he usually had for breakfast, how often he washed up. In the end the judge becomes quite testy and asks him where this is all going, and though Charles blusters about all becoming clear, he soon moves on.

'Were you worried by this phrase, 'She might try to do me some harm'?' he asks.

'How do you mean?' Rachel replies.

'Well, you said yourself you thought your brother was in some danger. Did you suggest he take some precaution? Go to the police? Arm himself?'

'No, of course not.'

'Were you worried, at the time, about John being in danger?'

'Not really. I suppose I thought Clarrie might go around slagging him off, or try to mess up one of his deals, something like that.'

'So not a physical threat.'

'No.' Rachel always was honest, I have to admit. 'No, I wasn't thinking of that.'

'And John wasn't either?'

'I don't know. He knew her better than I did.'

'But he didn't seem frightened?'

'No, of course not. He wasn't like that. Nothing would have scared him, certainly not the idea of Clarrie doing something stupid.'

That phrase again. Don't do something stupid to John, like telling people what he did to me, or scratching the side of his car with a key, or shooting him dead. Don't do something stupid to myself. I have a snatch of song going around in my head as I imagine I'm standing by a huge steel-framed window, climbing out on to a ledge, miles above the ground. Or maybe off the pitched roof of D Block, though how I'd get on to the roof I've no idea. I could lie there, missing, everyone running around below trying to find me, and I'd be hidden away up there, listening to songs on my Walkman, or listening to the birds, or to nothing. Lying in the sun, with my eyes shut, or maybe watching the clouds crossing the blue of the sky. The wind should be rushing past, it should be very frightening, but the air is calm, I'm calm, I go to the edge, look out into the blue and step forward. As simple as that.

★ ★ ★

Selena Baxter lives in Marsh Lane, Normanton, she tells the court, and she and her husband sold a paddock at the back of their garden to John Grant as part of the development. This was in September, and she'd heard somehow that I was seeing John, and so she mentioned it to me when she saw me at the sports centre. I was visibly shocked and angry. This was on a Monday evening. Yes, the seventeenth of October last year. Three days before John died.

She must be in her forties, though she looks younger. She has a teenage daughter who used to have a pony until a year or two back, and I suppose the paddock followed it, both turned into cash. I know her a bit through my mother and through the badminton club, and I've never taken against her or liked her much either. She has such a different life. She doesn't work, but has hobbies instead, mainly gossiping and sports that allow her to buy lots of flattering clothes, and she and her husband take lots of holidays, skiing and the Algarve. She certainly has an excellent tan for May. Much more John's sort of person, now I think about it.

I remember seeing her at the club that night. Sarah and I were waiting for our court and she came over specially to talk to me, which was odd. She asked when I'd last seen John, and then went on about 'the paddock' so that I had to ask her what she meant, and then she made such a fuss about how there was no reason that I should know about it. Of course, that only made it worse that John had said nothing to me. She must have had some idea something was up to start with, and been pleased she got such a good reaction, because I certainly didn't manage to cover up how surprised I was.

I watch Gerard asking his questions, Ruth watching him, and then notice that Rachel and John's parents are now sitting behind the Crown lawyers, listening intently, their faces set in looks of sullen anger. John's father has a horrible dusky colour to his face, like hating me is making him ill. I sense they are getting some satisfaction from all this and I make sure they don't see me looking their way and that I don't catch their eyes. David and Andy Calder have joined them too, so there's a little block of Clarrie-haters all helping each other through it. I look away to my own family, and Nick smiles at me, and my mother too, though she still looks near to tears, and my friend Emily is there too, which is a real surprise and she gives me a covert wave and I smile back as much as I dare. I hope to see Claire too, but she isn't there, which disappoints me as she hasn't nearly as far to come.

But I can't feel too down, seeing them there and knowing they are trying to help me through this, whatever the outcome. There's such a contrast between them and John's family. They don't exactly look happy to be in court but they don't look so screwed up by it either. I suppose the difference is that my family still have something to believe in. They must know the evidence looks bad — and Andrew would have made it clear to Nick at least — but there's always the hope that the jury will believe me, or something will turn up. But for John's family there is nothing to keep them going except making me suffer.

★ ★ ★

I've watched the clock drag out another hour, and I have spent most of it with my head down, supposedly looking at the document bundle, but in fact letting my mind wander again, thinking about school, of all things. But now I hear a familiar voice, and look up to see Sam Tyson, the landlord at the Royal Oak, shambling into the box and holding the Bible in his hand as he peers at the card the usher holds. He looks ill at ease in an unfamiliar suit instead of his usual shirt-sleeves or cardigan. He looks around him as he gives his name, address and occupation, and gives a sort of half-nod to someone in the gallery, the sort of nod I've seen him give a hundred times to a regular who comes in while he's serving someone else.

'Did you know Mr Grant?' Gerard is asking the questions. Perhaps they think he knows more about pubs. I can't see Ruth, sitting poised and elegant and who's wearing another beautifully cut suit under her gown, in the Royal Oak, slobbing around in jeans.

'Yes, I'd known him for years. On and off, like. He wasn't a regular customer.'

'And do you know Miss Morland?'

'Oh, yes. Her brother better, perhaps. He's been coming to the pub of a Saturday night for years. She doesn't come in quite so often.' He nods towards me, and says, a little gruffly, 'I hope we'll be seeing more of her soon.'

It's the first time anyone has spoken up for me, and my eyes fill with tears. I want to hug him, beard and all. For a moment I feel I am back there, in the warmth of the fire, the curtains pulled against the winter night, Nick and his friends talking and laughing about nothing. Some familiar faces from the village. I can smell the place, the mixture of beer and damp coats and polish and wood smoke and dog. Now, even the feel of the smooth wood of the dock is like the aged, dark oak of the tables.

I remember summer evenings in the beer garden, after a day wasted in chat and soaking up enough sun to last through another winter, sitting on the wooden picnic benches, drinking, Claire driving away the midges with cigarette smoke, watching the end of a cricket match on the green, Woodwalton losing again, and smelling the barbecue getting going. At the time, it was just what we did, a place to go for the evening, always the same, sometimes a little dull. Now, I feel sick at the thought of it being taken away for years. For ever.

'Did you ever see Mr Grant and the accused together?'

'They came in together a few times. Midweek, I think.'

'When was this?'

'The end of last summer. Maybe September. They maybe had a sandwich one time.

159

Otherwise, just a couple of drinks, and then they went off.'

'Would you say they were meeting for business or pleasure?'

'I'm sorry?' Sam tips his head to one side to hear better and Gerard has to repeat the question.

'Well, given this was in the evening, I'd say pleasure. They seemed to be getting on well. But one time, they were looking over some papers. So maybe a bit of both.'

Gerard looks over his notes. I wonder what the point of all this is. Perhaps I should have read Sam's evidence before now.

'When was the last time you saw Mr Grant?'

'Well, it would be the night before he was killed.'

'Wednesday, October the nineteenth?'

'That's right.'

'And he came in for a drink?'

'Not exactly. He was after buying a bottle of wine.'

'Had he done that before?'

'Once or twice. But I don't carry the kinds of wine he likes, so it's only if he wants a bottle of claret or something.'

'He had fine tastes?'

'He did in wine.' One or two of the jury smirk.

160

'But this evening, he did come in?'

'Yes. He wanted a bottle of champagne.'

'Did he speak to anyone?'

'He said hello to one or two people. I don't remember him saying much. But then, I was out the back.'

'And he left straight away.'

'Yes.'

'What time would that be?'

'That he left? A bit before nine, I'd say.'

'Did you see anyone else with Mr Grant?'

'Well, he came into the bar on his own, sure enough, but he may have had someone in his car with him.'

Sam alone doesn't seem to feel the atmosphere he has created, the stillness, the expectation, let alone the buzz of questions in my head. *What was John doing in Woodwalton? Why did he want champagne? Why didn't he come to see me? And who the hell did he have with him?* He tells the story as if he were standing behind his bar, polishing a glass or rearranging the shelves of tonic water and ginger ale.

'Well, I went out the back, see, to get the champagne. I keep a few bottles in the fridge, in case it's a birthday or someone wins the Lottery. Anyway, the fridge is in the kitchen, and the window there looks out over the car park. I keep a light on there, though there's

161

not much risk of thieving. So, I saw this car was sitting in the car park. I think the side lights were on, and the engine might have been running.'

'Do you know whose car it was?'

'Well, it were a Range Rover.' Sam is becoming more confident, getting into his stride. 'Which is what he used to drive. Anyway, I could see there was a woman in the passenger seat. She had the mirror down — the one on the back of the sun-shield thing — and was using a lipstick. She had the light on, so I could see it was a woman.'

'Did you recognize her?'

'No, I didn't. I couldn't see her that well.'

'So it wasn't anyone you knew?'

'I think it was. I'm not sure. She seemed familiar, somehow.'

'Was it Miss Morland?'

'No. I'm sure it wasn't her. The woman in the car had longer hair,' Sam adds, gesturing to his own balding head to demonstrate. 'Down her shoulders. Fair, blonde probably.'

I can picture the whole scene so clearly, I can't believe it and I know it to be true all at once. There was another woman, someone more his 'type'. I should be pleased. Whoever it was with John that night, they haven't come forward, which is suspicious in itself. It must muddy the waters, perhaps even help my case. But I feel so upset, despite everything that has happened since, and every chance I've had to think of John as a shit and a bastard. I am still upset to find out he was seeing someone else. I thought that he ripped me off because he was greedy, or because our relationship was going wrong. I'd convinced myself, without really knowing it, that he couldn't help himself when he saw the chance to make some money, but that he was faithful when we were going out. But no, it was all lies from the start.

I have sat in that same seat in his car a dozen times, perhaps. John always used to wait for me in his car in the Market Place in Oundle, usually on the phone, then we'd head off to wherever he'd picked for us to go. For a meal, to the cinema, back to his house, or mine, or even to stop in some quiet lane, not because we needed to but because it made it seem more exciting, more illicit. Now I have to know that another woman was there in my place, before he even told me it was over. Or maybe he'd been seeing her all along. There were times I couldn't find him. He'd be evasive, say he was working. There was the weekend he went away, supposedly to look at some property in the South West, but was that all lies too?

'Did Miss Morland come in that evening?'

'No, she didn't.'

'Miss Morland lives at 6 Main Street. How near is her house to your pub?'

'A few doors away. Less than a minute.'

'If she came out of her front door, could she see anyone coming in or out of your pub?'

'By the front door, yes.'

'Which door did Mr Grant leave by?'

'The front door.'

'Does the entrance to the car park lead on to the same street?'

'It does.'

'So again, Miss Morland could have seen Mr Grant and his companion come and go, couldn't she?'

Charles objects that this is a leading question, and the judge agrees, and Gerard puts it again in the proper form, but the answer is the same. I could have seen them leaving the car park, if I'd been at my front door. Gerard has no more questions, and Sarah stands to cross-examine. I guess it's a point of pride that if the prosecution junior examines a witness, the defence junior has to cross-examine. But Sarah is looking a little too obviously casual, and I wonder how much of this she has done before.

'Mr Tyson, you've known Miss Morland for a number of years,' she says.

'That's right. Four or five, maybe.'

'And Mr Grant, perhaps even longer?'

'Yes.'

'When did you first hear of Mr Grant's death?'

'The day it happened. Someone came in at lunchtime, one of the workers off the estate, and he said how the police were round asking questions. A couple more people said the same thing, so we put on the radio and it was on the local news at one o'clock.'

'You must have been surprised?' Sarah asks, seeming more confident.

'I'll say. You never think that sort of thing'll happen to someone you know.'

'And were you surprised to hear that Miss Morland had been arrested?'

'Oh yes, I was . . . well, I couldn't believe it. You hear a lot of rumours and gossip in a pub, and I don't tend to pay too much attention to it, see, and with the murder being so near and with everyone knowing John Grant there was a lot of wild stuff flying about, people trying to make out what had happened, but no one ever said it were Clarrie. Not before we heard.'

'What was the general reaction to that news?'

'One or two said about how with John there'd always be a woman at the bottom of it, but most people thought the police had got it wrong.'

Charles is looking like he wants to strangle Sarah for asking such an open question, for going off the line they must have agreed beforehand, and for a moment I think he is going to pull her back into her seat, but Ruth has stood up anyway.

'M'lud, I would submit that my learned friend is asking the witness to repeat hearsay.'

'I agree.' The judge is crisp, and a little irritated. 'Could you try another line of questioning, please, Miss Martin. This one seems to be getting you into trouble all round.'

There is a little laughter. Charles looks like thunder and Sarah blushes, but she ploughs on. I know I should be listening to her, but all I can do is think of how John betrayed me. How can I have thought there was ever anything in it? How could I have been so stupid, after everything, as to think that he wanted to go out with me because of who I am? Or that when we were together, it meant something? How could I have even thought that for one moment? I hate myself for being so stupid, so weak. All the time, he was seeing this woman. Screwing her. I know it. In the same bed. Doing the same things.

I look over at Ruth, watching me with her faint, irritating smile. She's probably working out new questions to throw at me, new ways to humiliate me. I hate her too for making me sit here and live it all through again. I want to strike out at her, break that cool poise, to hurt her as she is hurting me. I imagine I jump over the side of the dock, grab one of the heavy water jugs from the clerks' table and stand above her, bringing it smashing down on her head, again and again, like crushing a snake. Beating it long after it is dead.

Just as quickly it passes and I sit back, gulp more air and close my eyes. Now I feel sick at myself for thinking these things. They must all be watching me, seeing inside me, knowing what I'm capable of. That I could have killed John, and enjoyed it too. I'm sure I am going to be sick, my stomach heaves, there's bile burning my throat. This sets me coughing, and I lean forward, and eventually one of the guards passes me a glass of water. I sit up, head down, my face flaming with embarrassment.

'Miss Morland?' One of the guards nudges me and I look up. The judge is leaning forward, scrunched over his bench. 'Would you like to break for a few minutes?'

It takes me a moment to work out what he is talking about, but then I nod, and they lead me below.

Downstairs I am offered another glass of water, and then I sit and the two guards stand around awkwardly, not knowing what to do, how to deal with a break in the routine. In the end one of them asks me if I am all right. I nod, and she makes a discreet phone call, presumably to tell the ushers we can restart. Then Andrew comes in, smiling, and asks if I am OK.

'Fine,' I say.

'I'm sorry if it's all been a bit much. I thought you'd know what was coming.'

I shake my head. He stands awkwardly, clearly thinking how to put something.

'If you're going to ask,' I say carefully, 'I don't know who she is. I've no idea at all.'

He nods, and wisely doesn't say anything. Just then, the signal comes from the judge's clerks and we climb back into the court.

★　★　★

The first thing I am conscious of is being stared at by the whole court, the audience, the jurors, the lawyers. I hesitate and have to be guided into my seat by the guard. I glance around and John's mother gives me such a look of hatred that it is like a blow. I look away and see that my mother isn't there, but my brother and his girlfriend Sophie are in their usual seats, and my gran has joined them again. She gives a little wave, her hands in gloves, the same ones she wears to church. There's also a friend of hers from the village, large and wrapped in a fawn coat with a hat. She is always taking her dogs for a walk, two spaniels, but I can't remember her name.

Sarah takes Sam over his story again, but it doesn't matter what the court thinks, or even the jury. I know it would be so much in John's character, if he was cheating on me, to go into my local, to have her sitting in the car while he bought the champagne they were going to drink before going to bed together.

I wonder who it was. Maybe it was someone from Normanton, someone he met while he was going around trying to put the deal together, a wife or daughter he could screw. Maybe it was Victoria, though I don't think so, not from the way she talked about him. Or maybe it was the woman on horseback I saw him stop and talk to one time. He certainly wanted her bad enough. But I don't want to think about her.

★ ★ ★

Charles and Ruth are going through some more written evidence, papers about Lioncrest, the shell company John set up to develop the Doles. I haven't been following it, but now Charles seems to be in some kind of argument with the judge, leaving Ruth seated.

'I don't disagree with your interpretation of the articles of association, Mr Everard, but I don't agree that they are relevant.'

'Yes, my lord, but I have said the reason — '

'Mr Everard,' the judge snaps, 'you have said your piece, and I have said mine. Can we move on?'

A voice in my head is saying *fuck*, over and over. Everything seems to be going wrong at once. Even I know that if he pisses off the judge, Charles is going to help put me away. Maybe Charles is screwing the case up in some way, and getting rattled, or desperate. All I can do is watch. I want to shout and scream and tell him to stop, but instead I sit quite still. I can't focus on what he's saying now, or what the expert witness says in reply. It's like being in a glass box, one of those they have in Italy for the Mafia trials. If I tried to get out, I'd be hammering on thick glass, my words stifled.

★ ★ ★

Next they call Brian Lindsay. His farm is over towards Woolford, the other side of Upton, right next to where my father's farm was. He sometimes does his own milk round, if the usual man is off, and he was the first to find John that morning. But he doesn't appear, and the usher and the clerk of the court, and then the clerk and prosecution team, go into a huddle. Andrew stands beneath me and whispers that Brian is ill, so they'll call the next witness on the list.

'What's wrong with him?' I ask, but Andrew isn't sure.

'I don't think he's been well for ages. I saw him the other day and he looked — '

He breaks off as PC Derek Sowerby walks briskly up the aisle, out of uniform, but still his boots clatter on the wooden floor of the witness box. He stands with much more assurance than any of the other witnesses, even Tony Peston, and answers the questions briskly. Ruth hardly needs to steer him at all as he tells the story, checking in his notebook from time to time. His shift was from 6 a.m. to 4 p.m. He drives a patrol car, covering an area from the edge of Peterborough down the A1 to Alconbury, and up to the Lincolnshire border to the north. He was driving along the A405 back from Peterborough towards Oundle when a call came through on the radio to attend at Manor Farm near Upton. He knew the farm because there'd been a robbery there a couple of years ago — one of the first crimes he attended when he joined the force. The call said there had been a reported shooting. No other details. It was timed at 6.38 a.m.

'I got there about ten minutes later. I didn't have the siren on. I saw the milk van and Mr Lindsay sitting beside it parked by the gate. He looked like he was in shock, quite ill, but he jumped up and waved to me. He said that John Grant was up by the front door. He'd been shot and was dead. I drove up to the farm quite slowly. If there was someone there with a gun, I didn't want to surprise them or panic them. So I rolled up, quite slowly, and round the barn towards the front of the house. I could see the door standing open, so I called into the control room. They told me the ARU — that's the armed response unit — was on the way, and should be there in a few minutes. I walked over quite slowly to the front door, and could see the body of Mr Grant lying in the front hall. He had been shot, and from the look of the wound and the pockmarks in the wall I guessed he had been shot with a shotgun. I felt his neck but there was no pulse. There was so much blood I didn't think there was anything I could do so

172

I called up the SOC unit and then shouted out in case there was anyone else around. I had a quick look around the downstairs. Nothing was out of place that I could see. There was a teapot that was still warm, and three or four lots of cups and plates out. I was about to go upstairs when I heard a car outside. This was the armed response unit. Sergeant Allington and PC Liddle. They began to check the upstairs and the outbuildings. I went back and spoke to Mr Lindsay and took a brief statement from him.

'Then DI Halliday arrived with some more officers and we sealed off the lane and I spent the rest of my shift checking who was coming in and out of the lane.'

'When you got the call to go to Manor Farm, you turned off the A405 and came towards Upton through Normanton?'

'That's right.'

'Would you have passed anyone who left Manor Farm and turned towards Upton or Kingsthorpe and Woodwalton rather than Normanton?'

'Not once they were past the gate, no.'

'Would you have passed anyone going the other way, towards Normanton?'

'I might, but I didn't see anyone.'

The jury, who have looked more and more puzzled by the endless succession of places they don't know, look blankly at their maps. The judge seems to sympathize with their restlessness.

'Miss Acheson, would this be a good moment to adjourn?' he asks. She nods, and that is that.

★ ★ ★

We are back in the interview room, Charles and Sarah and me. We each have our plastic cups of coffee in front of us. They are discussing Sam's evidence, have been for half an hour or more. It's interesting to watch them work, turning over each piece of information, every angle. They get on very well together when they are working like this. I start to realize what they've been doing on my behalf these last few months.

'Who was in the pub that evening? Is there anything in that?'

'I don't think so.' Sarah leafs through the police evidence. 'Tyson could remember eleven people who were there at the time that Grant came in, and several more who came in later.'

'Are any of them giving evidence?'

'They aren't calling any of them. But Brian Lindsay is one of those who came in later, so maybe you'll get something out of him.'

174

We all look up as Roisin, Andrew's clerk, comes in.

'Have you given any more thought to giving evidence?' Charles is still stirring his coffee, carefully dispensing a single sweetener into it, stirring it some more, all to make the question as casual as he can. 'I don't think we can rely too much on the medical evidence.'

'Why not?' I reply. He sighs because I can't keep the aggression out of my voice. Sarah helps him out.

'We would have to argue that there was clear medical evidence that you were unable to give evidence, or at least that your inability to give evidence for the time in question was based on a genuine medical condition. This would mean the judge would direct the jury to take no account of your failure to give evidence in reaching their verdict. But the prosecution would be able to advance medical evidence too, particularly picking up the point that it is fairly rare for amnesia to remain total for such a long time unless there's real brain damage. So the judge may rule that the jury can take into account your failure to give evidence. That wouldn't be good at all.'

'Even if the application were successful,' Charles adds, 'we would only be back where we were a few years ago when defendants had the right to silence. It doesn't matter what the judge says in his summing-up. The jury will expect you to give evidence. To try to clear your name. They'll think it odd if you don't. Suspicious. They're bound to. And that would be profoundly unhelpful.'

'But I can't remember.'

Just then Andrew comes in with more papers, but he sits down without saying anything.

'It would be much better to give evidence to that effect than not give evidence at all,' Charles says, quiet but insistent. 'You stand there and when it's something you don't remember, you say so. Don't try to invent anything. Simply say you can't remember. Hopefully you'll make the right impression.'

'What if I don't?' I think of the prosecution counsel. Gerard with his arrogant, hectoring voice. Or Ruth, enjoying putting me through it, trying to pin me down with question after question, all put with a sugar coating, until I was trapped. 'What if I'm made to look like I'm lying?'

'I have to be frank. I don't think you are at all likely to end up worse off. The Crown has a very strong circumstantial case. The jury will expect you to be able to say, 'I can explain everything.' Now, you are not in a position to do this. So we have to be very,

very careful. We have to remove any thought that you are deliberately trying to hide something. Giving evidence will be one way, probably the only way, to do this.'

The last time we talked about it I ended by refusing point-blank. Now, I say I'll think it over. They seem happy with this, and as they pack up I feel for the first time we are part of a team and I don't want to disappoint them, so I add that I'd like to if I feel I can. Charles says we could try out some cross-examination one evening, if I'm not too tired. I say thank you.

Andrew stays behind when the others have gone off, still looking through the bundle of papers. He looks tired, a little worried, not his usual smiley self.

'Is it not going well?' I surprise myself by sounding so calm, so detached.

He looks up, puzzled for a moment.

'Sorry, I was miles away.'

It is strange having him sitting here, in his suit, looking much like he did when I went in to see him about the original contract. I was all for signing the deed of sale which John had prepared, but Nick had nagged at me to go and see Andrew about it. At first I had refused, and thought Nick was trying to have a go at John. He was quite open about saying that he liked John enough to see in the pub every few weeks but he didn't trust him and he wasn't happy that we were going out together. In the end, to shut him up, I sent the deeds to Andrew and asked him to check them over.

He had asked me to come into the office a few days later, and had as usual given the impression of being amused by it all and serious at the same time. He'd asked me some questions about the deal, about what I wanted from it, what John had said. At the end, he'd sat back and looking a little pleased with himself he'd said he had to advise me not to sign.

'What's wrong with it? What's the problem?'

'Well, the main thing is that you are putting this land into the new company, you're going into partnership with John in effect, and yet he's got effective control of the company. He can do almost exactly what he wants with it, and there's no mechanism for you to protect your interests.'

'But legally there's nothing wrong with it? Nothing crooked?'

'No.' He thought about this for a minute, twirling his pen around his thumb, looking down at the thin green file. 'No, you're selling for a fair price for pasture. The valuation looks OK. But you'd get more for it if the land had outline planning permission.'

'So there's nothing to make you think I shouldn't go ahead.' I'd said it as a statement, not a question, trying to push him into agreeing it was a good idea. But he didn't.

'From your point of view, I wouldn't recommend this arrangement at all. In effect you will be a sleeping partner, leaving him in control. The way the company is structured, he could build a nuclear power station on the land and there's nothing you could do to stop him.'

'But I'd still own a quarter of it, wouldn't I?'

'Oh yes, you still have the share in the value. But you can't say what direction the company should take. And there's no need for that. I'd be very happy to draw up an alternative company structure, and to talk it over with John, explain my concerns to him if you'd prefer.'

'How much would that cost?' I can hear my voice clearly, even though it was a year ago, sounding strange, choked. Andrew looked a bit fucked off at the idea that he was making work for himself.

'I'd happily do it at no charge. That's not the point.' He'd looked away, his cheeks flushed with embarrassment or anger. I sat in silence, and he tried again. 'Will you at least think about it?'

But I'd had the answer I'd wanted to hear, and I could tell Nick and my mother it was all OK. I signed the papers and took them round to John the same night.

★ ★ ★

We are waiting for the van again, Josie and I. The guard has gone off and left us alone in the holding room. Despite the no-smoking signs, the floor is pitted with the marks where cigarettes have been stubbed out. Josie sits on the floor, against the wall, and lights up, sucking the smoke into her lungs, and then blowing it up to the ceiling.

'How did it go?' I ask. She snorts, mutters something, then turns to me suddenly with her startling gaze.

'My bastard boss stitched me up. Told them all about the fight. He was there in his suit, looking like butter wouldn't melt. I've seen him headbutt a punter one time who was giving him aggro. He's a real nutter, but the brewery've looked after him all right.'

She looks away, smokes on. I don't really follow this, but I don't fancy asking her to explain.

'What about you?' she asks, after a while.

'I think my barrister's fucking it up for me,' I say, surprising myself.

'Yeah, they do that.' She starts tapping her foot, mouthing something again and again. Only now does it occur to me that Charles wants me to give evidence so that, when I screw up, he can blame me. I can almost hear him saying to his colleagues '*Well you have to have a witness who can stand up to cross-examination. She fell to pieces — I knew she would, but what can you do?*'

'You've been here before,' Josie says accusingly. 'How long d'you have to wait for the van?'

'Half an hour, perhaps.'

'I don't know why I'm in a hurry anyway. No hurry to get back there. I hate it with those loonies all around. They give me the shits, I tell you. Screaming and talking to themselves. Or the ones who don't say anything, like that Toots woman. Has she ever said anything?'

'Not to me.'

'Fuck 'em all. You're better off talking to the screws half the time.'

I already know that she sees herself as a cut above the others, with their unpaid fines and petty thefts and drunk and disorderlies. Wounding, affray, a two-day trial all mark her out as in an elite. One I'm in by default.

'D'you know what Harrison said?' Harrison must be one of the prison officers, one I don't know. 'I told her I couldn't stand the loonies and could she get me on to another landing and why weren't they in some hospital somewhere. And she said she was glad to have a few in because they freak out the other prisoners. Makes being inside even worse. More of a punishment. Can you believe it? Wankers, the lot of 'em.'

She walks around the room in frustration, mutters to herself a bit more. Perhaps she's taken something. Lots of people do, because they think they need it to help them through.

'You're in with Baz, ain't you? She's all right, she is,' she adds, nodding her head wisely.

'Yeah.'

'D'you know that all that stuff she says about her life, it's all shit, y'know?' She sits on the table, kicking her legs about, staring at me almost as a challenge.

'I guessed a lot of it must be,' I say. I'll probably hear something spiteful, but I can't help wanting to know more.

'Oh yeah. Someone was here months ago, knew her back in Middlesbrough or wherever she's from. She was never in care. She ran away from home. And it's her first time in the nick. Did a bit of thieving and dealing on the

182

side. Had too much gear on her when she was caught, the silly bitch.'

That's all I hear before they come and take us away. Locked in the van, I think about what Josie was saying about Baz, and how people from your past could always turn up like that, and how it might happen to me. They might produce more witnesses claiming I'm unbalanced or violent. Shooting John in cold blood — shooting him twice. Could I have done it? Maybe I could — that's what everyone else seems to think, anyway. I know I have a temper, I've hit out at people before. I have a sick feeling, thinking of who they might drag into the witness box. Who might come all too willingly to stick it into me. Someone like Michael.

I was at a party, one of those cheerless student parties with too many people getting drunk on cheap wine and cans of beer and own-brand vodka. I can't remember whose house we were in — they were all the same — terrace houses, smelling of damp and stale cigarette smoke and mouldy food because no one had taken out the rubbish for days on end. Everything — the wallpaper around the light switches, the brown three-piece suite, the kitchen floor — everything had a glaze of ingrained dirt and grease. This party was no different from a dozen others. Drinking cold red wine from a plastic cup, chatting to friends on my course, pushing past people to get a plate of pasta salad and dry bread from the kitchen. Hoping I wouldn't need to go to the loo, with the queue already halfway down the stairs.

I was sitting in a dimly lit front room, the tinny noise from the stereo jarring with the muffled heavy dance music from the bedroom right above us. I was eating to soak up the acid red wine, and drinking because the party was worse than usual, far worse, because Michael, my boyfriend the week before, was there with his new girlfriend. Everyone knew this, it was one of the things people were telling each other, a bit of gossip to pass around. People thought he shouldn't have come, or I shouldn't, or that he'd been a slag, or that it was just one of those things and good luck to him. But everyone knew I was the victim, the loser, even my friends who had formed a small female defence league around me at one end of the room.

I had to stay for a while, to make some kind of point I didn't really understand, and the others went off for a bop but I didn't feel up to it so I stayed chatting to my friend Emily. Then I knew that he was there, in the room, and a moment later he was sitting on the arm of the chair, saying hello, playing the

184

'let's be adult about this' card. We had to talk, apparently. I didn't look at him. Emily went off and he started to explain himself, justifying himself, in a low, confidential voice, a bedroom voice, which hardly carried over the music. I endured this shit, no more, and stared at the food on my plate, and pushed it around with my fork. He began to rub my back. It was supposed to be soothing, to match his smooth voice telling me how it didn't have a future anyway. 'It' being our relationship. And he was right, I now know, because 'it' consisted of him hanging round with me, and sometimes screwing me, until he found someone else. I felt sick with anger. My face was burning, but he didn't notice as he leant closer, his ridiculous beard brushing my ear so that I flinched. And he didn't notice because he'd been drinking.

He put his hand on my knee and at once, without thinking, I drove the fork deep into his arm. He screamed, fell back off the arm of the sofa and scrambled up to gaze at his arm, expecting blood to be welling out through his shirt, though there was nothing there. *You fucking bitch*, he was saying, over and over again. I sat watching the wine run out from a bottle knocked over beside me. Michael was standing over me, wanting me to look up so that he could hit me. Then he turned to the others in the room, I could sense them standing about, unsure what had happened, wary, embarrassed. So I pushed past him, head down, into the hall, and was gone before he could follow me.

I'd left my bag and door keys upstairs in the house, my coat too, so I wandered the streets for hours, waiting for someone to come back to our flat. Emily found me in the end, shivering on a bench in the park opposite, and took me home.

Tuesday Evening

This evening, when I got back to my cell, I tried the usual line about having a shower on the duty PO and got the shock of my life when he said yes. I didn't ask why, when something like that's offered you take it before it goes again. So he let me into the washroom and told me not to be too long. The place was empty, a big tiled hall, with rows of jets jutting high up from the wall and taps that usually turned the water from chilling to tepid, except that tonight the water was scalding hot. I used the last of my shampoo and tried to get really clean, using as much water as I could, letting it run over me, taking my time.

But then I started to wonder why the PO had said I could come down here and whether he was searching my room. Or maybe the stories of being watched — and worse — by the male screws was true, so I finished off quickly and wrapped my robe round me and met him at the door coming down to see where I was. I thanked him, but all he said was he wouldn't do it every day and not to tell anyone else or they'd all want one.

After the shower I felt much better, and when I was dressed again I went and collected my supper from the canteen. They'd served up their own take on chicken chasseur with duchesse potatoes and mixed vegetables, kept warm in a hotplate. The sauce was a bright red with uniform slices of button mushroom in it. The chicken skin was tough. I stuck my fork into it savagely and remembered doing the same to Michael with some satisfaction.

I wonder now if what they say about the system and even the screws themselves respecting murderers is really true. Would they all respect me because I'm on a murder trial, or because I have actually murdered someone? Could they tell I am the type, just by seeing me eat or hearing me speak? And I worry too, that I am starting to become paranoid, thinking that people are watching me, or out to do me down, that things can't be taken at face value. That's something that happens to people inside, they tell me. Or maybe it's because so many of them are on dope.

Cleaning the steel tray, I remember something about the evidence Rachel gave, when Charles was asking her about John's living habits. *Was he very tidy? Would he leave stuff lying around overnight or always wash up?* I could've told him that John couldn't leave anything dirty on a table or even in the kitchen. If he was cooking he'd always be wiping down the tops and washing up pans and spoons and so on as he went. And he wouldn't leave glasses, they'd always be put in the dishwasher. Rachel was surprised by the questions, and said much the same as I would have done, but what I think of now is the way she softened as she spoke, her whole face lost its hardness, and for a moment she was as I remember her. She was thinking of him, amusing and exasperating at the same time, the same way I do when I find that, despite everything, I still miss him. I wish I had a photo of him here in my diary, because the image I have of him in my mind is fading as the trial goes on.

Seeing Rachel helped bring him back a little. It was eerie, though, to hear her speak. Her voice is so close to his.

★ ★ ★

Back in our cell, Baz seemed her old self and kept asking questions about the trial, how it was going, what all the witnesses had said, what I reckoned about the judge and the jury and the lawyers most of all.

I told her about Victoria giving evidence,

and how Charles had made her look stupid, so that Ruth and Gerard had been looking daggers at the CPS solicitors who'd prepared the case, and so that even if I was put away I'd have one good memory from the trial. And how Andrew had dug up this stuff about Mountgrove, had fed Charles the right questions, and that I had passed him a note afterwards saying he was great, and he'd passed one back saying 'Not great — supremely gifted!'. Baz thought this meant he was a tosser, and typically I couldn't explain why it was funny.

I suppose she wanted me to talk, to distract her from thinking about her release. She lay on the bed, restlessly turning a plastic mug she'd picked up over and over in her hands, banging it against one foot. She said she wanted to get out, more than anything, but she was scared too.

'What if I screw it up? I'm clean now, but I'll never get a job. No one'll take us when they see my record.'

'Sure they will.' I tried to sound confident. 'You've got a trade now. No one has to know anything about what you did before.'

'Yeah, right.'

She kept coming back to saying she wouldn't find work. I thought it more likely she was worrying about meeting up with her old friends, who from the sound of it couldn't even get it together enough to nick things any more. She wanted me to say something reassuring, or to take her mind away from getting out. I thought about telling her about the flat, but maybe she already knew about it and resented it in some way, which would be just like her.

Now she is staring out of the window. I can hardly see her now in the gloom. It is like we are children, visiting each other's house, staying the night and sitting up talking about all kinds of things.

'Tell us more about Karl,' she says.

'What's there to tell?' Karl was an ex of mine, brief and long past, but he was glamorous — or at least Norwegian — and of all the people we talked about in hospital he was the one who caught Baz's imagination.

'Did you write to him like I said?' This makes me shy. I hadn't seen him for more than four years, but Baz had gone on about him so much that I'd asked Nick to find his address and I'd written him a card asking how things were going, not telling him anything about what had happened to me. He was from a town called Tonsberg, which the way he described it sounded like Peterborough, but placed on the side of a seventy-mile fjord, surrounded by mountains and ice rather than fields of carrots.

'Yeah, a couple of weeks back,' I admit.

'Oh man, there's still plenty of time. He's probably on a ship. Catching fish. Whales.'

Baz had embroidered the story, turning my trainee lawyer into a bearded seafarer, a young-stud version of Captain Birdseye.

'What about his sister? Did you mention her? If she was blonde and had a nice smile I could even put up with the rucksack.'

'What rucksack?'

'Norwegians. They all wear rucksacks. I've seen 'em in London, on the tube, like tortoises. With pans and stuff hanging down. Long legs and rucksacks.'

'I never met his sister.'

'Sure you did,' Baz insists.

'Oh yeah. Is it Helga?'

'No, Inga.' So I make up Inga, and her lodge in the Norwegian mountains, with the days of skiing and then the sauna and the jump into the cold mountain stream and then Inga drying her long blonde hair, lying stretched out on bearskins before an open fire. Then I leave the rest of the story to Baz.

★   ★   ★

This night, I try to stay awake for as long as possible, to avoid the dreams. I have my radio

192

turned on very quietly, right next to my ear, soothing. I doze for a while, and then comes the end of the news and the shipping forecast, and I feel like I am on a ship, and I try to keep the feeling going, remembering how we once took the overnight ferry to Hamburg, imagining — except not an image but more a sensation — the shudder of engines or the slow pitch and roll of the ship in the North Sea swell. Tonight the forecast is for calm seas and clear visibility, and the sea seems the most peaceful place you could imagine, dark save for the cabin lights and the wake washing along the side. *Tyne, Dogger, Fisher, German Bight.* The names roll by, meaningless and yet loaded with associations, images. It reminds me of the coast, family holidays, staring out to sea from the cliffs by the lighthouse, watching the bare horizon, gulls wheeling, and always the breeze and always the suck and draw of the waves on the beach below.

With the sound of the forecast, the incantation of names, I remember one New Year's Eve, staying in the flat at university. I was staying there because I couldn't face a whole Christmas and New Year at home, and because I was doing some bar work to earn some extra money. Karl, one of Nick's friends from work, was staying for a couple of days as he wanted to travel round England rather than go back to Norway. He'd come into the bar quite a lot, it being pretty dead after Christmas, and he'd sit chatting, very calm and sorted, and surprisingly funny in a dry sort of way.

On New Year's Eve I wasn't working and I'd said I'd take him to a party, and cook us something in the flat first, but in the end we got chatting, and he was telling me about his home, and his job, and his sister who was serving as an aid worker with the UN in Croatia, and I was telling him some stuff, I can't remember what. So we just sat listening to records in my room, and talked about places we'd been, and drank the remains of a bottle of aquavit he'd brought with him, and ate some sausages I'd burnt earlier, and then it was midnight, with distant cheers from the houses around us, and further away the sirens of the ships in the docks, blasting out the new year. We kissed, lying together, taking such a time to hold each other, to touch each other, and then to lie together, on the threadbare carpet, naked in the light from the street, warmed by each other and by the drink.

We screwed for so long, and he had such a strong, slow rhythm, that it was like being rocked in a dream, the sensation lasting long after, like being on a boat. And I can feel it now. With my eyes shut I can see the desk with my books piled on it, the glint of our glasses on the floor, the feel of the carpet rough under my back, and then later his face beneath mine, as he looks at me in the wash of the street light coming up through the open window, and for that moment I feel beautiful. I remember it all, I am there, and I feel that same fire now.

I think of the card I wrote, and what I couldn't write. I wanted to tell him I am in trouble. I wanted to say that I should never have run away from him, that I shouldn't have been scared of having ties. I want to escape, to go back. But I could say none of these things.

Wednesday Morning

Alone in my cell in the van, I can only see the sky but I can imagine where we are, the view over the fens, the fields of black earth turned ready for the next crop, winter wheat or cabbages or whatever, fields all the way to the horizon. And to the other side the river sliding between the long straight banks. I used to come out skating here, or I can remember one winter at least, when the fields were flooded to stop the river bursting its banks, and the ice lay in one smooth sheet, dotted with the black specks of other skaters, Nick and I shouting at each other, trying to go faster and further, and my father calling us back. He'd told us how when he was up at Cambridge, in the fifties I suppose, he'd skated ten miles along the Cam in a day, almost as far as Ely.

I wonder if he would have been disappointed that we didn't go to his college. I don't remember him ever saying anything about it, but he told us such stories, he'd had such a great time there, that I'm sure that's what he saw us doing — or Nick, at least. But Nick went to London, I went to Hull. I wonder where our children will go. Nick will be OK. I guess he'll marry Sophie, have lovely children, they'll go to a good school, to Oxbridge, wherever they want. Maybe they'll be Euro-kids, studying in Paris or Berlin. But for me? I could be in prison for ten years or more, I could be too old to have children by the time I'm let out. And then who'll want to go out with me? A killer? Not even in a rage, but in cold blood. Who could fall for me, knowing I'd done that to my lover? Who could wish that on their children — growing up knowing about their mother the killer?

I hum a song to myself to try to blank out the thoughts. I have to tell myself that maybe the trial's going OK. Charles has got the jury thinking about John being killed in a protection racket. He made Victoria's evidence look iffy. I tell myself it's always bound to seem worse when the prosecution are making all the running. All the witnesses have been against me, more or less, but that'll be different too when they start to put my case. No point worrying about the evidence to come today.

I put the tape back on, turn it up and try to lose myself in the music again. Baz was quite impressed that I had this tape, because she thinks I've got weird musical taste. I have a really random selection of tapes. I hear something and I like it, maybe because of where I was or who I was with when I first heard it, and then I buy it or copy it. She follows all the fashions, she likes bands because they play well and have cool lyrics and are part of a scene. She told me she used to be in a band, playing bass, though she says they were crap. She used to have over two hundred records — vinyl, not CDs, she was very insistent about that — but she'd sold them all and her hi-fi too to buy drugs.

'Good thing I did, too,' she'd told me, ''cos they'd have sold the lot to pay our fine. Better to smoke it, get some fun out of it.'

There's a loud bang, and the truck brakes sharply. I'm thrown against the wall of the cell. We weave from side to side a little, then the brakes come on again, pitching the front of the truck down. I try to grab on to something, my hands scrabbling at the sheer walls before I slide to the floor. I'm shouting, I can hear someone else scream, but already we're coming off the road. The truck sinks down on one side, sways. I wait for us to start to slide into the river.

Even when we have stopped I am tearing at the door, waiting for the cell to fill up through the fucking skylight I can't look through and can't climb up to try to shut. I wonder how long it will be before we are flooded. But we are still upright. I hold my breath, listening for the creak as we begin to tip over.

Then a voice says, 'I'm sorry but you've failed your driving test.' Someone starts to clap. I let out my breath, and hug myself, sitting on the floor, my back to the door. And after a few moments one of the guards opens the door, so I half-fall at his feet, and says they've got a flat tyre and it'll be a few minutes' waiting. He's about to shut the door on me again but I tell him I've got to get out, I've just got to, and I don't swear or scream but it must be all the more effective for that because — even though I'm sure he isn't supposed to — he takes me outside and sits me down on the grass verge, looking out not at the river but over the fields, empty fields, with a low shed in the distance, while the other guard and the driver are looking at the wheel on the truck. It's a twin axle, a good tyre on the outside of the blown tyre, and to change one they'll have to remove the other one. The truck must weigh ten tons and they know they'll never shift it themselves.

'Bit of a shock, eh?' he says. I nod. 'No real danger, though.'

From time to time cars speed past. The other prisoners call out, mocking. I guess he knows who I am, and maybe about my crash too, because he offers me a cigarette, which I take, though I haven't smoked in years. I feel OK, sitting here, chilled by the wind, looking at a field of grey-green plants. Perhaps they're potatoes. I'm not sure. I take a drag on the cigarette, then I cough and remember why I gave up. I don't stub it out, though, because I can stay outside as long as I'm smoking it. Instead I play with it, stretch it out, enjoying the grey skies and the slight hint of chicken shit carried on the air from the distant sheds.

I could make a run for it. If a car came along and stopped, or I could run off over the fields, or even swim across the dyke. Would they follow me? Only one of them at most, and if I could get away, flag down a car, convince them I'd broken down or got lost and wasn't a murderer on the run. I could get to Peterborough, and then . . .

Then what? Go and see my mother? My brother? The police would be there before I was. Go on the run, with no money, no passport? Find some clues, talk to people, work out who the real killer was? That's the biggest joke of all. Anyone I saw would phone the police, same as I would in their place. And while I don't want to believe that I killed John, I've still no idea who it could have been.

So I sit here, by the side of the road, and I have to smile as a tractor crawls into sight, rumbles past, pulling a trailer of silage, tempting me to run after it, swing myself into the back. Even a van with a flat tyre could catch up with a tractor. I guess it would be the shortest prison break in history. I wouldn't even be late for court. The only difference would be that I'd probably end up covered in pigshit.

The driver stops kicking the good tyre and moaning about how badly the vans are serviced and reckons he can drive on as it is, so the guard helps me back into the truck, into my cell, and after ten minutes of the cold March winds I'm glad to be inside.

* * *

I hadn't really appreciated until this morning how much better it is here at the Crown Court than it was going to the magistrates' courts for the remand hearings. There, they had so many people going through the cells and the holding rooms that at times it was really scary. You'd end up parked in a corner while they sorted out the paperwork, and the male prisoners, some of them, they'd shout and say things, sick things, though they probably thought it was just a laugh, and some of the other women prisoners would shout stuff back too, and the guards seemed to think it was funny, half the time. One time I was in a cell on my own, and there was a man, a prisoner, hanging around outside, handcuffed to a custody officer, and he was staring at me with this horrible look and whispering stuff to me, and although I knew he couldn't get to me, he was on the other side of the bars, it was really, really frightening and I called out to the guard to make him stop, but the guard told me to shut up, and the prisoner went on and on about what he wanted to do to me, and it freaked me out. I think it must have been my first or second time there, and by the time I was in court for the hearing I could hardly stand, or answer my name, I was so scared.

I suppose Andrew must have been there, at some point, down in the cells beforehand, and my family in the court itself, but I can't remember that at all. I can only remember the look on the man's face. It reminded me of something I'd read in the papers about what it was like being in a mental hospital, how the inmates were left running around, not really supervised, and some of them would take advantage of the women, molest them or rape them or anything. If they complained they wouldn't be believed.

Someone told me in the new prison at Peterborough they'll be able to give evidence by TV, without having to come to court. I don't know what's worse. Having to come, and sit about, and be pushed around and in and out of the van and maybe have a brief glimpse of real life, of people going shopping or buying a paper or cycling to school, and maybe of family and friends, only a minute or two as they bring you up and the magistrates see you're still kicking and they remand you, send you back for another month, back into prison. Or maybe it would be worse to never even have a taste of freedom, a glimpse of reality. That's what it will be like anyway, if they find me guilty.

Andrew has been on to me again about giving evidence. I know I have to, if I'm going to have any chance of getting off. But I don't think I can. I have a very clear image of the cross-examination. Ruth standing a little beneath me, looking at me very evenly with her wide grey eyes, occasionally turning the pages of my previous evidence, asking me what I meant by this or that, trying to catch me out. If I say nothing I know I am done for, but if I try to remember, if I say more than I have before, she will claim I am making it up, ask me why I hadn't said it before. And all the time she'll be sizing me up, looking for weaknesses, and worst of all I know she will be enjoying it. Enjoying playing me, playing with me, and beating me.

I don't think I can win. How can I when I think I may be guilty? I've nothing to say except I can't remember doing it, I loved John, and it isn't the kind of thing I would do. It isn't the kind of thing anyone would do, shooting someone down, standing over them, watching them die, finishing them off. I don't want it to be me. How could I live with myself if they said it was me?

★   ★   ★

While I'm waiting in the holding area, I pick up today's *Sun* and see with a shock my own name standing out from one of the inside pages. Andrew had warned me they might pick up on Victoria's comments, and now I'm the 'rollover lover', the Lottery Tottie, spread over a whole page, going on about the case, and quoting chunks of what Victoria had said about me, with photos of John and the farmhouse and one of Victoria coming out of court. The photo of me is years old, showing me smiling wickedly and holding what I'm sure must be a water pistol, which was a craze one term at university, but it could be any kind of gun and the paper doesn't seem bothered enough to explain. I am captioned as 'Jilted lover Morland accused of shooting',

John as 'Millionaire Grant 'seeing mystery woman''. I start to read the text, but at once I see one of the headings, standing out in bold: 'Randy couple had sex in car park'. I can't read on, and I feel a bit queasy, and shy away from thinking of anyone I know reading it, my friends, my mother, but it's only the *Sun*, I tell myself, and I'm surprised I'm not more upset. It doesn't seem as if it could have anything to do with me.

I stare at John's picture for a long time, trying to get his image clear in my mind again. I don't have his photo in my diary, and as the months have gone by I've found it more and more difficult to remember what he was like. His picture is a bit posed, although the smile is there, the broad chin and the short curls of dark hair, and it gets just right the way he held his head. The one of me is much more grainy, so my hair looks black and my skin quite white, and my mouth dark too where I'm laughing as I point the gun at the camera.

* * *

The court looks different this morning, and I look over the jury and the press and public gallery before noticing that they have put up a board with a plan of the area around John's farmhouse on it. Another map next to it shows the familiar web of villages and woods linked by roads and paths. Woodwalton, Kingsthorpe, Upton and Warmington. The road from Woodwalton to Campsworth and Peterborough, crossing the river Nene at Wansford. The green of Forty Wood, Hang Wood, Norfolk Purlieus and the other scraps left from the medieval hunting grounds of Rockingham Forest. The sweeping red line of the A1 running from London to Edinburgh. All so familiar.

I think about the way I would have gone that day. Stepping out of my front door, straight on to the pavement, then running downhill, past the church, to where the road crosses the Ashbrook. Beyond the edge of the village, the road is long and straight with glimpses of bare, empty fields over the low hedges. A mile, then the pub and the pine trees at the edge of Kingsthorpe. The village is tiny, little more than a hamlet, and there's never anyone about. I run on, another bridge, then through the wood, the road making a long curve before climbing out of the valley. There, less than a mile ahead, the road running dead straight towards it, the squat tower of the church half-hidden by the rise of the land, is Upton.

At the edge of the village, the back lane to join the Wansford Road, out of the village past the row of red-brick council houses, half a mile alongside the verges and the hawthorn, three miles into the run, then reaching the turn into Sulehay Lane, by an old-fashioned fingerpost sign that says only 'Byroad'. I would have run down there, as far as the cottage where old Miss Meadows lives, then turned right into the track up to Manor Farm.

I can imagine the mixed mud and gravel beneath my shoes, the rasp of the cold air as I draw in each breath, the cry of the rooks, wheeling above me from the tops of the avenue of trees, and maybe the trees themselves creaking in the wind. Finally, the road opens out into a neat farmhouse, painted white with a fresh thatched roof, outbuildings tastefully converted into an extra cottage for guests, an indoor pool, a garage and a storeroom for the drive-on mower. There would be a car parked in the drive, a Range Rover, in a discreet dark colour. Everything would be quiet, except for the rooks, and the wind, and my steps on the gravel.

★　★　★

Halliday was the policeman in charge of the case and it gives me a shock to see him again, walking up briskly to take the stand. He is sworn in, looks around, then glances at me with an expression I cannot fathom.

'Could you state your name and position?' Ruth asks.

'Yes, of course. Detective Superintendent David Halliday, Cambridgeshire CID, based at Parkside station in Cambridge. I was asked to take charge of the investigation into John Grant's death.'

'And you were responsible for the whole of the investigation process?'

'Yes.'

'Could you give a brief outline of what you found at the scene of the murder?'

He starts off on a long description of the investigation on the day, how he looked around the farmhouse, the surrounding area, collected evidence, interviewed several witnesses himself. It builds up slowly into a picture of John's last movements, the clues to what had happened that evening, the contents of the bins, the state of the bed, the number of towels used, what plates and cups and glasses were out, even how hot the tea was in the kitchen when he was found.

'Mr Grant appeared to be a methodical man. The kitchen was fairly neat and tidy, and the plates, pans and glasses had been stacked in the dishwasher. We only found one champagne glass and one brandy glass in the living room, though to be fair we can't be sure when he cleared away the rest of the glasses and we didn't rule out the possibility of someone else being present.'

The jury are paying full attention to this. The Builder has leaned forward, as if to catch every word. Miss Marple is looking more alert, and the Student has polished his glasses and stopped slouching. They are finally hearing something close to being a coherent account, after two days of fragmented statements by individual witnesses. They are bound to put a lot more weight on what he says, if only because it sounds so sensible and logical in comparison to what has gone before.

'We made a very thorough examination of Manor Farm itself and the surrounding area over three days following the discovery of the murder. It was immediately clear that little if anything had been taken. Mr Grant had a fairly modern and well-made wall safe, containing a passport, some cash, and various papers, but there was no evidence of any attempt to tamper with it. There weren't the number of antiques and paintings and the like that one might often find in a property of this value, but nevertheless I checked with Mr Grant's parents and with his sister, neither of whom were able to spot anything missing. His wallet containing credit cards and a considerable quantity of cash was untouched on his bedside table. So if we were looking at a robbery, the obvious conclusion was that it had gone badly wrong at the very beginning.

'We also took account of the nature of the killing itself, the method if you like.' This is to the jury, who are lapping it up. It's better than *Inspector Morse*. 'Mr Grant was shot at his own front door, which it is reasonable to assume he opened as there was no sign of any attempt to force it, or indeed any of the doors or windows, and it was a Yale lock so he wasn't likely to have left it open. So my firm view from the start was that it was an odd setting for a killing which was the result of a bungled robbery. Had Mr Grant surprised armed intruders within his house, perhaps suddenly, perhaps even armed with some weapon of his own, the thieves might have panicked and fired. But it was far less likely that they would be standing outside his front door to be surprised, or that had they been surprised, that they would have killed him in a panic when the obvious course was to escape empty-handed but, as you might say, with no harm done.

'I could also see that some time must have passed between the first and second shots, as there was a trail of blood where Mr Grant had moved from the front door, where the first shot took place, down the corridor towards the kitchen, where he turned and was shot in the face.'

He stops as Rachel Grant stands, head down, clutching her coat and bag. We all watch in silence as she clacks out of the room, almost at a run. I wish I could do the same. I don't want to hear any more about the second wound.

'Although I did not know what state Mr Grant was in,' he goes on, in a more subdued tone, 'how mobile and so forth, it must have taken him a considerable period of time to do this.'

'More than a few moments?' Ruth asks.

'Perhaps as much as a minute.'

'Did you take any steps to establish how long it would have taken an assailant to reload and fire a second shot?'

'Yes, I tried it myself both with a single- and double-barrelled shotgun. With a double-barrelled gun, one can fire the second shot immediately. And even with a single-barrelled weapon, one would be able to break the gun, remove the spent cartridge, and replace it all in about five or six seconds.'

'What did you conclude from this?'

'I didn't reach any conclusions at this stage,' he says cautiously, to show how fair he is. 'But the only explanation which I found easy to square with the facts was that the assailant deliberately waited before firing the second shot. This might be to see if Mr Grant survived the first shot, but this wasn't wholly convincing. Why wait? Why not fire the second shot anyway? Instead, I formed the working hypothesis that the assailant spent the time watching Mr Grant, perhaps even talking to him, and that we were dealing with a revenge attack or an attempt to force information out of Mr Grant.

'Later on the morning of the day of the incident, I arranged for Mr Grant's office premises to be sealed and for all his business and personal accounts to be opened. I was aware that Mr Grant had substantial business and property interests, and it seemed a promising avenue of inquiry. At the same time, we started routine house-to-house inquiries, and these quickly threw up several leads.

'Acting on information received, I went with DS Jordan to interview Miss Morland in Woodwalton, but she wasn't there. I spoke to a neighbour, Jane Kennedy, who informed me that she had seen the accused driving off seemingly in some distress at round 7 a.m. that morning. I alerted neighbouring forces and all ports and airports, and several hours later one of our officers made the connection with a road traffic accident over the border into Lincolnshire.

'I was also aware by then from information received that Miss Morland and Mr Grant had been conducting an affair. Unfortunately, Miss Morland's injuries were such that we weren't able to interview her for several days, though obviously we examined the car and its contents, her house, and other material to see what evidence we could obtain.'

He goes on to describe the route they think I took on that day, leaning out from the witness box to point to the map on the easel. He also mentions a map in the bundle, and when I unfold it I find it shows a route from my house to John's farm, but not the way I'd imagined. Instead at the Woodwalton bridge it leaves the road and follows the River Ashbrook, skirting to the north of Kingsthorpe, and to the south of Upton, then crossing a green lane which leads to Normanton. From there it is a quarter-mile to Snag's Lane, and the track to Manor Farm.

At the bridge, there is a path worn through the brambles and nettles down to the

Ashbrook, but after a few yards this runs out and both banks of the stream are overgrown along most of its length. I know because I have run that way years ago at 'hare and hounds', laying a trail along the river, splashing through the shallow water as it runs over beds of smoothed rocks. You really can go all the way past Kingsthorpe and beyond, if you don't mind wading here and there. You wouldn't be likely to be seen because the trees, the poplar and willow and alder, follow the line of the river. I know that, but I don't know how the police could have known. Perhaps someone has told them: one of the 'hounds', maybe. Perhaps they plan to spring this on me, ask me if I give evidence if that was the way I went that morning.

'The circumstances surrounding Miss Morland's car accident were also of interest as she was expected at work that day and yet was driving away from her place of work. There was also no obvious explanation for the accident, as there were no other cars about, the weather was good, and there was no evidence of any mechanical failure in the steering or brakes and so on.

'Finally, our records revealed that Miss Morland held a shotgun licence. I also recovered a 20-bore shotgun with the matching serial number from a steel cabinet in the spare bedroom of the accused's house, which I sent for examination at the regional forensic laboratory at Huntingdon.

'Following the initial interview carried out by DS Jordan solely about the accident, on the twenty-fifth of October I cautioned Miss Morland and began a series of interviews. A member of the hospital staff was present on each occasion, and the accused's solicitor was also present for most of the subsequent interviews. These formed the basis for a report to the local Crown Prosecutor, and a decision was made to charge Miss Morland and she was duly charged at Peterborough District Hospital on the fifth of November.'

The court silently digests this succinct account of the downfall of a master criminal. I look over towards the jury, but although they have all been looking at me, none meet my eye. They have heard the truth from an honest, diligent copper, and now they know.

'My lord,' Ruth says, 'I would like at this point to submit transcripts of the interviews and to play extracts from the tapes themselves . . .'

'M'lud.' Charles rises. 'As you will know I have an application at this point which I would wish to make without the jury being present.'

'Certainly.' He turns to the jury. 'I am sure

215

that the members of the jury will indulge we lawyers in a small procedural matter.'

The younger woman and the Student smirk at this unexpected judicial joke, and they all file out. Charles and then Ruth go through their arguments, and the audience are soon mystified and then bored. They shuffle and whisper and one or two people squeeze along the rows and slip out of the double doors at the back, to the loo or for a fag, and then sneak back in again. I recognize Andy Calder, who gave his evidence against me on Monday and is now here to watch me suffer, and he catches my eye and gives me a little 'fuck you' smirk as he pushes his way back to his seat, next to another of John's friends, David Brewster, who everyone calls 'Brewers'. He's one of those clubby types I used to come across in London, who were in dining societies or ran May balls and had their own dinner jacket and are terrible company. First they are loud, then they are lechy, then they get ratty, then they fall asleep. But he was always OK to me, perhaps because of Nick. It was Andy who was the one I actively disliked, and let it show. He might not have been the most stupid, but he was certainly the nastiest. Once he put his hand up my skirt and got a pint of lager in his groin. I should've kicked him, or pushed the glass into his horrible leering face. He couldn't have done any more to get me back than he did this week.

'Now,' the judge says briskly, waving a pencil which he holds between his first and second fingers, like a cigarette. 'In summary, you, Miss Acheson, want to play the tapes now. You, Mr Everard, object on the grounds that you should have the opportunity to cross-examine Mr Halliday before the tapes are played, so that any light you might shed on Mr Halliday's conduct of the investigation will be available to the jury before they come to consider the interviews themselves. Is this a fair summary?'

Wisely, neither dissents. The judge is clearly at his most brilliant today, as he thanks them for their written submissions and explains why he prefers Charles's view. Charles looks pleased, and whispers his thanks to Sarah, who actually prepared the submission. They even get nods from Ruth and Gerard, and I realize that in their legal world this is quite a significant point, a neat piece of argument. Meanwhile the jury are filing back in and shuffling back into their usual places. Each now has a preference where to sit. Miss Marple nearest to the door at the back, next to the old bag, and the Student at the end of the row, half-hidden behind the Pig and the Bank Manager, as if he's too cool to take any part in what's going on. As they squeeze past each other to get to *their* seats, I notice the back of the Pig's head for the first time, the sandy hair cut short into bristles, showing the rolls of fat on his neck. Not a pretty sight. He settles down, and shifts in his seat until he is comfortable.

Now Charles stands and starts his cross-examination.

'Superintendent, at what time did you first hear about the murder of Mr Grant?'

'It would have been at about 8.30 of the same morning. When I reached the office I was asked to phone Commander Tennant at home. He told me what had happened and asked me to take on the case.'

'Did you know Mr Grant?'

'No.'

'Did you know any of the people concerned with the case?'

'No.'

'You presumably left Cambridge fairly quickly and travelled to the scene?'

'Yes. I got there at about 10.30. I was accompanied by DS Jordan.'

'You also mentioned in your evidence that you first began to form suspicions around Miss Morland in the late morning of the same day. Could you be more precise?'

'Well, one of the officers making house-to-house inquiries called in to say he had a positive ID on a named suspect. Clearly this was an excellent lead and I immediately followed this up.'

'And when was this exactly?'

'At about midday.'

'So, within two hours of arriving on the scene, you had a prime suspect?'

'We had a strong lead, yes.'

'That seems like very fast work. Would you not say that it was surprisingly fast?

'No, I wouldn't.'

'I put it to you that having stumbled upon what might have seemed like a promising lead, you decided that the case was in the bag and failed to investigate other leads thoroughly.'

'Not at all. And we didn't have only the one lead.'

'No, you spoke in your evidence about 'information received'. What information?'

'We were told that Mr Grant had been having an affair with Miss Morland, and that this affair had recently ended and that Miss Morland had taken it very badly.'

'This information came from where?'

'From . . . well, from Mr Grant's parents.'

'You went to see them on the same morning?'

'Yes. I asked them if Mr Grant had any enemies, or had received any threats, or whether there were any other people who might have wanted to do any harm to Mr Grant.'

'And they named Miss Morland?'

'Yes. That was the only name they could come up with.' I almost wince. This doesn't seem to be helping, but Charles carries on.

'Who was present when you talked to Mr Grant's parents?'

'Could I check my notes on this point?' The judge nods, and he flips open a slim black notebook and leafs through the pages, showing slight nervousness for the first time. 'Yes, here we are. Myself, Sergeant Jordan, Mr George Grant, Mrs Audrey Grant, and Miss Rachel Grant. We were all together in the kitchen.'

'And who first mentioned Miss Morland?'

He looks through the notes for a while. 'It was Miss Grant.'

'Miss Rachel Grant?'

'Yes.'

'Were you aware at the time that Miss Grant and Miss Morland were at school together?'

'No. I wasn't.' He shifts his weight from one leg to another.

'Or that they had a mutual dislike of some years standing?'

'No.' Nor was I. I wonder if Andrew has told Charles this, or if he's made it up himself.

'Would you have placed such reliance on her evidence at the time, had you known it could have been based solely on malice?'

'Clearly I would have treated the evidence cautiously, but at this stage I was only collecting background information, if you like. There was no question of relying solely on the unsubstantiated statements of one or two people.'

'But isn't that exactly what you did do? You heard Miss Grant say her piece, and you had this allegation from Miss Meadows, and then you started to look for Miss Morland. You started to scour the county, you visited her house, you sent an officer to her place of work, all on these two snippets of information.'

'They were more than snippets,' Halliday replies calmly.

'Didn't you consider the possibility of a robbery gone wrong?'

'Yes, naturally. That was almost our first thought. But as I explained, there were several aspects to the case which pretty soon made this into very much a second-rate option. For example, the timing was all wrong, as robberies tend to take place in the full daylight or after dark, but not when people are starting to get up and coming and going. Then again, there was no sign that anyone had tried to force an entry, and it would be a pretty strange villain who knocked on the door, shot the owner when they answered it, and then decided not to rob the place after all. And also we knew from Miss Meadows that no vehicles had come and gone at the time under consideration.'

'*Knew?* That puts a lot of reliance on Miss Meadows as a sort of gatekeeper to Manor Farm. Surely she could have missed a car or a van leaving, particularly if the occupants hadn't panicked and were driving in a normal way?'

'She might have done, we didn't rule that out, but she said that no vehicles came in or out from about six o'clock onwards.'

'The lane from Manor Farm to the road between Upton and Elton isn't the only way in or out, is it?'

'No.'

'There's a track that runs past the farm, past Forty Wood and out to the road between Upton and Glapthorne, isn't there?'

'Yes.'

'So you can't rule out a bungled robbery?'

'No, there was no conclusive evidence one way or the other.'

'Do you know the average number of robberies in Cambridgeshire each year?'

'Not offhand.'

'Robberies of isolated farmhouses are fairly common, aren't they?'

'Fairly, yes.'

'And the fact that Mr Grant's farm happened not to contain much in the way of valuables might be the kind of information which thieves would not, in fact, know?'

'I suppose so.'

'You suppose so. In the light of this, what steps did you take to pursue the possibility that Mr Grant had been killed during the course of a bungled robbery?'

'Well, we checked the farmhouse for fingerprints to match against our records, and we looked for car tracks, and of course we made house-to-house inquiries in the surrounding area.'

'But nothing specific about robberies.'

'What do you have in mind?'

'Well, did you for example ask the Metropolitan Police if they had received any intelligence about bungled robberies? I understand that many such robberies are committed by London-based teams.'

'No, we didn't.'

'Did you liaise with the National Criminal Intelligence Unit?'

'We sent them the usual reports.'

'But specifically on the question of burglary?'

'No.'

'So, in short, apart from the routine, one might say mundane, work of checking for fingerprints and asking around, there was nothing specific that you did to explore further the possibility of a raid that went tragically wrong?'

'No.'

Charles is throwing these questions with a fine mixture of anger and amazement, as if he's trying to suggest to the jury that they too should be angry at this bodged investigation. They are looking interested, but no more than that. Miss Marple is leaning forward, perhaps gratified that alternative theories are making the case a little more like a proper detective story. The Builder is curious as well, perhaps angry too, as if he has been burgled recently and would like them all hung, whether they shot John or not. This is all good, but the Pharmacist is smiling faintly and I think she is amused by these attempts to muddy the waters.

'Would I be right in thinking that you and your colleagues must have spent quite some time looking over Mr Grant's business affairs?'

'Quite some time, yes.'

'You would have looked over various other transactions as well as those involving Miss Morland?'

'Yes.'

'How many people had entered into financial arrangements over the land deal that Mr Grant was putting together with Mountgrove?'

'About ten.'

'You aren't sure how many?'

'Well, most were married couples, so if you count both of them but not other relatives, children and so on, it's ten.'

'And you interviewed all of them?'

'Not all, no. We didn't interview both the husband and wife in each case.'

'Only the husband?'

'Er . . . ' For the first time he senses danger. 'Yes, I think so. I would have to consult my notes and perhaps my fellow officers to be sure, as I didn't conduct each interview myself.'

''You didn't conduct each interview yourself'? I find that rather odd. Didn't you think that these were important interviews?'

Halliday remains outwardly confident. 'Important, yes, but I had full faith in my officers to conduct the interviews properly.'

'Can you tell me how many hours you

spent, during the whole investigation, interviewing my client?'

'Oh,' he says as he blows his cheeks out, 'it must have been thirty or so, all in all.'

'And how much time did you spend interviewing the other people involved in the same deal?'

'Perhaps a couple of hours.'

'In total?'

'In total.'

'Tell me, Inspector, how many other people involved in the deal with Mr Grant at Woodwalton got the full market price for the land or other rights they sold?'

But Halliday can't be sure of that. He has to concede that any of them might have got more for the land if they'd known of the land deal. Just like me. He also has to concede that any one of the wives — or even the daughters — could have been having an affair with John — just like me. His face looks more and more stony. He becomes more formal, more the stage copper.

'Mr and Mrs Felton, for example. They live at Woodside Cottage, Church Street, Normanton. Do you know what colour hair Mrs Felton has?'

'No.'

'She has shoulder-length blonde hair.' Halliday says nothing. 'So you would be able to tell the court the exact financial position of the Feltons at the time of the murder?'

'I would have to refresh my memory about the interviews, check with my officers.'

'What about the Birds?' Halliday looks blank. 'Jonathan and Caroline Bird, who also live in Normanton. They sold a paddock at the back of their house to a company called Firesteed Developments Ltd in August of last year. Mr Grant approached them, saying the company was looking to buy land for development and offering to act as their agent. He carried out negotiations on their behalf, even though, unbeknownst to them, he also owned fifty-one per cent of Firesteed Developments. He recommended Jeremy Varley of Varley and Stokes, chartered surveyors of Oundle, to carry out an independent valuation, and on the basis of that valuation of £22,000 for the land, the Birds were very pleased with Mr Grant's efforts to secure a deal with Firesteed of £61,000. Does this sound at all familiar?'

'I'm sorry, but it doesn't.'

'Were you aware that the other shareholders in Firesteed Developments were Rachel Grant, John Grant's sister, who owned five per cent, and Roger Turner, who owned forty-four per cent, both of whom gave evidence on Tuesday?'

'I wasn't aware of that, no.'

'These three acres would, by the same method used to value the Doles, put the value of the land they sold as nearer £200,000.' Charles looks at Halliday, as if expecting a response. Halliday stares back. 'Have you any comment at all to make?'

'My officers spoke to everyone who had dealings with Mr Grant over the Normanton development. If there had been any lead, any suspicious circumstances, even the sniff of some possible further link, they would have reported it.'

'Can we really be sure? This brings me on to the question of Mr Tyson. We heard yesterday that he may have seen a woman sitting in the passenger seat of Mr Grant's car on the evening before his murder. A woman with blonde hair. A woman who he was absolutely certain wasn't Miss Morland. Now, this woman must be the most material witness it is possible to imagine, who was presumably the last person to see John Grant alive, who may have been present at his murder, may even have killed him. Now you — '

'My lord,' Ruth says, as if pushed beyond endurance, 'my learned friend is commenting again.'

'Yes, quite. Mr Everard,' the judge says

228

with the driest of smiles, 'could you try to find a question from somewhere in your speech?'

'Yes, m'lud. Inspector, you haven't been able to trace this witness, this possible suspect, have you?'

'I think you are putting too much emphasis on this possible witness.' Halliday assembles his answer carefully, trying to break the momentum of Charles's questions. 'I think that we clearly would be happier if we could have identified this woman, who she was and what she was doing. But she may well have no connection with the case. After all, Mr Tyson himself is uncertain about the identification, might be genuinely mistaken, might have misremembered the day on which this happened, or may have mixed Mr Grant's car up with another car. Range Rovers are fairly common in the countryside. So it is a significant piece of information, and I very much regret that this woman hasn't come forward to be eliminated from our inquiries, but I don't think it affects the case significantly.'

'Are you still looking for this other woman?'

Halliday clearly isn't sure whether to say no, and look slack, or say yes, and risk weakening the case against me.

'Well, we'd like to interview her, yes.'

'Do you not think it a fairly bizarre situation, to be in the middle of a trial for murder with the police still hunting for someone who is a potential suspect and certainly a key witness?'

Halliday wisely interprets this as a rhetorical question. Charles has to let it hang in the air. The judge is looking restless.

'Now there is one final point I would like to cover, and that is the evidence you mentioned as to the length of time between the first and second shots. Now, there was no evidence as to the timing of the shots from eyewitnesses, was there?'

'No. No one overheard the shots, as far as we know.'

'So all we have to go on is the forensic evidence, from which you drew some conclusions.'

'We drew tentative conclusions, yes.'

'*Tentative* conclusions, then.' Charles is mocking him. 'You concluded that this might have been a revenge killing. That Mr Grant was left dying while the assailant gloated or taunted Mr Grant.'

'Something like that.'

'Did you consider that another possibility was that the first shot was fired in surprise, that both assailant and victim were equally surprised, which would also explain the markings on Mr Grant's body which you suggested were the result of his knowing the assailant but which could equally be the result of his having no time to react?'

'Yes. But . . . '

'And if the first shot was fired in surprise, and the assailant ran off, he might after a few seconds have stopped and realized that he had shot a man, that this might mean a lengthy jail sentence if he were identified, and that the safest thing to do was to go back and finish him off?'

'That is possible.'

'Then why didn't you follow it up?' Charles and Halliday square up to each other again. There is real animosity now.

'We did follow it up.'

'You didn't contact the Metropolitan Police and ask for information on possible rumours of shootings in the underworld.'

'We both circulated reports and read intelligence received from other forces.'

'Did you contact the Met Police?'

'You don't seem to understand the way the police works.'

'It seems to me a fairly obvious line of inquiry.'

'With respect, you don't understand. We have procedures. We don't work on the basis of hunches. It isn't like *The Sweeney*.'

'And is the standard procedure to find the first likely suspect, the first person that someone else mentions, through spite or whatever, and then work to pin it on them?'

'No, of course not. That's a quite objectionable thing to say.'

'Well, I'm very sorry that you object, but there's something here a little bit more serious than your sensibilities. My client's whole future is at stake.'

'I know that,' Halliday snaps, and oddly I believe he means it. Anyway, Charles is sounding a bit pompous. He senses this, and goes on in a different tone.

'Inspector, you carried out a series of interviews with Miss Morland over nine days before she was finally charged on the third of November. These were all taped, and you intend to play extracts of these tapes by way of illustration to the court, and you have also made full transcripts available. Taken as a whole, what do you think they add to the case?'

Halliday looks puzzled. 'Well, they help to build up the picture of what happened. The relationship between the accused and Mr Grant. The business relationship, in particular.'

'Did Miss Morland, at any point in these

twenty-seven hours of interviews, ever say she had committed the crime?'

'No, she didn't.'

'Did she co-operate in making clear the nature of her relationship with Mr Grant?'

'I suppose she did, though there were some points on which she was evasive or could have been more forthcoming.'

'If someone tried to drag out the most intimate details of a relationship in which they had been cheated and made a fool of, do you think you would perhaps share that reluctance?'

'This was a murder investigation.'

'Perhaps only an innocent person, who doesn't think it will ever get as far as her being charged, let alone going to court, would therefore try to hold back those personal or intimate details.' Halliday says nothing. 'So Miss Morland told you everything about her dealings with Mr Grant, with a perfectly natural modesty, but never admitted the slightest guilt.'

'She kept saying she couldn't remember what had happened. I don't think that's the same as maintaining your innocence.'

'People are presumed innocent,' Charles says with a note of triumph.

'And if we hadn't had the eyewitnesses, and her having the right kind of gun, things would have been different. And there was already strong evidence about motive.'

'But in terms of the interviews, the information you gained was no different than that which might have been gained from any of the other people who had had dealings with Mr Grant?'

'It was much more detailed.'

'Was it any different?'

'No.' Halliday has to concede.

'So, on reflection, do you think that perhaps you should have made equally thorough inquiries of the other people who had dealings?'

Halliday is clearly caught again between saying no and looking cavalier and saying yes and suggesting someone else might be equally suspect.

'We could have interviewed all kinds of people for days on end, but it wouldn't have meant that our end result was any different.'

'Can you be sure?'

'No, of course not, but when you have a clear lead there is no justification for inventing new possibilities to waste time on. We could speculate about all kinds of motives and possible suspects, but we had a clear lead and we followed it up and put together one of the strongest cases I have come across.'

They run on like this for a while, without adding much. Charles keeps on about alternative theories and about other supposed sloppiness in the inquiry. Halliday repeats his view that the case was strong, but it sounds a bit too much like bluster. He has a habit of saying 'I' when he is being confident and 'we' when he is defensive or less sure of his facts. I wonder what I could have made of this if I'd ever had to interrogate him. Perhaps I would have made quite a good detective. Eventually, they wrap up and Ruth stands to make up some of the lost ground. She starts by taking him back to this mysterious woman. Was there anyone of this description who was part of the case?

'Well, the description is after all pretty vague. A woman with longish fairish hair. Almost half the women in Britain could be covered by that description.'

But not Miss Morland. For once I'm the winner for not having long blonde hair. Not that I find that much of a consolation just now. I can picture the scene, the woman sitting in the dark, lit by the faint green light from the dashboard, looking into the pub from time to time, wondering how he could take so long. Even if he was only a minute or two it would always seem much longer, waiting for your lover. Perhaps she'd be wondering whether he might have got talking to some friend of his, or business partner, or crony, and it would be twenty minutes before he'd be out again. So she'd look away, check her make-up in the mirror, pull her coat up around her throat because even with the engine on and the heater going it would seem cold, sitting in a car park in the middle of the night, in late October, the wind blowing perhaps. Then, at last, he'd come trotting out, waving the bottle of champagne and grinning triumphantly, and then all her annoyance and petulance would melt away, and she'd only smile, and want to kiss him and hold him.

★　★　★

Ruth is taking Halliday back over how his team had checked every possible lead in putting together the case against me.

'How many people were in the pub when Mr Grant came in?' she asks.

'There were at least twenty, as far as we were able to tell. We traced most of them, sixteen people in total, but in these kinds of investigations people don't always come forward for a variety of reasons. They don't want to have anything to do with the police, they think they may be wasting our time, they want to keep a low profile for some completely unrelated reason, or they never read the papers and don't even know about the murder.'

'Is there anything sinister in not being able to trace all those present in the pub?'

'No.'

'And the same might apply to the passenger in the car?'

'Yes, that's quite possible. For example, someone driving through the village might pull into the pub car park, the driver might run into the toilet and out again without ever going into the bar of the pub at all. There might be a passenger in the car which Mr Tyson saw. But those people mightn't even have known the name of the pub or the village, or remembered it at all, or linked it to the murder. They may live hundreds of miles away. So no, the fact that they haven't come forward may mean nothing at all.'

★　★　★

The re-examination goes on until lunch. When they take me down to the cells there's a pause and I find a paper lying around.

MYSTERY WOMAN SOUGHT IN FARMHOUSE MURDER

The Farmhouse Murder trial heard dramatic new evidence yesterday of a 'mystery woman' who could hold vital evidence.

John Grant, 34, might have been with an unknown woman the night before his slaying on the doorstep of his £750,000 farmhouse near Peterborough, a court heard yesterday.

The woman was seen by local landlord Sam Tyson while Grant came into the pub to buy a bottle of champagne. He wasn't seen alive again.

Mr Tyson, popular landlord of the Royal Oak in Woodwalton, near Peterborough, told the court that the woman had long blonde hair and was certainly not Clarissa Morland, now standing trial for Grant's murder.

The pub is only yards from Morland's house. The prosecution claim she may have seen her lover with the woman and followed both of them back to his house where he was killed.

Asked why he thought she hadn't come forward, a spokeswoman for Cambridgeshire CID said: 'She may be worried about the publicity. Or she may be a married woman.

We can't guarantee her anonymity, but we have repeatedly asked her to make herself known.'

The court earlier heard evidence that Grant and Morland were lovers as well as business partners. Victoria Asprey, who worked for Grant, said the pair had met after work and mixed business and sex. But a property deal both were involved in went sour and Grant ended the relationship days before he was killed.

The trial continues.

Wednesday Afternoon

'Will you state your full name, please?'

'Clarissa Abigail Morland.'

'And your occupation?'

'I work for a housing association, managing their stock.'

'The Forest Housing Association?'

'That's right.'

'And how long have you worked for them?'

'About four years.' I break off to cough. 'After university, I took a diploma from the Institute of Housing, and then worked for the New Islington for two years.'

'New Islington?'

'It's another housing association. In North London.'

'And your current position is a responsible one?'

Easy questions, to settle me down, like in an interview.

'Yes, I suppose so. I'm now what they call the Head of Lettings. I have three staff and we have about three hundred and fifty properties to look after.'

'Have you ever had any disputes with colleagues at work, or any cautions from your managers or any other disciplinary action?'

'No.'

'And with your previous employers?'

'No.'

He turns over a page, to start a new line of questions.

'Have you ever suffered from any mental illness? Depression? Anything like that?'

'No.'

'Or any losses of memory or blackouts? That is, before now?'

'No. Not that I can remember.'

There's no reaction to my joke. He makes a note.

'And have you ever come into contact with the police, in any form? A caution? Or the police coming to your home because of any disturbance or violent act or anything of that kind?'

'No, nothing like that.'

'Now, Miss Morland, you said in your evidence that you had known Mr Grant for some years, though not well. Is that correct?'

'Yes.'

'Your brother knew him?'

'A bit.' I speak up, trying to rid my voice of its hesitancy. 'They were at school at the same time. They still had some friends in common.'

'But he was nearly two years older than your brother, and six years older than you.'

'Yes.'

'You started going out with Mr Grant in July of last year. You would have been, let me see, twenty-six?'

He makes a play of looking at his notes, but of course he knows already. He knows exactly where he is going.

'Yes.'

'Were you, how shall I put it, *seeing* anyone else at the time?'

'No.'

'You were single?'

'Yes.'

'How long had you been single before you started to see Mr Grant?'

'Some months.'

'As much as a year, perhaps?'

'It might have been.'

'More than a year?'

'I don't know. Perhaps.'

He relaxes a bit, checks his notes, then goes on.

'Could you describe how you started your affair with Mr Grant?'

It wasn't an 'affair', I want to say. *I don't know what it was, but it wasn't that.* But I bite back the words, and try instead to explain.

'Well, as I said, we met from time to time, at parties and things. But it all started at an

242

exhibition a friend of mine was involved in at a gallery in Oundle. I was going round looking at the pictures, and he was doing the same, and we got chatting. Then he suggested going to get something to eat. So we did. We just hit it off.'

'Why do you think that was?'

'How do you mean?'

'You'd known him for several years, on and off, hadn't you?'

'So?'

'What did you think of him, before you met him that evening? Did you like him?'

I try to think of how to explain what I felt. I must have been attracted to him from the start. He was pleasant enough to me, if we all went out to the pub in a group, Nick and his friends, though he never showed the slightest interest in me or what I did or what I thought. He'd buy me a drink if he was going to the bar, but he'd never have anything to say if we were alone together. In a group, he was great company, always a joke or something interesting to say. I suppose I had more of a problem with him. I didn't like him because of what he was and what he did. He spent too much time trying to make as much money as he could, however he could, as quickly as possible. That's what I thought then.

'No. I didn't particularly like him.'

'So what made you change your mind?'

'I don't know. He'd changed.'

I can see the gallery quite clearly, a big converted barn, the walls painted white, the pictures brought out by the bright lighting, and lots of people standing around, some looking at the pictures, but most chatting to each other, getting louder the more white wine they drank. I'd been chatting to Tim Johnston, a local artist I met through Philip and my mother, and John had come over and sort of carried me off. He'd said a few words to us both, asked after me, my mother, and said it was amazing how we hadn't seen each other for ages, as if we were close friends. Then he asked Tim if he could borrow me because no one he could trust knew as much about pictures as I did.

I went along with this, more through surprise than anything, and he led me over to get me a fresh drink, asking about my job, and making noises about the responsibility and how interesting it was talking to someone in the same line of work. Then he insisted that I show him the pictures I liked the most. So we walked around, and he was much more aware about art than I'd expected, he seemed to know all the artists by reputation and some of them personally. He had lots of stories about them, funny stories, and for once he wasn't entertaining a crowd but just me, leaning over as if we were conspirators.

I know now that he hadn't changed, or if he had that wasn't the point. It was that now I interested him, and all his energy and personality was being aimed at me. He wanted to please me, and so I wanted to be pleased.

The questions go on, and I answer them, but I am also thinking through the evening, living it again. We chatted on, he encouraged me to tell him what I thought about the paintings, which I liked, which I thought would be a good investment. And suddenly it was nine o'clock, long after I'd meant to leave. Perhaps something had told me I should go, while I still could. Maybe I just felt hungry. But when I said I'd be off, he found out I hadn't asked anyone for a lift, then said he'd drop me off — after a 'quick bite to eat'.

As we left together, he stopped to have a word with the gallery owner, then caught me up in time to open the door for me. I laughed, told him he was far too smooth, a dinosaur, and he protested he was far too old-fashioned to change. A victim of my upbringing, he said. But then he took me by the arm to guide me towards his car and it made me shiver, as I do now at the recollection of it, as the questions go on.

'Well, what was it about him that you found attractive?'

'I don't know. He was fun to be with. Very polite. Very charming.'

But it wasn't that. I shivered because he was sexy, he was a turn-on. It wasn't the way he looked, although he was quite handsome, tall with curling dark hair cut very neatly and well washed. It wasn't the money, although he dressed very well, looked prosperous without being showy. It might have been something to do with his assurance, because he was very plausible and he acted as if he would succeed in anything he put his mind to, including taking you to bed. But it was more than all of this.

I can see us both sitting in the restaurant of the Great Northern Hotel. At his suggestion, of course. I'd never been, and the widely spaced tables, the crisp tablecloths, and the way he managed to order a bottle of champagne without a trace of self-consciousness or ostentation seemed to be from a different world. He was relaxed, confident, and I sensed he was secretly amused. I knew he was chatting me up, and that directness, putting us as adults, equal partners in a game, was part of the charm. I was used more to clumsy overtures, half-hearted efforts which were too ambiguous to lead to anything more than embarrassment. He was more adult, more exciting, more together than anyone else who'd ever shown any interest in me. And as we ate, and chatted about the usual things, films and books and the like, I thought that I deserved this. That I had changed too.

I would have slept with him, that night. As we left, he took the coat from the waiter and put it on me himself, and I imagined him folding his arms around me, pressing against me. The whole evening was like that, a kind of dream, totally new and unexpected. We drove to my house in silence. He was concentrating on his driving, going much faster than I ever would down those country lanes, the hedges whipping by, but he drove so well and we were high up in this big box of a car, that I was surprised at myself for enjoying being driven like that, thrilled but feeling quite safe. He saw me to my door, then just said goodnight and was gone. I was left listening to the engine of his car, the faint reflection of the lights along the road.

'Could you answer the question?'

'Sorry?'

'When was the next time you met?'

'A week later. Maybe ten days. At a party a

friend of my brother's was having.'

'Peter Barnett?'

'Yes.'

'You met several times after that?'

'Yes.'

'He sent you flowers?'

I felt myself blush, just as I had on the day afterwards, when the flowers arrived. They were roses — not the usual mean arrangement from a florist, but real garden blooms, heavy with scent. The others in the office said nothing about it, but smiled a lot.

'Yes, from time to time.'

'And how often would you see him, in an average week?'

'Well, we'd speak on the phone quite often, and perhaps meet up one or two evenings. Depending on what else we had on.' What time he could or would spare would be more honest.

'Mainly on Wednesdays?'

I nod, thinking of the headline in one of the tabloids that morning. 'Lottery lover 'killed Romeo who rolled her over''. The picture of me with the water pistol next to one of the farmhouse looking dark and sinister.

'Did you sleep together?'

I realize now that someone I was at college with must have sold my picture to the papers. A friend, supposedly. Whoever had taken the picture. It could have been Emily, Josh, any of them. I can't speak with anger. Humiliation. I want to stop all this happening to me.

'Would you answer the question?'

How could someone do that to me, betray me like that? One of my own friends. Like the queue of people ready to say what a fantastic bloke John was, nicest chap you could imagine, and just by being there show I was an evil witch who should never be let out.

'Look, I can't do this.'

'Come on.'

'I can't.' I'm crying now.

'You have to answer the questions.'

'Look, fuck off. I'm not answering them.'

I sit with my head down, crying, gulping in air, while they sit in silence.

'I'm sorry.' The silence goes on. 'I'm really sorry. I am. I was thinking of the paper today. What they said.' In the end, Andrew puts his arm round me and talks to me in a low voice.

'Come on, it's only a rehearsal. It doesn't matter. Much better to go through it now than in court, yeah?' I nod. I know it's what they want. 'We'll do this another time, eh?' I've got my head down but I sense him look at Charles to check this. 'Come on.' Now Sarah has produced a bottle of mineral water from her bag which she passes to me. I take a sip and choke. Tissues follow. When Charles thinks I'm ready, he starts off again.

'I do appreciate that this is difficult, and if you do start to cry in the witness box no one will think it out of the ordinary.'

I notice that he has given up using my name. I guess that he finds Miss Morland too obviously formal and Clarrie or even Clarissa too intimate. Or perhaps it's another clue that he thinks I'm guilty, or going to lose, or both, and he wants to keep his distance.

'But one outburst like that could leave a very bad impression on the jury,' he goes on, pompous and hectoring. 'Very bad.'

'I'm sorry. It's just that all this stuff is so horrid.'

'I do appreciate this. But lots of people do manage very well under even the toughest cross-examination. And the judge will — '

'You don't understand. I can't go through with this because I don't know what happened.' They all look blank now, but I have to get them to see. 'Look, I don't know what happened. Maybe I did kill him. I just don't know. I can't remember. So how can I answer all these questions? I don't know I'm innocent and I can't even know that I'm guilty and lie to try to get off. I don't know what they'll produce and what they'll say next. What they'll drag up from my past, like that bloody photograph.'

They don't know what I mean, but I'm tired, I've said it all and I can't be bothered to explain. But Charles won't let it drop.

'What picture?'

'In the paper,' I reply, without expression. Andrew silently pushes the folded paper across the table. I hear the rustle as Charles reads it.

'I would imagine,' Andrew says, 'that if people were digging stuff like old photographs up from my past life, I'd wonder what else they'd find.'

'I suppose so.'

'Mmm, but if I were the defence team of that imaginary person, I'd be wondering that too. And I'd also be wondering whether something was being kept from me. I mean, this is nasty and you must feel a bit let down by whoever gave them the picture, though these journalists are very good, very plausible, I mean it's their job to get stuff like this from family and friends. You know how it works. They'll have said that a photo with you smiling and looking normal would help give the right image. It would be helpful. Anyway, my worry would be that there's something you're keeping back — past violence, something like that — perhaps even buried from yourself and that's what's really worrying you.'

The silence rolls on for a bit, and for a moment I really hate Andrew, he's really got under my skin. I say that I want legal advice, not amateur psychology. I'm a bit upset and on edge and that's all there is to it, and there's nothing I'm holding back. And just in time one of the dock guards comes in to take me back upstairs. First they take me to the toilet, and the guard stands beside me as I wash away the tears, dry my face, take deep breaths. In the mirror, under these lights, I look pale and ill. We are supposed to have an hour of outdoor exercise each day, but by the time we are all gathered together and trooped out and got back in again we're only outside for half that time. And if it's raining, or they're short-staffed, then it can be called off altogether. In the hospital, I'd hardly been outside at all.

Sarah comes in to join us. She doesn't mention the scene, just says she thinks I'll want some make-up. She produces powder and lipstick from her handbag, and hands them to me. The guard seems to know that Sarah is a barrister and though it is probably against some rule she shrugs, glances at her watch and says we should be quick. My hands are shaking and I can't even open the compact, but Sarah takes over, puts it on my face, turns my head one way and another, like being made up backstage before a performance. She doesn't say anything, only smiles her secret smile. With the make-up I look different, not so ill, but I am so unused to it that I think it makes me look strange.

'There.' Sarah admires her handiwork, then hands me the make-up, still smiling. 'Why not keep these?'

The guard shrugs again. I look at it more closely. It's some expensive brand. You can only buy make-up from the prison shop, and then only one cheap brand if you're on remand. If you are there for a long stretch and earn the conduct points you get to choose from a bigger range, which is something to look forward to. I don't suppose she knows this, though.

'Thank you,' I manage to say. She laughs.

'Think of it as my reward for you telling Charles to fuck off.' I must look surprised, because she smiles again. 'If I'd caught your eye, or Andrew's, I'm sure I'd have laughed out loud.'

'I thought you liked him.'

'I do, but he can still be horrible when he wants to be. He's always moaning about this and that. But he is very good.'

She offers me a brush, and as I quickly flick my hair into place she says she's surprised I can get such a good haircut in prison. I explain that it's one way prisoners can earn a few pence. I add that it's a bit odd having your hair cut by a convicted murderer, and that's why I asked for the clippers rather than scissors, but either she doesn't understand or doesn't think this is funny.

Coming back into the courtroom a minute or two later, up from the strip-lit depths into the sunshine is a relief, and I look around with an odd sense of belonging, feeling everything is familiar and safe. Charles and Andrew are seated neatly in their benches, talking quietly as the judge sits and Ruth stands to call the next evidence. Neither of them look at me.

'My lord, the first tape in the sequence was recorded on the evening of the twenty-fifth of October at Peterborough District Hospital and is entered as Exhibit J/22. The transcript of the tape is also entered in evidence as Exhibit P/41.'

As one, the judge, counsel and I all turn to Exhibit P/41 and the tape is switched on. There is a clatter, then a voice.

'This is a recording of an interview recorded at Peterborough General Hospital on the twenty-fifth of October. Present are Clarissa Morland, Detective Sergeant Annette Jordan, and me, Detective Inspector David Halliday. Also present is Dr Alice

Greenwood, a member of the hospital staff.' A chair scrapes, and someone coughs. 'Now, Miss Morland, earlier on today you gave a statement to my colleague here about the car accident and I'm very grateful to you for that, but I'd like now to ask you a few other questions if I may. Is that going to be all right?'

'Yes . . . yes, of course.' I hardly recognize my own voice, it's so lifeless.

'Now you'll see that I've brought a tape recorder with me, so we can get everything down on tape. This is quite normal. And also like I said a moment ago I'm going to give you a caution, which is also a formal thing we need to do, because there is the possibility of some kind of criminal charge, and it wouldn't be fair to be asking you things unless you were aware of that. OK? That was a nod, I take it?'

'Yes, sorry. That's OK.'

'Right.' He changes voice and reads quickly through the clumsy words of the caution, which makes no more sense to me now than it did then.

'Do you understand?' he says at the end.

'Yes.'

'Thank you.' More rustling, then he goes on in his friendly voice. 'Now, Miss Morland, you live at 6 Main Street, Woodwalton, is that

255

right? And you live there alone?'

'Yes.'

'Have you ever been burgled?'

'No. Why?'

'Only routine, you might say. No break-ins, or attempts, or people wandering around, or anything like that? Something you mightn't have bothered reporting to the police?'

'Nothing like that.'

'Fine. And have you had any other dealings with the police in recent years? Say in the last three years?'

'No, I don't think so. A couple of parking tickets.'

'Right, those would be in Peterborough, would they?'

'Yes. I paid them all at the time.'

'Good, that's fine. And what about any other dealings?'

'Well, I have a shotgun licence. You have to get that from the police.'

'Right. A shotgun. Why do you have that, then?'

'I go shooting from time to time. Clay pigeons. Sometimes with the local shoot.'

'I see. And this shotgun, you keep it at your home?'

'Yes, in one of those steel cabinets.'

'You wouldn't lend it to anyone, would you?'

'No. I've never done that.'

'And it's there now, I suppose? Not off being mended?'

'No, it's there. Why do you ask? Has someone broken in?'

'No, not at all. But maybe we should keep an eye on your place, just in case. If it's known locally you're in hospital, someone might try to take advantage.'

'Yes, I suppose so. That's very kind.'

'You'll sort that out, will you, Sergeant?' There is a grunt. 'Now, perhaps if we could go back to the accident on Thursday. Have you a clearer recollection of it than when you spoke to my sergeant?'

'Not really. I can't really remember anything. I went out for a run that morning, I think, like I normally do. I don't remember anything very clearly, 'til I woke up here.' There is a pause, and then I go on. 'Except for a bit after the crash.'

'Yes?'

'Afterwards. Being in the car. Being cut free.'

'How about the night before?' he asked. I remember being puzzled that they didn't want to know more about the crash.

'I think I was supposed to be going out. I got back from work about six, but in the end I stayed in and had something from the

257

freezer and watched TV. I think I had an early night. Fairly early, anyway.'

'Did you have much to drink?'

'A glass of wine with my pasta. And a whisky before I went to bed. Not much.'

'Who were you planning to see that night?'

'What do you mean?'

'You said you were planning to go out.'

'Oh, well, it was a sort of tentative thing. To meet up with a friend and go to the cinema. I probably got the dates wrong.'

'Who was that?'

'Umm . . . John Grant. He's er . . . He lives nearby.'

'A friend?'

'Yes. I've known him for years.'

'So you won't mind if we go and see him, ask him about this supposed meeting?'

'No . . . no, I suppose not. If it would help.' There's a pause, then I add, 'He may not be easy to get hold of.'

'What do you mean?' Halliday asks sharply. Another pause. 'What do you mean by that?'

'Well, he's out and about a lot. He isn't always easy to get hold of. That's all.'

The whole court is silent, save for the faint whirr of the tape player. I glance at the jury, and find they are all looking at me, the Bank Manager shifting in his seat, Danny Boy scratching the back of his ear in

258

embarrassment. They must be wondering if I was making a secret joke about John being hard to talk to because I'd killed him.

'Right, now, on the Thursday, you woke up, got ready for work, all in the usual way?'

'I suppose so. I think I can remember listening to the news on the radio, then going for a run. But it might have been a different day.'

'And you work in Oundle?'

'Yes, in the high street.'

'You drive there?'

'Yes, most days. Occasionally, I'll cycle or take the bus, if I'm going to stay there in the evening for a meal or something.'

'Do you always take the same route to work?'

'Yes, I suppose I do. Through Kingsthorpe and Upton.'

'That's about eight miles.'

'Yes, it usually takes me twenty minutes door to door.'

'And what do you wear to work?'

'How do you mean?'

'What clothes do you wear to work?'

'A suit. Or skirt and jacket. Maybe jeans and a sweater, if I'm going on to a site.'

'Would you wear a tracksuit?'

'No.'

'Or a T-shirt?'

'No. Except in summer, perhaps, with a skirt. But it's quite traditional at work. I certainly couldn't wear a tracksuit.'

There's a beeping noise on the tape.

'Sorry.' The new voice is Dr Greenwood. 'I'll be back as soon as I can.' There's a scrape, a crash, a door opening, and a thud as it shuts.

'Miss Morland, what kind of sports do you do?'

'Running, mainly. And skating in the winter, if there's ever any ice. Why?'

'You couldn't go to work in your running kit and get changed there?'

'No.'

'So how do you explain the fact that you were involved in a car crash near Thorney, the other side of Peterborough, miles away from your normal route to work, and that you weren't dressed in your work clothes but in your running clothes?' There's a different kind of silence now. Accusing.

'I don't know.' I had wondered about this before, but it hadn't seemed important. Now Halliday's questions made it seem sinister, like I'd crashed on purpose. 'It doesn't make any sense.'

'No, it doesn't, does it?' he replied.

There is a pause. I remember that he made a long note at this point, scrawling away on his pad with a cheap biro. I found he often did this, leaving me worrying about what I might have said, or let slip, and building up a sense of drifting into deeper water.

Once when we were on holiday in Norfolk, I was swimming a few yards from the shore when I realized the current was carrying me along. The shore looked odd, I couldn't see my brother or the camp my parents had set up by the dunes. I can still remember the rising panic, my feet scrabbling to touch the bottom, feeling the current strong against my arms and legs, and swallowing great gulps of water. I knew I was a good enough swimmer to reach the shore, but somehow that didn't help. Then I felt sand and pebbles beneath me for a moment, just in reach, and I could catch my breath and calm myself down, and swim back to the beach.

I had felt that same panic as I lay in my hospital bed and Halliday questioned me and I knew something was dreadfully wrong. I feel it now, sitting in court, waiting for the next words.

It was then that he told me that John was dead.

* * *

More tapes.

'Interview resumed, 9.56, evening of Saturday the twenty-ninth of October, at Peterborough Hospital. Present myself, DI Halliday, also Sergeant Jordan, Clarissa Morland and Andrew Macleod, her solicitor. Miss Morland has been informed of her rights.' His voice is tired, irritation now giving it a sharp edge, as he asks me about the route I'm supposed to have taken to reach Manor Farm that morning.

'If you went out for your normal run, where would you have gone?' he asks.

'It depends.'

'Well, what would you usually do?'

'Sometimes I'd go along the . . . er . . . the old railway to Normanton, take the footpath to Sulehay, then cut back to the Wansford road.'

There's the sound of someone shifting in their seat, the squeak of a chair leg on the lino floor. I think it was Andrew, worried by what I'd said, but Halliday had already seized on it.

'So, if that's your most likely route . . . ' There's a rustle as he unfolds a map. 'You'd have been . . . oh, say, a mile, less than a mile, from Manor Farm. *And* you'd be there at about the right time, too.'

I don't speak.

'Can you remember what you did that morning?'

Silence.

'Miss Morland. Clarissa. You're an intelligent girl. You can see the facts as clearly as we can.'

'I might have gone another way.'

'But you didn't, did you? You weren't seen by anyone on any other route. But you were seen by two people running away from Manor Farm around the time of the murder. And one of them saw you carrying a gun. So there isn't much doubt, is there?'

There's a faint noise on the tape, which I know was me saying *no*.

'What was that?' Halliday asks sharply. 'What did you say?'

'Could you not bully my client, please,' Andrew says calmly.

'There's no question of anyone bullying anyone.'

There's another long pause, but whether it was Halliday writing something out or planning his next move, I can't remember now.

'I want to go over this land deal again,' he says. 'I still don't understand. To be honest, I really do need to get this clear in my mind. Now, you said that the development at the Doles was your idea?'

'Kind of.' My voice is as tired as his, but heavy, blunted. 'We both thought of it.'

'Chatting it over.'

'That's right. He was always saying that I should buy a place, rather than waste money renting. First he said I should sell the Doles, but I didn't want to as I'd always had this idea that one day I would build my own house on it. I couldn't afford to, of course, but I didn't want to sell it off when my grandparents had turned down offers over the years. Then he worked out that we could build two houses on the Doles, and that the money from one would pay for the other.'

'You entered into an agreement with Mr Grant on the thirtieth of September. You set up a company in which he owned seventy-five per cent of the shares and you owned twenty-five per cent. The structure meant that you had a substantial share in the value of the company, but day-to-day control was in the hands of Grant. You were in effect a sleeping partner. Is that right?'

'Yes.'

'You placed a lot of trust in Mr Grant, didn't you?' Silence. 'After all, he had effective control over the business.'

'Yes.'

There's a pause on the tape, and I think back to that afternoon in his office, John

264

playing me off against Victoria, enjoying his little games, and my being too embarrassed to think about what I was agreeing to. He'd explained it briefly, something to do with access and collateral, and when I'd asked him about what it was for he'd said to Victoria rather sarcastically that I would soon be joining him in the business. So I'd just signed.

'OK,' Halliday says. 'There's one other thing I want to ask you about. This shotgun. Why do you have that?'

'I explained that before.'

'Tell me again,' Halliday says, quite pleasantly.

'I go shooting sometimes. Not often. With the village shoot. And clay pigeons.'

'Would you say you were a good shot?'

'Not really. I'm OK. I know what I'm doing, but I hardly ever go these days. I don't get much practice.'

'When did you last go shooting?'

'In September. The second weekend in September. At Hill Farm.'

'And what did you shoot?'

'I don't know. A couple of pheasant. A pigeon, I think. And two rabbits.'

'I've never gone shooting myself,' he says. I say nothing in reply. 'I suppose sometimes the animal isn't dead. Only . . . winged, is that the word?' He waits for me to say something, then goes on. 'You go and finish them off, I suppose?'

'Yes.'

'You've no problem with that?'

'Of course I've got 'a problem' with it,' I snap, though still with a croak. 'It's really upsetting. But it doesn't happen very often. And you couldn't leave an animal in pain like that.'

'No, you couldn't.'

'Is there a point to these questions?' Andrew asks. We all know there is, but Halliday changes tack.

'The gun was a present from your father, you said.'

'Yes.'

'Quite an expensive present.'

'Not really.'

I don't say that, unlike Nick's brand-new gun, it was second-hand, an old one that Uncle Brian had.

'That was for your fifteenth birthday. The same year your father died.'

'Yes,' I whisper.

'Could you tell me something about how he died?'

'Do I have to answer?' I ask Andrew.

'No, not if you don't want to,' he says.

'I don't want to.'

The tapes are merging one into another by now. I find it more and more difficult to concentrate. I have the same sensation of time being played over again. By this time there were three of them, sitting facing me, and Andrew wasn't there for some reason, I think they'd come by without telling him or me, and stupidly I'd believed them when they said it would only take a minute. Each of them would ask a question and then look disbelieving as I tried to answer. They showed that they were being reasonable, were trying to sort this all out, but that because I was telling the most obvious untruths and distortions it was more and more difficult to believe me.

'Let's go back to the morning,' Halliday says. 'Can you remember anything?'

'No. Nothing.'

'You went for a run?'

'I suppose I must have done.'

'Which way did you go?'

'I don't know.'

It carries on, with me answering every question the same way, *I don't know, I can't remember*. They change from patient, to bullying, to cajoling, anything to try to get me to vary the story, or reveal some loose end they can exploit.

'Why were you carrying the gun?' This is Annette, the sergeant, being understanding.

'I don't know.'

'So you were carrying it?'

'I don't know. I can't remember anything.'

'You might have been, then. You don't know. Why might you have been carrying it?'

'I've really, really no idea.' I am pleading.

'Have you carried the gun before when you go running?' she asks.

'No, of course not.'

'Can you be sure?'

Then the other one breaks in, the one with the rough, sarcastic voice whose name I've forgotten, if I ever knew it, impatient with this. 'You were seen, though. Miss Meadows saw you. She knows you, has done for years. She says that she saw you at the time of the murder running away from the scene of the crime, shotgun in hand. So why were you carrying it, eh?'

'I don't know.'

'But you were carrying it?'

'No.'

He makes a snorting noise, then there's a pause, just the noise of the tape running through the machine.

'Miss Morland.' It's Halliday again. 'Clarrie. We want to help. We have to get this all cleared up, you know that, and all the evidence points to you. I know you can't remember anything, but you can't get away from the evidence. I've been a police officer for more years than I care to remember and this is the clearest case I can think of. Witnesses, forensics, the lot. Now, the only thing that we don't know is the 'why'.' His voice becomes even more fatherly. I can picture him now, leaning forward. He looked like if I talked to him, told him what he wanted to hear, he would hug me and everything would be fine.

'You see, it could have happened in a lot of different ways. Say you went round there, and he was there, he should have phoned you and he hadn't. So you argue, and he says things, and you say things. And then there's the shotgun there. Perhaps you lent it to him, and maybe it's sitting by the door or he brings it to you because he doesn't want to have it any more. And maybe he tells you about the business deal, throws that in your face, tells you how it was all a sham and he never loved you. And you have the gun in your hands, you don't mean to do anything, only frighten him, pay him back. So you point it at him.

'Maybe he laughs at you. He doesn't believe you mean it, he mocks you, he says some more things, hateful things. And you pull the trigger. You don't mean to, you just do.'

I know I whispered No, but the tape doesn't pick it up.

'And then it all becomes real, he's there, there's the wound, the blood. You stand there, stunned, the time's passing, and maybe he's screaming, shouting, whatever, and the time goes on and the screams are worse and worse and finally you have to stop them, any way you can, you have to stop him from screaming, and so you fire again.'

The tape rolls on. I am sobbing on the tape, and I am crying here in court too, silently, reliving what he said, or what happened, I don't know which.

'Is that what happened?'

'No.' Pause.

'Is it?'

'No.'

There's a pause, a chair creaks. A cough, then Halliday's voice, further away, stronger.

'You see, the other way we can see it is that you went up there in a cold rage, because you'd found out about him, you'd heard he'd been saying he was only screwing you for the money. You took the gun with you, went to the farmhouse, knocked on the door, and as soon as he opened it you shot him in the balls. He didn't even have time to say or do anything, or explain himself. You shot him in cold blood.

'He's lying there, he's screaming, and you watch him. You watch him as he tries to get up, as he writhes around in agony. I think you talked to him, told him what you've done, and why, and what you'd do next. You make that minute of his into an eternity. He's dying, but all you do is tell him that you're going to blow his head off. And then that's exactly what you do.

'Even then you're cool. You pick up the cartridges, you check you've left no trace, you clean the gun out and then you run off. It's early, you know you shouldn't be seen. It's just your bad luck you are. Perhaps you know you've been spotted, perhaps you catch a glimpse of Miss Meadows at the kitchen window. You start to panic, you run back and lock up the gun in your house. Then you decide to make a break for it. You aren't thinking, you drive off with no money, no passport, nothing. Or maybe there's some incriminating evidence you want to dump, maybe in a river out in the Fens. Then the crash. You wake up in hospital, but you think you can still bluff your way out of it. There's this head injury, so you claim you don't remember anything. Play dumb and we'll never prove a thing.

'Is that how it is?'

'No.'

'But you don't know, do you?' Mocking. 'You can't remember, can you?' Silence. 'The thing is, are you someone we should feel some sympathy for, who has been used, betrayed, and did something totally out of character in the heat of the moment? Or did you plan it, do it knowing exactly what you were up to? Now you're simply going to pretend it never happened. That your hands aren't stained with blood.

'So which is it?'

'I don't know,' I whisper.

'But you know you killed him?'

'No.'

We listen to the tape, to my sobs, then there's a low mutter, and Halliday's voice, suspending the interview at 22.08. The usher switches off the tape player. No one in the court says a thing.

★   ★   ★

I remember when they arrested me, in my hospital bed. They came in and read out the formal notification, and then the WPC who had been sitting by my side or just outside for the last few days was no longer there 'in case I remembered anything' but to stop me

272

running away. Not that I could run anywhere, with my leg in plaster and my ribs stoved in and my arm so I couldn't button up a shirt. But they were obviously nervous about me being in hospital, they wanted me under lock and key, and they applied several times to have me transferred to the prison hospital. Dr Greenwood saw them off for a week or two, but in the end they won and I was wheeled down into an ambulance and driven out to Whitemoor. I could sit up and see the familiar streets over the shoulder of the driver, until the policewoman told me to lie down.

At the prison we drove round to the hospital block and I was helped on to another trolley, all solicitous care until the ambulance crew were gone. Then I was wheeled along to a plain room, nothing in it but a single folding table, a chair and a bright overhead light. There were two guards and a doctor and they looked me over, did some pointless tests with a light pen and making me look at a pencil being passed from side to side. The doctor was absolutely colourless, no human side at all, he hardly looked at me but spoke when he was looking down at his notes or searching in his bag.

Then I was strip-searched, a bit like being examined in hospital again, but this time they were rough, pulling me about, prodding me, all the time when I was lying on my back they were talking about something else and I knew they didn't expect to find anything, they were doing it just to show me they could.

★ ★ ★

More tapes. By playing them, I realize, the prosecution have set out my own attempts to explain all this. Even if I don't testify, the jury will be able to draw their own conclusions. Every now and again Ruth stands up to introduce a new section, from another interview, another day. They run for the whole afternoon, a series of questions put to me, and my own voice giving answers, the same answers, or with tiny variations to be taken up and picked apart. *Why did I phone John on the Wednesday?* To talk about the property deal. *I knew he had misled me?* Someone had told me about the larger development plans and I wanted to ask him if it was true. I wanted to talk to him about it, that was all. I didn't know what to think, and I hadn't seen him or spoken to him properly for days. That's why I was upset. *Did you speak to him?* No, but he phoned me back later. He said he was really sorry he'd been running

274

around so much and hadn't talked to me properly but he'd have everything sorted out in a few hours' time. He promised me he'd phone that evening. Absolutely promised.

Did he phone you?

I spent those days before the murder in a state of deep misery, trying to convince myself that everything was OK, that he would ring, that he wasn't losing interest, but at the same time gnawing at myself with worry, giving in to my fears, waiting desperately for him to write, or call round, but most of all for a phone call. Sitting looking at the phone in the office, my heart turning over every time it rang, constantly checking my answering machine, carrying my mobile phone everywhere with me in case he called.

I sound defeated as I say, 'I can't remember.'

There's another long pause while the lawyers go over some point, and the whole atmosphere in court changes, relaxes again. The guard next to me is looking up at the windows above, just as I do from time to time, and for one moment I think about making a break for it, vaulting over the dock rail, sidestepping the court officials down the aisle and through the double doors into the lobby, where surprised witnesses and coppers are rooted to the spot. I burst through the glass doors into the cool, breezy air outside. But then I'm left standing in the car park, unable to think what to do next, where I should go, knowing I should keep running, that they will be after me, but my mind is frozen.

So I sit quietly, looking at the same strip of blue sky, wiggling my toes to try to warm them up, shifting a little to stretch my back, and thinking about how it will end. I flick through my diary, looking at the cards, the picture of the skaters whose feet can't be any colder than mine, and the postcard of the whale, and another of a bear eating raspberries which my cousin in Canada has sent me, and then I decide to write something in my diary:

Today is the third day of my trial. Now it's for real, I'm so frightened of what will happen. Kate has sent me a card telling me about being pregnant, about how excited she is, and I look up to see the jury and all the rest of them who are here to put me away and then I'll never have a child of my own, I'll never have a scan or have to stop eating blue cheese or feel it kicking inside me or go through any of that. They all want to find me guilty, the crowd who've turned up to watch, John's family, his friends, all

276

lining up to give evidence, the press people wanting a good story. And everyone who's heard about the murder, read the papers or listened to the radio or seen the pictures of the farmhouse on the TV news, who could imagine it, thought about someone being shot on their own doorstep, then taunted as they bled to death, then shot again, finished off like that. They've all felt the horror, they're still carrying it with them, and it will only go away when the jury say that I am guilty and I am taken away to begin my life sentence. I can picture the scene so clearly, I've seen it dozens of times myself. There'll be a reporter in a fawn mac standing outside the court, describing how I stood impassively in the dock as the verdict was brought in, or maybe I broke down in tears as the judge called it a ruthless, cold-blooded execution, and describing me as wicked and evil as he handed down a life sentence. Then there'll be the usual shot of the prison van speeding off through the crowd, and that will be that.

The usher hands a file of photographs to each member of the jury, as Ruth tells them to prepare themselves for a very unpleasant experience. As they start to open them, I can see that they are every bit as shocking as she said. The old dear looks at one or two and pushes them back into the envelope, the Builder and the bloke in the sports jacket exchange glances.

The usher hands an envelope to me, and I hold it in my lap, unopened. I don't want to look at them but Ruth, is directing everyone's attention to the first one and I steel myself and pull them out.

They are in colour, far worse than I could have imagined. They start with a series of shots of the doorway, the door standing open, dark stains peppered over the walls, and a dark heap beyond the threshold. The next shots come closer in on the body, first on to the face, one eye half-open, staring upwards, blood all around the mouth, the rest gone, and everywhere the black spots from the pellets. Then they close in on the other wound, a shiny patch of mangled flesh and the remains of a bloodstained dressing gown around it.

The walls and the banisters are the most shocking, with palm prints on both, smeared where John had tried to pull himself along. The body is nothing human, but the palm prints are like writing, recording the last moments of his life. Despite everything he did to me, I can't bear to think of even one moment of that time.

I feel the blood thumping round my head, and that is all I feel, and I have to lean forward and one of the guards puts his hand on my back so that I can catch my breath. I hear him ask if I am OK, and then he nudges me and helps me sit back up and I see that the judge is leaning forward, his head on one side as he looks across at me, and the usher passes me a glass and the warm metallic taste of the stale water helps me to recover.

The pathologist is explaining what the photographs show, what he discovered through the post-mortem, piecing together the whole story of John's death, but I don't take any of it in. I can't face it.

If I were to look up and across the court, I would see his family watching me. They haven't missed a minute, father and mother and sister sitting in a single group, staring intently at whoever is speaking, hardly looking my way. His father looks ill, sunk in on his heavy form, no longer the confident successful businessman. He is hating every minute of it, unlike the others, who are spending every minute hating me.

They have all aged, but his sister most of all. She used to be happy, in a superior, offhand sort of way, the sort to have her oversized sunglasses always pushed up into her hair. Now she looks soured, her mouth pinched as if always tasting something bitter, eyes dulled. I can't look at any of them for more than a moment in case our eyes meet. I couldn't bear that.

⋆　⋆　⋆

I thought that nothing could be worse than the pictures. But they have videotapes of the scene of crime to show. The lights are turned down, and the room is lit only by the strip of sky in the windows far above and from the screen.

The film starts with a long shot of the farmhouse, the colours washed out, the view slightly shaky as it moves in on the porch, the front door standing half open, then takes in the windows at the front. It pans round in a circle, around the trees, the garage and other outbuildings, a carelessly parked police car, the drive leading away through the trees, then back to the farmhouse. Without the date and time displayed in one corner of the screen, this could be some low-budget horror flick.

It blanks out for a second, and then comes the view in from the doorway, at first dark, then as the camera adjusts to the interior light, the colours burst out, whites from the walls and carpets, rich woods from the furniture, and red and black from the blood. In the middle is a heap, horribly mangled by the shots, the legs and one arm all that is recognizable. The eye of the camera jerks forward, closing in on individual prints and smears on the walls and the banisters, then circling around the body lying on a deep stain of blood which has soaked into the thick carpet.

When I can look back, the camera has moved away further into the house, looking around the kitchen at glasses and plates, recording the position of the kettle and the coffee jar, then moving into the sitting room, neat and characterless. The sofa cushions need rearranging, and there is a single brandy glass left on a table, but otherwise the scene could be from the pages of *Country Living*, down to the neatly piled logs in the grate.

We are led on to the study, the reproduction desk with pull-out computer keyboard and monitor, the antique-effect filing cabinets, the camera operator zeroing in on each window, on the latches, for signs of forced entry, then on past the downstairs toilets, where I catch a glimpse of a pile of cartoon books, the one personal touch, one the rest of court must surely have missed, and then we are heading back to the stairs.

A subdued soundtrack of muffled voices,

steps, thumps, accompanies the film. The words are hard to make out, but the tone is clear, the tone of professionals going about an everyday job of recovering evidence, recording the scene. Once or twice a furtive figure scuttles out of shot, and as the camera returns to the kitchen there is a muffled crash followed by a burst of laughter quickly suppressed. One more unexplained look at the kettle, then the screen goes black.

* * *

I look at the jury. They are looking grave, still a bit shocked at what they have seen and what they are still listening to, as the pathologist starts off again. Miss Marple is very still, very composed, except that she is so dead white. The bloke in the sports jacket is leaning over towards the Pharmacist, protectively, though I doubt either of them have noticed. Danny Boy has his hands planted on his knees. Beside him the Builder and the Rat both look uncomfortable, their legs crossed, and another time I might have found this funny. But the sight of them all sitting there, going through this with me and yet a million miles away, makes me feel cold.

Occasionally one of them looks over to me, then looks away at once. I know that they are now looking at me like a murderer for the first time. The whole atmosphere of the court has turned, like a change in the weather, the wind backing to the east, cold with the promise of snow.

★   ★   ★

The day ends, and I'm grateful to be able to climb down towards the cells, out of sight of the audience and the judge and above all the jury. I am led down to the usual holding room. I try not to think about what I have seen and heard, but I can't stop it coming back, the talk about John's wounds, of him lying in agony, the fear, the idea of him facing the gun at the last moment, it all goes round and round in my head. I shut my eyes, but then I see the pictures of his body, with the blood making his face into a black disk, so he hadn't a face at all. Nothing there but blackness. I know I will dream of it tonight. Like when I was a child I always knew if something scary was going to give me nightmares.

Does he know that I did it? Would he come back for revenge?

Even here, in this bright clean cell, with a guard down the corridor and bars around me, not even a window, I still imagine him coming in, or me turning around to see him sitting there, watching me; or worse, his head the same as in the photos, his hands reaching out, and me trapped in here, unable to cry out or move.

The door opens, and I jump, spilling the dregs of the tea, and I am about to scream when I realize it is Andrew, and I run to him and bury my head in his suit, and he holds me as I cry, talks to me, soothes me. After a long minute, he gently prises my fingers from his coat and sits me down.

'Come on. Couple of deep breaths.'

He lends me his handkerchief, lets me sit for a moment, then says he'll be back in a moment. He knocks on the door and goes out for a few minutes, so I can catch my breath, wipe my eyes, and by the time he comes back with a cup of coffee I am ready to face him.

'This filth'll take your mind off feeling upset,' he says, putting the cup in front of me. He doesn't have one of his own. 'Charles and Sarah said they've got some material to go through so they've gone straight back to their hotel. Is there anything you'd like to talk over?'

'Yes.' Too desperate. 'I'd, er . . . I was wondering about what'll happen tomorrow.'

'Sure. It'll be expert witnesses all day.

That's why Charles wants to go through it all again. What we want to do is show the investigation to be a bit shoddy, the police jumping to conclusions, not following up all the avenues, that kind of thing.'

Someone has carved into the top of the table the phrase 'the hurt'. It is horrible and makes me shiver.

'The interviews with you in hospital are one possibility, though he's not so sure about that.'

Andrew sits down, but says no more. He's still wearing his coat. We are both on edge, looking like we want to take up smoking. I want to talk about anything or nothing, rather than be left alone. I guess he knows this, and compassion has won out over his desire to get home early.

'Have you thought what you'll do when this is over?' he asks.

'That rather depends if I get off, doesn't it?' I can't keep the bitterness out of my voice, but he doesn't seem to notice. Instead he settles back in his chair.

'Look, I've not worked on a murder case before, but I do know my way around the law and I think you've got as good a chance as anyone of getting an acquittal.'

'Like you said that other time, it's down to luck.' I don't really believe him, but even being lied to is a comfort. 'Not that it matters much, anyway.'

'What do you mean?'

'If I'm acquitted, half the people round here will think I did it and got away with it. They'll nudge each other and go quiet when I go into shops and restaurants. Say things behind my back, about all the stuff in the papers.'

'No one takes any notice of what's in the *Sun*, do they? Anyway, no one we know reads the tabloids.'

'Yeah, well, what about the broadsheets?' He looks at me in surprise. 'They have the same stuff as the tabloids, only they do it as 'media analysis' or as a comment on the court system. The *Guardian* yesterday had a piece about how the press were only interested in this case because I'm middle-class. But they took the chance to rake it all over again, Victoria's stuff and the waiter and all that, so their readers don't miss out on the smut. The *Telegraph*'s the same. I'm on page five of that.'

I know I shouldn't, but I feel pleased that for once I'm the one who knows how the system works, and it's Andrew who's on the receiving end of a lecture. But he looks so crestfallen that I wish I hadn't been so aggressive.

'I'm really sorry,' he says. 'I should have thought about it. I've not been reading the papers.'

'It's OK. I have more time on my hands.'

'I'd thought we'd have a statement ready.'

'Better if I make it myself.' Though I don't know how I could face speaking to anyone. I don't even know if I'll be able to give evidence in court.

'Yeah? Well, I'm sure you'd put on a good show. I've seen you perform.'

'What do you mean?' For a moment, I am scared that he thinks I have been lying, that I'm guilty.

'Oh, years ago. At school.' I stare at him. I had forgotten that he would have been at school at about the same time as me. 'I saw you in a Noël Coward play. I can't remember which.'

'*Hay Fever.*'

'That's it.'

'My God, that must be ten years ago.' I remember the way the cast had been one gang, going out for food after rehearsals together, sitting drinking coffee and practising our lines. Exams over and not a care for the summer ahead. Ten years ago.

'And I saw you in *The Merchant of Venice* too,' he goes on. 'You were Jessica in that.'

'That's right.'

'Miscast, though. You should have played Portia.'

'I never used to get the lead parts.'

'Until now.'

'But I can't understand why you'd have seen it.'

'I was going out with Nicola Cairns. Do you remember her?'

'Yes, of course. She played . . . Oh, I can't remember the name of the part.' Andrew looks blank. 'She used to laugh a lot. Went off to do medicine. I never knew she went out with you. Where were you?'

'At the sixth-form college.'

'Of course.'

'I saw her a few months ago,' he says. 'Bumped into her at the station. She's got a kid now. Six months old.'

We talk on, finding people we know vaguely in common, looking back. The sort of conversation I would have thought so boring, before all this happened.

'Have you done any acting in prison?' His question is just as friendly and matter-of-fact as all the others.

'No.' Too abrupt. I try to relax. 'If you're on remand or have a short-term sentence, you're in a different block and there are fewer activities. No drama. But if I'm convicted, perhaps I'll have the chance to play Lady Macbeth.'

'Do you think you'd be any good at it?' he asks in his usual way, interested and concerned, but also amused, as if I am a reliable source of entertainment.

'Do you?' I reply. Suddenly, it matters what he thinks.

'I don't think so.' He laughs. 'I don't think you're a murderer, if that's what you mean. Or going mad.'

'I don't think your colleagues would agree.'

'How d'you mean?'

'Charles goes on like I'm guilty and he's just putting his great skills into trying to get me off. Sarah thinks I did it too, but John deserved it so that's OK. But Charles really doesn't like me or like talking to me. He never says my name. He thinks I'm the thing that's going to stop him winning the case, because I won't testify and because he thinks I'm going to crack up.'

All this hangs echoing in the air for a bit, but Andrew keeps smiling.

'Perhaps Charles isn't so good with women. I reckon he still misses his nanny. I don't know about Sarah. She was telling Charles she thought you'd be very impressive in the box so maybe you've got one fan at least.'

'And you? Do you think I did it?'

'Oh no. I don't think the case makes any sense. That you loved him so much you killed him? Revenge? It's all a bit melodramatic. That you ran round half of Rockingham Forest carrying a shotgun? That you went home, cleaned the gun, locked it away, and then drove off in such a complete state that you went and crashed your car? Frankly, I think the case just doesn't stack up. It's crap. Even if I didn't know you, I'd still say it was crap.'

★ ★ ★

There are two other prisoners waiting for the van back, and I don't know either of them so I guess they are on remand for something or other. One is about twenty, though looking prematurely aged, and has a dreadful bruise down one side of her face. The other looks lost, vacant, and as we set off she starts to cry, slowly and silently. The first one says something to her, a change from hostility to something approaching tenderness, then looks at me, sees my unspoken question.

'It's 'er kids.' she says. 'Nine, six and four.' I realize she knows who I am, and is according me some respect. I just nod, thinking how if I got out in ten years, I'd be thirty-seven, and it'd be hard to find work or somewhere to live. To get a job I'd have to explain where I'd been for ten years. I could end up like the rest of them, in and out of jail, taking up with some bloke, maybe being knocked about, but going back to him because there's no one else. I guess there's not much of a future for her kids, passed around her relatives, or maybe taken into care, where they'd be running riot, getting into drugs and the rest of it. If they got a move on, her children could be in prison before I got out.

Looking around the room, at the scuffed paint and the pattern of stains across the floor, I wonder what I would do if I had a child, would I want them in here with me, or looked after by my mother or even by Nick, though I smile at the idea of him struggling around with a pram. Or maybe it would be better for the child to be adopted, so they made a fresh start, didn't know what their mother had done. Maybe then they could have the kind of childhood I had. Maybe they wouldn't screw it up the way I have.

When I was very young I used to have a cuddly rabbit. I took it everywhere with me, to nursery school, out with my parents, out when I was playing in the garden. One day I was walking along with my father and my brother, down by the river, and we were mucking about and I threw the rabbit at Nick and it went straight past him and into the water. The current took it away, and I saw it floating off downstream and I cried and cried. And although my father told me he'd go along the banks and there was every chance he'd find it in some reeds downstream, I knew it was gone and I had that terrible empty feeling. It must have been the first time I really understood about how some things can't be made better, by yourself or by adults. It was gone for good.

It's the same now. I know if I get out, life won't be the same. I won't be able to go home to my house, go back to work, and find everything the same. My old life has gone.

Wednesday Evening

Back in Whitemoor we have to wait to be escorted back to the cells individually, and I am the last to go. Miss Elliott is the reception officer and she suggests I make a cup of tea for us both. She fills in some forms while I find a couple of clean mugs, slosh the bags around in the hot water, then pull them out with my finger because someone's pinched the teaspoon.

'Put it down there.' She waves at her desk. Most POs make a point of never saying thank you. You have to know they're grateful from the tone of voice. She sits, nods to me to sit, and I realize she wants to chat.

'How's it going, the trial?' she asks.

'OK.'

'Will it go into next week?'

'Oh yeah, definitely.' I wonder what she's working herself round to.

'It's not so bad, being back on the wing, is it?'

'No, it's OK.' And I mean it. I hadn't realized how much the hospital was getting me down. It's the sort of place that makes you feel ill, or like you're going mad, by the way they treat you and the feel of the place. That, and the other inmates.

'You're going to miss your friend Baz.'

'I suppose so.'

'It's not ideal, having you sharing for only a couple of days, but we're all at sixes and sevens at the moment, as you know.'

'It isn't a problem.' I sip the tea.

'It'll be a wrench when she goes, though. You must be pretty close.'

I know what she wants to say now. They must all know that I sorted out Baz's flat for her.

'Yes. It will,' I say, looking her in the eye.

'You can get very attached to people in here,' she says. 'That can even go for prison officers too, though not so very often. It's a hothouse. You're smart, you can see that. The thing is, it doesn't last when you leave. Whatever you feel for people in here, and it's not to say it doesn't matter at the time, but it goes once you leave. You're all ordinary people again.'

I look at her more carefully, trying to see beyond the uniform. I know she is doing her best, as she sees it, telling me things for my own good. She reminds me for a moment of my mother.

'I expect the next few days'll be difficult, with the weekend and the trial and everything. So if you need to talk to someone, you ask for me. OK? If you feel it's getting you down.' She drains her tea.

'Thank you. I appreciate that.'

'I'll take you back to the wing now.'

'Do you know when you're moving over to the new jail?' I ask as we walk along.

'Next month. I'll be here until the end. I expect I'll switch off the lights.'

'When will that be?'

'In two weeks we'll have the last of the prisoners out. Then we'll finish packing up the offices, sorting out the records and equipment, all that.'

As we walk along we hardly see anyone. The building is starting to look derelict, with odd piles of old chairs in the corridors and some of the ceiling tiles taken down, leaving loops of wire trailing.

'You'll have to make do with sandwiches this evening. The canteen's out of action.'

'That's OK.'

'The sooner we're all gone, the better.'

'Will you be sorry to go?'

She is unlocking one of the barred gates in the middle of the corridor, and she stops and straightens up while she thinks about this. She looks at me searchingly, trying to see why I've asked.

'No. I don't think I will.' She says it so

seriously, she must feel she has to explain, because she adds, 'When I came here I was much younger than you, I'd only been a PO for a couple of years, and we thought Whitemoor was going to be the test bed for all the new approaches. Rehab, drugs unit, mother and baby unit, proper training, the lot. And it's all gone, bit by bit, or it never happened in the first place.' She unlocks the gate. 'Half the rooms downstairs have been shut for years. No staff to run anything. There was even talk of a language lab when we first moved in.' She laughs. 'Can you imagine that now? It's all about costs per prisoner and lowest staffing ratios and containment and more bloody reorganizations.' She locks the gate and leads me along to the gate through to D2, where Miss Walters is standing.

'Clarrie here has been asking if we'll be pleased to leave.'

'I will, for one. D'you know the bloody canteen's closed again?'

*   *   *

Baz is sitting in her usual perch on the window ledge, looking out at the security lights.

'Your last night, then,' I say, but she doesn't reply. She must still be thinking about her flat. When I came back from court she gave me a crushing hug and said she could never thank me enough and asked how had I managed to swing it and started telling me about her plans for decorating it and how she'd get hold of some furniture, all before I had a chance to answer. We chatted on like that for hours, because it stopped me thinking about the trial and her thinking about getting out tomorrow. She kept asking me what the flat was like, though all I knew was that it needed some work, but it was pretty sound and only a few years old.

'It's really quiet round there,' I tell her. 'Lots of old Victorian terraces, lovely stuff. Lots of young professionals.'

'Yeah, that's me. Young professional sounds better than old lag.'

'If I was going to live in Peterborough, I'd live in Woodston. You're near the river and there's a supermarket. If you don't mind the smell from the sugar-beet factory.'

I thought of her settling in, getting a job that paid enough to cover the rent, the odd meal out, even a holiday. She'd sort out the flat, make it lovely, maybe meet someone. While I could be here for fifteen years or more. What would it be like coming out then? I'd never be able to work for a housing association again. I'd probably never get a decent job, all my friends would have moved on or forgotten me or not want to remember. I couldn't go back to Woodwalton, so I'd live in Peterborough, or move further away, somewhere I could be anonymous, I'd just be a strange woman and then someone would whisper who I was. No one would speak to me, the kids would be kept away. I'd end up drifting like a ghost around the town.

So the mood changes, we both fall silent. I lie in the dark, watching Baz watching whatever is outside, sorry for myself and angry with her for a moment because she won't be here tomorrow, her trial is over and the punishment paid. It's all starting again for her.

'D'you know,' she says suddenly, 'why you were put in here?'

'I thought you asked.'

'What good would that ever do in here? If I'd asked for you to come in here, they'd have put you in a cell on the moon.'

'Why, then?'

'Because they were worried you were . . . y'know. At risk.'

It takes me a while to work out what she means. 'You mean they think I'd try and kill myself?'

'Yeah.' She sounds like she thinks I might too.

298

'But that's stupid. I'd never do that.'

'You just bloody make sure you don't.' I can't see her face but I think she's crying.

'I'd never do it. I know things can get bad in here but I'd never do that.'

She doesn't say anything so I go over to her. She won't look at me, won't let me see the silent tears, though it's obvious they're there, so I hold her and she hugs me back. She's freezing cold under her T-shirt, as cold as the little metal cross she always wears.

'You'll come and see me, won't you?' she says. 'When your trial's over?'

'Yeah. We'll go clubbing.' But the joke falls flat.

★   ★   ★

Later, when we are lying in our bunks, and I am worrying about my mother, about whether to ask her to visit this weekend, and whether I would be more upset to see her or not, Baz whispers to ask if I'm awake. I grunt.

'What was he like?'

'Who, John? He was . . . ' I stop, because it matters that I get him right. 'Well, he was very proper. Quite conventional in the way he spoke, his clothes, and the things he did. And at the same time he was kind of dangerous. You could tell he was ambitious, even ruthless. But with it he had this amazing energy. He was always having ideas, plans, always phoning people up, sorting out things, arranging to go off and have a meal or a drink or a game of squash. He was really exciting to be about.'

'Was he nice? I mean, kind?'

'I suppose so.' I hear the doubt in my own voice. 'He took trouble about things. Little things. Flowers, saying thank you. Remembering things. He had one of those stupid handheld computers filled with stuff about all his friends, his business contacts, what their girlfriends' names were, what sort of drinks they liked. If they mentioned something they liked, he'd make a point of getting it — a bottle of wine or tickets for a concert, that sort of thing. That was really typical of him.

'And he always used to clean his teeth before doing it.'

'You're joking!' She snorts.

'No, he did, whenever it was, during the day or anything.'

'Better than bad breath, anyway.'

'Yeah. But mainly he was a lot of fun. All week, his friends have come into court and said how great he was. And the worst of it is, it's true. He was so exciting, so full of life. And everyone loved him. All the women because he was a real lasher, I mean to look at and in the way he acted. And the blokes all reckoned he was a good bloke like them.'

'Not so good for you.'

'No.'

'Is that why you went out with him?'

'It must be,' I admit. 'But it was more than that. I really fell for him. Loved him. He'd phone me up, and I'd feel all flushed and silly. You know.'

'Yeah,' she agrees.

'And I suppose I was a bit bored. Work was a bit routine, I was quite settled, doing the same thing every week, out on Friday, maybe a film midweek. Fun, you know, but not enough. When I met him I was thinking about taking six months off and going around the world.'

'Where to?'

'India. Or maybe South America. I didn't want to go on my own, so I was working on Claire and Joanne and trying to get them interested in going.'

'I'd love to go abroad like that.'

'What's to stop you?'

'Money, for one thing.' She thinks. 'And what would I do when I got there?'

I can't answer that.

She changes the subject. 'D'you miss him?'

'Yeah. Sometimes.'

'If he was still alive, you'd have him back?'

'God, no. I don't know. Maybe. But I'd hate myself if I did.'

She doesn't say anything, and I think for a moment she has fallen asleep. I wonder if it's true. If he'd come to me and said it was all a mistake, said he was sorry about the land, but he still wanted to see me, what would I have done? Would I really have told him to get stuffed? Or would I have let him win me over? Would I have enjoyed it a little? Would I have let him screw me? Again.

Then Baz says, 'What was he like in bed?'

Maybe it's the dark, but I don't mind telling her.

'He really knew what he was doing. Sort of controlled, though it wasn't creepy or anything. That was, most of the time. But he could be a bit offhand as well when he was in the mood — when he'd been drinking, maybe. Then it was just a quick fuck, no more than that.'

'Nothing wrong with that.'

'No.'

'And he was screwing around?'

'Yes.'

'You poor girl,' she says, and something about her voice, though it's dulled by sleep, makes me think that something similar must've happened to her one time. But she doesn't say anything more, and soon I hear

302

her soft breathing like she's fallen asleep. But I can't do the same, because I keep wondering who it was John was seeing. The woman in the car park must've been the same one he chatted to one time. We were driving somewhere together, and John slowed to overtake a woman on a horse, all dressed in white but with her back to us so I couldn't recognize her. Then he stopped, lowered the window and they chatted to each other easily for a few minutes, exchanging pleasantries, something about a puppy she had bought from someone he knew. I thought it was someone I knew, but I still couldn't see her face and I couldn't bring myself to ask him who it was, then or later. I couldn't see John's face either as he leaned out of the window but I could tell he was looking her over in her white jodhpurs and her cream sweater, her long fair hair falling over her shoulders as she talked and laughed.

I think of the sign saying 'Byroad', pointing the way to his house, an old-fashioned fingerpost set at just the right height for a rider. Did I run up there, perhaps along the footpath with the screen of trees so he wouldn't see me by accident, and then see — what? Her leaving? A last lingering kiss after a night of passion, then him helping her back into the saddle?

(I know this is ridiculous. What would the horse have done all night? There are no stables at the farm. But the thought stays with me.)

As we drove off, he looked back at her in the rear-view mirror and I knew from his careful lack of expression that he was thinking about screwing her.

That evening, I wanted to teach him a lesson. So I played up to him, with a passionate, pressing kiss in the doorway of the restaurant, and then sitting demurely across the starched white tablecloth from him. Slipping off my shoe to play footsie with him, then putting my foot up into his crotch, kneading his stiff dick as he struggled to order our food from a girl years younger than us both. Asking him about his deals, his future plans, so that the rest of him swelled up too. Loving the wine, the food, the place he had found. Asking if we could skip the dessert and coffee and leave at once. All this to lead up to the moment when I licked his ear and asked him to drop me off at my house on his way home.

But the fire in me was for real by then, I was the one he wanted, not the bitch on the horse, or the waitress, and so instead of leaving him wound up as I planned I leaned over to whisper that I needed him now.

We went into his farmhouse kitchen because he wanted coffee, and I started playing with him as he filled the kettle and in the end we screwed on the floor. I began to bite at him as he pumped away, and he pushed himself into me even harder so I cried out. He loved that so much he came at once with an odd kind of bellow, and then rolled off me to lie on the tiles beside me, saying *Fuck, that was good,* almost with surprise, which looking back I shouldn't have found very flattering. Yet for that moment it made me feel so sexy and so vulnerable and I made myself come too. But quietly.

We lay there, cooling on the cold tiles, both sticky and speckled with crumbs from the floor, and then we noticed the cat looking down on us and we laughed together, and took a shower and dried off in the deep comfort of his bed, and I thought as I listened to him breathing in his sleep that I had found out something important. That it was my fault that he looked at other women, or that I'd had trouble meeting men who would love me, and that I should have thought more of them, done what they wanted, dropped my inhibitions, not thought of it as playing the tart but knowing them better, more closely. I slept with that in my mind.

Thursday Morning

I hardly notice the van journey. I don't feel tired, just strange, sort of detached from everything, for once not worrying about court. I ignore the other prisoners and the POs and watch the square of sky I can see through the window, high and blue.

It was beautiful at dawn, cold but with the same fresh sky without a single cloud. I had my run without even having to ask. The duty officer came and woke me at the usual time. Prison is like that — anything to establish a routine. The POs like it just as much as the prisoners.

On the way back from the showers, someone hands me a well-thumbed copy of yesterday's *Sun*, creased and the ink smeared from being passed from hand to hand, the one with me as the star of page six. Two other prisoners were hanging around outside their cell and they watched me pick up the paper with a strange mixture of excitement and sympathy on their faces. Any drama is welcome in here, and the outside world comes to have as much reality as the TV or the tabloids. I said something about how they'll print any crap, like I didn't care, and they took my mood and agreed and dismissed it, and wandered away.

I had a letter from Seb this morning. It was mainly about a book he'd read, and what'd been on the TV — all things I might do despite being inside, which is very sensitive of him. But at the end he'd written, 'I know you can never be sure how things will turn out, but if it was a jury of people who knew you, I know they would find you innocent. So whatever they say, I want you to know that I will go on believing in you, and I'm sure that goes for everyone who really knows you.' He didn't mention the papers, but he must have realized it's looking bad.

Andrew has said that if the press got out of hand, printed too much stuff like this, then we could apply for a mistrial if the verdict went against me. I think he was trying to cheer me up, but it made me wonder what might be in the next day's papers, and whether I'd be able to face going through all this again if there was a retrial. The way I feel now, I think it would kill me.

Back in my cell, I'd looked again at the paper, thinking how I'd changed since the photo was taken, how much paler, older and more tired. I was rubbing at the dark smudges around my eyes when Baz asked me what was wrong.

'I'm worried I'm looking guilty. Like in the paper.' I threw it on to her bed and started to get dressed. She must have seen it before because she turned straight to the right page.

'They're wankers, this lot. Journalists. How can they say this shit?'

'It's just a job.'

'No way. No one makes them do it. It's like being in the police. Some people get off on it, the uniform, pushing people around, all that.'

I shrugged. 'If people didn't buy the papers . . . '

'Yeah, like fuck.'

'Anyway, aren't you getting up?'

'I might not bother,' she said, pulling the blanket up to her nose. 'Can't do much to us now, can they? Take away my association? Put us back on bins?'

'I suppose not.' I fumbled with my collar. 'How do I look, then?'

'I'll come and visit you.'

'Back here? I don't think so. I'll write to you, tell you how everything is here.' I already had her address, written into my diary in her strong, thick script, stylized so that it was as difficult to read as graffiti. 'How we all are.'

'You look great,' she said, watching me as I put my jacket on and stepped into my skirt.

Her look reminds me of one time, when I was at university, I was outside the faculty bar on a bright mid-morning, and I happened to see one of the other students watching me hitching up my skirt as I got on the bike. She was looking me over, her expression halfway between a smile and a leer. It was a strange sensation. I felt very sophisticated to have been eyed up by another woman. But with a friend I felt shy, blushed, looked down and smoothed my skirt out. I didn't want her to know I'd seen.

'I'd like to give you something.' She threw back the blankets, came over to me and adjusted the collar of my jacket. Then she took off the chain she always wore around her neck and linked it together again behind me. The little silver cross lay bright against my jacket. I knew that she wanted me to kiss her properly but I couldn't and I didn't know what to do or say until she said, 'You say *thank you, Baz.*'

Then, laughing, I hugged her until tears came to us both.

Now, sitting in the van, fingering the cross, I find I miss her more than I knew. I wonder how I will get through tonight, or the weekend, knowing no one in this half-derelict prison. I can't think beyond that. I picture her, feel her, standing in my cell, in front of me, her arms around me. I wish I had kissed her the way she wanted.

* * *

Thursday is market day in Oundle. If I was back in my office, I'd be listening to the calls from the stall-holders in the street below, enjoying the absence of cars. There'd be that excitement about, a bit like a funfair, more than simply the attractions of being able to buy fresh fruit or cheap clothes, or for Julie the receptionist the trip to *John Jakes the King of Rock*, selling every kind of sweet imaginable from his gaudy trailer.

I might lean back from my computer, stretch, glance out of the window at the buildings opposite, the spire of the church beyond, all the same as every day, and think of taking a walk at lunchtime down to the river. Perhaps I can picture it all so clearly because one of the psychologists was really interested in it, asking me repeatedly about my desk, the decoration of the office, how I got on with the other staff, whether I cleared my desk every evening. I had to listen to his suggestions too. *Was I prone to ideas of escape? Was I always planning holidays to distant countries? Did I read a lot of romantic fiction? Did I keep the postcards to impress people with how many friends I had?*

★ ★ ★

Andrew is alone in the interview room when I arrive. He is looking tired, and I wonder how late he was up. But he is still cheerful.

'You OK?' he asks.

'Yeah.' Today, I don't want to chat to him, but to keep it businesslike. 'I've decided I . . . Well, I definitely want to give evidence.'

'That's great. That's really good,' he says, expecting some explanation for my change of heart, but I don't say anything. 'We can find a time this afternoon to go over the kinds of things you'll be asked. The way it's looking, you'd be called sometime tomorrow, or possibly last thing today, depending on the forensic evidence. How does that sound?'

'Fine.'

'Good.' The question still hangs in the air. 'I thought it would be useful to go over a couple of weak points in our evidence, from what we've seen so far.' He has a pad open in front of him, covered with scrawls and arrows and underlinings.

'There's something I wanted to tell you first,' I say. 'I thought of it last night. They say John was killed with the same kind of gun and ammunition that I have, right?' He nods. 'Well, the type of gun may not be very common, but there's a few people have them, men as well as women. Smaller men, or the ones who like to show off.'

'Why's that?'

'Well, with a 20-bore gun you've got a smaller cartridge, so less shot, so you have to be more accurate. Like a sharp-shooter. So it's a bit flash to use a 20-bore.'

'Do you know anyone who has one?'

'No, but everyone I know goes to the same shop, Jarrolds' in Stamford. It's the only one around, so everyone in the shoot, all the farmers, everyone round about goes there. That's where I go. So if John was killed by someone local, chances are they'd have got their gun from there. And they'd have a list of who they sold what kind of gun to.'

'That's excellent.' He makes some notes, and asks me about the shop, the manager, when I last went there, and who he could speak to on the shoot to back this up.

'That's really, really helpful,' he says at the end. 'If you have any more thoughts like this, you let me know.'

'I will. And I'm sorry if I'm a bit out of it recently,' I add. 'I haven't been sleeping so well.'

'Are you having nightmares again?' I nod. 'Have you spoken to the doctors at the prison?'

'There's no point doing that. It's because I've moved back into the main prison, I think. And my cellmate was let out this morning.'

He is concerned, wants to help, but I can't begin to explain it all to him.

'Never mind,' I say. 'Shall we sort out this evidence thing?'

'Sure.' He nods, but is still thinking about me, still concerned.

Then he picks up his pen, sits back in his chair, becomes the lawyer again.

'It's about Claire Pattinson's evidence.'

'Is she still going to testify?'

'Of course. Probably next week. Unless you know something I don't.'

'Well, I'm only thinking . . . I mean, she's my best friend, but she hasn't been in court. So I thought that maybe the idea of it sort of freaked her out. Put her off. It isn't like her, but maybe that's that.'

'But she can't come into court. Look, Clarrie, if you have any worries like this, questions about anything, you must tell me. She can't sit in court because she's a witness and it would compromise her testimony. So she has to wait outside. But I think she's been to speak to your mother after court every day, most days anyway. Don't think she's running away from it.'

'I don't think I did think that . . . '

'Is there anything else you're worrying yourself over?'

He's concerned and exasperated at the same time, which is so sweet, so lovely, and for a moment I think of asking him about John, and what I should say about him when I testify. I still don't know what I think of him. There's all the stuff I've heard in court, the horrible things he'd said to his friends, and the way he'd set out to rip me off. But I can remember him being such fun, so lovely and so exciting. Maybe I'm no better placed to judge him than all his friends coming to court to testify against me.

'Anyway, you've got a pretty good fan club in court,' Andrew says.

'Yeah?'

'You look at the difference between your lot and John's family, I know who I'd rather have supporting me.'

'I know. It's awful having them there. I think they could kill me by just looking at me.'

He changes the subject.

'Tell me, what do you think of when you're sitting in the dock?'

'Nothing much. I try and follow what's going on. A lot of the time I'm thinking of how what people are saying isn't really the way it was. Why d'you want to know?'

'Most of the time you look like you're having a terrible time. Which is really good, from the point of view of the jury and the press. Makes you look like a martyr being burnt at the stake. Like Joan of Arc. And then sometimes you look interested, or you even smile. I was only wondering what you were really thinking.'

After the committal hearing, my mother had come to see me in the prison and told me that I'd sat looking ill and frightened and all she'd wanted to do was hold me, and she felt so awful because she couldn't. But once during the hearing, which had lasted an hour or so, something had made me smile, and it reminded her so much of when I was young, how it changed the way I looked, she wanted to cry all the more but it also convinced her I'd be all right, whatever happened.

'Some of the time I think about being in prison,' I tell him. 'What would it be like if I lose. Or I think about getting out. Not from the trial, but walking out of the court, or being outside, not on trial and not being recognized, but doing ordinary things like going to the market or going for a run.

'Like yesterday. You know the way the railway runs past the court building? Well, I heard the horn of the train as it went past, and I thought of all the times I took that train when I was going off to university, or afterwards to see friends, or even going down to London. And I imagined I was on the train, not just the idea of it, but I could picture it as clearly as if I were there. Spreading out over the seats, maybe having a cup of tea or hot chocolate for a treat, reading a crappy book or *Marie Claire* or staring out of the windows, watching the fields or backstreets of towns, or a scrapyard, anything. Just seeing things, moving on.'

'Getting away?'

'It's more than that. It's like trying to find something. To add something to what I've already got. I mean, I love my family, my friends. I love living round here — or I did — and it isn't about wanting to leave it. It's about still having it, but finding something else.'

Andrew has his mouth open to reply when the guard comes in.

'Five minutes, sir,' he says, and Andrew nods.

'Oh yeah, I've got a bit of bad news,' he says to me, and it makes my stomach lurch. Maybe it's my mother, or Nick in a car crash, or Baz run over in the street. 'Someone broke into your house. Messed it up a bit.'

'Is it bad?' I say, breathing out with relief.

'It could've been much worse, Nick said. There's some graffiti on the walls, and stuff's been thrown about and broken in the kitchen and the front room. But they didn't go upstairs, so everything there's OK. Yeah, and the fridge is a goner.'

I know I should feel awful, but it doesn't seem real. Maybe it would be worse if I didn't already know I have to leave anyway. And at least they didn't mess about with my bedroom, and my clothes.

'Do you know who did it?'

'No. No one saw a thing.'

*   *   *

We're waiting to go up to the dock. It's comforting that Claire must be sitting somewhere in the court building, waiting for her call to give evidence. She's so kind, and so funny, that I can't believe that anything bad will happen if she's around. All the times we've spent together, at school, messing about, flicking things around the class, then going on holidays together, drinks and meals and films, evenings of gossip, all that must count for something. She must be able to

317

convince the jury what I'm really like.

One time, it must have been about the last time she came round for dinner, I told her about the time I'd gone to the Hayloft with John, and what had happened afterwards, and she'd found it so funny, and spent the evening trying to imitate the noise John had made, and we'd cackled about it over our wine as she tried different variations, each more stupid and walrus-like than the next. And for weeks afterwards, she'd make these noises when we were out together, and I'd go red and she'd look all innocent and we'd both try not to crack up.

The guard next to me notices that I'm smiling, and tells me that that's the spirit.

★   ★   ★

As soon as the judge is sitting down, we start where we left it the night before. Ruth is continuing her examination of Dr Beale, the Crown's second pathologist, who is surprisingly jovial and normal-looking for someone talking about wounds and blood and what he found when he 'opened the body'.

'Comparing the extent of bleeding between the two wounds and the pattern of the shot allowed me to reconstruct with confidence the sequence and, to a lesser degree of

318

certainty, the timing of the wounds.

'The first shot was fired at the victim's groin from a distance of approximately three feet. It couldn't have been much closer than that, judging from the spread of the pellets and the lack of scorching marks from the powder — the combustible material — in the shotgun cartridge. I would also doubt it could realistically have been more than a couple of feet further away, although there is a little more room for uncertainty because we have to rely on the spread of the pellets alone.

'From the travel of the pellets, I concluded that the shotgun was being held at waist height, by the hip, pointing slightly downwards. Again, I wouldn't wish to be dogmatic on this point, because it is perfectly possible that it was held lower down by a taller person, or higher by a shorter person, but if one takes the most comfortable, most natural position for holding such a gun, then it would be held at the hip. Like this.'

'Would it be possible to conclude anything about the assailant, their height and so on, from this?' Ruth asks.

'Yes, it would. Assuming this stance, I would say the assailant would have been between five foot eight and five foot ten in height, and right-handed.'

Three or four of the jury look over at me,

trying to work out how tall I am. I wonder if I should stand up. No doubt Ruth has plans to come back to my height later on.

'Did you conclude anything about how Mr Grant was standing from the pattern of the wounds?'

'Yes I did. I could see at once, and the PM confirmed this, that the pattern of the first wound corresponded to Mr Grant having stood with his arms close to his sides, not raised, or perhaps with one arm holding the door. He was also facing his attacker straight on. I formed the tentative view that he knew his assailant, or at the very least had no clue as to what was about to happen. You see, if someone believes themselves to be about to be shot, they tend to do one of two things. Most of the time, people will instinctively put up their hands to protect themselves, protect their face above all, and they also tend to crouch over and to turn away. Sometimes, though less rarely, people make an effort to get hold of the weapon, and again the pattern of wounds from a shotgun will be distinctive. He seems to have done neither of these things, at least before the first shot, the shot to the groin.'

'Could you describe the wounds them-selves?' Ruth asks.

'Well, the first wound caused considerable

damage to the lower trunk and the upper portion of each leg. There was limited damage to both arms, mainly the left arm, which led me to the tentative deduction that the right was partly shielded by the door, and very light injury, only a few pellets, to the lower legs and to the head. The damage to the trunk was sufficient to cause death due to loss of blood, though not through direct damage to any vital organs.'

'So it was potentially a fatal shot?'

'Oh yes, it was clearly sufficient to kill. The rate of blood loss, as far as one can tell this from the state of the body and the scene of the crime, was very heavy. I wouldn't have expected the victim to live more than, say, half an hour at the outside. Even if medical attention had been immediately available, I doubt that the victim's life could have been saved.'

'And Mr Grant would have lost consciousness immediately?'

'Not necessarily. The loss of blood would have had a cumulative effect, and would eventually have brought about a loss of consciousness and, in time, death, but not at once. The handprints made by the victim were consistent with his having pulled himself along the hall towards the rear of the property. It is extremely difficult to be exact about these things, but it would have taken him the best part of a minute to do this, at the least.'

'And the timing of the second shot?'

'At a guess, and it has to be little more than that, I'd say after one minute.'

'What can you tell the court about the second shot?'

'I think it likely that it was fired from a standing position, about three feet away from the victim, aimed downwards towards the victim's head. Again, this is based on the spread of shot, the nature of the wound, and so forth.'

'Which way was the victim facing when the shot was fired?'

'That's quite an interesting point. If we assume that the assailant followed Mr Grant down the passage, stood over him, and aimed the gun at his head, it would be most unlikely that he would be facing the gun. Firstly, Mr Grant was on his side at this point, and the natural thing would be to be looking down, letting the head hang down, or to be looking straight ahead, that is towards the opposite wall. Further, if someone is threatened by a gun and has reason to believe it is about to be fired, their normal reaction is to flinch, or look away. But Mr Grant was looking almost directly at the gun when it was fired.'

'Do you think this was solely a matter of chance?'

'That is possible.'

'But would it also be consistent with the facts that the assailant waited until Mr Grant looked up, or that she was speaking to Mr Grant or in some other way attracting his attention.'

'Certainly, that would be wholly consistent with the facts.'

Having seen the video, I can picture the scene, the hall, the blood, even standing over John and pulling the trigger a second time. But I don't believe it was me. I can't believe that.

'Would Mr Grant have been conscious for any length of time after the second shot?'

'Oh no. Death would have been quite instantaneous.'

I don't want to listen to any more of the evidence, particularly because Dr Beale is coming on to the autopsy. So I open up the bundle of documents and find the copy of my first statement to the police, written out by the sergeant in painfully neat longhand rather than typed because we were still in the hospital. At the bottom of the second page is a shaky version of my signature.

My name is Clarrie Morland and I live at 6 Main Street, Woodwalton. I have known John Grant for several years and I had a relationship with him from approximately the middle of July until his death. The relationship was happy. He was not seeing anyone else, as far as I know. I was not seeing anyone else. We were on good terms. We did not quarrel.

As well as that relationship, I was a shareholder in a company with him called Lioncrest Developments Limited, and I sold a plot of land in Normanton which I inherited from my grandmother Mrs Anne Morland three years ago to that company. We planned to build two houses on this plot. We had no disagreement over the business.

I last saw John Grant on Friday 14 October for a drink at his house. I did not stay the night. I last spoke to him on Wednesday 19 October in the afternoon. He phoned me to say he could not meet that evening as arranged as he had to go to London on business. He wanted to meet up at some point over the following weekend instead. He said he would phone me that evening to fix it up.

I work at the Forest Housing Association offices in Oundle. I left work on the evening of 19 October at about six o'clock and went straight home. I had something to eat and watched TV and phoned a friend of mine, Claire Pattinson. That was at about 9.30 and we spoke for about half an hour. I then cleared up and went to bed. I do not remember receiving any phone calls that evening, or the next morning. I do not remember anything from going to bed until I woke up at the hospital in Peterborough on the afternoon of 22 October.

I own a shotgun which I keep in a secure cabinet at my home. I have not lent it to anyone in the last year.

I do not know why I was driving along the road to Market Deeping on the morning of 20 October. I do not remember anything about the accident, or being taken to the hospital.

I do not believe that I had anything to do with John Grant's death. I was in love with him and would not have done anything to hurt him. I have no idea who would have wanted to threaten or injure him and his death was a complete surprise and shock to me. I do not believe that I went near to Manor Farm on the morning of his death or the evening before. I did not spend the evening before with him.

Charles is arguing with the pathologist over some of the detail of his conclusions. I'm surprised, because there's no doubt as to what happened. The photographs show it all too well.

'So this aerosol effect would have left residues on anyone within several feet?'

'Yes, it would.'

'Did you find traces of this aerosol effect at the scene of the crime?'

'Yes, on the carpet, walls, banisters, and on the clothing of the victim himself.'

'So you have no doubt that the aerosol effect took place in this case?'

'No.'

I remember Andrew explaining that one of the best points about the forensic evidence was that there were no traces of John's blood on me. Apparently a shot from close range should have created a mist of blood which should have covered me, and would have shown up in the analysis of my clothes. So Charles is trying to push him into conceding I might have been closer than he said, and can't have been further away than he said. The pathologist is cautious, and admits he can't be definite, but doesn't really shift at all.

I take the chance to look around the court, at the audience and the press box, where some of the faces are becoming familiar. I wonder which of them works for which papers, which writes the nastiest stuff. I risk a quick smile for my family sitting just behind Andrew and Roisin, avoiding a look at John's family, and then I look over to the jury. Miss Marple has changed her scarf, and the bloke who was wearing a sports jacket has abandoned it for a sweater, otherwise they seem the same.

But the mood has changed a little from last night. Then, you could feel the shock of the pictures and the film on the jury and the audience. Now, I might still have a chance of convincing them it wasn't me. Not I, the sweet girl next door, the sort of woman you'd be proud to have as a daughter. Andrew is always going on about this, making it into a joke but meaning it as well, about how I have to look alert and intelligent but not calculating, how I shouldn't smile more than once a day, but do it really sweetly. How I should look innocent.

I look again at the jury, sitting hunched forward or lying back or leaning on one arm, baffled and bored and interested and alert all at once. Any of them could look as much a murderer as me, only they are sitting in the wrong place. If you are in the dock, where the guilty people sit, you are bound to look guilty. Sit in the jury box, you look ordinary and slightly bemused, even if you have more intelligence than the lawyers or the judge himself. The witness box is more ambiguous, because not all the witnesses can be telling the truth, or at least telling the same truth. Perhaps that is why I want to give evidence. To step down from the dock, take my place as a non-convict, someone worth listening to, someone who might be believed.

But then, I still don't fancy facing Ruth. I watch her stand to re-examine her witness, and she is cool, relaxed, as if the grisly subject matter means she has to be even more poised than normal. Charles must have raised some doubts about the final position of the body, something to do with bruises and this settling of blood in the body. I guess that a post-mortem must be pretty thorough, and I wonder what John looked like when they had finished. I suppose the coffin must have been sealed anyway. The video showed that there would have been nothing they could look at. It must have been so bad for his parents, not being able to say goodbye, knowing that what happened to him was so awful they couldn't even see him.

I try to imagine John being dead, but it

doesn't seem real. Maybe if I'd gone back to any of the places we'd been to, or I'd visited his house, or his parents' house, or I'd met up with his friends it would be different, but I have done none of these things. I know now I have never really grieved for him as I should. I can still remember bits of our time together, driving along with me in the passenger seat. Or working at his desk with this look of utter concentration on his face. Or coming into the bedroom with a tray of coffee, smiling, full of energy, but also wanting to be up and gone.

The thing about John was he was always so alive, in everything he did. One weekend he arranged for us to go and stay on the south coast, Havant or Hayling Island, and during the afternoon he hired some jet skis and we messed about on the water, bombing up and down, and because he knew what he was doing he'd go much faster, racing off down the harbour and then coming back, weaving in and out of the marker buoys, circling around me, and then helping me up out of the water when I fell off. And all the time he'd be shouting something out or laughing or coming up with some words of advice.

Afterwards we went back to the hotel, which was part of a marina on the waterfront, and we had dinner looking out over the harbour lights. Then we ate in this starchy restaurant, showered and dressed and hungry. I wore my best navy silk blouse and the fawn skirt I knew he liked, and I was thinking about later on, how good it would be. My muscles were aching all down my legs and up my back from the exercise and my skin tingling from the salt water. That was what being with John was like all the time, the mix of him being so formal and so exciting all at the same time.

I wonder what the funeral was like, where it was, what they said about him in the eulogy. Perhaps Andrew was there. I should ask him. I wonder also where John is buried. I've never asked, never been told, but it matters now. I imagine that he would be buried in the churchyard at Upton, but perhaps he was cremated. I can picture the service, the figures in black clustered around the grave, his parents and his sister looking much as they do at this minute, dressed in mourning, looking tearful and grim.

★   ★   ★

Dr Beale has gone, but the judge is still making notes. People wander in and out. Then one of the clerks lifts a package wrapped in clear plastic on to the documents table beneath me. It is my gun case.

Meanwhile, the other clerk is swearing in another witness, Dr Fairbrother, who runs through the affirmation with practised ease. He has a balding head, fringed with reddish hair, and the same on the back of his hands, where he is holding on to the front of the witness box. He must be forty or so, bulky, with blunt fingers. Though he is wearing a sober suit, he looks like a science teacher. In a light Yorkshire accent, he gives his credentials as an expert witness on firearms.

'I work at the Forensic Science Service's regional laboratory in Huntingdon. On the twenty-sixth of October of last year I was asked to examine a shotgun.'

'This has been entered as Exhibit 14J,' Gerard adds.

The judge nods. Everyone looks at the gun, inside the brown canvas case. I have had it for ten years or more, since I was fifteen. It was too large for me then, and is a little too small now, but I don't — didn't — go shooting often enough for that to matter too much. I started because my father used to go, and Nick and I would join the beaters, making as much noise as possible walking through the thickets, flushing out the birds, then picking them up as they fell. I can still remember the welcome warmth from their bodies in my chilled hands. There was never more than a

331

smear of blood, no sign of how they had died. But even as a child, you could never think they were anything but dead.

The days were always cold, frosty, with snapping twigs, driving the birds forward with shouts and banging sticks against trees, and then the sharp cracks of the guns. When Nick got a gun, I wanted to learn to shoot too. My mother didn't want it, perhaps because she thought I was enough of a tomboy, but I went on about it until she relented. I loved the shoots even more then, Nick and I standing around, very serious, as the men smoked, leaning on the Land Rovers, swapping jokes, or took nips from their flasks, then set off for the woods.

'It may be helpful if I explain how a shotgun works,' Dr Fairbrother says. 'It's not like a bullet, in that there is not a single projectile. Instead, the shotgun cartridge contains dozens or even hundreds of pieces of metal or pellets, which is collectively termed shot, and also a propellant. You pull the trigger, this ignites the propellant, and the shot flies out of the gun.' His stubby hands play all this out before us. 'The shot is usually made of steel, and it comes in a whole variety of sizes and weights, and these are all graded. The reason for that is that different weights of shot perform differently in the air. They travel further or faster, or give a different spread, or cause more or less damage to the target. In practical terms, if you were trying to shoot a large duck, say, you'd want a different weight of shot, a heavier shot, than to bring down a smaller bird. And if you were shooting a bird flying high, you'd want to use more of the propellant. So there are a range of cartridges on the market.'

He has a wide flat face and a sandy beard, neatly trimmed, so that he looks like Henry VIII in a suit. His voice is flat too, as he describes his analysis of the pellets removed from the wounds. He adds, to be fair, that it would be possible to dismantle a cartridge, and so alter the charge or the shot it contained, so his conclusions are not absolute.

'But this aside,' he says, 'I would think there is little doubt of the weapon used.'

'Which is?'

'A 20-bore shotgun, probably double-barrelled, firing 8-gauge cartridges.'

'You had reached this conclusion before you were asked to examine the accused's shotgun.'

'That is correct. I have checked my notes very carefully on this point.' He taps the blue book. 'I completed the examination of the material from the scene of crime four days before I received the weapon for examination. That same day I prepared and sent my report to the police officer leading the investigation, by fax.'

'And could you remind the court of the type of shotgun owned by the accused?'

'A double-barrelled 20-bore shotgun.'

'And the ammunition?'

'8-gauge Eley cartridges.'

'Thank you. No further questions, m'lud.'

And with a bow he sits down. Charles starts off very relaxed, establishing that double-barrelled 20-bore shotguns are not so uncommon, that 8-gauge shot would be the normal type of cartridge to choose, that they don't have the same evidential quality as handwriting, or fingerprints. Dr Fairbrother cheerfully goes along with all this.

'Eley is a very common brand, is it not?'

'Yes, it is.'

'And if the local gun shop stocked Eley, or even recommended it, then a very high proportion of local gun owners might use it?'

'They might.'

Charles is well pleased by this. It's odd to think I might have helped him make this point. Maybe there's other stuff I could try to think of.

'Did you also test the gun to see if it had been fired recently?' Charles asks.

'I did, but I was not able to reach any conclusions as the gun had been cleaned since it was last fired.'

'This would be the usual thing to do after using the gun, for example if you went clay-pigeon shooting.'

'Oh yes, you'd typically clean the gun the same day, to avoid the risk of corrosion and keep the workings in good order.'

'Nothing sinister about the gun having been cleaned, then?'

'Nothing at all.'

'How long would you say it would take to clean a double-barrelled shotgun?'

'That really does depend how well you do it. How thoroughly. Same as cleaning anything.' Smiles all round.

'The gun looked like it had been cleaned properly?'

'Yes, I'd say so. You'd have had to spend, say, five minutes or so cleaning it, at the very least, I would think.'

'So it isn't a matter of someone rushing into a house and giving it a quick wipe before locking it away.'

'Oh no. You have to use an oiled rag, see, and then wipe off the excess oil, and pull the rag down both barrels, as well as dealing with the firing mechanism. A couple of minutes' work at the very least.'

'No further questions.'

Gerard then re-examines him, to elicit that cleaning a gun is a simple operation that could easily be done in a car or by the side of the road. He then goes over the cartridge issue again, and instead of listening I picture the farmhouse on a late winter dawn, the light grey, and the air cold and still. Behind the farmhouse, in the bare trees, picked out in skeletal black against the grey sky, rooks call. Walking up the drive, footsteps crunch on gravel. The door, freshly painted, stands closed. The peal of a bell, then a surprised stillness. Perhaps a curtain twitches above in the bedroom, the same curtain I have pulled back, watching John leave to go off to some early morning meeting. But standing in front of the door, you are hidden from sight by the roof of the porch. So there comes the sound of feet on the stairs, fast and angry. The bolts are pulled back, the key turns the lock, all sharp and loud on such a still morning. The door opens, and John stands there, tucking his shirt into his trousers with one hand, holding the door ready to shut with his other. He stands surprised, until his eyes are dragged down to the gun. He gapes, backs off one step, looks up in disbelief. Then comes the shot. He falls back on to the stairs, his shirt and trousers dark with blood and mess, screaming, his arms waving. He is swearing, pleading. He watches the barrel move, looks away, looks back. A second, careful shot. More blood, far more blood, splattered over the wall, bloody hand-prints on the banisters, and blood staining the pale carpet.

In the yard again, the rooks, disturbed by the shots, are wheeling to and fro, their caws raucous. There is no other sound.

★ ★ ★

I'm taken down to the holding room, and there's an unexplained delay, and I sit in the corner and listen to the guards discussing a story in the *Mirror*, about a woman getting her bag caught in the doors of a tube train during the rush hour. She was dragged along the platform, and before anyone could do anything she hit the mouth of the tunnel. One of the guards says 'Nasty,' and the other agrees, and the first one reads on, looking for the next story, and I am left thinking about that woman, and what went through her mind as she was dragged along, and if she saw the tunnel mouth coming, faster and faster. I can picture it so clearly, the shoving, uncaring crowd, the sudden drama, a hundred faces watching or turning away, wanting to see and not to be seen.

I see the scene play out again and again, the train setting off, pulling her suddenly off her feet, the moment of realization, struggle. Then what? Pain? Darkness? A moment of knowing?

I shiver, feeling sick and cold, and I find I'm crying. I haven't got a handkerchief, no handbag like the woman in the paper. One of the guards notices, and they are both embarrassed, as if I'm letting the side down, that they'd expected better, but one passes me a tissue without saying anything.

Thursday Afternoon

The jury are already in their places when I am brought back into court. The guy who wore the sports jacket and the Pharmacist are getting on really well, chatting about something, laughing even in a discreet way. He probably isn't that much older than her, maybe five years, so perhaps something will come of this, they'll arrange to go out for a drink, a meal. It seems funny that I may be acting as a matchmaker. Miss Marple and Danny Boy are talking too, but otherwise they are sitting in silence, looking around the court or staring in front of them, lost in thought.

The witness box is empty, though they are now calling the first witness. This morning, Andrew warned me that I'd have a hard afternoon, not as bad as yesterday perhaps but still there'd be the rest of the forensic witnesses and then the medical evidence to go through. Doctors talking about me, my psychological state, my capacity for violence. He told me I should try not to let it get to me. I wish he'd come down during the lunch break, but he had another client to see.

Charles and Sarah were busy too going over some papers, but Roisin from his office came down to see if I needed anything, which was brave of her because it's pretty intimidating in the cells, even today when there aren't many other prisoners around. In a way, the guards were just as bad because they were either leering at her or winding her up, showing her the panic button in the cells, saying they would be there as soon as they could if I turned violent, that I was known as a biter.

She didn't seem to mind, and we chatted for twenty minutes or so, mainly about Andrew and what he was like to work for, and how I'd known him for years, back when Nick and he were students and spent a summer taking American tourists around Italy and trying to get a rock band together, which she found really funny if difficult to believe. And we talked about why she had moved to England, what she wanted to do next, and how she had ended up working in Peterborough.

'I was living in Nottingham, and there weren't many vacancies for articled clerks going there, and I wanted to move on anyway. Then there was this advert for a job at Andrew's firm, and here I am.'

'Didn't you want to move to London?' I asked.

'In a way, but then, well, it seemed too easy, too obvious, you know? I came over and met Andrew and thought he'd be great to work for, which is a bit ironic.'

'Why's that?' I asked, and she gave me this funny look.

'Well, he's Protestant for one thing.'

I hadn't known that, nor even thought that she must be Catholic, with her name. I remembered now that Andrew's father had come over to work for the City Council, bringing his family, fifteen years or so ago.

'Could you not work it out from his accent?' she asked in surprise.

'No.' I felt so stupid, and it made me realize how little I knew about Andrew, and how I'd come to depend on him, not just as a lawyer but as a link back to Nick, to my family, my friends.

Now the two of them are sitting in silence, Andrew slouched back, looking around, and Roisin with her head bent forward. She has the most lovely colouring, blue-black hair, dark blue eyes, full of life, but he seems quite unconscious of her, though their shoulders are almost touching.

The next witness is being sworn in, and Andrew heaves himself forward and makes a note. Then, sensing my gaze, he turns and smiles, and gives me a covert thumbs-up sign.

It reminds me of the sort of good-luck wishes you get backstage, from the crew or the stage manager, as you wait for the curtain to rise.

'My name is Alicia Hamnett,' the next witness says. 'I work at the regional forensic science laboratory at Huntingdon. On the twenty-fourth of October last year I received several items from Cambridgeshire police for examination. These were marked and sealed in the usual way.'

'These are the items in bags marked RJ1 to RJ3?' Gerard asks.

'They are.'

The usher holds up the first bag, which holds the stuff that mainly used to lie about on the floor of my car. Tapes and maps and chocolate wrappers and a can of de-icer and my mobile phone and a box of Kleenex, a bottle of moisturizer, part of a mudguard, scraps of paper and cardboard are all mixed up together. Most of it is a sodden mass, but I can recognize the cover of an old copy of *Housing Today* and a Neneh Cherry cassette. Dr Hamnett briefly describes her examination of these items, which apparently turned up precisely nothing of interest.

She is dressed in a plain, dark blue roll-neck sweater with the arms rolled up. She isn't wearing any jewellery, except for a silver bangle she occasionally pushes up her arm.

Her face is equally severe, and she appears to be deeply unimpressed with Gerard.

The second bag is produced. Dr Hamnett consults her notes.

'These were the contents of the glove compartment of the car. There was a plastic wallet holding the instruction manual for the car and a guide to Ford dealerships in the UK. There was a copy of the *Independent* dated the tenth of September, a street atlas of Peterborough, a large-scale map of Peterborough and Oundle, a can of Halford's de-icer, almost full, a screw-driver, several cassettes, a Michelin guide.'

I recognize at the bottom of the bag a compilation tape which I've had for years, since college. I loved being given them because they're really personal. The idea of someone choosing music you like, or they like, or a mixture of both. A bit romantic, though I said this once to Claire and she laughed and said that once you made a tape up you could copy it to lots of friends and they'd all think the same. Then she started teasing me about which tape in particular I meant, who it was from, and did I perhaps fancy them something rotten? I can see her now, sitting at the kitchen table, in the candlelight, plates piled around, screeching with laughter.

'What would be the main things you would be looking for?' Gerard asks.

'Any unusual marks, particularly if they looked fresh, and traces of mud, paint, skin, finger or palm prints, traces of chemicals, including explosives and ammunition propellants, oil, blood, fibres. Anything that looks out of place.'

The third bag holds my clothes from the day of the accident. Under the polythene, they look like evidence from a victim, torn and stained with blood. I imagine her in a white coat, her sleeves rolled up and her bony hands picking over them, taking swabs and samples. If I had died in the crash, they would have had me on a slab and done the same to me. It leaves me cold to think of it.

The evidence goes on. All the bloodstains are from my blood group. None the same as the victim. Various fibres on the shirt and leggings, but no matches. Various smears of mud and stains from dirty water, all but one of which match the area around the crash site. No match for the other mark. No traces of having handled or used firearms. She agrees that such traces wouldn't be likely to survive a prolonged immersion. Traces of mud on the trainers and on one of the socks, with a good match to traces taken from

344

Manor Farm. Impossible to say reliably if they were fresh.

Gerard makes a brief note, asks a couple of other pointless questions, and then is finished.

'Dr Hamnett,' Sarah begins, 'would it be fair to say that the main conclusion you reached is that Miss Morland may have been in the vicinity of Manor Farm recently, but not necessarily on the day of the killing?'

'Yes.'

'And that although you specifically looked for traces of blood from Mr Grant, you didn't find any such traces?'

'No.'

'I take it that you are an experienced forensic scientist?'

She raises an eyebrow and looks even more frosty.

'Would you say it was likely that being briefly and only partly immersed in ditch-water would erase all trace of such stains, if they had ever existed?'

She pauses, thinking, for what seems like an age, before saying that she wouldn't wish to offer an opinion. Sarah tries again.

'Did you find any trace of any such contamination?'

'No, but any contamination is often very light and susceptible to erasure. Their presence is positive evidence that someone wearing them has used a firearm, but their absence isn't positive proof that someone has not.'

Thanks for that.

'And would bloodstains, not being water soluble, be more likely to remain?' Sarah asks.

'Yes. But the shirt was pretty much drenched in blood. This would make it very difficult to know one way or the other if other blood was present, albeit in very small quantities, but masked or even washed away by the wearer's own blood.'

Sarah gives up at this point, and the jury look bemused, which is better than nothing. I even see the Student say something to the Pharmacist, who shrugs, as if she had no idea why the evidence was being discussed at all. But then Gerard stands up again.

'Dr Hamnett, could I clarify one point?'

'Certainly.'

'It is this. Although you didn't find direct traces of residues from a gun or blood from the victim, would you agree that such traces could have been present but then later erased or masked by the quantities of blood which the accused lost during the crash, and from the immersion in water at the scene of the crash?'

'I don't understand your use of the term

'direct traces'. There were no traces of any kind.'

'I'm sorry, traces then. They could have been erased or marked? In your opinion.'

'Yes.' She remains unmoved, but is clearly suffering a prize fool.

'Dr Hamnett,' the judge asks, 'perhaps you could help me and the jury by making clear the relative weight which you would ascribe to different parts of your evidence?'

'Certainly. The only evidence on which I would place the slightest reliance is that concerning the traces of earth from around Manor Farm.'

That's that. As she leaves, still stony-faced but walking with surprising grace, she passes Professor Emery, the next witness, bustling in. He holds the door open for her with a flourish, and I imagine her smiling despite herself because he is the kind of man who so obviously wants to please, not so he can get anything but because he enjoys it. He saw me once in the prison hospital and once at the Royal Free in London. I liked him a lot, he was very cheerful and friendly, and the trip out of prison was something in itself, even though it was a few days before Christmas and seeing the shoppers in Hampstead made me think afterwards of what I was missing out on, being locked up. I try to catch his eye as he takes the oath but he doesn't look at me.

Ruth and he hit it off, she taking him easily through his qualifications and experience, and asking him to describe the medical background to amnesia.

'In essence, you have two types of memory loss,' he says. 'You have temporary amnesia, which may last for a week or two, which comes about from a blow to the head sufficient to cause bruising. In effect, the brain is shaken about inside the skull, the brain is bruised, and the bruising interferes with the memory.' I remember now that he made a point of never using medical jargon. 'Quite often this is associated with very short-term memory loss, which leads to people forgetting the events covering the hours before their accident. As I said, this is fairly common, and it is also the common pattern that the memory returns in stages progressively over the succeeding days or, on occasions, weeks. The return of memory may be fragmentary, but it is highly unusual for there to be no recall whatsoever.'

He is enjoying himself, with an audience to lecture.

'There is also a more permanent amnesia which comes about from a more serious injury to the brain. In these cases, the bruising is such as to actually cause longer-lasting damage to the tissue of the brain. Or some other form of injury, such as bleeding or a blood clot, may result in the damage. The outcome is more permanent injury, as I said, which can lead to a whole range of damage to the memory functions, though these more permanent injuries are also capable of regeneration so that full function can be restored in time. One possible outcome might be the loss of particular memories, but again it would be rare for the symptoms of the head injury to manifest themselves solely in the form of the loss of one block of memory. Further, such serious injury would be capable of diagnosis by means of a brain scan.'

'Do you mean that the injury would be so serious that it would be almost certain to have other symptoms?'

'Yes.'

'And would it also be visible through a brain scan?'

'Precisely.' He is pleased to have such a bright student.

'You examined the accused on two occasions. What conclusion did you draw about the nature of the injuries and the apparent loss of memory?'

'On my first examination, I was surprised by the tenacity of the memory loss. The patient claimed to be able to remember nothing whatsoever of the twelve hours or so up to the crash — that is, from the evening before — but otherwise her memory was unimpaired. She had no other memory loss, and her short-term memory wasn't impaired in a physiological sense. Further, I knew from the scans carried out at the district hospital in Peterborough that there was no tissue damage. So the fact that no part of the memory had returned was curious, to say the least.

'I was also struck by a considerable latent hostility towards my efforts to probe her memory for these days. She became emotional, and often refused to answer questions, either becoming distressed or claiming to feel unwell. She seemed to be suffering from some fairly well-entrenched form of psychological trauma, although as that isn't really my field I couldn't be more specific than that.'

He talks on about the second examination, a week later. Further scans, further tests, all inconclusive, but suggestive. Ruth leads him up to the punchline.

'Do you believe that the accused's physical injuries can explain the memory loss which she claims to have experienced?'

'No, I don't.'

'Might she be lying?'

'Either that, or suffering from some kind of psychological state of denial.'

'Have you formed a view as to which?'

'I think it highly likely that it is some mixture of the two.'

'Thank you, Professor Emery. I have no further questions.'

Charles tries to get him to shift his ground, to admit there is far more uncertainty than he might have suggested. Emery is happy to agree it is all very difficult, but maintains his position. I am lying, or I have suffered some strong psychological trauma, or possibly both.

'The car accident alone would be a considerable trauma, would it not?'

'I quite agree a car accident might. And the patient's injuries were considerable. But against this I note that she didn't have any difficulty in remembering some events around the accident. My notes contain a fairly detailed and accurate account of her being cut free from the car.'

They weave on like this, Charles making little headway, and in the end he has to leave it. He has medical experts of his own lined up to refute this. I hope Ruth doesn't make a better job of shaking their assurance. Meanwhile the Professor steps down cheerfully, his reputation intact.

Ruth calls another doctor, Dr Willett, a consultant psychologist, who says much the same, but with more medical jargon and more about my mental state. He is more cautious by nature, more cerebral, matching his clichéd bow tie, his dome of balding head with his features scrunched into the bottom half of his face. Charles manages to get him to admit he has never in fact dealt with any cases of trauma resulting from either being a witness to a murder, the perpetrator of a murder, or the victim of a road accident. Nevertheless, once Ruth has run over his evidence again, the impression is the same. He thinks I'm either mad or bad.

It makes me think ahead to when I will have to give evidence. It will be like reliving all the police interviews, but even worse than that, being in court, in front of all these people, John's family, my family, without Andrew to intervene on my behalf. I suppose Ruth will cross-examine me. I watch her now, looking through her notes, one hand calmly turning over the pages. She frightens me.

★ ★ ★

There's another long delay and I sit back in my chair, try to ease my back, which is starting to hurt again, and I'm so tempted to slip off my shoes and rub my toes to warm them up, but there's the judge and jury to think of. So instead I look at the patch of sky, the odd patches of sunlight coming in, and I dream of sitting like a lizard in the sun, soaking up the heat, and remembering a holiday in the south of France one Easter a few years ago with Emily and Josh and some others, staying in a stone cottage with no heating, so that however many blankets we piled on ourselves we were still freezing, but each morning we'd come out into the sunshine and warm up over croissants and coffee.

In Whitemoor, there's never the chance to sit in the sun. We have exercise, when the weather is OK and there are enough staff around, but we'd always be doing something, playing netball or rounders, never free to stop or sit and rest in the sunshine. The only ones who are left alone were the LTIs, the lifers, who you see sitting quietly, a breed apart. That could be me, I suppose, unless Charles can pull something off.

★   ★   ★

It's almost four by the time the next witness is called up, and the jury are restless. Danny

353

Boy is so slumped in his seat I think he might be asleep. I remember reading about a trial where one of the jurors was asleep a lot of the time, or maybe they were ill, and the whole trial had to be started again. A retrial. The idea of months of waiting, more months in jail, and then the whole process to go through again, is horrible. I want it to be over.

Next up is Dr Gilbert, a psychologist specializing in aggression studies, whatever they are, who prepared a psychological profile of the killer and who interviewed me in prison. Charles at once asks the judge to rule his evidence inadmissible, and as the jury file out and he and Ruth start to argue I look again at the profile itself in the bundle of documents, odd phrases standing out: 'neurosis of penis-envy . . . desire to dominate . . . insecurity of gender'. And later: 'The assault on the penis may be a 'male' act, the destruction of a competitor, or as a 'female' one, motivated by revenge, the desire to punish and to destroy.' And worst of all, on the final page:

To attempt to summarize the foregoing without recourse to technical terms, the profile of the assailant is likely to contain most or all of these elements: an experience of having used weapons on live targets,

354

such as in hunting or in the army; a sexual relationship with the victim, or a sexually related obsession about the victim, or both; a strong sense of grievance against the victim, perhaps combined with paranoia about the victim as a potential source of threat; a strong moral sense of being superior to the victim, perhaps linked to a belief that the victim has deviant or criminal behaviour patterns such as to create the belief that 'he does not deserve to live'; and the assailant is also likely to have a conformist and even a repressed personality, but who has committed previous acts of explosive aggression, that is aggression not arising directly from a dispute but from an inability to deal with emotional conflict and to release repressed emotions.

Dr Gilbert had come to visit me in prison. I was still ill and on painkillers. I answered his questions for a while, but they became more and more personal, and I had this strong impression that there was something weird about him. I remember that he had small round glasses and bad skin, a really bad shaving rash. It was like a nightmare, because in prison you feel you have to talk to people, you have to let them pry if that's what they want, so I sat in this plain white room, with no windows, with a prison officer outside, perhaps listening in, perhaps the rooms are bugged for all I know, and he was asking me about the kinds of sex we had, John and I, and how I felt before, and afterwards, and during it. By the end I wouldn't answer any of his questions, and he got angry and I shouted back. I may have thrown something, a cup of coffee, though not at him and only one of those plastic ones, and that was the interview over.

I can't bear to look at him, as he waits in the box. I'd much rather do something to him than to Ruth or John's family or even his friends. Maybe I'll block out what he says by thinking of ways he could die. A car crash on his way home, or trapped in his burning house. Shot on his doorstep.

I told Andrew about his visit. Not the details, just that this doctor had come in and I'd got really upset, and he'd said he'd make sure it didn't happen again. Now I think about it, it was odd that the prison staff didn't say anything about it. I don't even think they made me clean up the spilt coffee. Maybe they should've made sure I had a solicitor there first, or something, and didn't want to take it any further.

The judge has heard Charles and Ruth out,

and is now looking over Dr Gilbert's witness statement — apparently much worse than the profile — with a hint of distaste.

'Miss Acheson, did your witness produce this after his interview with Miss Morland?'

'He did.'

'And after discussing the case with the police?'

'Yes. He had to ensure that he had all the relevant details about the crime, so that he could put together this profile.' She waits, Kerr says nothing, and for once she seems a little unsure of her ground and adds, 'Although the use of such profiles for single crimes is a relatively new technique, it is only a development of psychological profiling techniques widely used in police work.'

'This interview with Miss Morland,' the judge asks after further thought, 'did anything come of this?'

'It allowed Dr Gilbert to gauge the accuracy of the match of his profile against the accused. It also has allowed him to build up a picture of the mental processes which the Crown submits lie behind the accused's actions.'

'But as I explained,' Charles interjects, 'my client wasn't informed of her rights before that interview, she wasn't accompanied by her solicitor, and she wasn't aware of Dr Gilbert's status.'

'Yes, I think these are telling points, Miss Acheson. I am not at all happy that this witness and his rather lurid conclusions will serve to assist the jury. Given the doubts about its . . . provenance,' he smiles at having found exactly the right word, 'I will rule it inadmissible. I don't think we need trouble Dr Gilbert further.'

One usher asks the jury to come back in and the other calls Dr Greenwood, who looked after me at the hospital. I look over to where Charles and Sarah are shuffling papers and looking pleased, and Andrew has turned to speak to my family sitting behind him, who I hope haven't seen the profile and don't know what they have been saved from hearing, and then I see Halliday and his sergeant at the back of the court. He looks pissed off, and she is saying something to him, perhaps reassuring him I'm still going to be convicted. Then Dr Greenwood comes in, looking much younger without her white coat, far too young to be a fairly senior doctor, but she takes the oath without any nervousness. Ruth stands to examine her, seemingly untroubled by losing a witness, still all sweet reasonableness.

'Dr Greenwood, you are a registrar neurologist at the Peterborough District Hospital, are you not?'

'Yes.'

'You were on duty on the twentieth of October?'

'Yes, I was.' She nods.

'And you examined the accused when she was brought into the hospital?'

'Not exactly. First she was examined by Dr Riley, the duty house officer in A and E, and by Dr Birch, the registrar anaesthetist. I first saw her about half an hour after she arrived at the hospital, at about 11.10 a.m.'

'But you carried out a thorough examination of your own?' Ruth asks.

'Oh yes.' Her voice is too soft for the whole court to hear her easily. One or two of the journalists look restless.

'Could you describe the nature of the accused's injuries? In lay terms, if at all possible.'

'Yes, of course.' She turns to the judge. 'Is it all right for me to look at my notes?' There must be some court official who tells them all to do this. The judge nods with his half-smile.

'Well, the injuries were pretty typical for a car crash. She had extensive contusions, with the most serious to her head, to her right arm, her torso and her left leg. Her leg had

359

been very badly wrenched and there was severe damage to the muscles and ligaments, though an X-ray confirmed no break to the bone itself. Both knees were heavily bruised — probably by the underside of the dashboard — and there was a hairline fracture to the left patella. The left knee-cap. She had five broken ribs on her left side, and a wound which required — ' she checks her notes ' — seventeen stitches. That was probably the steering wheel. She also had a break to her left arm just above the wrist, and had broken her left collarbone.

'The leg injury was sustained from being thrown forward and probably from the left foot being caught between or under the pedals of the car.

'Finally, she had a severe contusion to the front of the head. The other injuries were serious but her body functions were stable and there were no indications of serious internal injuries of the kind you often get with car accidents at speed. She had lost a lot of blood from the wounds to the ribs and the head, but the head wound was the thing that worried us most. I knew from the paramedics that she had been conscious at the scene and had since lost consciousness. Accordingly I arranged for an X-ray and a brain scan.'

'Were you responsible for the accused's

care during her stay in hospital?'

'In effect, yes, although she was in fact operated on by Mr Asher, who is the orthopaedic surgeon attached to the ATLS — '

'ATLS?'

'That's the advanced trauma life-support team.'

'Oh yes,' Ruth says vaguely. 'Now could you say some more about this head injury, as it appeared over the next few days?'

'Well, the patient was under a general anaesthetic for the operation and came to early the following morning, but was in considerable pain and was under sedation for the next three days. The scans and ECG monitoring suggested some bruising to the brain but nothing too worrying, but then it isn't always easy to predict these things from scans.'

'You have to wait until the patient wakes up properly?'

'Yes.'

'Now the accused was in hospital for twenty-three days, and as the neurologist registrar you presumably saw her from time to time for the whole of this period?'

'Yes. Most days. Though most of her treatment was for the injuries to her leg.'

'How quickly did the accused begin to regain her full faculties?'

'How do you mean?'

'Well, able to speak, or eat, or move about. That kind of thing.'

'She was able to speak on the twenty-second, after she woke up from the operation. She asked the nurse where she was. Later that day I spoke to her and she could remember and describe quite clearly the events after the crash, though not before and not anything about her time in hospital.'

'Did you ask her about the crash?'

'Yes. Not because I wanted to know,' she adds, as if she's worried we'll all think she was pumping me for information to pass to the police, 'but more for an idea of how serious her loss of memory was. I asked about her job, her family and friends, that sort of thing. But she was deeply upset and emotional, which is fairly common with a patient with heavy injuries. She would cry, couldn't follow questions, and would easily lose attention.'

I feel cheated that I told these doctors everything I could, as honestly as I could, and they come here and testify against me. Just like John's friends.

'Would you say it was unusual to have this pattern of amnesia?' Ruth asks.

'I haven't come across it before. But every case is unique. I wouldn't draw too strong

362

conclusions from this pattern of symptoms.'

That's better than the other two, anyway. I should have known she'd be OK. She tried to stop me being transferred to the prison, and after they brought me back to the hospital for a check-up and she refused to examine me until they'd removed my handcuffs.

'If that's what Professor Emery says, then I wouldn't disagree with him directly, but my own view remains that many cases have these kinds of unusual patterns and I wouldn't say that there is any evidence that I have seen which leads me to think that Miss Morland is deliberately exaggerating the symptoms.'

'But to be quite clear, you found no evidence of the serious and permanent damage to the brain that Professor Emery indicated was associated with the permanent loss of memory.'

'That's quite right.'

'Thank you, Dr Greenwood.'

Charles cruises through the familiar questions. Diagnosis is very difficult. Even more so with head injuries. Very unwise to generalize. Every case unique. The best we can say is that we only understand a small part of the working of the brain. The jury look dulled by all this. I think the Old Bag may have started to doze off. Not much brain-stem activity going down. Only the bloke with the sports jacket and the socks is still alert, looking intelligently at Dr Greenwood as she talks on, her ponytail flapping as she nods in agreement with something Charles has put to her.

'Could it be that the attempts on your part — and I don't mean to criticize your medical judgment at all by suggesting this, Dr Greenwood — but could it be that all these questions, from you, from the other doctors, from the police as well, could have exacerbated the effects on Miss Morland of the trauma of the crash?'

'Well, there is always the risk of this sort of thing. I was worried myself that she was being pushed to remember too far or too fast.'

'Were you present for all the police interviews, Dr Greenwood?'

'No, not all the time.'

'Isn't that rather unusual?'

'I would have preferred to be there, yes, but at the time I understood that the police wanted to know about the RTA.'

She explains that she was on call and was bleeped by one of the duty doctors, and thought she should check for herself that I was well enough to be interviewed.

'Did the police say why they wanted to talk to Miss Morland that evening?' Charles asks.

'They said it was urgent.'

'But they'd spoken to her earlier that day?'

'Briefly, yes. She wasn't able to say much.'

'But when they came back' — he flicks through to the transcripts of the interview in his bundle — 'I see there were three of them, and they had a tape recorder, and they cautioned her.'

'Yes.'

'Did they say what they wanted to question her about?'

'The accident.'

'Not the killing of Mr Grant?'

'No. They never mentioned that.'

'I see.' Charles pauses, takes a sip of water, then starts off again briskly. 'Now, have you heard the tapes of the interview?'

'No.'

'Or read or had sight of the transcripts?'

'No.'

'Did you know that Miss Morland and Mr Grant had had a very close relationship?'

'I'd heard that, yes.'

'Breaking news of that kind could be a shock, could it not?'

'Certainly.'

'It would need to be handled sensitively?'

'Yes, of course.' Like me, she seems puzzled where this is going.

'Do you know who broke the news to Miss Morland that Mr Grant was dead?'

'No. I assume it was her family. They were the first visitors she had.'

'So you were not aware that Detective Inspector Halliday informed Miss Morland of Mr Grant's death during the interrogation that evening?'

'No. Did he?'

Behind her, the Builder and the one who might be a taxi driver in his leather jacket are whispering together, perhaps agreeing that this is the kind of sharp practice you'd expect from the police. Maybe it could nudge them over to my side.

'With someone in hospital,' Charles says more slowly, 'someone suffering from the after-effects of major injuries, would you say this is how you should break news like that? From a police officer in the middle of a tape-recorded interview?'

'It sounds quite wrong to me.'

'Well, yes.' Charles smiles. 'It might sound wrong. I meant from a medical point of view. Would you say it could have had some kind of effect on Miss Morland's response to questions?'

'Yes, it could have done. I wouldn't want to be too certain without thinking it through. It's very difficult to predict. But it's certainly possible, yes.'

'So, again, you would question the

reliability of evidence collected in this way?'

'Question, yes. Not rule it out, but yes, you'd want to be cautious with it.'

'Do you consider that the police tried to bully the patient, or take advantage of the fact she was still suffering from a major accident and from a serious head injury?'

'No, not exactly bully. Not while I was there, in any case. It's more that they shouldn't have been asking her these questions while she was so ill.'

'Subsequently, the police questioning generally was quite intensive, wasn't it?'

'Yes, although in fact I asked them to cut short several interviews because the patient was tired or on one occasion quite distressed.'

Dr Greenwood has the same determined expression she had when she was arguing with Halliday about whether I should be questioned — the look of someone unshakeable in their view of right and wrong, but who also knew she could only go so far. She and Halliday had sparred, but both had had to give ground. I wonder if that is why they wanted me out of the hospital. The prison service doctors wouldn't have been so bothered.

In the end, Ruth stands to re-examine her, as relaxed and charming as ever despite Charles's success.

'To clear up this point about the first police interview, you received a call from a junior doctor about the police making a request to interview the accused.'

'Yes.'

'She had already been interviewed that day?'

'Yes.'

'You didn't feel the need to pass this request further up the chain of command? To a consultant, perhaps?'

'Oh no, there was clearly no need for that. I'd treated her from when she arrived, and I've done a lot of work with head injuries before.'

'All quite routine?'

'Yes.' The doctor bites her lower lip.

'And in your judgment, the patient was well enough to be interviewed?'

'She was awake and alert, yes.'

'You examined her beforehand?'

'Yes. I carried out the usual tests, and spoke to her. She was quite willing to be interviewed, though — ' She tries to find the right words, but Ruth ploughs on.

'And you sat in on the whole of this interview?'

'No. I was bleeped and had to go to look at another patient during part of it.'

'At no time did she say she was distressed

or feeling unwell?'

'Not while I was there, no.'

'And at the end of the interview, Miss Morland showed no ill-effects?'

'No.'

'Thank you, doctor. I have no further questions.'

★ ★ ★

'How well do you know Mrs Tomkins?' Charles asks.

We are back in the cells, he and Sarah and I, preparing for the next day. Charles is going on about how shoddy the Crown case is, how their solicitors haven't put it together properly, how their witnesses keep coming up with stuff which Ruth and Gerard don't know about. I suppose I should be pleased, as they seem to think that if the case seems chaotic, I've a better chance of getting off. And maybe I will be able to convince the jury that it wasn't me, that I am not the kind of person to have done it.

But that means giving evidence, and I don't want to think about that. I am more tired than I can ever remember, and the whole trial is a dead weight on me now, everything from being unable to sleep properly to the journeys in the van to sitting in court, stiff, cold, and having to listen to the evidence, and worry about when my turn comes, and be stared at by the audience, and the stuff in the papers too, and then these sessions with Charles afterwards, it's all too much. I'm tired, and fed up, and I can hear the disinterest in my own voice.

'Mrs Tomkins? She works in the shop in the village.'

'She is going to give evidence that a week or two before the murder, you talked to her about murdering someone with a shotgun.' He waits. Eventually, I force myself to reply.

'It wasn't like that. She . . . she's making it into something it wasn't.'

'Clarissa, it's very important that we counteract her evidence as far as we can. If they can show that you were talking about murder before it happened, it's bound to influence the jury.'

'But it wasn't like that. It's just that she hates me.'

I look up at him and he doesn't hide his look of deep irritation quickly enough. I try again.

'Look, she had something against me for years. Ten years or more. When I was young, she accused me of shoplifting. It was really horrid. Anyway, nothing came of it, but she's never liked me since. I think she's trying to get her own back.'

I can feel myself tense, remembering the fear when she grabbed my arm and started shouting at me in the shop. I have the same taste of metal in my mouth now. I hardly hear what Charles is saying.

'I said, what did you say to her about this shooting?' he repeats, rather too patiently.

'I asked her what she knew about Cross Wood. When I was at school, people used to say that years ago it was the scene of a murder. One day I was talking to someone about where I went running, and they mentioned Cross Wood and I said I never went up there, and I thought later it must be because of this old story. So I thought I'd find out if it were true or not. And Mrs Tomkins has been living in the village for years, and knows everything that goes on, so one day I asked her about it. That's all.'

'And had there been a murder?'

'No, not as far as she knew. She said she didn't know, and asked why I'd been out at Cross Wood anyway. In a sort of suspicious voice. Typical of her, really, wanting to know everyone's business.'

'So it was simply an off-the-cuff remark.'

'Yes.'

He sighs and makes some notes.

'So you think she's blown this up into

something sinister out of animosity?'

I take the witness statement from the table and read out a passage. ''Clarissa then asked me about a murder at Cross Wood. Was it true that a man had murdered his wife and her lover for being unfaithful. I said I didn't know. She said that I must, that the man had lived locally and found out that his wife was sleeping with another man, and he spotted the other man's car parked by the woods, and went in and found them together having sex. And that he shot them both dead.' Here we are. 'All the time she had the strangest manner, was very insistent and eager about it. It was very frightening, the way she kept going on about killing them both.' Well, that isn't true. I asked her about it, but that was all. I was interested, sure, but it was just curiosity.

'Anyway, if it was a week or two before John was killed, why would I be thinking of killing him? I didn't even know he'd ripped me off.' Now I say this, it strikes me as a pretty good point, but they don't seem at all interested.

'And I didn't go on about it,' I say, still trying to make them see. 'I just asked her, and she said no, and that was that.'

'She might have embroidered it, I suppose, in the telling?' His face is grey, tired, but also with a flicker of anger.

'Well, she'd have told everyone about it. Everyone who came into the shop. Until the next bit of dirt came along for her to spread round.'

'If you are asked about this in your evidence, I suggest you take a less hostile line.'

Charles stares at his notebook for a minute or two, not saying anything or writing anything down.

'Look,' I say in the end, 'she's the one who's made this up. I didn't do anything. I didn't take her sodding cakes and I didn't tell her I wanted to kill John.'

'If we let her evidence go unchallenged, it could make the difference between conviction and acquittal. It could also make the difference between a conviction for man-slaughter, saying you were suffering from an emotional outburst, a moment of jealousy, and premeditated murder. That you planned the whole thing, worked it all out in advance. If the judge and jury go for the latter, you will go to prison for at least ten years. If you survive that — and some don't — you won't be the same person.'

'I know that.'

'So if that's what you want, fine, but if not you'd better start telling me the truth.'

'I am.'

'You are not. I can read you like a book. I think you took these cakes, or whatever they were, she caught you, and since then you've hated her for catching you and giving you what was probably, until all of this, the worst fright of your life. Now she's getting her own back, consciously or not, and you have to work out what to do.'

I can feel his eyes on me, and I stare at the table, at the witness statement, willing him to go, making him go, and in the end he does, they both do, shuffling their papers together and putting them in their bags. Sarah says goodbye, he says nothing, and I ignore them both. Only he leaves the witness statement on the table.

* * *

Later, the guard comes in to take me to the van but I won't go. I can't take any more being told what to do or say or think or go or when to stand or sit or eat and drink. I tell him I won't go. I don't know why, I don't really care if I go or stay but I don't want to do what they tell me.

So he grabs me by the arm and I grab the table and the chair falls and I shout at him to let me go and try to shake him off, but in a second or two another guard comes. They have me by both arms, flat on the floor, my cheek against the scarred lino. One has her knee in my back, the other holds my legs. I can't see anything but the chair across the room and the toes of a boot.

I try to get free, roll over. One of them is shouting in my ear, telling me to listen, listen, and saying how they could bash me around.

'D'you want a black eye?' one of them shouts in my ear. 'How would that look in court tomorrow, eh?'

'Come on now,' the other one says. 'Let it go, just relax.'

I do, and after a moment, when I can hardly breathe with the weight on my back and the pain in my arm and I think I'll have to try to push them off before I pass out, they step back and get me up and start to dust me down. I can't even whisper that I'm sorry as they lead me down to the van. We pass Bill, looking on with a mug of tea in his hand, perhaps thinking without any real surprise that I'm just like the rest, you never can tell.

'It's so nice here that no one wants to leave, eh?' he says, laughing, and we walk on as he says it again, don't want to leave, ha, ha, ha. One of the guards mutters how it's my fault we'll have a week of listening to him tell that joke. I nod and smile and wipe my nose on the back of my hand like a schoolgirl and everything is back the way they want it.

★ ★ ★

Back at the prison, as I am led out of the van, Miss Barker takes me to the holding centre and I'm put in a windowless cell, no furniture at all, with the inevitable lino floors and bare painted walls. I guess it is some kind of punishment cell. There is no clue as to who has been there before, no graffiti, none of the usual names and dates and lines from songs and filthy stuff about POs and other prisoners. Just blank walls. With no watch, I have to let the time flow over me, and work out how long I have been there from my stomach. Perhaps it is only half an hour or so.

I remember chatting once to Baz about this idea I have of there being other Clarries. If I miss a bus, or don't make it across the road at the lights, then there will be another Clarrie who did, who will be on the bus or walking along a minute or two ahead of me. It's like that now. I can imagine another me, heading home from work, perhaps already home, thinking about what to have for dinner, starting it off, frying some vegetables, tipping in a tin of tomatoes, putting the whole thing in the oven, then maybe walking down to the village shop for some cheese or some red wine. I can see myself going along the shelves, thinking of other things I need, some bread, some washing liquid. I get back just in time before Claire and Seb and Lisa turn up, each with another bottle of wine, and Lisa with flowers and Claire with chocolate too. An ordinary evening for the other Clarrie, the one who isn't in Whitemoor. I wonder what the point was where the split happened, where I was set to end up here and the other Clarrie could go on living her life. The day John was killed? Or before that, when we met in the gallery, or when he first knew my grandmother had left me the land that he wanted?

In the end they take me back to D2, without any comment or explanation. My cell has been turned over while I've been at court. Everything is in roughly the same place, but moved around and pawed over so that you know it's happened. Sometimes, like this time, they do it because you've caused trouble. It's the same with strip-searches. It's another way of getting at us. Some relatives won't visit if they think they'll be searched. Like Sarah, my badminton partner, who came to visit me once, but was strip-searched for no reason and who hasn't been back since.

* * *

Now I am staring into the dark, at the ceiling
lit by the floodlights outside, blue like stage
moonlight. I think of a line from a play I was
once in. *On such a night as this* . . . Except
that in the play it was a warm evening, with
lovers meeting in an enchanted forest under a
silver moon. This light is cold like ice, so I
huddle under my blanket a bit more.

It was almost a full moon when my father
died, and I can remember lying in bed like
this. Uncle Michael had fetched me from
school. Mrs Bruton, the headmistress, came
into class and asked me to come with her,
and I knew at once that something terrible
had happened, and I walked down the empty
corridors beside her, like a small child on the
point of tears, not because of anything that
they know has happened, but only because of
the atmosphere. We went home but I couldn't
see my mother because the doctor had given
her something to sleep, and I couldn't see my
father — I never saw him, because of what
had happened — and I went to bed, tried to
sleep, stared at the ceiling, read children's
books as if that would make everything all
right again.

The cell seems much larger and certainly
more empty with Baz and her stuff gone, and

I wonder how she is, whether she's sorting out her new flat at this very moment, perhaps thinking of me, or whether she's off on the piss, celebrating her freedom. I wonder if I will ever see her again. I couldn't ever say that I knew her very well, she was always too closed up for that. She'd tell all these stories about herself, which made her out as some kind of urchin, never going to school, taken into care, nicking stuff to pay for food, and then for drugs. But once I asked her something about her family, and about being in care, and she snapped back at me about how I knew nothing about it. She forgave me soon enough, but that made me think all the stories were some kind of cover, so she didn't have to talk about herself, or about her family. A bit like changing her name, always being known as Baz.

I never talked to her about my family, either. Not really. Now I wish I had, or that I had someone I could tell now. And I wish I'd told her about stealing the cakes, too, because I like to think she'd have understood. It was only a box of jam tarts. I don't even think I liked them very much, and I certainly haven't been able to eat them since. When Mrs Tomkins grabbed me, I fought her off and wouldn't let her look in my bag. I managed to run away, and went up on to the hill beyond the village and ate the lot, one after another. They were in three lurid colours, and flavours so artificial that it was difficult to tell if they were strawberry or raspberry or blackberry, and as I ate them I was feeling more and more sick, but still stuffing them in. I had to swear to my mother and to Mrs Tomkins that I hadn't taken anything. I kept saying this and in the end they let it go. By then, I suppose I believed it myself.

Friday Morning

The jury file back in. None of them looks at me, as if they are embarrassed by their decision. The judge asks them if they have reached a verdict. The man in the sports jacket stands and says that they have. The judge — it is his voice, but also a different voice, as familiar as my own though I don't recognize it — asks him what it is. And without looking at me, the foreman says something which I don't catch. The whole court breaks into uproar, and half the people are cheering and others crying out and I still don't know which way it's gone, if I'm guilty or not. I try to call out but I can't, no sound comes, and then the judge calls for silence and begins to speak. Hands grab me from each side, but it still doesn't sink in, and I shout that it must all be a mistake. Then I look at the judge, and when I see who it is I begin pleading and crying, as they take me away.

I wake in the dark, in my cell, still crying, with the bedclothes on the floor, and no one comes.

By morning I feel terrible and look worse. I have my run and stand under the shower for minutes, and it does me some good, but I know that as soon as I am sitting down again the tiredness will come back. It's odd getting dressed on my own, and I miss having Baz there to tell me I look OK or wish me good luck. Even the room seems colder without her, and it reminds me to put on a black polo-neck under my jacket so I won't get cold sitting in court. I can't eat anything when I think about giving evidence, and in the end it is a relief to be taken down to the van.

I get four letters this morning, which I keep unopened until I am on the van. The first is a card from Seb. This time he's drawn a hare which looks a bit like me, bounding up a hill, and looking back at a group of hounds milling round a tree, puzzled and lost. It makes me smile.

Seb's message is brief. 'Dear Clarrie, Thanks for your PC. I'm supposed to start on another set of illustrations for Picador this week and can't face it yet, so here's something I did to put off the evil day. Hope this finds you well and feeling good. We are all thinking of you here and have the fizz ready in the fridge. It will be the mother of all

382

parties when you're back. Love, Seb. Lots of love, Lisa, xxx.'

I lean the card against the door of the cell so I can still see it as I look at the other three letters: one postmarked Peterborough, one marked Brussel-Bruxelles, and the third without any postmark at all. I don't know anyone in Brussels, so I leave that until last, to string out the excitement. The first one's from my mother, written in her slanting handwriting on cream notepaper with flowers on, surely a gift from the National Trust. Perhaps I bought it for her myself when I was young. She wishes me luck, says I'm making such a good impression on the court, that she's proud of me, and that my father would be proud of me too. 'Andrew has told me you may be giving evidence this afternoon. I know that I would find this so difficult, and I cannot offer you any advice of any use beyond the thing I've always said — that you should tell the truth. If you do, I know they will believe you.' She says how much help all my friends have been, how Andrew has been such a source of strength. Once I would have been embarrassed by a letter like this, but now, here, they matter more than I can say. I fold it up carefully and put it in my jacket pocket.

The next letter is a creased brown

envelope, overprinted with the Prison Service logo, but inside on a sheet from a notepad Baz has drawn an invite, with bottles and musical notes and glasses and a series of dancing couples circling around the single word PARTY, all done really well. There's no date, but she's written something on the other side: 'Dearest Clarrie, It's a party just for us! When the trial is over and you're back on the streets. And I'll take you clubbing after. Luv 2 u. The Menace to Society (Baz!).'

I stand this next to Seb's card and for a moment I think about seeing her, having a drink, a laugh, seeing a band. Helping keep her away from her old friends. I hate them because of what they'll end up doing to her, getting her back on to the shit she smokes, back into nicking stuff and into jail. Not that it matters, as I doubt I'll have the chance. Though I tell myself that if I was let out, I'd see her again.

Then I open the letter from Brussels, and a photograph falls out on to the floor of the truck. It shows a small child, perhaps two years old, though I'm no good at guessing ages, smiling up from the floor, her face a little pinched where she is losing her baby fat. She is dragging a large furry seal around by the tail.

Dear Clarissa,

You were right that your letter is a surprise, but it is great too. I am happy that you are well, but you tell me nothing of your life now. Very mysterious! What are you doing? Write and tell. I am married now, since two years ago. We had our wedding here in Brussels where I now live. My wife is Karolina. She is Swedish and works here for the Commission. I work for Tractabel, which is OK. We have a baby, too, who maybe you will meet one day. Maybe you have a daughter too now? Write soon. Karl.

Then, in another pen,

Karolina and Anna.

I put the photo alongside the cards in a row along the base of the door. They all fall over straight away, as the truck brakes and swings into the loading bay of the court.

* * *

Andrew is waiting in the interview room, alone. When I ask him why he's smiling he tells me it's because I'm smiling, which I hadn't realized.

'That's very good,' he says. 'And I've some good news too. Mrs Tomkins won't be giving evidence.'

'Why not?'

'No idea. One of the CPS solicitors told me on my way in, but wouldn't say why. I guess they've got cold feet about how she'd come over, if she's got a grudge against you.'

In the night I'd imagined her self-righteous bulk filling the witness box, and I'd tried to prepare myself for what she might say. About me, or my father. Now, all that is gone.

'Does it help with the case?' I ask.

'Not really. She was never that important. But it's a good sign. It shows they're worried about how it's going. It also means you should be on this afternoon, if all goes to time. Oh, and I got you a coffee.'

Instead of the usual instant stuff from the canteen, he has brought in two huge cardboard cups from a coffee bar.

'Seattle coffee in Peterborough?' I say.

'No, I had it flown in straight from the US. Come, eat, already.' He produces some flattened pastries from his briefcase. I open the coffee to find a mountain of whipped cream, dusted with chocolate.

'Is this to make sure I testify?'

He ignores my question. 'Normally, before someone gives evidence, I go over with them what they're going to say. Not coaching, which is completely unethical, as you know, but to help them know what'll happen. But frankly, the only thing that matters is what you were doing between six and eight that morning, and you can't remember. So you have to be clear in your own mind that you're not guilty.'

'But if I can't remember?'

'This one's got apple in.' He stops sniffing the pastry and passes it over. 'It's not a matter of remembering, it's about thinking 'Am I the kind of person who would do this?' and concluding that you're not. So then the rest of your evidence will be coloured by your belief in your innocence. 'Cos if you're in any doubt the judge and jury will pick it up, perhaps without thinking.'

The apple filling is sharp, real, not like the sugary stuff in prison pies. Andrew goes on in the academic tone he uses to make what he wants to say seem less personal.

'Think about it. John Grant led a complicated life. He was putting together a deal worth a lot of money. Money attracts villains. He was having an affair with you, but perhaps he was seeing someone else either before, during or after that affair. We have Sam Tyson's evidence for that, and John's own character as well. I mean, let's face it, he was exactly the sort of bloke who would. His private life may have been as tangled as his business life. Who knows who he might not have crossed? Whose husband might not have had good reason to want to threaten him, or even to go further?

'Say you went over there on Thursday morning and found him snogging another woman on his doorstep. You might have been really upset, distraught, so you go home, drive off you don't know where, trying to think it over, decide what to do, and then a moment's lack of concentration and you crash the car.

'Or say you went over and found John dead. The photos are bad enough, I couldn't begin to think of the effect of seeing him like that for real. So the same thing happens, you panic, you run away, you're upset, drive off, and then the crash.'

He is pleased by his rhetoric. Maybe it was like that. John promised he would phone and he didn't. He said he was in London, but you could never tell with him. He'd never say what he was doing, or where he was going, but only give an impression, so that if you ever challenged him, he'd explain himself and turn it round so that it was my fault for asking him, for not being able to trust him. I go for my morning run, and it takes me within a mile or so of his house. Once again I can picture myself so clearly, standing where the track runs from the main road up towards the farmhouse, catching my breath, looking up at the sign, the fingerpost saying 'Byroad', white with black lettering, black and white bands on the post, not built for runners like me but for people on horseback, people like that woman I saw John speak to, the one I think he was screwing.

'There's one pastry spare,' Andrew says.

'Would you do this for all your clients?'

'How d'you mean?'

'Well, if I didn't have any money, hadn't got the right background, education and everything, would you still be buying coffee then?'

'I got it because I thought you'd like it,' he says, and I feel ashamed. I know I shouldn't take it out on him. 'Look, Clarrie, you can't stop people liking you. You'd do things for other people if you could, so let them do the same for you.'

I nod.

'Anyway, it's an excellent sign if you're back to wanting to put the world to rights.'

I smile.

'And you can feel safe from any more arguments about nicking cakes, as well. Sarah told me about it. I think everyone was a bit tired last night. Charles has been up each night working on his questions and so on, and he gets a bit ratty, but he's all right really.'

'Yeah, I know.'

'And he's really pleased with your idea about checking up on that gun shop. He keeps going on about it.'

There's a bit of a silence.

'There's one other thing I should say before Charles arrives,' he says. I've a sick feeling in my stomach, knowing what he is going to say.

'It's about my father, isn't it?'

'Yes,' he says gently. 'Charles will have to ask you about it. You didn't find him, did you?'

'No, my mother did.'

'But you knew what had happened?'

'Yeah, they told me at the time. My uncle did.'

I form the words in my head long before I can say them.

'He shot himself.'

'And you were fifteen?'

I nod, and he makes a discreet note. I take a big slurp of coffee, and look at the pattern of the cream down the side of the cup.

'Did you ever see him? Afterwards?'

'No. He, er . . . He shot . . . Well, in the head.'

'That's all he'll have to ask you,' he says. 'If

you need to stop for a bit, you'll be allowed to. You've only to ask.'

I swill the coffee around, trying to wash away the rings of cream, but they won't be shifted. I look up, and am a bit surprised that Andrew's smiling at me, until he touches his nose, and I do the same and find a blob of cream on mine.

'You'll be OK,' he says.

Charles comes in at just that moment, Sarah too, and he looks less stressed and is very proper and courteous to me as we talk over the evidence for the day. He asks who Miss Meadows might have seen. Was it me? Would I have run along that road? How often did I do so? Did I ever meet anyone else running? I try to answer his questions, but I can't come up with anything of any help. We've been over it all so many times before. I might have passed a couple of cars. I usually did. I don't remember anything about that day.

'Tell us about your neighbour, Jane Kennedy.'

'She lives opposite, she's married with two young kids. I don't know any of them very well, just to say hello and the odd cup of coffee. I babysit for them, too. Used to, anyway.'

'In her witness statement she was quite — '

Charles looks about, trying to find the right words ' — unhelpful. Determined to portray you as deeply upset.'

'Her statement was taken when she thought it was about the car accident,' Andrew says. 'She didn't know about the murder. She was probably trying to be helpful.'

Charles makes a note in his blue notebook, then turns back to me.

'What about the gun? Miss Meadows' evidence? Any innocent reason you might have been carrying it?'

'No. I'd never take it running. Anyway, I'd always have it in its case. It's against the law to carry it around without it being in a case.'

None of them seem impressed with this argument. I see their point.

'Could you have been carrying anything that looked like a gun? A stick?'

'I don't think so.'

Andrew unfolds a map, smoothes it on to the table and traces a line with his finger.

'The police say you could have followed a route out of Woodwalton up a back lane, then gone along the banks of the Ashbrook past Kingsthorpe, then gone up this footpath and across these fields, then joined the track at the back of Manor Farm here.'

'I'd still be taking a real risk, with a

shotgun in my hand.'

'Their other suggestion will be that you hid it near to Manor Farm beforehand. That you'd have known where to leave it where it wouldn't be found, and you picked it up on the day. Or even that you'd left it with John Grant, perhaps by the door. You could have crept in, using some keys.'

'I never had any keys.'

He never gave me a set — which maybe shows how much he thought of me.

'You could have made a set. They're only a Yale and a deadlock, easy enough to get copied.'

I'm still unconvinced by all this.

'But if I was so careful getting there, why did I panic and run down the main road holding a gun? And why didn't Jane see me with it when I got back to my house?'

'They'll say you cut down Kiln Lane, threw it over the back wall into your garden and then picked it up later.'

'I wouldn't have had time. I'd have had to unlock the back door, get the gun, clean it, lock it up.'

'Perhaps you had help. Perhaps you told someone where you hid it, along the road from Upton, and they found it and cleaned it and put it back in your house.'

'Who'd do that?'

'You brother would've, wouldn't he? If you'd phoned him and asked him,' Charles says, almost impatiently. 'But anyway, the main problem is still Miss Meadows. She says she saw you with the gun. Unless we can show that she was mistaken, or is motivated by malice, or has been got at in some way, then the jury will have that in their minds and you will be in some difficulty. So might she have something against you?'

'No. I don't think I've talked to her for years. We were both in the choir when I was young. But I don't really remember much about her. My mother knows her a bit, but only as neighbours.'

'I've spoken to your mother about this,' Andrew says, 'but she'd nothing more to add.'

'We'll probably have to stick to the idea she was mistaken,' Charles says. 'If the police planted the thought in her mind, we might get somewhere in reducing the reliability. That's our best line.

'Anyway, once the prosecution has closed, I'll make an application to the court that there's no case to answer. These applications are rarely successful, though the jury won't be present so there's no harm in having a go. But if we assume the worst it'll then be your turn to give evidence.

'Now if we take Miss Meadows out of the equation, and I'm fairly confident we can dent her evidence, if not get it thrown out altogether, then all the Crown have done is linked you to the scene of the murder, not to the murder itself. All the evidence is two-way, once you accept the premise that you could have been at the scene but that it was someone else who killed him. So what we need is for the jury to want to interpret the evidence in your favour. And the judge too, though I'll come back to that in a minute.

'Clarissa, I don't need to tell you that your role is absolutely crucial. Where we want to end up is here: with the jury thinking that they can quite understand why the case was brought, but that you are nevertheless innocent. Rubbishing the case won't do. We have to work with the grain of the evidence, explaining why all it amounts to is your involvement in some way with the events of that day, but not in any sense proving your guilt. Are you happy with that?'

'What do I have to do?'

He looks surprised, perhaps because despite my own fears I sound really competent, in control.

'Well, first of all you have to be frank. You have to say that you simply can't remember anything at all about the day. It's important that this doesn't look like you are saying this purely for your own convenience, to avoid incriminating yourself, so I'll ask you several questions about people you might have seen on your run, or who might have seen you return to your house, and show that if you could remember these people it could help to show that you didn't have a weapon. It's this kind of line of attack which should help to dispel this idea that you could have run around the countryside in broad daylight with a shotgun and not expected to be spotted.

'After all,' Sarah chips in, 'they can't both claim you are a cold-blooded murderer planning the perfect crime, and so insane as to have put yourself at such risk.'

'Then it's the prosecution's turn. It's very important that in the cross-examination you don't try to control the direction of the questioning or try to argue back. Don't get angry, don't get rattled, and never say more than you need to. Short answers are good, because there are less words to come back at you on, and because it sounds like you're being honest and helpful. That's something else — always try to be helpful. But don't worry if you forget all this and make a complete hash of something, we can pull it back later. After the prosecution have finished with you — ' *unfortunate choice of words, Charles,* I think to myself ' — then I'll have a chance to re-examine you, and we can pick it up there, I can go over it and give you a chance to set it straight.

'What she'll want you to do is condemn yourself in your own words. She'll want to get statements out of you that are at variance with the evidence, or which she can put back to you. It's all about comparing one statement to another, pointing out inconsistencies. That's why you have to say as little as possible without appearing unhelpful or too scheming. And don't volunteer anything. You're there to answer questions, not to try to explain anything.'

They talk on, sounding confident, trying to pass some of that confidence on to me, but everything feels flat. It's the end of the week. I feel so tired, and I've only had to sit and listen. How Charles and Sarah can be so full of energy is beyond me.

It's almost quarter to ten by the time they go. I go back to the waiting area, and sit listening to Bill and Joe and the others swapping comments. I flick through my diary again, and think about writing something but nothing comes, so instead I look at the picture of my house Seb did, the letters from my friends, the cards, all the rest of it, and I think that I just want my life back.

That means convincing the court that I'm not the kind of person to kill someone. Then Charles can put forward alternative stories for the jury, to show that the facts were just circumstantial, that if you shook them around they could show another explanation. The gangland killing. The cheated husband. The robbery gone wrong.

I hardly notice as they lead me to the steps up to the court, I feel like I am going on for just one more stage appearance: tired, but at least I know my lines.

★ ★ ★

The day starts quietly. Ruth calls Terry Allsop, the van driver and leads him through his evidence, though what he says isn't crucial one way or the other. He was driving to a building site on the other side of Oundle and saw me running down the road towards Upton. Why did he look at me? Nothing else to look at along the road, he says, grinning. What was I wearing? White T-shirt, blue leggings, white socks, white trainers. Was I holding anything? Can't remember. Sarah asks him whether I looked distressed or upset. He says, no more so than anyone fool enough to go running at that time in the morning, and gets a laugh, and steps down.

Now it is Miss Meadows, who lives in the cottage on the road from Upton to Normanton. In the last ten years I have only ever seen her in her own garden, looking over the hedge, or on the Oundle bus, off to do her weekly shopping. We know each other, but I doubt we've spoken more than a dozen words since I stopped going to church, when my father died. Now she is standing in the witness box, dressed in her church-going clothes, holding the bible not tentatively like the other witnesses, but with confidence. She looks at the prosecution lawyer, and at the judge, and at the jury, but not at me.

'I was up early. I usually am up early, by six o'clock, and I make myself some tea and listen to *Farming Today*.'

None of the jury looks as if they're the type to be up and dressed at 6 a.m. They look as if early rising is next to godliness, and about as unobtainable. They are going to believe whatever she says.

'It was just after six. I know because I'd just listened to the headlines on the radio. I went out into the garden to see what the weather was doing and to pin out my towel. I had come back in and was by the sink when I saw her.'

'And who did you see?'

'I saw Clarrie running down the road.' I look up, surprised after a week in court not to be called Clarissa. Or *the accused*.

'I see. And which direction was she running?'

'Well, she came out from Snag's Lane, and turned into the road by my house, and then ran off towards Upton.'

'Snag's Lane leads to Manor Farm, doesn't it?'

'Yes.'

'Does it lead anywhere else?'

'Yes.' This clearly isn't the answer Ruth wants. 'After half a mile or so it joins the Kingsthorpe road.'

'But there are no other houses or businesses along Snag's Lane?'

'No, only fields.' This time Ruth has the right answer. There's nowhere else I might have been going, so I must be the murderer.

'Can you say what she was wearing?'

'Oh, yes. She was wearing a white T-shirt, long and loose, and blue trousers, the kind for jogging, and those white pumps. Trainers.'

'Did you notice anything else about her?'

She looks blank for a moment, then realizes that this is her cue.

'Yes. She was carrying a gun.'

'You are sure it was a gun?'

'Oh yes.'

Everyone knows she's going to say this, but there's still a stir around the court.

'And are you sure that the person you saw was the accused?'

'Oh yes, I know Clarrie very well, and I'm quite sure it was her.'

I try to picture the scene she is describing. I can picture the house in the early morning light, the deep green hedges starting to lose their leaves, the slight early morning mist hanging in the trees, and the figure in blue and white running along the lane, long loping strides and maybe sliding a little in the mud as she turns on to the road, and then running away uphill. But I can't see what it is in her hand. My hand.

'Miss Meadows,' Charles begins, 'you said that you saw Miss Morland from your kitchen window, at about ten past six in the morning, running down Snag's Lane, and that she turned and ran up the road to Upton. Is that right?'

'Yes.' She is quite calm.

'You were at the sink in your kitchen at the time?'

'Yes.'

'What were you doing?'

'I was filling the kettle. To make tea.'

'And you said in your evidence that you thought that Miss Morland was carrying a gun. Which hand was this gun in?'

'Oh, in her left hand,' she says, pleased she can remember.

'And as Miss Morland ran down Snag's Lane, and turned on to the Upton road, she would have turned to her left, wouldn't she? So that she would have her left side, and her left arm, away from you. Isn't that right?'

'Yes. I suppose so.'

Charles consults his notes.

'You said in your evidence that it was a gun that this figure was carrying.' He pauses. 'Miss Meadows, could you say what you did next, after you say you saw this figure?'

'I wasn't mistaken,' she says sharply. 'It was her.'

She looks my way, no expression on her face. I turn away.

'I know you want to make clear that that is what we should think,' Charles says with a show of patience. 'I will come back to this later. For now, could you answer the question. What did you do next?'

'What do you mean?'

'It's very simple,' he says, kindly now. 'What was the next thing you did? You were filling the kettle, I believe.'

'Well, I boiled the kettle and made some tea.'

'You made some tea?'

402

'Yes.'

'Did you do anything else?'

'I don't know what you mean.'

'Well.' Charles waves an arm to show the range of things she could have done. 'Didn't you think it was odd to see someone running around with a shotgun at six in the morning?'

'Yes, well, yes, I suppose I did.'

'So what did you do?'

'Well, nothing. What should I have done?'

'You didn't think to phone the police?'

'No.'

'You didn't open the window to watch this figure running further down the road?'

'No.'

'Or go out into your garden to see?'

'No.' Her replies are becoming monotonous.

'It doesn't sound as if you were very curious about this figure. Did you do anything at all about what you had seen?'

'No.'

'Did you speak to anyone about what you had seen, before speaking to the police?'

'No.'

'You didn't phone a friend? See anyone passing to chat to?'

'No.'

'No.' Charles echoes her. 'You see, when I looked at your written statement, this was a

403

fact that struck me particularly strongly. You had just seen a figure running past your house. This figure was carrying a gun. But you didn't do anything about this. You didn't try to get a better look. You didn't even think about phoning the police.'

'I did think about it. I thought about it, but I didn't like to. I wouldn't have known what to say.'

One or two of the jury, leaning forward to her faint replies to Charles's booming questions, now sit back again as his line of argument slips away. But he carries on.

'You were saved the trouble, then, by the arrival of the police some hours later.'

'Yes. They came round at about eleven o'clock. I was out in the garden and saw the car pull up outside. And the dogs started barking.'

'And could you describe what the police did?'

She looks puzzled, makes an effort to remember. 'Well, they introduced themselves, and came in and asked if I knew Mr Grant, up at Manor Farm. And I said I did, but only to nod to, not well. And they said he'd been killed, shot on his own doorstep. And I said what a terrible thing it was. They wanted to know if I'd heard anything that morning, or anything suspicious, and I said

404

I hadn't. And then — '

'If I can stop you there.' Charles has one hand raised, and he is tensed up, like a dog that's smelled a rabbit.

'You just said that the police asked you if you had seen anything suspicious, and you said that you hadn't.'

'That's right.'

'What about Miss Morland?' Silence. 'You are supposed to have seen her with a gun, to have thought about calling the police, but when the police turn up on your doorstep and ask you if you have seen anything suspicious, you say no. How can that be?'

She says nothing, but Ruth comes to her rescue by protesting that Charles is commenting instead of asking questions. The judge agrees with her, but when he asks Charles to rephrase the question there's no hint of a rebuke.

'Let me put it this way,' Charles says. 'Did you tell the police that you had seen nothing suspicious that morning?'

'Yes, but — '

'And once you had told the police that you had seen nothing suspicious, what happened next?'

'Well . . . ' she says, licking her lips. 'Well, then they asked if I had seen anyone passing by early in the morning. When I told them

405

about Clarrie Morland running past, they were very interested, and they took a statement down, and I signed it. And then later on, the Inspector, or something like that, he came round and I made another statement, with more detail. And . . . '

'Can I be absolutely clear about this, Miss Meadows? The police knock on the door, you open the door, they tell you their business. They tell you that Mr Grant has been killed. They ask if you have heard or seen anything suspicious. You say no. They then ask if you have seen anyone passing your house earlier that morning. You tell them that you did see someone. Is that correct?'

'Yes. I told them I'd seen Clarrie run past.'

'And this conversation took place on the doorstep?'

'Oh no. When they said what they'd come about, I asked them in.'

'Perhaps you were making tea again?'

Cheap. A few sniggers come from the press and the gallery above, but not from the jury.

'Now I assume that they asked you to remember everything about the figure you had seen. What they were wearing. Where they came from. Where you were standing when you saw the figure, that sort of thing.'

'Yes.'

'They sound very helpful.'

'They were very considerate. I'm not at all used to this kind of thing. I've never been mixed up in anything like this.'

'I'm sure not. So one or other of these officers would prompt you to remember what the figure was wearing?'

'Yes.'

'And whether she was carrying anything?'

'Yes. She was carrying a gun.'

'Did you say that, or did they ask you if she was?'

'I'm not sure.'

'They asked you what the figure was wearing?'

'Yes.'

'And you said she was wearing a tracksuit and a T-shirt.'

'Yes.'

'It would seem quite natural for one of the police officers, helping you to remember what you had seen, to ask if she was carrying anything.'

'Yes. They may have done. I can't remember. But she was definitely carrying something. I saw it glint in the sunlight. I remember quite clearly.'

'Is that what you told the police?'

'Yes.'

'That she was carrying something which glinted?'

'Yes. Something metal.'

'And they asked if it was a gun?'

'Yes.'

'Had you thought it was a gun until they suggested it?'

'But it was a gun.'

'Had you thought it was a gun until they suggested it?'

'I can't think what else it could have been.' She is becoming a bit flustered.

'You said it was 'something metal'. You said that only a few moments ago.'

Her mouth shuts hard. She must have been warned by Ruth in the same way Charles warned me about what the other side's barristers will do. Trying to undermine your confidence, twist the words around you, make you doubt your own memory. She looks as if she is going to hold on grimly to what she remembers.

'How was she holding what you think was a gun?'

'In her hand.'

'I mean, how did she grip it? At one end? In the middle?'

She screws up her face, trying to remember. 'I'm not sure. At one end, perhaps?'

'How long would you say the thing she was carrying was?'

'Er . . . about this long?' She holds her hands up vaguely, only a few inches apart. Charles looks genuinely surprised.

'No longer than that?'

'I can't be sure.' She sounds so worried now.

'This is important. Please try to remember. How long was the gun?'

'I'm sorry. I don't know. But I did see it. I'm sure.'

'What sort of gun was it?'

'A shotgun,' she says promptly.

Charles points to my gun, the one my father gave me, lying on the table in the middle of the court, still wrapped in polythene.

'Like that one?'

'I suppose so,' she says doubtfully.

'Could you take the gun, Miss Meadows, and show us how this figure was carrying it?'

She takes it from the usher, holds it fearfully, at arm's length.

'It isn't loaded,' Charles can't resist saying.

'What do you want me to do?'

Charles asks her to hold it in the same way as the figure, but although she tries different ways, in the middle, by the butt, she looks uncomfortable. Or perhaps puzzled.

'Is there a problem?' he asks.

'Well, there wasn't nearly so much of it

showing. Perhaps she had part of it up her sleeve?'

'A shotgun?' Charles sounds genuinely astonished at the idea.

'Or like this. Along the length of her arm.'

'Perhaps I could remind you that, according to your own evidence, the figure you saw was wearing a T-shirt. And holding the gun that way looks extremely uncomfortable, even as you are standing there, let alone if you had to try to run.'

Miss Meadows, with her hand clasped around the lower barrel of the gun, and the butt waving around near her face, has to agree.

'Are you in some doubt about what you saw?'

'I saw her carrying a gun. She ran past me, she wasn't far away, and I saw it quite clearly, glinting.'

'Can you remember the exact words you used when you first described the thing that Clarrie was carrying to the police?' Even with the court watching intently, and even as I wait for her words, I have to admire Charles for choosing the right moment to use my name, Clarrie, the little girl who sang with her in the choir.

'I don't know. I think I said that she was holding a gun.'

'But you can't remember the exact words?'

She shakes her head. She has gone a strange colour, both blushing and pale at the same time. Perhaps she senses the doubt around her, or within her, because she cries out, 'I know what I saw.'

But she doesn't know, not any more, not after all this time, and after the police and the prosecution and now the defence and her own conscience have finished with her.

Charles waits for a moment, but she says no more. He is about to try another question, when the judge speaks, a courteous voice after the needling of the last few minutes.

'Miss Meadows, perhaps you can help me on this point. If I look at something, I may at once see what it is. I may look at this pencil and at once know it for what it is, without the need for conscious thought. On the other hand, there are occasions where one needs to look and to think. Where one deduces what something is from the evidence, one might say. A little like one of those photographic puzzles, where you have to work out what an object is from a photograph taken from an unexpected angle.'

She smiles weakly, relieved by his pleasant, conversational tone and his familiar comparison. I imagine she does a lot of puzzles, alone in her cottage.

'In this case,' he goes on, 'did you see a gun, or did you see something that you later deduced was a gun?'

She is deferential. 'It was the second, my lord.'

'And this process of deduction took place at the time of the police visit?'

'Yes.' She is pleased to agree, grateful for his help.

It's going so well, I can't believe it. I could have been holding anything. Perhaps it was my mobile phone. That's metallic. Maybe I was carrying it in case John tried to phone me, like he'd promised to.

But I'm determined not to get my hopes up. So I sit, looking at my feet, breathing slowly, humming a tune to myself. The jury are watching the judge, so I risk a quick smile to my family, who smile back brightly.

'So you said that the defendant was carrying something which glinted, something metal,' the judge says, waving his pencil. 'The police suggested that this might have been a gun, and you agreed.'

'Right.' Kerr makes a long note, then nods to Charles. 'Thank you, Mr Everard. Do carry on.'

The evidence rolls on, all about how good her eyesight is, when she last had her eyes checked, was she wearing her glasses, the view from the kitchen window, how light it was. Endless, boring details. *Was the light on inside the kitchen? No, she kept the light off in the morning, if it was light enough to see. Could she have mistaken the day? No, it was certainly the same day as the police came around.*

I can picture the kitchen, warm from the stove, the light through the windows enough to make the tea, a sense of virtue hanging in the air from that little saving, the radio on, she standing in front of the steel sink, running the water, looking out past the spider plants and the bottle of Fairy Liquid and the soap in its china tray, seeing a figure running down the lane and into the road, sliding a bit on the mud, putting a hand out to steady themselves, then away towards Upton. I know it was me, for what that is worth.

★ ★ ★

Jane, my next-door neighbour, is the last witness called. I have known her for three years, ever since she and her husband Mark invited me round for a meal the first week I moved in, and I have never seen her look so unhappy, almost ill. Her face is drawn and white, and as she stands in the box she looks about her as if waiting for an attack. Her voice is too quiet to hear properly as she is sworn in.

'Mrs Kennedy, your house is opposite Miss Morland's, isn't it?'

'Yes.'

'You were at home on the morning of the twentieth of October, weren't you?'

'Yes.'

'Could you tell the court what you saw on that morning?'

Ruth is being particularly brisk, as if she knows Jane is nervous and needs to be pushed.

'Well . . . ' Jane looks about her, as if waiting for someone to save her from speaking. 'I was in the kitchen, making some toast I think, and I looked out of the window, which is at the front of the house and looks over to the road, and I saw Clarrie come running down the road and go through her front door.'

Ruth pauses for a second, as if waiting for more, and then prompts Jane.

'What time would this have been?'

'About seven o'clock. I usually am up by then because of Pippa and Marco.' Her kids, six and four, who I used to babysit.

'Can you be more exact?'

'No, but it must have been before ten past seven.'

'And what happened after the accused went into her house?'

'Well . . . after a few minutes she came back out again and got into her car and drove off. That was at ten past seven. I remember looking at the clock.'

Again, Ruth seems to expect some more.

'What state was the accused in when you first saw her?'

'Er . . . she looked quite tired. I mean, she'd obviously been running.'

'Distressed?'

'I don't think so. Maybe. She was leaning over a bit as she opened the door, like she was breathing heavily, but no more than that.'

'I see. And how long was it before she came back out again?'

'A minute or two.'

'Can you be more precise? This is a very important point.'

'It seemed like only a minute or two. It couldn't have been much more than that. The alarm went off a minute or two before seven, and I came straight downstairs, put the kettle on, and I was making the toast and rinsing out some cups by the sink when I first saw her, and that must have taken several minutes.'

'Could it have been as much as five or six minutes?'

'Maybe.' She looks doubtful.

'But certainly several minutes?'

'Yes.' So perhaps I could have had time to clean the gun.

'How did the accused seem when she came out of her house and got into her car?'

'How do you mean?'

'Did she seem normal? Or upset, or crying?'

'Upset, I think, though I didn't see her for long.'

'Which way was her car facing?'

Jane screws up her face, trying to remember. 'I think it was pointing towards the right, as I was looking at it. Towards Kingsthorpe.'

'So she would have had to come around the front or the back of the car to reach the driver's door.' A statement, not a question. 'And you would have had several seconds to see her, wouldn't you?'

'I suppose so.'

'What was she wearing?'

'Er . . . her tracksuit. A white T-shirt. And a headband.'

'The same as when she came back from her run.'

'Yes.'

'And you thought she looked upset?'

'Yes.' She nods.

It goes on like this, seemingly for an age, and it is worse when Charles starts his cross-examination.

'Mrs Kennedy, I have a couple of questions on the timing.' He makes this sound as if he's asking her permission. 'You said that it was possible that Miss Morland was in her house for longer, but your own view was that she went in and came out in a minute or two.'

'That's right.'

'You saw her open her door and enter the house.'

'Yes.'

'She closed the door after her.'

'I'm not sure. I don't think so.'

'And a minute or two later she runs out, pulls the door shut, and runs round to get into her car.' She nods. 'Was she carrying anything when she left?'

'No.'

'You are sure?'

'Yes.' She closes her eyes again, and I can imagine the vision she has in her mind. Me, leaning against the door, breathing in great gasps of air as I turn the lock and half-fall across the lintel. I go into the house, out of sight, maybe I fling myself down on the sofa in the kitchen. Thinking about John having deceived me, two-timed me, screwed me in every way he could. Crying perhaps. Then something reminds me of John, a phone message, or no phone message, and I want to get out again. I pick up the car keys from on top of the night-storage heater in the hall and run out to the car, drive off anywhere, just to get away, to have something to do, to try to stop myself thinking too much.

'No, wait, she was carrying something.'

Her face has a look on it of triumph that she has dragged up something more from her memory. Charles looks back at her with his alarm well masked. Behind her I can see the jury looking at her. The whole court is hanging on her next words.

'Yes. She had a phone in her hand. A mobile phone. She was leaning with one hand against the door jamb, and had a phone in her other hand with her key, which made it difficult for her to unlock the door. I think that's what first made me notice her there.'

Despite the relief, I still feel sick at the thought she might just as easily have said it was a gun in my hand. Then, that would have been that. Another week of the case, perhaps, but no doubt of the outcome. Premeditated murder. Life imprisonment. I try to calm down, to maintain my outward composure, while Charles takes her through her morning routine, tries to pin down the times more exactly, to show that I couldn't have had time to get the gun from the back garden or wherever else I might have hidden it, and then clean it, put it away in the cabinet, and run back out to the car.

Ruth re-examines Jane briefly, ignoring the phone and the question of the gun, trying to undo Charles's work on the time I was in the house. The Builder is sitting with his chin down on his chest, his arms folded, annoyed as if everything is being twisted round and around solely to prevent him following the case properly. The Rat and Danny Boy exchange a look and a shrug. Jane steps down, with one last look over to me and I smile, even though I know I shouldn't.

Then, almost before anyone realizes it, the Crown's case has closed. The whole court relaxes for a moment, hardly listening to Charles as he makes the application to the judge. As the jury leave, Andrew looks over at me, smirks, puts his thumb up, as if the worst is over. Charles then starts to explain why the case should be thrown out, despite the week of evidence against me. I can sense how unimpressed the audience are by this, even if they don't follow the legal arguments. The judge starts picking holes in what Charles is saying, and when Ruth comes to answer she doesn't seem too bothered by it all. More distracted, really, as if she's already planning

419

how to cross-examine me. I try to remember what Andrew has told me about the witnesses who'll be called in my support, how this should change the atmosphere, and how the judge at least must have been impressed that two of the prosecution witnesses went out of their way to be nice about me.

'No, I don't think I have any need of that,' the judge says, though I've missed what he is talking about. 'Perhaps this would be a convenient moment to break for lunch.'

*　*　*

Lunch is fish. Some random fish, a sliver of white flesh between the orange breadcrumbs and the black skin, the whole thing desiccated, then dampened again by water coming off the peas, fish as served (I start to suspect) every Friday in every prison, hospital and asylum in the country, which means that if the rest of the trial goes wrong I'm unlikely to escape from it for years to come. Even if I cut my wrists or put my head through the bars or try to hang myself with my own bra, or even lose it completely and end up being sectioned, there'll still be fish every Friday. I pile up the mash, then use the wrong end of the fork to carve it into the rough shape of a castle. Maybe I'll start to find it comforting, no need to think about anything, no break from the routine, like being a child again. Or maybe I should pick up the tray and throw it against the door.

Andrew said that I was likely to find waiting really stressful. So I try to relax, deep breaths, all the rest, and try to think what I am going to say. *You've got to look innocent*, he said. I wish I had a mirror so that I could practise.

I remember Baz saying that the worst part of her trial was waiting over the weekend. If you were in court again the next day, that was bad enough, but it was worse to have two days with nothing to do but think over what might happen, what might go wrong, getting more and more worked up. And because there are fewer staff around there's no exercise or activities, and no one to check up on prisoners they think might make an 'attempt'. It's odd the way everyone calls them 'attempts', even the ones which succeed. Like the time my friend Natalie came into the prison and said to me when she was going that everything was going to be OK and that I shouldn't do anything 'stupid'. I didn't realize what she meant until she was gone, or I'd have laughed or said something. But it doesn't feel so funny now.

I know that I'm thinking this way because

I'm scared about having to give evidence. I'm scared by the judge and the jury and what they will think. I'm scared about Ruth and what facing her will be like, with her smiling as she pulls it all out of me. I'm scared about what I will say.

Then Andrew and Roisin come in and I jump up, guilty, amazed by their cheerful expressions, and I realize that they are much later than usual, that I've been sitting here for almost an hour, we'll be restarting in only twenty minutes. Roisin has a tray of coffees piled with chocolate bars too, and she explains that no one knew which my favourite was so she got one of each. I can't think of anything to say, I'm still a bit out of it, so I smile at them both and sip my coffee while Andrew paces around and Roisin quietly sorts through a bundle of papers which I guess Charles has spent the morning messing up.

'Nick asked me if you wanted any more books,' Andrew says at last.

'No thanks. Tell him no.' I find I can't concentrate in prison on reading, or much else. Once I had thought how great it would be to be ill for a month or two, not actually feeling bad, just laid up so you couldn't be distracted and could catch up on all those books you'd never read, letters you hadn't

422

time to write. But inside I become restless, or tired, or find my mind drifting away, running over the same worries again and again, about the trial, about my mother, my house, what I will do if I get out, or if I don't. It was the same in hospital. I still have half a bag full of books I've started and not finished and which the prison rules mean I can't even lend to anyone.

'Are you nervous?' I nod. 'Ruth can be quite a terror. But Kerr won't let her bully you, and if she is aggressive, then you'll win from having the jury on your side. I don't mean to criticize Charles, I mean, I think he's great, but when he was really laying into Halliday the other day I think half the jury were saying to themselves that he was only a copper doing his level best and he shouldn't have been pushed around like that.'

'How long will she question me for?'

'There's not really any limit. But she has to have something to ask you, she can't drag it out. Again, Charles will say something if she's being unfair. I doubt it'll be more than a day, but you can never tell. And you'll be surprised how quickly it goes.'

'It won't be over today, will it?'

'No, we'll finish your evidence on Monday or Tuesday, then call our witnesses. We should be through by Thursday.'

Andrew looks really on edge, much more excited than normal. I ask him what the matter is but he's evasive and says he has to go off and see Charles.

'Where is he?' I ask.

'Oh, he's in with the judge.' I must look puzzled, because Andrew goes on to explain that they sometimes have little conferences in the judge's rooms during the recesses.

'Is there any chance of this application working?' I ask, trying not to sound eager. Andrew stops and thinks carefully before he replies.

'Yeah, there is a chance. But don't get your hopes up. Most judges would leave it to the jury. Less controversial that way. It all depends on what he makes of Miss Meadows' evidence.'

I think about this.

'And they can't try me again, if it goes my way.'

'No.'

'But everyone would think I got off on a technicality, wouldn't they?'

'Well, you'd be acquitted, just as if the jury had heard your side of it as well.'

'But people will still wonder if it was me, won't they?'

Andrew shrugs and looks away, and I start

to play with my lunch again, mashing the potato around.

'I'll be one of them, won't I?' I say.

'How do you mean?'

'Well, unless I start to remember, I won't know if I did it, will I? I'll always wonder if it was me that killed John.'

Now I've said it out loud, I realize it's worse than I thought.

'And I'll worry about remembering, won't I?' I look searchingly at his sombre face. He's already worked this out. 'I'll wake up each day and think, maybe this is the day that I'll remember that I'm a killer. I'll always have this fear that one day I'll remember exactly what I did, how I felt when I killed him. Won't I?'

He still won't look at me.

'And there's fuck all I can do about it, is there?'

'I don't know. Maybe.'

It's odd, but I find I'm really angry. As if I'd been conned into thinking there was a way out.

'So it doesn't really matter if I'm found innocent or guilty, does it? Either way, plenty of people will still think that I did it. My home's been trashed, I've lost my job and I won't be able to find another one because everyone will ask where I've been for the last nine months. Even if I move away, everyone will know who I am, thanks to the papers.'

What I don't say is that I've no chance of meeting anyone, not with them thinking what I might have done to John. And me wondering if they're some kind of weirdo, like those people who write to Myra Hindley. But I don't want to say this to Andrew.

'So all in all, I'm pretty much fucked over, aren't I?'

'You've got lots of people on your side. Your mother, Nick, all your friends. They'll be there for you.'

'But what about me? What about inside my head?'

'Do you think you killed him?' Roisin asks, and at first I have no idea what to say. None of them have asked me this before. We've always danced around the question. But once said, maybe it's not so difficult to answer.

'No, I don't think I did. At the start of the week, I thought I must have done, because all the evidence looked that way. Now, I think I probably didn't. I don't think I'm the kind of person who would have done it. Or done it like that. Or maybe I would do it now, but the person I was then wouldn't have been able to do it. But thinking it wasn't me isn't enough. I've got to *know*.'

I look from one to the other. I suppose I

want them to tell me that it's all going to be OK, so that I can shout at them that it won't. I want the comfort so I can throw it aside.

'Unless you remember,' Andrew says. 'Or they find who really did it.'

'No chance of that. They won't even try.'

If I was acquitted, I can imagine Halliday going on TV and telling everyone that the police won't be looking for anyone else. Saying, in effect, that we know we got the right person even if the jury were conned.

'You'll be OK. Stand up and tell them the truth and know in yourself that you didn't do it and you'll be fine.'

I nod.

'Do you want any chocolate?' he asks.

I shake my head. I feel a bit sick, thinking about giving evidence in a few minutes' time.

'Never mind.' He sweeps the little pile of brightly coloured bars into his briefcase. 'I'll give them to you later. But have one of these.' He produces a bag of Fisherman's Friends.

'We used to have these before we went on stage,' I say.

'Thought so. Clears the passages. Stops you snuffling like a pig during your evidence.'

'Thanks very much.' I have to laugh despite myself.

'I'd better go. But what I thought I'd do is fix up to come in over the weekend to run over what's going to happen next week. We'll not have much time on Monday morning. OK?'

'Sure. I'd like that.' I know the weekend won't be easy, and the idea of a friendly face, especially now that Baz has gone, is such a comfort.

'Break a leg.'

'I'm sure you'll do just fine,' Roisin adds as they go.

I sit still for a moment, listening to their footsteps down the corridor, and then to the clatter of crockery being cleared in the canteen above. I imagine the staff wandering around, collecting the last stray cups, a few people lingering over coffee or cake, choosing whether to finish the paper, go for a stroll, whatever.

The warder comes back and we go back to the holding room, and after hardly a pause we are back in our places at the foot of the stairs. There is that same anticipation, waiting in the wings, but this time I have lines to speak, not just a walk-on part. I hum a tune under my breath, another song from the tape Baz gave me, which I already seem to know by heart.

'What's that song, then?' Bill asks.

'I don't know. It's going around in my head.'

I hum it for him, but he shakes his head.

'I prefer the Rolling Stones any day,' he says.

I climb back into the dock.

Friday Afternoon

The judge sits, settles himself, draws out some papers, and begins to speak.

'Members of the jury, before lunch counsel for the defence made an application that the defendant had no case to answer. In other words, that there was now little prospect of there being sufficient evidence, taken at its highest, for you the jury to convict. I also heard counsel for the prosecution reply to the application.'

He pauses, and I look at Charles for some clue as to what this means, but he and Andrew and the others are all looking fixedly at the judge. There are whispers, and someone says mistrial, or maybe retrial. I feel sick at the thought of having to go through it all again.

'Miss Acheson,' he goes on, 'I understand you have something you wish to say?'

Ruth stands, calm as always.

'The Crown has had the opportunity to consider further Miss Meadows' evidence, and other information recently brought to our attention, and in the light of this the Crown wishes to withdraw the case.'

The judge pauses to make a note, one of the ushers is talking to the jury. Charles and Sarah are deep in conversation, and Andrew and then Roisin come over to join in, and the huddle is so thick with gowned backs and nodding wigs that I can't even see their expressions. I don't understand what the judge is saying, and look around at the jury, the press, Nick sitting near the back, but their faces are as blank as mine. I wonder if I'll be freed. But I can't believe they'll just let me go after all that's happened. Maybe I'll be sent back to Whitemoor. Another six months, then another trial.

'Mr Everard?' the judge says, as Charles stands.

'I would be grateful if my learned friend could be clear as to whether she is proposing that the case be ended but the charges lie on the file, or whether she is proposing an acquittal.'

'Oh, I think we are talking about an acquittal. Aren't we, Miss Acheson?'

She is on the point of disputing this, but thinks better of it.

'As your lordship pleases.'

The judge goes on to say how the prosecution's action in ending the case is in the highest traditions of the criminal bar, and how he hopes that the police will soon be able

431

to bring the real culprits to book. He sympathizes with Mr Grant's family and friends and he is deeply sorry that their suffering is to continue but that justice must be served and it is his clear duty to end the proceedings without further delay.

And all the time the court is silent, except for a voice, John's father, I think, muttering in disbelief.

The guards help me to my feet. In the end I have to look up. The noise in the court has died down. Everything still. All eyes on me, mine on the judge.

'Miss Morland,' he says, turning towards me, slouched forward, with his strange imitation of a smile, 'you too will wish to know the implications of this. You have in effect been found not guilty by this court. You are free to go.'

He stands and begins to leave amid complete silence, people standing and bowing but unable to speak with the suddenness of it. Then someone shouts out from the back, about how this is a fucking joke, how I clearly did it. The judge pays no attention, but barely has he left than the noise rises like a wave, a babble of voices, amazement and outrage and swearing and crying too. I look over at the press, penned in by a couple of guards, all shouting as one, a chorus, *Miss Morland,*

Miss, just a word, how do you feel, Miss, were you expecting this, what are you going to do now, love? any chance of a statement?

The clamour continues as the jury is ushered away into their own room. One or two look back at me. The Codger and the Old Bag have already gone, and Danny Boy is stepping down, holding both rails on the stairs carefully as always, and behind him the Builder shrugs as if to say how he can't believe they've let me go. The court officials and the stenographer are starting to pack away their papers, and Ruth is doing the same, looking calm, except that there's something about her which makes me think that no one would dare speak to her. Halliday is talking to Gerard, shaking his head, waving one arm about, and I can imagine all too easily what he is saying. Then Nick is below me.

'Are you OK?' he asks.

'I don't know. I don't think so.'

The guard opens the door of the dock and shows me down the steps, and Nick gives me a crushing hug. But over his shoulder I can see John's mother staring at me, and the others around her, and I can hear voices saying how this is a mockery, someone arguing and trying to get past one of the police, sounds of a scuffle, and I ask Andrew to get me away from here.

They must be used to this kind of thing because the guards quickly hustle us through into a side room and shut the door behind us.

In the quiet I can catch my breath. Nick goes off to phone our mother while I try to get Charles to explain what's happened. He beams at me, every trace of his awkwardness with me now gone.

'With Miss Meadows' evidence so compromised, there was no realistic chance of conviction. So the Crown packed it in. Simple as that.'

'We'd guessed before lunch,' Andrew adds, 'but we'd not wanted to raise your hopes.'

I can hardly take all this in, and I don't want to ask any more. It seems like tempting fate.

Charles and Sarah seem keen to get going so I say my thank-yous. She gives me a faint hug, hardly spontaneous, and Charles shakes my hand more warmly than I expected and wishes me well. Then one of the court officials asks me what I want to do, and I'm a bit thrown because I haven't had to make any decisions like that for months.

'You can go out the front, but there'll be the press and it might be a bit of a scrum,' the woman says.

During the last week I'd imagined walking

out of court a hundred times, dodging past the guards, or tripping down the steps and running on to the grass, maybe a cartwheel, or walking calmly out, like any other member of the public, a law-abiding citizen that no one would pay any attention to, walking out and into the city centre and disappearing back into my life. Now I realize I can't leave like that. I feel trapped, hunted, as if the nightmare is due to start again. Like in the courtroom, they'll shout out, they'll ask questions, they'll all be thinking that I did it after all, that I got off on a technicality. I can see myself being pushed at, booed, spat on, grabbed at, and then bundled into a car with a coat over my head, like any other criminal.

'Or we can take you out the back,' she adds, seeing my hesitation.

That would mean going through the loading bay, through the security doors and past the cells and the reception area. Waiting behind the smooth brick walls and the steel-mesh gate and the razor wire, with the smell of diesel and bins. It would be like going back to prison.

'I'll go out the front,' I say. 'But can I have a few minutes first?'

'As long as you like, love,' she says.

I tell Andrew I'll talk to the press on the way out, and he goes off to sort it out. Then they show me into a loo, and for once there's no guard with me as I drink some water from the tap, splash more on my face and round my neck, then bury my face in the clean towel on the roller. As I put on a bit of lipstick and straighten my jacket, I start to realize that I've done it. I've got through. I feel this elation bubbling up inside me. Even the reflection of the bruises under my eyes, the way I look older and more wary, is part of who I now am, and doesn't worry me any more. In a minute I'll walk out of here, and know that John's family and friends, who were laughing at me all the time I was seeing him, and who came out with all that stuff about how I'm supposed to be bitter and twisted and fucked up, and then about how I killed him, have lost.

I come out again and Sarah pulls my clothes about a bit, and Andrew and Charles nod and smile, and I feel as ready to go as I ever will. The guard leads us out into the main corridor, and it seems like no time before I'm standing outside the wide glass doors of the court, blinking in the light, sniffing the fresh breeze. In front of me is the line of press people, TV and radio too, and a couple of police holding back a small crowd. Beyond them all is the car park, the trees in the park and along the river, and away to the

436

right the ring road and the rest of the city. All I'd have to do is push through the cameras and notebooks and I'd be there. Despite the snatches of sunshine the wind is cold, buffeting, but it is so welcome after being inside for all this time.

In front of me the journalists are in position, in their suits and anoraks, with cameras and lights and furry boom mikes and a forest of tape recorders held out at arm's length, and the jostling dies down, heads are eased out of the way of the lenses behind. I recognize some of them from the court. One or two others are strangely familiar until they resolve themselves into faces from local TV.

I have no idea what I am going to say.

Andrew tells them that his client wants to make a short statement. They shuffle a bit more, then go quiet.

'Thank you,' I say. Then there is silence, except for the whirring of the tape recorders and cameras, and far away the noise of the everyday world of ring roads and buses. I look at my feet, take a minute to concentrate.

'I want to say how grateful I am to the judge and jury for the verdict today, and of course to my legal team, who have been fantastic, and to my family and friends and well-wishers for all their support. I am pleased that my name has been cleared, after what has been an awful six months. It was a terrible thing to be accused of, and I am more thankful than I can say that it is over. I'm now looking forward to returning home and picking up things where I left off. I just want to get on with my life.

'But I want to say that I've no grudge against the police or the authorities for what has happened. I am sure they were acting for the best. I only hope they can now try to find who really did kill John. I don't want to say any more now, except to thank you all for this chance to say what I think.'

I step down and the scrum drives forward, shouting questions, cameras flashing, and I'm hemmed in, jostled, and then somehow we're in the car, speeding away, around the ring road and on to the Oundle road. And now I have the time to be angry that the judge didn't even say sorry that I've been locked up for six months. I wonder what to do about my few possessions in Whitemoor. I worry about what will happen next. And all the time I stare at the things I've missed, the shops, the people walking past, the road signs, the adverts on the bus shelters. They all seem different, brighter, like coming back from a holiday abroad.

'You were pretty good back there,' Andrew says, without taking his eyes off the road. 'I'm starting to wish we could have put you in the witness box. You'd have made a great impression.'

'Yeah, we'll have to watch it on the news,' Nick says. 'I thought we'd take you home so you can get sorted out, and Ma and Granny'll come over. Everyone's going to be down the Oak later on. Did you know Sam was in court this afternoon? He made a point of saying we should all come down. If you felt up to it,' he adds, with a touch of concern.

'That would be brilliant,' I say, though even the thought of going home scares me.

'I can't believe it,' Nick says, turning to me. He at least looks his old self, even if the rest of us are different. He's so happy, with this wide grin, that we could be sitting on the back seat of our parents' car on the first day of the holidays, heading off to the coast. 'I can't believe it's really all over.'

But I don't think it is.

★   ★   ★

We drive through Upton, past the church where John might or might not be buried, and down the long stretch of road into gloomy Kingsthorpe, the firs surrounding it looking threatening even in the fitful sunlight, even with the hawthorn in bloom. We go on in silence, past the familiar village sign — 'Woodwalton' — in old-fashioned black letters, then over the bridge, between the flat-fronted houses, the church, the pub, all in the same honeyed stone, to pull up in front of my own home. Just before four o'clock on a Friday afternoon. No one's about, as I step out of the car, feeling not a sense of homecoming but of being watched, monitored. I wonder if I might be shouted at, or attacked, or if there will be some other charge so I could be rearrested. The front door sticks where the wood has swollen with damp, and as we stand about, with Nick shoving at it with his shoulder and in the end kicking it at the bottom, I'm glad to have the others with me. It feels so odd, so exposed, to be outdoors like this.

Inside it is cold and a little damp. The pilot light on the boiler had gone out, but Nick gets the heating going and Andrew finds some tea and goes off to get some milk and biscuits from the shop and I pace around each of the rooms, picking things up, looking at my books and pictures, rearranging things, looking out of the window at the garden where the daffodils are pushing through the carpet of dead leaves. The kitchen looks much the same as before, only there's less in it, and the door of the fridge has been torn off. Nick and Claire have cleaned everything up pretty well, the broken plates and glasses and smashed pictures, and they've even painted over what had been scrawled on the walls, although from the shapes of the blocks of new paint and the blurs beneath I can guess what they said.

We have our tea and the phone starts going, friends, people from work, and some journalists. After a bit Nick unplugs the phone and Andrew leaves to go back to the office and for the first time it's possible to think that it never happened, that I had never gone away, with the water bubbling in the pipes, bringing the house back to life, and with Nick talking about work, about friends of his in London, and what needed doing to the flat he's bought with Sophie, what they plan to do with the kitchen, and the damp in the bathroom.

There's a knock at the door, and as I run to answer it Nick calls out sharply to leave it. I ignore him, and of course it's only my mother, bringing Granny and Emily and my cousin Caroline. Soon after that, when we are still hugging each other and talking at each other, Seb and Lisa turn up too, and the house fills with chat and noise and questions, and it is lovely and painful all at once, like coming in from the cold, warming your feet on the radiator, and getting pins and needles. So it's a relief when I go upstairs for a bath, filled as hot as I can stand, topping it up with extra water and piling in the bath salts. Then back to my room, smelling the familiar scents of wood and old plaster and eiderdown. It's been empty for too long, and the cold has settled into the walls, but I am so hot from the bath that I can lie on my bed, thinking of nothing, while it turns to night outside.

★　★　★

It took me ages to dress, now that there was no one to shout that I was late, or bells to hurry me along to a meal or to exercise. I pulled out all kinds of clothes, old jeans and favourite shirts and the like, but in the end I put on a loose white T-shirt, like the one I was wearing the day it all started. I remembered seeing my clothes in that polythene bag, thinking of how it would have been the same if I had died instead of John, how they would have been bagged up, torn and bloody, for the coroner. Dressing the same way was one way of showing I'm still alive. That I'd survived it all — prison, the trial, the crash.

I decided that tomorrow I'd ask Nick to drive me over to where my father is buried. I guessed that's where I was going that day, after I'd found John's body and run home in a panic. Only I was in such a state I never made it.

At the back of the bottom drawer I found an old grey sweater which is far too large for me, so that the arms hang down loose. It was one my father had, that he used for gardening, and which I rescued from the bags of clothes my mother put out for Oxfam, without her knowing.

Ready to go, I felt shy, reluctant to go downstairs again, to face them all, and instead I listened to the hum of voices, and then to a sudden hush, a faint sound from the TV, the local news. My moment of fame.

Eventually, my mother came upstairs to find me. I felt odd about having the sweater, but she only smiled and said she was surprised I still had that old thing. She chatted on about coming over tomorrow to help me give the house a good clean, and how kind it was of my young friend to come and see her after court yesterday to tell her I was OK — it takes me a while to work out this must have been Baz — and how well I'd done on the local news. Everyone had said so, and agreed I'd make such a good journalist, much better than the ones they had on now. But behind the bright smile she was different, seeming smaller than I could ever remember her, and anxious, as if waiting for some other catastrophe to hit her. It made me think again of what I had made happen to her, to everyone. But when I tried to tell her how sorry I was she only held me and rocked me and stroked my head and wept even more than me as she said how much it meant to have me back.

Then Nick came up to tell me we were all going to the Oak. Nick and my mother, and all of them downstairs must've known they should let me be on my own for a bit, but they couldn't help themselves, and that was nice in itself. That they wanted me to be OK again. The old Clarrie.

★   ★   ★

Now I am perched on a bar stool, telling Claire about the food in prison, comparing it to the stuff we ate at school, trying to make a joke of it all, asking her about what's been going on, how her job's been, if she's seeing anyone, has anyone in mind. I find it so restful to watch her watching me, to see her so pleased that I'm here again. I'm speaking between bites of yet another sandwich from the pile that Sam's wife Jenny has made, salty ham she has cooked herself between slices of real bread with proper burnt crusts, a million miles from the squashy cellophane sandwiches Andrew used to bring down from the canteen. I am washing them down with sips of Guinness, taking it slowly because I'm not used to the alcohol. Everyone else is mostly drinking champagne, but I thought of Sam getting it from the fridge for John and I've hardly touched the glass I got when we first arrived. I suppose there will always be these little nagging reminders, for as long as I live.

There's a snuffling by my feet as the pub dog comes around. I slip her the rest of my sandwich, and her dark mournful eyes are then fixed on me, pleading for more food.

The pub is packed, and again I could almost imagine nothing had changed, except that I am the centre of attention, so that everywhere I look, people, neighbours, friends, they all look back and wink or raise a glass or come over and tell me how well I've done — as if it was anything to do with me — and they knew it would all be OK and only a fool of a copper could have thought any of this had anything to do with me. It's as if it's my birthday, everyone wishing me well.

Emily asks what I'm going to do, and I say I might go away. I have an image of rocky shores, blue skies, the same daydreams I'd had sitting in court. Or a big city, somewhere I could lose myself in the crowds.

'Don't do that,' Claire says. 'You've only just got back. There's plenty of time to go away later. Stay here. Enjoy yourself. Get out more.'

Baz used to say the same thing, when she found out I'd never been to a club, never taken drugs, never had what she called a laugh. She'd used the same phrase — how I should *get out more* — and being where we were, this became our in-joke. So our reply to anyone moaning about anything was *you should get out more, girl*. She'd meant it seriously, too, saying I shouldn't rush to settle down. She'd once told me she'd bet me a tenner I'd be acquitted, and then married in a year. Three kids to follow. Perhaps she knew it was what I wanted to hear. But she's half-right, so far.

'Yeah, maybe you're right.'

'Andrew,' Claire calls to him as he comes to the bar, 'Andrew, tell her she can't go away.'

'Oh, I couldn't do that,' he says, smiling. 'She'll not take any advice from me.'

'That's not fair,' I protest, but she carries on saying how I ought to stay, how once they get the right person everyone will forget all about the murder, and Andrew and Sam exchange glances, like they know something.

'We've all missed you so much,' she says.

'Don't run away now.'

Her words bring tears to my eyes. Andrew puts his arm around me. The dog snuffles at my hand. She says something about us maybe going away somewhere hot for a week or so, maybe to Spain. I think of how much I want to go away, knowing I can come back here whenever I want. I have enough people here who believe in me, who trust me, that it doesn't matter that John's parents and his friends and all the rest of them are still around. They can't do anything more to me now. There may always be people who say that of course it was me and I was lucky to get away with it. But none of that is being said here tonight, and I am grateful for that.

I look around the pub, noticing the things that are different, like my gran sitting by the fire, with a glass of port or something like that in front of her, chatting to a village neighbour. I've never seen her in a pub before in my life. Or how Roisin is behind me, chatting to Claire's younger sister Izzy about what passes for a night life in Peterborough.

Even Baz is here, I've no idea how but I expect Andrew arranged it. She is playing pool through in the other bar with my cousin Joe and some of Nick's friends. Andrew himself is fetching a drink for his wife Hannah, who has set up her own little circle by the fire to admire their baby Rose, fast asleep in her lap despite the noise. They arrived an hour ago, and though I've hardly met her before, almost the first thing she did was ask me to hold Rose for her for a minute, and that act of trust means so much.

Now, for a moment, it is all too much. I tell Claire I'll be back in a moment, squeeze her hand, and I go through to the back, past the toilets, to the back door.

Outside, I step into a blue-black world, midnight blue for the sky, and black for the bulk of the building next door, the scatter of cars, the beer garden, the mass of trees beyond. I walk across the gravel, between the cars, and then climb over the fence to reach the field beyond, and the oak tree in the middle.

It's still only early May, and a cold cloudless night and coming out of the warmth of the pub I feel exposed, vulnerable, like a snake that's just shed its skin. But my sweater is big and heavy enough so it doesn't matter. I look up at the stars spread across the night sky, seeing them for the first time in months, no longer lost in the glare from the security lights. The moon is starting to rise beyond the chimney of the house next door. *On such a night as this* . . . It must have been like this when John was here on that last night, with the same warm glow spilling from the windows of the pub, the occasional roar of voices from the bar. But then it was autumn and now it's spring.

It's so quiet out here, but inside I'm seething with excitement, like listening to happy music really loud. I could shout out that I'm free, as loud as I can, shout it to the whole village and beyond. Or I could say it quietly, to myself, because the night seems too peaceful to disturb.

There's a rustle behind me and I turn to see Baz climbing cautiously through the gap in the hedge, peering about in the dark. I call her name quietly.

'What are you doing out here?' she hisses fiercely.

'It's beautiful out here. Look at the stars.'

'Are you OK?'

'Yeah. I feel so good. Is this how you felt when you got out? That you could do, I don't know, whatever you want?'

'Something like that.'

'Does it last?'

'I don't think you should be out here.'

She looks worried. Maybe it's being in the country, somewhere unfamiliar, and the night-time noises of rustling bushes and scampering animals scare her just as a dark alley in the city would me.

'I'm OK,' I say. 'Honest.'

'It's not you . . . ' She looks about, moves a little closer to me and to the bulk of the tree trunk. 'Look, you didn't do it, right? But all his friends think you did, right? So what are they going to do?'

'Nothing. Look, they're not the sort of people to do anything like that. They may slag me off, sure, maybe even to my face, but they wouldn't do anything more.'

I smile at her reassuringly, but this only seems to irritate her.

'Yeah, well, maybe. But there's something else. You went there that morning, right? So maybe whoever did it is thinking that you might have seen them and that one day you'll remember. Someone local. Someone who knows you. They've already killed John, so why — '

'Come off it. Nothing like that's going to happen.'

She looks away, across the grass to the dark hedge beyond.

'Your friend Andrew's leaving in a few minutes,' she says. 'He's giving us a lift back to town.'

'Do you have to go? We've hardly spoken.'

'You know where I'll be.'

'Yeah, but . . . '

'You'll be fine,' she says, brushing some

450

stuff from my sleeve.

'Why don't you stay with me?' I say, amazed and pleased at how calm I sound.

She looks at me closely.

'You sure that's what you want?'

'Yes.' She is shivering a little, so it's the most natural thing in the world to hold her.

'Only for tonight?' she asks, and I nod.

'Yeah,' she says. 'I'd like that too.'

After a while, we go back to the pub and meet Nick at the door. He looks at me in surprise, almost suspicion, and I notice I still have bits of bark stuck to my sweater, and a patch of green lichen on one leg.

'We went for a walk.'

I stand there grinning like a schoolgirl and trying not to catch Baz's eye.

'Ma's taken Granny home,' he says.

'Good. She looked so tired.'

'Are you OK?' he asks, and I nod, giving him a big hug, trying to pass on to him some of what I'm feeling.

'Come on,' I say, linking arms with them both, 'let's get into the warm.'

We go through into the bar, where the crowd has thinned out, the noise dropped although the air is still thick with smoke from the fire and from the cigarettes and from the fumes of alcohol. Our little group is sitting in a circle around the fireplace. I stand looking at them all, Seb, Claire and Izzy, and Philip scratching the ears of the pub dog, and Roisin dangling some keys in front of little Rose, catching the red of the flames, so that she waves one hand about in delight, and Andrew and Hannah looking on. They make room for us in front of the fire.

Saturday Morning

It's early when I wake, only just after dawn, but I know I won't go back to sleep. Yesterday's fears about getting out all seem to have faded, and I lie back watching the sunlight come and go and hearing the wind rattle the window and the hot water starting in the pipes. Instead of the shouts and forced laughter and tannoy announcements of Whitemoor there's only birdsong.

It's strange to be back in my own bed, even stranger that Baz should be lying next to me, still asleep. I watch her for a while and then decide to make tea for us both — not the coffee I'd have had in my old life — and even think about going for a run. I dress as quietly as I can and try to find my trainers, until I remember I was wearing them on the day John died. Then I put on my sweater and pad quietly down stairs.

There's no milk left, but while I'm trying to remember what time the local shop opens I hear the whirr of the milk float coming down the street, and the clink as it stops a few doors away. There's some change in a saucer on the window ledge which has escaped the carnage, so I grab it and step outside.

The sky is clear and it's fresh rather than cold, but I'm still glad of my sweater. I walk towards the float where Uncle Brian is dropping empties into a crate with impressive speed. He is as spruce as ever, his tie — worn to show he is a farmer and not a hired hand — neatly tied, but he seems much older, with deep bags under his eyes and flecks of grey in his combed black hair. All the cockiness has gone, and I remember then that he's been ill.

He looks up, sees me, and the last bottle falls from his hand. It smashes to pieces on the kerb, but neither of us looks at it. He stares at me with a look of shock and surprise and even horror, like I've crawled out from under a stone. Or returned from the grave. *God*, I think, *what have I done? Will everyone be like this?*

'They let you go.' It's a statement, but I still nod in reply.

He moves his head a little to one side, so he can read my expression more clearly.

'What do you want from me, then?'

I try to say that I only want a pint of milk, but no words come. Behind him, the early morning sun makes the stone of the houses glow like honey. There's a smudge of smoke against the blue of the sky above one of the chimneys. It's so quiet and so beautiful, just the same as I remembered, but this only makes Brian being so weird seem even more horrible. He stares right at me, waiting for me to speak, though I've no idea what I'm supposed to say.

Then I know.

I know all of it, all at once.

He was there, the first on the scene. His wife, Sue, must have been the one in the car that night, the one John was seeing on the side. He must have found out, waited, picked his moment and then . . .

'It was you, wasn't it?'

He looks away, shakes his head.

The street is empty. No one about, no cars, not even a cat on a window ledge.

'It was. I know it was.'

The pieces crowd into my head. He drives around with a shotgun in the cab so he can knock off any early morning pheasants. It's even the same kind of gun as mine. And he didn't want to come to court to give evidence.

He steps forward, his boots crunching on the broken glass.

'Leave it alone.' There's a hint of cunning behind the anger and the tiredness. 'You get on with your life and I'll get on with mine.'

For a second, it's so tempting that it hurts. Make the tea, go back to bed, pretend it never happened. No interviews with the police, no questions, no having to go to court again. But something — maybe it's thinking of my family, my mother, or Andrew, or Baz asleep upstairs, or even John lying in a grave somewhere — makes this stick in my throat.

I shake my head, and he walks past me to the cab of the float, muttering something.

'Why didn't Sue tell someone?' I say at random.

I can see the blood rushing to his face. It scares me because he's known for having a wicked temper.

'She took the kids,' he says. 'She said if I tried to speak to them, I'd never see them again.'

'Tell me you did it.'

'She even took the dog.'

'Tell me.'

'If you say anything . . . '

'You'll kill me too?'

He thinks about this, then shakes his head.

'No one will believe you,' he says.

'I'll take that chance.'

He turns away and leans into the cab. I can see the tension in the way he stands, and in the way he breathes in. And though I know I should let him drive off, I have to get him to say it.

'I'm glad she took them,' I say, thinking of

the children John will never have. Wanting some reaction. Wanting him to admit what he did.

But he's too quick for me. Before I can even think I am lying on the pavement, bright sparkles before my eyes, trying to drag in a lungful of air. When I try to prop myself up against the wall everything spins round and I feel sick.

He stands over me, holding the gun.

There's a smear of blood on it, where he must have hit me, and blood on me, and blood beneath his skin, turning his face a horrible dusky-grey. He says something, but I can't understand him. His words are slurred, his movements clumsy, as if he is drunk with rage. Or maybe it's me.

Then the ground stops spinning, I don't have to hold on to it any longer, the pain fades, and for a moment I'm filled with an amazing sense of elation. It runs right through me, as if I'd jumped into a pool of icy water. Now I know, really know, that it wasn't me. No more fears about remembering one day. Or what people will think. Or who might still have doubts about me.

He points the gun at my face.

I breathe in a great sob of air, then another, and I find I'm crying too.

There's a scrape as a window opens further

up the street. A head looks out, but only for a moment. I can taste blood in my mouth.

'You're like your father, you know.'

He says this in such a normal voice that I think I must have imagined it. I can't see his face very well against the light blue of the sky behind him.

Then Baz comes out on to the street and stops dead. She stiffens and I pray she'll get back out of sight while she can, but then the barrel turns towards her and the chance is gone.

'What have you done to her?' she says. I look down at my chest, half-expecting to see a ragged wound like in the photos of John, but there's nothing there.

Brian shakes his head, as if he can't understand what she is saying. I think of grabbing the gun, at least giving Baz a chance.

'Put the gun down.' Another voice, one I don't know, from behind him, further up the street. 'Brian. Listen to me. This isn't the way.'

The man is in his forties, balding, with heavy eyebrows. He has one arm out-stretched, the other holding his dressing gown together. He must think that Brian is threatening me because I got off. That he's angry because the murderer of his friend John is walking about free.

His feet are bare, and I want to tell him to watch out for the broken glass.

'Brian,' he says, his voice rising. 'Listen to me.'

'Fuck it,' Brian says thickly, and I shut my eyes.

And listen to the birdsong.

And when I open them again, Brian is yards away, walking purposefully down the street, past the war memorial and out of sight up Church Lane. He has the gun beneath his arm.

'Stop him,' I say to the bald man, between my sobs.

'Are you joking?'

'He's going to kill himself.' I don't know how I know this, but somehow I convince the man and he goes off at a half-run.

Baz helps me to my feet, swearing at me under her breath in her relief. A couple of neighbours gather round. Mark Kennedy is there and says he's phoned the police, and someone else asks if I want a cup of tea and I smile and say yes please. I've some blood on my lip, and on my hands, and I'm shaking a bit, but I know that will pass. Someone is even picking up the coins I dropped when Brian hit me.

You could think that it never happened.

Except for the way we all keep listening, and looking towards the church. And the shards of broken glass on the pavement. Later on, I'll come out again and sweep them into the gutter.

THE END

We do hope that you have enjoyed reading this large print book.

Did you know that all of our titles are available for purchase?

We publish a wide range of high quality large print books including:
Romances, Mysteries, Classics
General Fiction
Non Fiction and Westerns

Special interest titles available in large print are:
The Little Oxford Dictionary
Music Book
Song Book
Hymn Book
Service Book

Also available from us courtesy of Oxford University Press:
Young Readers' Dictionary
(large print edition)
Young Readers' Thesaurus
(large print edition)

For further information or a free brochure, please contact us at:
Ulverscroft Large Print Books Ltd.,
The Green, Bradgate Road, Anstey,
Leicester, LE7 7FU, England.
Tel: (00 44) **0116 236 4325**
Fax: (00 44) **0116 234 0205**

Other titles in the
Ulverscroft Large Print Series:

STRANGER IN THE PLACE

Anne Doughty

Elizabeth Stewart, a Belfast student and only daughter of hardline Protestant parents, sets out on a study visit to the remote west coast of Ireland. Delighted as she is by the beauty of her new surroundings and the small community which welcomes her, she soon discovers she has more to learn than the details of the old country way of life. She comes to reappraise so much that is slighted and dismissed by her family — not least in regard to herself. But it is her relationship with a much older, Catholic man, Patrick Delargy, which compels her to decide what kind of life she really wants.

SLAUGHTER HORSE

Michael Maguire

The Turf Security Division is surprised and suspicious when playboy Wesley Falloway's second-rate horses develop overnight into winners. Simon Drake investigates, but suddenly there is a new twist — someone is out to steal General O'Hara, the star of British bloodstock, owned by Wesley Falloway's mother. With a few million pounds at stake, lives are cheap; Drake finds himself both hunter and quarry in a murderous chase where even his closest associates may be playing a double game.

MERMAID'S GROUND

Alice Marlow

It's been five years since Kate Williams' beloved husband died, leaving her with two young children to raise. Now she's built a good life in one of Wiltshire's prettiest villages, and she has her dream job, as gardener at Moxham Court. For the last year, Kate has had a lover, roguishly attractive Justin Spencer, but he won't commit to more than a night here and there. When she takes in a male lodger, Jem, Kate's secretly hoping his presence will provoke a jealous reaction in Justin. What she hasn't reckoned on is exactly how attractive Jem will turn out to be.

A MORTAL AFFAIR

Stella Allan

Frances Parry seemed to have it made. She was married to a Harley Street consultant, she had a beautiful home, wealthy friends — including the fascinating Bernard, her husband's friend since undergraduate days — and a creative job. But suddenly Frances's world was turned upside down; her home was sold, her sideline job became a vital means of livelihood, and Bernard, who had become her lover, was exposed as a criminal. And then Frances found that she herself was indulging in criminal activities in a deadly duel with the law.

ONE BRIGHT CHILD

Patricia Cumper

1936: Leaving behind her favourite perch in the family mango tree in Kingston, Jamaica, little Gloria Carter is sent to a girls' school in England, to receive the finest education money can buy. Gloria discovers two things — one, that in mainly white England she will always need to be twice as good as everyone else in order to be considered half as good; and two, that her ambition is to become a barrister and right the wrongs of her own people. Ahead lies struggle — and joy. The road stretches to Cambridge University, to academic triumph and a controversial mixed marriage. Based on a real-life story.